Y0-CAP-447

Gen. Muhlenberg's Quarters

Pliny B. Fiske
Byron, N.Y.

Gen. Weedon's Quarters

GULPH RD.

KING OF PRUSSIA

COUNTY LINE RD.

Gen. Greene's Quarters

OLD EAGLE SCHOOL RD.

SWEDESFORD RD.

W. VALLEY RD.

1 Commander-in-Chief's Guard
2 McIntosh's Brigade
3 Maxwell's Brigade
4 Conway's Brigade
5 Huntington's Brigade
6 Varnum's Brigade
7 Woodford's Brigade
8 Scott's Brigade
9 Knox's Artillery
10 Wayne's Division
11 Deerkill Valley Ind. Co.
12 Poor's Brigade
13 Glover's Brigade
14 Learned's Brigade
15 Paterson's Brigade
16 Weedon's Brigade
17 Muhlenberg's Brigade

The Strong Men

BY JOHN BRICK

The Strong Men

JOHN BRICK

DOUBLEDAY & COMPANY, INC.

Garden City, New York   1959

Library of Congress Catalog Card Number 59–12617
Copyright © 1959 by John Brick
Printed in the United States of America
First Edition

This book is dedicated to the memory of

MARGHITA MacDONALD

who spent a lifetime trying
to make the dreams of youth come true.

THE STRONG MEN:

The Highland County Independent Company of Rangers, serving with the Continental Line, in winter quarters at Valley Forge from December 19, 1777, through June 28, 1778.

Captain Marion Hawk Hill
Lieutenant Matthias Hill
Lieutenant Harmanus Tallman
Ensign Walter Luckey
Sergeant John Curran
Sergeant James Dutcher
Sergeant Jared King
Corporal Tobias Garrison
Corporal Peter van Houten
Quartermaster Frederick Youngblood

Private Soldiers

Archer, Derrick
Babcock, Thomas
Bill, William
Blancher, Jeremiah
Blauvelt, Gerret
Bogert, Isaac
Conklin, Aaron
Curran, Samuel
Ekerson, Teunis
Felter, Samuel
Ferguson, Benjamin
Halstead, Timothy
House, Peter
Hutchings, Gilbert
Johnson, John
King, Silas
Knapp, William
Leecraft, William
Lowry, Ebenezer

Martin, John
Mott, Mordecai
Osborne, Jonathan
Palmer, Benjamin
Perry, Garret
Polhemus, Teunis
Remsen, Thomas
Rider, Justus
Secord, Andrew
Secord, William
Smith, Edward
Tallman, Teunis
Tallman, Woodhull
Van Buskirk, Henry
Van Houten, Hendrick
Waggoner, Tobias
Welch, James
Welch, William

The strong men keep coming on.
They go down shot, hanged, sick, broken—
They live on fighting, singing, lucky as plungers. . . .
. . . .
Call hallelujah, call amen, call deep thanks.
The strong men keep coming on.

—CARL SANDBURG

BOOK ONE

BOOK ONE

CHAPTER ONE

The deer run followed the pass that twisted between the twin mountains. Lying on a rock shelf above the pass, I could see the run clearly. It was a ribbon of rich brown oak leaves, a foot or two wide, winding through the tumbled boulders. No shrubs or grass grew on it; the sharp hoofs of the deer that traveled it day after day cut away all vegetation. Here and there on the run the leaves were disturbed, where the deer had shuffled them in moving through the pass during the previous evening.

Some of the saplings that grew tall and straight along the run also showed the marks of the deer. The gray bark was rubbed away, at man's knee-to-hip height, to reveal white wood beneath. When antlers are maturing in the autumn months, the bucks lower their heads at smooth-barked saplings and rub vigorously, scraping off the soft velvet that coats the new antlers. The horns must be ready for fighting during the rutting season. How often have I heard the dry clatter of horn against sapling, a sound that, once heard by the hunter, will never be mistaken.

I lay in comfortable silence on the shelf, in a hollow filled with creeping cedar. The long rifle, hammer back, rested on the rocks before me. Slight movements of both hands would bring its dark stock to my shoulder; I had only to dip my head a few inches to sight along the octagonal barrel.

I waited patiently, my eyes fixed on the eastern slope of the pass. The wind was quartering from the northeast. Unless it shifted, the deer would be below and beyond before they caught my scent. There would be all the time in the world to pick out a fat doe.

There was no doubt that the deer would come. They bedded for the day on the western slopes of the twin mountains, where the sun threw its greatest warmth in the afternoon. Deer are creatures of fixed habit, as every hunter knows. That is why they are the easiest of all game to find and kill. I would as lief undertake, in a wager, to track and down a deer as to stake my money on bringing in a brace of woodcock in a day's hunting.

There was a further reason to believe that the deer would come. Harm Tallman was in the eastern valley below the pass, where the deer had browsed all night. Harm would take care to spook the deer toward the pass—not clumsily to put them running, but giving them a whiff of human scent, the crackling of brush at a distance. The deer would hurry up the foothill slope, bounding fearfully for a few hundred yards, until they were sure they'd left the human presence well behind. Then they would slow to their ambling, ungainly walk, pausing here and there to crop the tender brush tips. The does would come first, ears twitching and tails flicking. The buck that followed them would come suspiciously, ever willing to let his females go ahead of him toward whatever danger they might encounter.

There was no sport in it. We sought a winter's meat. Four deer, all does, were already hanging in our camp in the western valley. Two more would do the job. Bucks were not wanted, so long as the tender flesh of the does came so easily to our rifles' sights.

Idly I wondered at the wisdom of shooting so many does. We'd been doing it all our lives. Yet a yearling doe killed meant the loss of the fawn she would surely carry over the winter, not to mention the loss of all the fawns she would carry in years to come. Shooting the bucks did not reduce the herd. One prime buck could service as many does as he could find.

I shrugged the thought away, settling deeper into the cedar. Let the people who lived here a hundred years from now worry about their meat supply. Maybe, I thought then, the people to come will raise so much livestock they'll have no interest in deer meat. It was already so in the cities along Hudson's River to the east. There was little game of any kind in the farm lands that bordered the river.

Then there was a new sound among the noises of the forest. It came to me clearly above the distant squalling of jays, the whisper of the wind in the hemlocks on the mountain slope, the chatter of a noisy squirrel. It was the steady shuffling of dry leaves. I listened intently, assuring myself that it was not that same squirrel scampering from tree to tree. My hands moved to the rifle.

Four of them walked into the pass. All were does. Two looked like spring fawns. The others were full-grown and heavy from a summer's rich feed. They moved slowly forward. One of the big ones stopped, lowered her head, and lifted a shining rear hoof to scrape vigorously at her neck. The others moved around her, pausing every few seconds to study the terrain around them with nearsighted eyes. One doe stared steadily at the rock shelf for almost half a minute. I didn't move a muscle, knowing that she could distinguish me from the rocks only if I moved. At times I have stood motionless in the open, not ten yards from deer that took me to be a stump or a rock.

Finally they were all below me, heads down. I moved the rifle barrel a few inches to cover the big doe that had rubbed her neck. I hesitated a second or two before I aimed, then decided on the easy shot at the heart. I could have tried to break her neck and thus spoil less meat with the passage of the rifle ball, but an inch either way and she would travel for miles.

I held the shot .again, briefly, as the buck came into the pass, thirty yards behind the does. He was a big one, gray-muzzled, with a rack of eight or ten points. He held his head high, scenting the wind to be sure that the danger in the eastern valley had been left far behind.

The rifle cracked. Three does bounded away through the pass, white flags flashing. The buck vanished the way he had come. The fourth doe jumped once, twice, then ran lurchingly with her tail down.

My eye marked the spot where she passed from view on the slope of the pass, fifty yards away. She wouldn't go far.

I reloaded the rifle swiftly, then sat back in comfort to wait. If she was hit in or about the heart, she was already dead. If not, she would lie down and stiffen, dying quickly as the blood flooded her chest cavity. But if I followed her immediately, she might get to her feet and travel for miles. I had no mind to track a wounded deer all day.

Two minutes later, I heard a shot echo ringingly from the eastern valley. I smiled. That would be Harm, I thought. That big buck came plunging down the mountain, and Harm heard him coming, saw the size of the rack, and shot him without thinking.

Now he's down there cursing the deer and himself, I thought, because it's too far to camp to back-pack the carcass, so he's got to go get a horse, and that will take the rest of the morning and most of the afternoon. And we said we'd shoot six does, not five does and a tough old bruiser with a big rack.

Maybe, I thought. Maybe he shot a doe and didn't see the buck at all. Either way, the hunting is done, and we'll go home tomorrow.

I got to my feet and started slowly down the pass. I stopped at the spot where I'd seen the wounded doe disappear. Unless I could see her lying below me, I wouldn't go any farther for another twenty or thirty minutes. If she was lying down and I came up on her, she'd jump to her feet with whatever strength she had left and race down the mountain. I looked down the slope. I wasn't surprised to see the body thirty yards below.

I approached carefully, reaching with the barrel of the long rifle to touch the deer's wide staring eyes. If she had any life in her, that would set the hoofs to slashing with no danger to me.

The deer didn't move. I set the rifle against a rock, unbuckled the belt that held my tomahawk and hunting knife, and then unlooped my hunting bag from my shoulder. I peeled off my buckskin shirt and the warm woolen undershirt beneath. Goose flesh immediately roughened my arms and shoulders in the chill autumn air, but I'd rather be cold for a few minutes, until the work warmed me, than wear clothes sodden with blood.

There was a gnarled scrub oak that suited my purpose about twenty yards from the dead deer. I dragged the body by the hind legs to the tree, then bunched my muscles to pick up the clumsy burden. I wedged the neck firmly, after several attempts, into a forked branch. I was puffing when the body finally was swinging freely. It held. The hind legs trailed in the leaves.

A length of buckskin thong from my hunting bag served to lash the head securely into the fork of the branch. Then I took my knife and went to work.

It was a job I knew well. It was finished in fifteen minutes. The deer hung with the cavity propped open to the air; the entrails were tossed aside for the scavengers of the forest, and the heart and liver and kidneys—wrapped in birch bark—lay on a flat rock beside the tree. I walked several hundred yards to a spring that trickled down the mountain. I washed my arms and shoulders free of blood, shivering at the touch of the icy water. Then I returned to the deer, put on both my shirts, and picked a comfortable bed of moss among the rocks. I had the rest of the day to pack the deer to camp. It could bleed for another hour or so right where it was.

Tallman reached camp in midafternoon with the old buck lashed across one of the pack horses. I helped him to hoist the carcass to a maple branch alongside the five others that were swinging in the chill wind that swept the valley. The story he told was just about as I had figured it.

"I seen that big rack," Harm said ruefully, "and up comes the rifle and down goes the deer. Even if there'd been a couple of does with him, I would of knocked him. Like when the redcoats is coming across a field and you pick out one that's got a sword because knocking him will be something to brag on."

"It's a nice rack," I said.

"Sure it's a nice rack, although he ain't as heavy as you'd think to look at his head. But what in hell will I do with the buck? He ain't good for nothing but stew meat, and it would have to cook for a whole day at that."

I laughed. "It's not that bad, Harm. Somebody will take him off your hands—somebody that would go light on a winter's meat otherwise. Maybe Wisner at the tavern will buy him."

Harm shook his head. "Not Wisner. I stuck him too many times already. First thing he does now when I bring him a deer with the head cut off is look between the hind legs to see how much I had to cut away to turn a buck into a doe."

"All right, then. I'll take the buck home with me, and you can take one of the does in its place. My mother works wonders with tough meat. And Hawk will hang the big rack on the front wall of the house with all the others."

Tallman shrugged. "Maybe. Or maybe I can go out tomorrow and shoot another doe. The horses can pack one more. I'm hungry, Matt. What will we eat? Liver? Rabbit? Partridge? What you got in mind?"

"The big trout that was on the set line this morning. He's already baking under those coals. I put him in a clay jacket with onions and turnips in his belly."

Tallman grinned in anticipation and sat down on the needles at the base of a big pine. He shifted comfortably as his buckskin breeches slid on the smooth needles. He took out one of his clay pipes and began packing it with coarse dark tobacco. He viewed the campsite with a contented air.

Our three pack horses grazed at the ends of their tethers in a natural meadow a hundred yards away. A white-watered creek tumbled its way handsomely through the valley, broadening and deepening with each shelf of land into smooth deep runs or boulder-studded pools. From the pool nearest the camp, I had pulled the three-pound trout that was baking. The camp itself was a strip of sand and gravel that was leveled and smoothed by the creek's flood waters in spring and fall. A few hemlocks bordered the camp's edge, and behind them, tall pines climbed the mountain.

Among the hemlocks was a lean-to with a long fire pit before it. The shelter was simply built of hickory poles and slabs of elm bark, laced with alder withes. Our blanket rolls and gear were in the lean-to. It was a simple camp, like in all its details to the scores that Harm and I had made in this valley since our first boyhood hunting trips.

Tallman spoke softly through the cloud of tobacco smoke. "A lot of water has gone down that Neversink since the first time we camped here, Matt."

I looked fondly at the stream, surely one of the prettiest mountain creeks to be found anywhere. "It looks just the same as it did the day Hawk stopped us here and told us to make camp."

"We should of brought him this time. His leg would do better with some good walking on it. He gets around fine with it now. All that's wrong is the limp, and that will go away."

"He wouldn't come," I said quietly. "You know he wouldn't. Not with me. Not the way things are between us. Oh, he laughs and jokes with me. But if somebody says a word about the army, and how I brought the company home, he tightens his face and doesn't say a word."

"Yeh, I know what you mean," Tallman said. "I watched him." His long, black-stubbled face turned toward me. "Now's as good a time as any for us to talk about that, Matt. We ain't said a word about it since we left home the other day. We got to get it settled, one way or the other."

"We've been over it before," I said, feeling the anger rise in my voice. "Don't drive it into the ground, Harm."

"Got to talk about it. Got to change that pigheaded mind of yours."

"You're not going to change it by talking, and you know it. Besides, I'm sick of talking about it."

"If you won't talk about it, there's only one other way I know," Harm said easily. "Going to beat hell out of you. Hawk's the one should of done it, but he couldn't when you brought us home dragging our tails. He couldn't do it with his busted leg. I should of done it at Germantown, and then we might not of come home. I'll do it now, better late than never."

I felt the blood rushing to my face. "Do you mean I've got to fight you? Right here, for no reason?"

"Damn good reason," Tallman nodded calmly. "Been thinking about it for days. Hawk or me, one of us has got to beat some sense into your head. He ain't as young as he was, and now he can't move so fast on that leg. So it's up to me. Right after we eat that trout, Matt. We'll square off and let go until you can't get up no more."

"You think you can keep me on the ground?" I asked, grinning in spite of myself.

"I can," Harm answered. "You know I can. Knock you down until you're finished. Fair fight, too. No kicking, no thumbs in eyes, no jumping when you're down. Just fists."

I stared at him, both angry and wondering. "Have you gone off your head, Harm? You think that even if you can whip me, I'll change my mind?"

Harm shook his head. "I ain't fixing to change your mind on the whys of it, just on what you're going to do. Here's the way I look at it. We each got a stake in this. If I whip you, like I'm going to, you back down and come along with the company as first lieutenant, same as you done before, same as Hawk wants you to. If by some chance or a lucky punch, you whip me, then I don't ever mention it again. You do what you want to, and I won't say a word about it. Fair?"

"Fair, hell! I'll not be bound by any such bargain. I said it after we got licked at Germantown, and I said it when we got home— I'm through with a war that we can't win. I'm through with killing men for no reason that makes any sense. I'm done with fighting and running away time after time. I'll starve no more nor watch other men starve while we wait for the best army in the world to beat the hell out of us."

"Look. Forget all that. It's got nothing to do with this case, beside the fact that it ain't so. We beat 'em a few times ourselves, them great trained soldiers you talk about. This is real simple, Matt. Hawk Hill says we go back to the army. You're his son. You go with us, if I got to beat you every day for a month until you say yes. That's how simple it is. We do what Hawk says, whatever it is. We always have, and we always will."

I jumped to my feet and turned my back to Harm, staring across the creek. "I don't do what Hawk says—not any more! He's wrong, and you're wrong, and his precious General is wrong! Give up, I say, and stop fighting 'em. We can't win now, we never could, and we never will."

Harm's voice was mildly disputive. "What about the news from that place—Bemis Heights, Saratoga, whatever—how we captured a whole damn army of 'em? What about that? That's winning, ain't it?"

I snorted disgustedly. I was sick of hearing about Saratoga. "Five thousand men! Don't you understand they can send twenty thousand to replace 'em? Thirty thousand! Doesn't anybody understand that?"

He clucked his tongue. "Man's in an argument, he changes figures to suit hisself. I heard it was close to seven thousand. Anyways, we got twenty thousand, thirty thousand, too, specially in the summer. That ain't no argument."

"Trained soldiers, Harm. The best in the world. We've got a bunch of farmers that pull foot for home every time they hear a gun go off."

"You're a farmer, ain't you? I never seen you pull foot when they was shooting at us."

I turned to face him. "Use your head, man! You know damn well they whip us every time they set their minds to it. If Billy Howe had half the sense God gave a flea, the war would have been over a year ago."

Tallman nodded affably. "He ain't, though. And it ain't over, not by a long shot. Good thing I ain't a farmer, Matt. Some farmers might get real sore about you running 'em down like that. What's more—them farmers, some go home and more come back. They ain't so bad if you give 'em something to hide behind. I seen a Maryland farmer at Brandywine laying behind a dead horse, and when we all run I had to drag him out of there by the scruff of his neck. Said to me, 'Just lemme get that big bastard on the black horse. Had three shots at him, and every time I pulled trigger, he moved.' That farmer said that with them damn Hessians not two hundred yards away and coming fast."

I shook my head. "You know militia as well as I do."

"Some of 'em is not what you'd call fighting men," he agreed. "But we'll win in the end, Matt. Hawk says so. That's good enough for me. He never told me wrong all my life. So he'll take us back to the army and you'll go too. You think that trout is baked?"

"Maybe," I said sourly. "I'll dig it out. You going to stick to this crazy idea of fighting?"

"Sure, right after we eat." He eyed me appraisingly. "Be a real good one, too, long as it lasts. You can move around quicker'n a weasel in a henhouse, but I got the strength. Long as you don't run away, I'll whip you."

"The craziest damn idea I ever heard," I told him. "Come on, let's eat."

I raked the coals out of the fire pit, uncovering the hard clay shell in which the fish was baking. A few light taps with my knife knocked away the clay, and I rolled the fish onto a long slab of birch bark. Tallman grunted happily. The point of my knife probed to reveal the tip of the trout's backbone. Then I carefully split the trout by lifting the backbone clear of the soft white flesh. I tipped half the fish to Harm's mess plate and tossed the backbone, rib cage intact, into the fire. Each of us had half the big fish with a side serving of turnips and onions.

We ate in silence. Harm poured himself a cup of applejack from the jug in the lean-to, offering me a share which I refused. He drank one cup, then poured another that emptied the jug.

When he had finished his fish, he dug a pair of rosy apples from a sack in the lean-to and tossed one to me.

He chewed his apple with noisy satisfaction. I listened to the crunching with irritation, hoping that he'd make some remark about my sour face. Be damned if I'd fight him, but be damned also if he could whip me as easily as he thought!

He ate all the apple but the stem. Then he got up and stripped off his buckskin hunting shirt. He flexed his heavy muscles and breathed deeply, expanding his great chest.

"Come and get it, Matt," he said happily. "I ain't had a good fight since that time on Long Island when I whipped the blacksmith with them Jersey troops, the one that called me an appleknocker. He was a hard man. You got to go some, Matt, to be as hard as he was."

"Put your shirt back on," I said savagely. "Don't be a fool."

He walked slowly to me. "All it is, Matt, is a matter of what's right and what's wrong. So you get up now and raise your fists."

His moccasined foot came forward and tapped me lightly in the thigh. I stirred angrily. Again the foot came forward. "Make you mad enough this way," he said quietly, "you'll get up and fight."

"Get the hell away from me, Harm!"

"Come on," he said. "I don't want to think you're feared of me. But maybe you are. Maybe running off from the army has put some yellow in you." Once again the foot nudged me.

I leaped into a crouch, then came slowly to my feet.

"All right," I said through tight jaws. "I'll fight you. Whatever happens won't change my mind, but by God, I'll fight you!"

I stripped to the waist. The chill air prickled my flesh.

"Blows to the body will be enough," Tallman said in grinning anticipation. "I ain't going to knock out a single tooth on you, Matt. I wouldn't want you to smile at that pretty Peggy Remsen with a gap-toothed mouth."

We faced each other on the level ground of the camp clearing. To the casual eye we were probably badly mismatched. He was a big dark man with knotted shoulders that proclaimed his strength. His body was heavy, on thick legs, but I knew his speed from years of woodsrunning with him. He had the agility of a big bear.

He was a brawler, and I was not. Scarcely a month went by that Harm didn't show the marks of his latest tavern battle, while I had not had a fist fight since I was sixteen. He outweighed me by thirty pounds, and had an inch over me in height and perhaps two inches in reach. There was only one advantage I could count upon; if I kept out of range of those massive fists, he would abandon his fighting skills and try to crush me with strength. I knew him well, you see.

"Ready?" he asked, grinning.

"Ready."

He came forward swiftly, fists poised at chest level. His left hand shot for my chest, but I blocked it easily and then ducked under the right-hand punch that followed. I hammered two swift blows to his hard belly and pulled swiftly away. I wasn't fast enough—the left hand sideswiped my head and I went sprawling.

Jumping to my feet, I kept circling away from that swift left hand, knowing that I was fast enough to avoid the clumsier swing of the right. I kept my eyes fixed on his chest muscles, watching for the ripple of knotted flesh that would signal a punch. He pursued me methodically, shifting his feet quickly as I stepped around him.

I managed to hit him on the chest and in the belly three or four blows for every sidearm swing that he landed on me. The difference was that my punches seemed to have no effect, while even his deflected blows hurt me. My arms seemed numb from the hammering they took in guarding me, and another punch from his left hand sent me spinning again.

At the end of ten minutes, I was gasping to pull air into my burning lungs, and I was sure that my legs were losing some of the spring that could so easily take me out of Tallman's reach. Contrary to my hopes, he didn't lose himself in anger; rather, he moved in constantly, fists always ready to strike.

It enraged me to watch him grin happily as he stalked me. The damn fool! We were lifelong friends—why were we battering each other like a pair of maniacs?

Yet I knew that he had no sense of madness in this silent battle; he was having a good time while he beat some sense into me!

I should have held my own caution in check, in spite of his infuriating grin. Instead, I tried to throw punches past those sinewy arms, coming in close to him to add strength to my blows. I managed several hard thumps to his belly and ribs; he grunted with pain and surprise. I moved in again. This time his left hand rammed solidly into my shoulder and the right came around like the swing of a sledge. It caught me in the ribs of my left side. I slammed to the ground so hard that my head bounced. I couldn't breathe. My lungs sucked air while a black curtain seemed to flutter across my eyes. I needed a respite badly, but I didn't want him to see how close I was to being finished. With full effort, I pushed myself up until I was kneeling on one knee, as if ready any instant to spring to my feet and continue the battle.

Then suddenly the fight was no longer important. I stared past Harm Tallman at the perimeter of our campsite, where the pines formed a green wall. I tried to tell him what I saw, but still couldn't speak from the force of his punch. He must have read the warning in my eyes, for he looked quickly behind him, then spun around to face the pines.

There were five Indians standing there, watching us. They were all armed with rifles or muskets, but they weren't painted. They were thirty yards away; that was too far for me to pick out any features by which to place them for what they were. Tallman knew far more about Indians than I did. He'd lived among them at times during his woodsrunning life.

"Senecas," he said softly. "I know the big one. From the Allegheny country. We got trouble, Matt."

"Shall we try for the rifles?" I whispered. The weapons were in the lean-to.

"Not a chance," he said. "But they ain't painted, Matt. And like I said, I know the big one. Just stand still and see what they do."

The Senecas didn't keep us waiting. Their leader stepped forward. All but one of the others followed him. The fifth man went directly, swiftly, to the lean-to and picked up our rifles. Then he joined the others, seeming to glide along like some slim brown snake.

The big man, the leader, was dressed in wool breeches, fine black leather boots and a carefully decorated buckskin shirt. He wore a battered broadbrim hat turned up to make three corners. The others were garbed in dirty buckskins, with dyed turkey feathers aslant from swivels attached to their scalplocks. They eyed us malevolently as they fanned out before us in scimitar fashion.

The leader, however, smiled brightly as he neared us.

"Tall-man," he greeted Harm amiably, making the name two distinct words. "It has been a long time since we saw you in the Long House." His English was excellent, if halting. It seemed to have a European flavor to it, perhaps Dutch or German.

Harm nodded and spoke quietly. "I been soldiering, John. How does it go with you?"

The Indian shrugged, a white man's gesture. "The same as before. We hunt, we fish, we trade in Niagara. But we did not mean to stop you from killing your enemy, Tall-man. You go on and kill him. We will watch. Do you want a knife?"

Harm laughed. "I wasn't going to kill him, John. He's a friend of mine."

The Indian wrinkled his brow. "Then why do you fight like men wishing to kill each other? It seemed strange to me that when he was on the ground, you did not jump on his belly with both feet."

"You don't understand," Harm said. "We're friends. If I'd of jumped on his belly, I might of hurt him."

"But were you not trying to hurt him by punching him?"

"Nope. Just to settle an argument."

The Indian spoke rapidly to the others, explaining why the two white men fought without intending to maim or kill each other. I understood a few words of his rapid Seneca; Harm had once spent a winter trying to teach me the rudiments of the tongues of the Six Nations, most of which he spoke well.

One of the warriors spoke harshly. "I am glad I am not a white man. They are all as crazy as the loon."

The Seneca leader turned again to us. "So you want to finish your fight. Go on with it."

"I guess we finished it for now," Harm said slowly. He smiled in friendly fashion, as if it were quite ordinary for five Senecas to pop out of the woods in the Neversink Valley. "We have plenty of deer meat and rabbit and partridge. Will you and your men eat with us, John?"

The big Indian seemed to smile, although I wasn't sure. Perhaps it was a scowl. Without answering Harm, he snapped a few orders to his men, two of whom moved swiftly in compliance. One of them poked up the fire, the other went to our hanging deer with knife and hatchet. I turned to watch him. He grabbed a doe's hind leg, braced it between his knees, and began instantly to hack away at the joint with knife and ax. I turned to protest, anger flaring at the careless butchering of good deer meat.

Harm's thick fingers gripped my arm tightly. "Tell your men to take what they want, John," he said softly.

The Seneca bowed his head slightly, as if accepting a gracious invitation. Then he looked inquiringly at me.

"My friend's name is Matt Hill," Harm said. "His father is Hawk Hill of the Deerkill Valley."

The Indian tipped his head again solemnly.

"This chief is John Abeel," Harm said to me. "You have heard me talk of him as Cornplanter, of the upper Senecas."

I knew that Harm had often visited the village where Cornplanter had lived, in days gone by when it was safe for a woodsrunner from the settlements to move freely, trading and trapping in the country of the Six Nations. I looked with interest at the young chief, whose father was a white man from Albany. He was not so dark as his Seneca companions, those Indians generally having a deeper cast of bronze than the other people of the Long House. Nor were his facial features so prominent as theirs in nose, cheekbones, and jutting brows.

I felt relief at learning his identity. During the past few minutes since the Indians had appeared, I had pictured Harm and me left hacked and bloody in this wilderness, or at least goaded by unfeeling captors on the long rough trail to the Genesee lands of the Senecas. Now I reasoned that Cornplanter, for years a friend of Harm Tallman, would turn out to be an interesting visitor to our camp, even if by custom's code in wartime he was an enemy.

When Harm spoke again I knew that he too was speculating on Cornplanter's attitude toward us. His voice was controlled and slow, as if he chose each word carefully. "Why are you here, John, so far from the western door of the Long House?"

Cornplanter smiled slightly, a mere twitch of his heavy mouth. He waved his arm negligently at our hanging deer. "The hunting is good in your country, Tall-man. We have come to hunt."

Harm seemed to accept the answer. "There are many deer in these mountains. Few Indians from the Long House come down this far, and our farmers in the valleys below ain't likely to pack in here just to hunt. But you ain't had much luck, seems like, the way your men are ripping into that deer meat."

The Indian solemnly agreed. "We were not sure just where the deer were. Now we have found them."

Harm spoke even more slowly. "You have a camp? With horses waiting to pack out the meat you kill?"

This time it was a real smile. "We have a camp," Cornplanter said, looking casually around, "and we have horses. Three of them," he added, turning his gaze to the intervale where our animals grazed.

His four companions were already squatting at the fire, searing slabs of deer steak on the glowing coals. Motioning us to follow him, Cornplanter crossed the camp to some tumbled boulders near the lean-to. He sat down on one and leaned his back against another. "Sit," he told us, "until the meat is ready."

It was a command rather than a suggestion. We found rocks for ourselves, and Harm passed his tobacco pouch to the Indian. When they were both puffing, Cornplanter spoke easily: "And now tell me, Tall-man, why you are not with the army of the Bostonians?"

"We were," Harm said, not looking at me. "Almost two years—twice we went for nine months. Then we quit and come home."

"A wise thing to do," Cornplanter said. "It will be only a little time now, before your army is finished."

Oddly enough, although I agreed with him fully, these confident words from an enemy riled me. "Who told you that?" I asked sharply.

"I did not have to be told," he said, smiling. "I saw it. At Oriska. You know what we did at Oriska."

"You got whipped," Harm said with heated voice. "You and the British and the Tories skedaddled back to Niagara."

"Why not?" Cornplanter said equably. "It was a good fight, with many scalps and much plunder, although the Senecas lost many of our good warriors. But we killed old Herkimer. I think maybe I killed him myself. I shot at him with a good rifle. When the smoke was gone, he was on the ground."

"But you ran," Harm said doggedly.

Cornplanter shook his head. "The Bostonians ran from us. We just decided not to go any farther." His face darkened. "There are many women and children in the Seneca nation who face this winter without a man to hunt for them, without a man to bring them furs against the cold. More Senecas were killed than all the Onondagas and Cayugas and Mohawks together. The Bostonians will pay for those lives. The settlements will pay in blood and scalps."

Harm brushed aside the Seneca's words. "You went back to Niagara after Oriskany. St. Leger was kept from joining Burgoyne, and so Burgoyne give up his whole army to Gates. All you done was kill old Herkimer and some of his militia. We got lots of militia, although it ain't often that many of 'em gets theirselves killed. You lost as many, you Injuns and British."

Cornplanter fastened his dark eyes on our faces, looking angrily from one to the other of us. "Listen to me, Tall-man. Listen and take my warning. You will not hear it again before the fire strikes, before the tomahawks flash in the firelight!" He paused, staring at us again in turn, the muscles working in the angles of his jaw. "For two years we have had the British in our councils. They have said one thing, again and again: 'Fight with us against the settlers! Drive them back from the frontiers. They want your land. They want to destroy the Six Nations, the Long House of the Iroquois.' We didn't fight, Tall-man, because our old men told us to let the white men kill each other as they wished. But we waited. We hunted and raised corn and beans and fished in the lakes and rivers. Yes, some of our young men in small parties raided on the Mohawk and along the Susquehanna and Juniata. There were chiefs in all the nations who wanted to go to war. Joseph Brant, who was in England, came home and told us to fight with the British. But we listened to the old men and we waited.

"And what happened? The old fool Herkimer raised an army against us. Do not mistake it. That army was against us. The militia on the Mohawk marched into the Long House, saying they would burn the Onondaga castle and the Cayuga and Seneca towns. They should not have come, Tall-man! Now all the Six Nations will paint for war. All but the Oneidas, who are fools and slaves. Seneca, Mohawks, Onondaga, Cayuga, Tuscarora—all are mixing war paint! We are coming with fire and steel. We will drive you back to Hudson's River and there the British armies will finish you. The Six Nations can put two thousand fighting men on the trails to the settlements. We will not leave one house unburned in all the farm country that rings the Long House. Believe me, white men!"

His cold biting words made me shiver. I could picture the leaping flames, I could hear the screams, I could see the sprawled bodies.

Harm Tallman answered him, as it seemed to me, with foolish braggadocio. "You'd better keep your Injuns to home, John, same as you been doing since the war started. You put 'em on us, and our General will send ten thousand men to destroy every village in the Long House. Where was them two thousand you talk about when Herkimer whipped you? I heard you didn't have five hundred Injuns at Oriskany, and a good part of 'em was those flea-bitten Missisaugas from Canada."

I expected Cornplanter to rise up in anger, but I proved no judge of Indian temperament. The Seneca shrugged his broad shoulders, saying, "Two thousand in all the nations, yes, but they are like your militia. Often they have other things to do when the time for fighting comes. But we come, Tall-man. Remember!"

"Why ain't you painted now, John?" Harm asked. "This a war party or ain't it?"

Cornplanter evaded the query. "The meat is ready," he said. "Come and eat. There is plenty for all."

He gave the invitation as if he were the host and we were the guests, as if the deer meat had fallen to his rifle. We followed him to the fire, where his Senecas were already tearing at slabs of meat, charred blackly on the outside and dripping red within.

Neither Harm nor I ate much, being filled with fish and turnips. The Indians ate as if they had starved for a week before falling upon our bounty.

When the meal was finished, Cornplanter's four warriors took our rifles, Harm's and mine, and proceeded to have target practice on the head of the big buck that Harm had shot. One after another of them took my fine rifle, made by John Golcher in Easton at Hawk's order for my sixteenth birthday, and misused it so flagrantly that my blood boiled. They tapped the delicate cherry stock on boulders to seat the powder charge; one of them dropped it ringingly among the rocks; still a third picked curiously at the silver stock mountings with his hunting knife.

Harm cautioned me in a whisper that Cornplanter could not hear: "Hold your tongue, Matt! Let them weasels do whatever they want, long as they don't get mad at us. We ain't out of the woods by a long shot, no matter how sweet John Abeel talks."

It was evident that Cornplanter wanted to talk. He told us boastingly about his exploits and those of other Senecas at the battle of Oriskany in the late summer. He questioned us about our army service and about the kind of man the General was, as well as about some of our other noted commanders. He and Harm bragged shamelessly on whatever topic came up. For the most part I sat silently, waiting for darkness, and watching the four Senecas distribute our gear in the lean-to among themselves with much bickering and some threats of violence. I was glad that Harm had finished the jug of applejack. Drunken Indians are dangerous and unpredictable.

Finally the sun dropped behind the western mountains and Cornplanter yawned. He called harshly in Seneca to his warriors, who were now broiling sliced liver over the coals of the fire, gulping it down as it charred, as if they had not just finished a big meal of deer meat. When he spoke, they stopped their gluttony briefly, coming to take care of Harm and me. They trussed us tightly with strips of buckskin, so tautly drawn that there was no play between my wrists or my ankles. They hauled us near the fire but tethered us far enough away so that we could not reach it to burn away our bonds. They put a few logs to burn for the night, but Harm and I got little of the heat. Cornplanter and one of the others went into the lean-to and curled up in the blankets. The other two rolled close to the slow-burning fire.

Harm and I tried to inch closer to the heat, but we were bound too tightly. We were soon chilled to the marrow, and I feared that our hands and feet might freeze before the long night was over.

Dawn brought a cold wind that told of rain or snow, with thick gray clouds scudding low across the sky. Oddly, my first thought on rousing from drowsiness was that it would be a fine morning for duck-shooting on the Delaware or in the Drowned Lands to the east. This was probably because my feet and hands were so numb that I might have spent the past few bitter hours in a duckblind.

The Indians wasted no time with us as the light came over the land. First they built up the fire and had a gay time spitting and broiling the four partridge and two rabbits that I had shot some days ago. They cooked the partridge without plucking them, fouling the air with the smell of burning feathers, and they skinned the rabbits in a manner to make your stomach turn—by hacking off head and feet and then squeezing the body out through the skin by hand-over-hand pressure.

I had no desire for burnt partridge feathers or squeezed rabbit, so it didn't matter to me that they finished all but the bones. All I wanted was to be untied, so the circulation would return to my arms and legs, and I could stop shivering as if I had the ague. Harm said he was hungry, unplucked partridge or not, and damned the Indians for not feeding us along with themselves.

After their meal, the Indians trotted off to the intervale where our horses grazed. They brought the animals back to the trees where the deer were hanging, forthwith beginning to pack the carcasses on the horses.

Cornplanter came to us. He took his knife from his belt, and for a moment I thought that he was about to kill us. Instead, with a few deft slashes of his blade, he cut away our bonds. Then he sat on a rock, watching us trying to restore the flow of blood to our limbs. The pleasant expression on his face might have been indicative of sympathy, but I damned him silently, knowing that he was amused.

"So, Tall-man, we go now," the Seneca said. "We should kill

you, or take you back to the Long House, but you have hunted well for us and have supplied us with fine horses. We thank you."

"It ain't no way to do, steal from friends," Harm said.

"Not steal—just take," Cornplanter answered harshly. "And remember this: no more friends, between Seneca and Bostonian. I warned you last night. I tell you once more. We are coming. It will be soon. Next time you will see us painted."

He left us swiftly, walking like a white man in his fine boots and breeches. Bitterly I watched his Indians lead our horses away from the camp, westward toward the rolling mountains that were the natural barrier to the Long House, the land of the Six Nations. I saw one of the Indians jauntily sporting my prized long rifle, and knew that I would never have another like it, just as I knew that in his careless hands it would be scrap within a year. Gone also were Hawk's two prized bird guns, fashioned in Amsterdam in Holland, that he had purchased from a Dutch ship's captain in New York when I was but a boy.

"Well, Matt," Harm said matter-of-factly, "we got off with our hair. That's more than I bargained for. Let's see if they left anything we can eat."

"Three horses, six deer, and the two finest rifles this side of the Pennsylvania line! And Hawk's bird-shooters! We didn't lift a finger to stop 'em."

Harm laughed shortly. "Damn good thing we didn't! They ain't just Injuns, Matt. They're Senecas, and they'd kill you quick as they'd kill a coon in a corn patch. We're lucky it was just Cornplanter and them four puppy dogs of his, instead of a big painted war party."

I stared soberly at him. "So you think he was telling the truth? That they'll be down on the settlements with war parties?"

"Maybe. He ain't like most Injuns. He don't brag just to hear hisself talk."

"So that changes things," I said abruptly. "The company can't go back to the army now, with Indians coming."

Harm snorted. "Now hold your horses, Matt. Think about it. I ain't saying the Injuns won't come down on the settlements, but they won't come on our part of the back country. There's lots of places that's easier for 'em than the Deerkill Valley, easier to get to and easier to hit. Besides, what the company does ain't for us to say."

"Who, then, for God's sakes? He told *us* they were coming, didn't he? We know they were down here looking over the settlements, don't we? Who can say better than we can?"

"Your father, that's who. We'll tell him what's what, and he'll do all the deciding."

Harm turned stiffly away, trying his legs carefully to see if he had regained full control of them. "Come on, Matt, and see what they didn't find to steal. They left our hunting bags, so we got fish lines to pick up our breakfast with. Maybe we can pull out a few trout before we start that long walk home."

So my father would do the deciding, would he? Just as he's always done, I thought bitterly. Ask Hawk Hill, was the single answer to every problem that ever came up in the Deerkill Valley. Just ask Hawk, and you'll get the wise and provident answer. Hawk Hill knows everything there is to know, and then some.

Except in the small matter of fighting England, I told myself. A few words from a few demagogues, and Hawk Hill turns into a wild-eyed crusader. Just like *Richard Coeur de Lion*, except that Richard had trained warriors behind him, not a bunch of clodhopping farmers and shambling woodsrunners.

That's not fair, I told myself instantly, thinking of Hawk as captain of our company—leader and chaplain and doctor and nurse and lawyer and defender. Be fair to him. If they were all like Hawk, we could win—it's possible. But they're not all like Hawk. Very few of them are, that I ever met.

But he's wrong about this, about going back to the army. We can't put our faith any longer in the wisdom of Hawk Hill. Not when he says: Leave the valley to the women and boys. They can take care of the Indians. We must go back because the General needs us.

I took a deep breath as the words went through my mind: Damn the General! Damn his pigheaded refusal to admit that we were licked, that we were licked when the first shot was fired at Lexington! And I would be damned if I went back!

CHAPTER TWO

The distance from our hunting camp to the Deerkill Valley was about fifteen miles, which might not be very far in a country of hard roads for the comfort of any itinerant with a spring-fitted chaise. By way of shanks' mare, however, following deer runs through heavy timber, it is a good piece of wearying travel for two hungry and dispirited men.

Midway through the afternoon, Harm Tallman and I topped the long escarpment that overlooks our valley. Sweated and puffing, we each drank of the cold sweet water that bubbles from a spring on the rim of the ridge. Then I threw myself to the ground to rest my aching muscles.

Harm, with the stamina of an ox, looked down at me smilingly. "Even if we're damn hungry," he said, "let's not run right down there. I'll take a turn along the ridge here, while you get your wind back. Maybe I'll find sign that them Injuns was here to have a look at the valley."

He left, and I settled comfortably on my belly in a wind-drifted cushion of brown oak leaves. Far below, in the clear autumn air, stretched the rugged beauty of the Deerkill Valley. The vivid colors of fall had not yet given way to the coming of winter, and I looked upon a vast expanse splashed with yellow and red and brown, as well as the rich green of the pine and hemlock stands.

Through the center of the valley twisted the Deerkill, some sections of its length visible to me where it coursed through the plowed fields of farm land. Along the creek or set above it on the sloping hills were the houses and cabins of our people. I could see perhaps thirty of them in the length and breadth of the valley, while twice as many again were hidden in stands of timber or behind the shoulders of the hills.

South of the center of the valley was the village, if such it could be called. The church dominated the cluster of buildings, a strange sight to any visitor who might know that the valley had been settled by a mixture of New Englanders and Yorkers from along the Hudson. The church was built in the shape of a long house of the Iroquois, although logs and cedar shingles were its materials instead of the Indians' withes and slabs of elm bark. It had stood for twenty-two years, since my father and the first minister (an erstwhile missionary to the Oneidas) had built it together.

It was typical of our people that, after more than twenty years, the propriety of holding divine services in a temple of heathen inspiration was a prime issue in town affairs. The new minister, Mr. Ovid Cornwall, led the proponents of a traditional New England frame building. Their plans and scheming came to naught, however, because Hawk Hill liked the old church. That settled the matter. It may not be precisely true for me to say that my father's word was law in the Deerkill Valley, but it is proper to point out the inclination of our people to consider that authority and Hawk's opinion were one and the same thing.

There were other buildings clustered near the church: the mill, the blacksmith shop, the schoolhouse, Woodward's staples shop and trading post, and, well away from the House of the Lord, Wisner's tavern. The tavern was the largest building of all, built of gray and brown stone in the Dutch fashion of the Hudson Valley towns. It stood well within a tall stockade, fixed with firing platforms and loopholes. The Indians had not come so far down as our valley but once in all its history, yet the stockade had always been maintained.

It has been said in my hearing, and sometimes to my face, that York Staters will stretch the truth to its breaking point on any occasion. Be that as it may (although those who say it are certainly not familiar with men from Connecticut or the Jerseys), I will aver that my eagle's-eye view of the Deerkill Valley on that day in the fall of 1777 stands in my memory as the most beautiful of the many natural wonders I have been privileged to see.

33

Yet I suppose that I must qualify my appreciation of the beauty of our valley as I lay gazing fondly on it from my couch of oak leaves on the escarpment. My fight with Harm Tallman, our encounter with the Indians and Cornplanter's threat, and my hatred of the civil war we were engaged upon, each tended to bolster my conviction that all would be well if I were left alone to live quietly in this lovely place, to farm the land according to the science my father had taught me, and to hunt and to fish and to trap in the forests I loved.

I knew, however, that I could not freely choose to do so. When Harm returned, we would start down the mountain, and any illusion of placidity would go whistling when I once again faced Hawk Hill.

Who was Hawk Hill? That would appear to be a proper question to answer, since I have thus far directed this narrative to show that Harm Tallman thought him something of a god, while I, his son, have indicated that I seriously doubted both his omnipotence and his omniscience.

In 1753, during the year when I was born, Hawk Hill opened the Deerkill Valley to settlement. A man in his early twenties then, he led six families southwest from Highland Landing in Highland County on Hudson's River. The new Canaan to which he led them was then a remote valley cut off from the civilization of Highland County by the old mountains that crowd the Catskills' southern slopes. The Deerkill, flowing into the Neversink and down to the Delaware, offered fair access to the Jersey and Pennsylvania borders, but the ties of the early settlers in our valley were with the New York towns and villages to the northeast.

Hawk was a leader and became the guide and mentor of the new settlement, its unofficial governor until the county government crossed the mountains, and then King's magistrate until the colonies renounced His Britannic Majesty. More than that: my earliest memories, as well as those of youth, recall Hawk as master builder, competent physician, teacher, skilled hunter, militia captain, miller, tanner, and the wisest farmer in the valley. For the myriad problems besetting a frontier village, Hawk offered and executed solutions.

Some of those early years were desperate, he often told me, as did

34

my mother. But, as the Deerkill Valley settlement grew in population and in cleared land, Hawk Hill's stature grew as well. When I came to manhood, there were almost four hundred people in eighty-odd families for whom Hawk Hill's word was law. There were a few malcontents, of course, as every community must have to give it common sense enough to avoid arrogance.

These few questioned all my father did and said. They denied his right to rule our valley with what may be described as benevolent tyranny. Yet Hawk was friend and neighbor to them as well as to all others who lived there, and set himself above no man, by principle, although, even if it's his son who says it, in practice he was head and shoulders above most of them.

Those who opposed my father were usually found doing it in the tavern over sundry mugs of flip. Wisner, the tavernkeeper, often livened a dull evening by drawing out some criticism of Hawk, with seemingly casual questions, until a red-hot argument was going. (Harm Tallman, being by nature a frequenter of taverns, found these people to be fine opponents for his brawling. When they gained the wisdom to stop running down Hawk Hill in Harm's presence, he was constrained to keep at the subject until they made some real or fancied mistake in answering; then he would whip them, one or more, in good conscience.)

Until 1777, I suppose it must be said that I lived in the shadow of my father and was content to do so because I gained so much by it; he imparted to me whatever skills and wisdom I managed to attain.

He was beyond doubt the head of our household, as he was of the valley, but I can remember many a time when my mother's lifted eyebrow was all that was needed to alter his plans or course of action.

Since this narrative brings him fully to view, let it be enough now to say that, as I looked down into the Deerkill Valley while Harm prowled the ridge, I was thinking of my father with admiration and affection, although I faced the prospect of clashing harshly with him at the very moment when he would issue the call to our company of rangers to return to the army and to the senseless war against England.

Our house was built on a plateau, among tall oak trees, and it faced the morning sun above the central part of the Deerkill Valley. It was of stone and peeled log construction, the largest building in the settlement.

The first house my father and mother had lived in, where I was born in 1753, had burned one winter's night in 1765.

It might help explain Harm Tallman's devotion to my father to relate the circumstances of that fire. Harm was the son of a woodsrunner who had once gone to Canada and never come back, leaving the boy with an uncle who had seven or eight children of his own. My mother and father took Harm into our family, making him welcome for as long as he wished to stay. (That hadn't been beyond young manhood; Harm turned to woodsrunning as his father had.)

The fire that burned our first house started in the woodshed where Harm had perched himself on a pile of kindling to puff on a clay pipe. While the embers of the house were still glowing and sending bright sparks sailing on the bitter wind, Harm had stepped up to Hawk (against my advice) and confessed that the fire had probably been started by coals from his pipe, which he had dropped in his haste to get outside to relieve his stomach of the unpleasant effects of our strong dark native tobacco. Harm must have expected his orphaned world to fall apart with the words, since my father and mother were the only adults who had ever given him more than crusts and sharp words.

Instead, Hawk Hill had rumpled the boy's hair, told him that they'd managed to get almost everything out of the house, and that he'd intended to burn the place down anyway and build us a new one on the same spot. After these many years, I can remember the look of wonder on Harm's face that he was to be forgiven so great a crime; I can see the tears running down his grimy cheeks. I can hear Hawk's cheerful laugh as he spoke to the assembled fire fighters from all over the valley. "Well, boys, we kept our record perfect—we saved another chimney!"

My father had built a new house where the old one stood, and since he was by that time a man of means and estate it was the finest house anywhere west of the towns on the Hudson in our part of New York. It was studded square with four chimneys, so that each room had its fireplace against the bone-chilling cold of our mountain winters. There were windows by the dozen in its eight rooms, and a morning visitor might be dazzled by the glare of the sun from the glass as he made his way up the ridge.

My mother had free rein in furnishing, and I remember well how she and Hawk went off on the unheard-of journey to New York city to buy the things she wanted. They were gone three weeks, and for the next three months there were frequent arrivals of ox-drawn wagons that had crossed the mountains with the things she had ordered to be fashioned by the drapers and joiners and cabinet-makers and metalsmiths far off in New York. Through all the years of my youth we were the only family I knew who sat a dinner table of polished cherry with spindle chairs that seemed likely to collapse at the least shift of a body's bottom, the table covered with linen cloths finer than my Sabbath shirt. And woe to me or Harm, when he was with us, or later, to my brother Johnny and little sister Abbie, if any one of us spilled gravy or wild grape jelly on the linen.

Yet it must not be imagined that ours was a stiff, precise, a-place-for-everything-and-everything-in-its-place kind of house. In the huge parlor where we, unlike most families who had a parlor, spent a great deal of our time, you would have to step over various dogs and children sprawled on the bearskin throw rugs, and you would see our guns on racks of deer antlers. There were books everywhere, for Hawk used to say that no penny left in a bookseller's shop was ever wasted. In our parlor you might want to sit down before the fire, but first you would have to remove my mother's knitting—like as not with a kitten sleeping on it—or a half-finished black duck decoy that Johnny was carving, or a sack of seed corn that Hawk had been examining by firelight. Probably, as soon as you stretched your legs to the fire, our old black tomcat, scarred from a score of mid-night brawls, would be rubbing at your shoes.

The house had a long, white-picketed porch looking eastward into the valley, and it was here that Harm and I saw Hawk standing when we came through our cleared fields that stretched to the mountain shoulder. He did not see us at first, since he was facing the valley at right angles to our approach, but the barking of our dogs as they raced toward us alerted him. He came to the end of the porch and watched us approach.

I was reminded of the last time I had come home and found him waiting so. It came into Harm's mind, too, because he said softly to me: "This is the second time he's seen us come home dragging our tails."

I nodded, thinking about it, looking across the fields to the straight figure on the porch. The other time we had come home this way was after the army had been whipped at the battle of Germantown.

That time I had seen him, standing as he now stood, from the fork in the road below the house. There were only five of us left in a group, of the entire company. The others had dropped out of the march as we'd reached their homes in the valley, along the Deerkill and in the black dirt country that touches the Drowned Lands. Five or six, who hadn't cared how soon they saw their wives and families, had stopped at the Liberty Tavern. (Wisner had called it the King's Inn until '76.)

Harm was with me, and three others. They looked up the road as we said good-by to them. They saw Hawk waiting. They didn't say anything to me, but I could sense the grins and rib-pokings that were being passed behind my back.

While Harm and I walked up the lane, treading the gravel that we had washed and hauled through an entire summer from the pit high behind the house, the three men in the road stood silently, leaning on their rifles.

My anger grew as I walked that long straight lane. They were waiting to see if Hawk would take his fist to me.

The damned fools, I thought.

Yet he stood motionless on the porch, instead of coming down the lane to meet us. I told myself that they'd get a show for their waiting; I'd stand up to him if he had it in mind to lay into me.

I call him to mind, clear in the sunlight. He wasn't a big man; I stood a half head taller, and my brother Johnny at sixteen was already ducking his head to pass through doorways. Hawk stood big, though, in whatever company.

He had the look, appropriately, of the hawks of our mountains, yet he wasn't named for the bird at all—Hawk was his mother's maiden name. To call him properly, he was Marion Hawk Hill, but my mother was the one person in the world who called him "Marion."

His face was long and lean and his nose was hooked. He had the eyes to go with the hook—they were hazel, often seeming to flash with a yellow flintiness.

He had a thin, whiplike body with a strength that I had seldom seen taxed. His hair was black and coarse, and his body, winter or summer, was weathered brown. His voice was harsh, though in the main he used it gently.

He hadn't moved when we were twenty yards from the porch. I could be just as stubborn as he was. I made up my mind that if he damn well wasn't going to step down, I damn well wasn't going to reach up to shake his hand. As I look back on it, I expect that he'd decided he'd stay right where he was.

"Well, Matt and Harm," he said. "This is a good surprise."

"Hello, Hawk," Tallman said. "You're looking pretty good."

"Hello, Hawk," I said, stopping at the stone steps, noticing that he was thinner and had less color. He'd had a siege with the broken leg, I supposed.

"Your mother's cooking supper," he said, "and the youngsters are in the barn, milking. They'll all whoop when they see you." His eyes left us and fixed on the road at the end of the lane. "What are they waiting there for? They look like relatives at a burying."

I smiled. "They didn't say, but I think they're waiting to see if you'll try to whip me."

Harm laughed shortly, looking from me to my father.

"D'you need a whipping, Matt?" Hawk asked.

"No more now than I ever did."

"Well, then?"

"I brought 'em home, Hawk. The day after Germantown, we voted, and only Harm put in to stay. All the rest said come home since our time was up."

"And you, Matt? How did you vote?"

"I held my vote until last. I said come home."

"You did," he said calmly. "Well, come inside and kiss your mother.

39

Come on in, Harm. We won't give those boys in the road a show tonight. I'll decide about the whipping after you've done your talking. We'll eat first. Come inside."

"How's your leg, Hawk?" Harm asked.

My father flexed his right leg swiftly, as if to show that it was fully recovered from the wound he'd taken during a foraging trip in the Jerseys in the springtime. "I can get around pretty spry, Harm."

I spoke before climbing the steps. "Can't we even shake hands, Hawk?"

"Sure we can. Step up here."

So I leaped up the steps, we shook hands, and went into the house with his arm around my shoulder.

My mother cried happily when she saw me for the first time in more than nine months. She made a fuss about Harm too. He was, after all, almost another son to her. She held us close to her at the hearth, chattering gaily through her tears, and all the while stirring a rabbit stew.

It was quite a while before Hawk got around to it, and when he did we were alone.

"Why did you leave him, Matt?"

Face him and get done with it, I thought.

"I told you, Hawk. The men voted to come home."

"And how many of them did you speak to beforehand, telling your usual piece about how we couldn't win and how we'd be better off to quit before things got worse?"

"Not a damned one!" I flared angrily. "They made up their own minds. They voted!"

"You left him because the men voted. You were the officer I left in charge of 'em. Why did you let 'em vote?"

"Their time was up. I couldn't have stopped 'em if I'd wanted to."

"Nobody's time is up. He needs you now more than he ever did. Every soldier, every musket, every pound of meat, every loaf of bread. He needs all he can get to last another winter, and then another summer. That's the way he will win it in the end, by lasting longer than they think it's possible for a human man to last."

"Let be, Marion," my mother said, coming into the parlor and hearing his tone. "Talk about that war and your General tomorrow."

40

"We'll talk about it now," he said evenly. "Go ahead, Matt."

"Winter's coming," I said slowly. "We were out nine months this time. We had no winter clothes. Everybody thinks the fighting is over now, with the British in Philadelphia. The men wanted to come home for the winter to cut wood and store up provisions and fix their houses. But mostly they wanted to see their families and to live warm and dry and with full bellies."

"Did he tell the army he was going home for the winter? Did he get you all together and say 'good-by, see you when the snow melts in the spring'?"

"We weren't the only ones," I said, flushing. "All the militia left and most of the levies. The Continental regiments are cut down every day by men going home."

"He won't go home, though. He'll stay as long as there's one man left with him."

"He has to," I answered harshly. "He'll be the first one to hang when they have the trials. The army won't last the winter, Hawk. You ought to see 'em now. Ragged and hungry and sick and dirty. It's not an army, it's a walking hospital."

"They've been that way before. They'll last the winter. They'll last a dozen winters if they have to, so long as he's there to lead them."

"Half of 'em will die, and the other half will go home!"

"Stop this now," my mother said gently, putting one hand on Hawk's shoulder, the other on my arm. "Talk it out tomorrow, Marion. Matt has just come home."

My father had the last word. "He'll be there. As long as we need him, he'll be there."

Now, a little more than two weeks later, we were once more returning to face him in failure. He stood silently until we were within range of his voice.

"The hunters," he said gravely. "I guess all the horses went lame, so you left them to come home for a wagon. You killed that many deer, to lame the horses with the weight of the meat? And you left your rifles and the bird guns and the packs?"

"That ain't just it, Hawk," Tallman said lamely. "We had some trouble——"

"I can see it," Hawk said. "Harm, the left side of your face looks as if a big buck kicked you, and Matt, I'll wager you can't see out of that purple eye."

"No," Harm said hastily, "we done that to each other. That wasn't the trouble. It was worse than that——"

Hawk interrupted again. "Worse, eh? I can guess. Let's see. You piled everything on the horses, and a bear scared them. Or a panther. All right, Matt, I'll send your brother Johnny to track the horses, soon as he hangs the two deer he shot behind the barn this morning."

"Stop joking, Hawk," I said. "We were jumped by a Seneca war party."

"I wasn't joking," Hawk said. "Johnny saw the deer, a big buck and a big doe, from his window. He took my rifle and his. Dropped the doe where she browsed, and snapped a hundred-yard shot at the running buck and dropped him too. If it was a war party, how come you still have your hair?"

"Friend of mine was the leader," Harm said. "John Abeel. Jumped us at the camp up on the Neversink."

"Friend of yours, eh?" Hawk said. "So he left you the shirts on your backs. Come inside and have a drink of rum and tell me about it. Especially the part about the bruised jaw and the black eye. I want to hear about that, because I never knew that Senecas could use their fists that well."

"Listen, Hawk," I said abruptly. "They came down to look us over. Cornplanter said so. He said they'd be back, painted."

He let a grin twist his mouth. "I wouldn't blame 'em if they did. They might find you boys out hunting again. Three horses, two rifles, two bird guns, and how many deer? It would be worth their while. Let's go in and sit down, and you can tell me all about it. You look as if you could use that rum."

Hawk was never one to cry over spilt milk. The horses were his, and both Harm's and my rifles had been birthday presents from him to us, but he said not another word about them. When he heard our story, he nodded thoughtfully, tapping the stem of his clay pipe against his teeth, as he was wont to do in deliberation.

"That was mainly talk," he said. "They'll come down on the frontier, now that they've committed themselves to the warpath at Oriskany, just as Cornplanter told you they would. They'll hit all the way from the German towns on the Mohawk to the settlements in Pennsylvania on the Susquehanna. But a big party won't come this far toward the river. We can count on that."

"Count on it?" I said. "Count on it? How can you say that, after the warning he gave us?"

"Don't put too much stock in the warning. Would you tell an enemy you were going to attack him? But we'll take precautions. I'll send word to the militia in Highland and Ulster counties. And after we take the company back to the army, the ones we leave behind on muster duty can keep a constant watch on the northern trails. But they won't come, Matt."

I jumped to my feet. "How can you say it so calmly?" I cried. "You didn't see that Seneca's eyes when he told us. You didn't hear the hatred in his voice for all of us who are fools enough to live on the frontier. How can you talk about taking most of the men out of this valley when a Seneca war chief has told us they're coming to burn us out? What's the matter with you, Hawk?"

"Slow down, Matt, and listen to me. Item: winter's coming on fast, and no war party would take a chance on so long a trip. Item: in any season, an attack on the Deerkill Valley would force the Indians to carry heavy packs of supplies to get 'em this far. How much easier for them to attack settlements close to their own country. There are at least two dozen towns on the Mohawk that make better targets. Item: this valley is remote enough, I'll grant you, to make them think of by-passing some of those other settlements. But what of the return trip for them, with the militia on their tails? They don't like to be chased when they're loaded down with plunder. Item: even with the company gone from the valley, we'd have a hundred able-bodied men and boys to fight 'em, not to mention women like your mother. A war party would need three hundred warriors. Finally, item: Cornplanter is like all Indians; he dearly loves to brag about what he's going to do. No, Matt. The time to worry is when the settlements on the Mohawk and the Susquehanna have been hit hard and the frontier moves back. Until that happens, the Deer-kill Valley is pretty safe from Indian attack."

Tallman nodded agreement. "All you said makes good sense, Hawk. This is too far out of the way for 'em to bother with. Specially with snow in the air."

I had listened impatiently while Hawk talked, and now I glared disgustedly at Harm Tallman.

"You heard him," I said. "You heard him tell us what will happen to this valley! What has to happen before you believe it? Do you have to see the houses burning? Do you have to see the bodies of the women and children? How can you two talk about taking all the men fit to fight out of this settlement?"

My mother came in from the kitchen, bearing a tray with three tankards of hot buttered rum. She looked anxiously from me to Hawk. "Is this the same old argument, or is this a new one?"

"It's part of it," I stormed. "Part of the same idiocy that's done so much harm to all of us the past few years, that's killed thousands already and will kill thousands more before they're done with it, before they come to their senses and quit before we're all dead!"

Harm Tallman jumped to his feet threateningly. "You can't call Hawk an idiot! Not in front of me, you can't!"

Hawk held up a hand to stop Harm from moving toward me. My mother clucked her tongue. She set down the tray, then looked searchingly at Hawk.

"Hard words, Matt," said my father sternly. "Maybe it's time we had this out, once and for all."

"You wouldn't listen to me," I cried bitterly. "You never have, since you first clapped eyes on that everlasting general of yours. Let me have my say for once!"

He nodded. "Go ahead and have it."

"I say we're threatened with an Indian war. I say it's time to have done with the crazy idea that we can ever lick the British Army. I say it's time to stop listening to the mountebanks, the soothsayers, the self-seekers who tell us to keep on fighting for liberty. Tell me this! Tell me when we didn't have liberty? Right here in this valley? We always had it, and you know it. The British never mattered a hoot in hell to us. For God's sakes, Hawk, you know we never saw a trace of tyranny. The Bostonians, the New Englanders—they did all the screaming. Why? Because their pockets were being lightened by taxes we never heard of, let alone had to pay. What's Boston to us, or we to Boston? We've been fighting two years now on Boston's say-so. Two years, and where are we? I'll tell you where we are!

"We run from the British like rabbits through the brush, and never a chance to do anything but get a bullet in the back or a bayonet in the ribs or starve to death for our pains. I say end it now. I say there will be Indians on us, and whose fault will it be? Our own, because we've roused 'em with the wild idea that we can stand against the best troops in the world. Tell me one time we stood! Come on, tell me! You can't, because we never did. The militia always runs first, and we're hot in their tracks. I tell you this, Hawk: I'll not go back with you to starve and freeze, and what's more, I'll try to persuade as many others as I can to stay right here to be ready when the Indians come. Don't you see? If there's only a chance that they'll come, we've got to be here to drive 'em off!"

He nodded soberly. "You've given me a lot of points to answer. Where do you want me to start?"

"I don't want you to start! I want you to finish, to have done with it! I want you to tell the men they're to stay right here to defend their homes and familes, instead of high-tailing after that ragtag army. That's what I want, and if you won't tell 'em, I will!"

My mother's voice had a sharp edge to it. "Matthias Hill, you keep a civil tongue in your head when you're talking to your father."

"Looks like you and me, Matt, will have to tangle again," Tallman said. "If you can't take some sense from talk, you'll have to take it from my fists."

"Hold on," Hawk said quietly. "Matt's got a right to say what he thinks. We've always held to that in this house and we're not changing now just because I don't agree with him. You'll have your chance, Matt. I've already called a meeting for tonight. We're going to take a vote. Before we vote, you can tell 'em what you think."

"A vote on what? What will it bind us to?"

"It won't bind you to anything. It will be a vote to go back to the army, or stay at home. And each man may do as he pleases, no matter how the majority votes."

Fair enough, I thought. The arguments against the idiotic war with England marshaled themselves and paraded through my mind just as clearly as if I had written them down in preparation for speaking. I had it in mind that, given a hearing, I could persuade the sensible men of the Deerkill Valley that they had nothing to gain and everything to lose by returning to the lost cause.

"All right, Hawk," I said. "As long as I get the time to speak my piece."

"You'll have all the time you want or need, and an orderly meeting to listen to you."

"I'll be there."

"Good," he answered, smiling. "Now let's sit down, by Jupiter! That rum is getting cool, and I want to hear about the hunting."

CHAPTER THREE

Wisner's Liberty Tavern had an enormous tap-
room by the back-country standards of the time, but it was not
nearly large enough to hold the men (and some women) of the
Deerkill Valley who came to the meeting that Hawk called.

The place was packed when I arrived with my brother Johnny,
Hawk having preceded us a-horseback, going the long way round by
the valley road. Men were ranged two and three deep along the
walls, seated on benches and on tabletops, and were clustered thickly
at the long walnut bar, waving mugs to have Wisner and his wife
and two daughters fill them with flip. Pipe smoke hung thickly in
the room, adding the strong smell of the tobacco we grew in the
valley to the odors of rum and beer and boiled cabbage, and almost
but not quite hiding the unmistakable evidence that our people
were not accustomed to the free use of water on their bodies after
the first frost of autumn.

"I'll get us a couple of mugs of flip," Johnny said, turning to push
through the throng.

"You're not old enough to drink flip in a tavern," I told him,
eyeing his slim height and the soft bristles on his chin and lips.

"Hawk says I am," he answered. "Says if I can do the farming
while you're off, and turn out for muster day, and hunt a winter's
meat for us, I can have a mug of flip. Or more than one, if I'm
thirsty." He paused. "Long as I can pay for it."

I grinned. "What does Ma say to all this?"

"Hawk says it ain't strictly necessary to tell her just yet. And to
keep away from her when I get home, so she won't notice the smell.
But after tonight, I can. I'm signing the papers tonight to go along

with the company." He left me, elbowing his way good-naturedly to the bar.

I looked after him in dismay. Had Hawk gone mad? Johnny wasn't seventeen yet; he couldn't go to war! He was just a child, for all his mug of flip and his bristled chin. Why, I could remember that very summer when we marched off to Boston, two years and some months ago, when Johnny wasn't allowed to go alone into the Drowned Lands with a duck gun, when he played games with our little sister Abbie every day after school. He hadn't had a dozen chores of his own to do then, and now he talked of going to war. He wouldn't sign any papers. I would see to that, even if my father had taken leave of his senses.

Johnny returned with the flip, handing me one mug. "I didn't get the chance to tell you about those deer, Matt. I told you that I've been watching 'em browsing in that pasture behind the barn. They come in under those apple trees every night. This morning was the first time they stayed long enough for me to shoot before they moved back into the woods. I could have laid up in the woods, waiting for 'em to come back in, but then I'd have had a shot at only one of 'em——"

"Does Ma know about it?" I asked abruptly.

"The deer? Sure. Why shouldn't she?"

"This wild idea of yours—going to the army."

"No, she don't. Or I don't think so, anyway. What's wild about it, Matt?"

"You're too young, Johnny," I said as kindly as I could manage. "You're only a boy. There are grown men who can't last a month in that army."

"Like Billy Bill?" he said, pointing across the room.

I followed his gesture, seeing one of the veterans of the Deerkill Independent Company draining a mug of flip and impatiently holding his hand out for more. Private William Bill, just turned eighteen, tall and slender and seeming as fragile as a hemlock sapling, with a face like a handsome girl's, who had marched to Boston and fought on Long Island, in the skirmishing in the Jerseys, at Brandywine and Germantown. He'd been the pet of the company in the camp at

Boston, a cool and seasoned soldier in the hard fighting at Germantown.

"Billy's different," I said hotly. "Don't match yourself with Billy Bill."

"How is he different?" my brother charged. "I can shoot better. I'm bigger and stronger. Had a reason for it, I could lick him right now, fist fight or rassle. How come he's different?"

Billy Bill had been the valley's orphan, raised by the succession of ministers that had come to our church in the late sixties and early seventies, and had early grown to man's responsibilities and man's size. His parents had died of the smallpox when he was six or seven; when he was fifteen, he insisted on joining the ranger company that Hawk formed. Since there was a new minister who didn't yet know that he was to take on the care of Billy Bill, and since Billy was already running the woods with Harm Tallman, no one cared much if he came or went; it had seemed logical to take him along to Boston.

"Never mind why he's different," I said lamely. "He just is."

Johnny shrugged confidently. "You ain't the one to say, anyway. What Hawk says counts."

I flushed at that, but then was beset by Harm Tallman calling to me to come and have a drink. He was red-eyed and slack-lipped already from too many noggins of rum, and he insisted I join him while he recounted the story of our hunting trip to a dozen sober-faced men. They listened intently, because our people didn't take to the idea of Six Nations warriors coming so close, painted or not.

Harm held his listeners fixedly, telling a highly colored account of how we managed to escape with our hair, turning his head now and then to me to say, "Ain't that so, Matt?" In the middle of his tale, Hawk arrived at the tavern, and Harm's audience left him to join the group that crowded around my father. Harm went to get another mug of flip.

Alone, I watched my father exercise his magic on these people. What had been a jostling crowd, talking at the tops of their voices and spilling flip and rum over each other, now became a quiet audience, seated or standing to face the bar. Wisner and his family closed up the bar at a nod from Hawk, and the meeting started with three raps of my father's fist on the polished wood of the bar.

He leaned back comfortably, as always at his ease before a crowd, and started to speak, his voice low but seeming to fill the room.

"You all know why we are here. Most of you have been to the war with the Deerkill Valley Independent Company of Rangers. Those who haven't, some of 'em, can go with us when we go out again. The rest of you are on muster call for home guard. So there isn't a man of you who hasn't got his stakes pounded into the ground we're going to cover at this meeting."

He paused, motioning patience to a couple of men who lifted their hands for questions. He filled a clay pipe carefully from a doe-skin pouch. The room was almost silent while he tamped the pipe, save for a few clearings of throats and the slight shuffling of boots and moccasins on the sanded floor. I watched him work on the pipe with a growing anger. I knew that pipe trick from long ago. He was going to call on me to talk, and while I told them what was in my mind, he would sit there behind me with a bundle of pine splinters. He would make a great show of trying to keep that pipe lit and drawing, while everybody in the room fixed their eyes on him, wondering if he'd manage to keep the pipe going. Fully half of them wouldn't hear a word I said.

I'd seen him do it at village meetings, at councils of war in the army—whenever there was someone to speak in opposition to his views. Splinter after splinter would flare up in the flame of a candle without that pipe drawing one good puff. If I spoke long enough, he'd empty it and make a great show of refilling it carefully.

He lighted a splinter from the tall candle before him. "Before we go any farther," he said, "Matt Hill has something to say to you. Even if you don't agree with what he says, don't speak up until he's finished. Harm Tallman, if anybody gets out of order, you tap him on top of the head."

I looked at him and waited until the smoke began to roll from the pipe. "You first," I said. "I'll have my say when you've finished."

He cocked an eyebrow at me, looked at his pipe, shrugged, and put the pipe aside. I felt it was a small victory, since I'd interrupted the pipe act.

"I don't have much to say," Hawk told them quietly. "The General and the army are somewhere this side of Philadelphia. He needs men, and he has to know that there are some of us who will stand with him until we win, until the British are driven back across the sea. You should not have come home after Germantown. You would not have come home if I had been there. So we'll go back. We'll have one week to finish getting our families ready to face the winter. We'll leave a week from tomorrow. That's Friday week. We'll have a muster on Thursday morning here at the tavern, with full equipment. That's all I have to say, but for one thing. When we go back this time, we stay until it's finished. We'll all sign papers for the full term of hostilities."

He nodded at me, settled back, picked up the pipe again.

I stepped before the crowd. They gave me their friendly attention, as well as a few soft remarks to hurry up the talking so they could get back to the serious drinking. I knew them all well, most of them since childhood; others, recently come to our valley, had served in the company. I picked out a few to whom I would be talking directly: long-jawed Walter Luckey, ensign of the company, who had only one fault as a soldier—he was deliberative to the point of exasperation and sometimes danger; Quartermaster Fred Youngblood, who knew better than any of them the rigors, the privations of another winter in that bobtail army because he had to do his best to see that they were kept from starving and freezing; Billy Bill, who had learned his deer-stalking from me, whom I had had tagging after me for ducks and coons and partridge almost from the day they took dresses off him and put him in breeches; Sergeant Jared King, hard and tough and wise in the hit-and-run tactics our ranger company excelled in. I spoke to these men.

"My father says you should not have come home after Germantown. He's wrong. You voted, didn't you? Every one of you threw his ballot in my hat, and no man knew how you voted until the count was made. There were thirty-six votes. The count was thirty-five to go home, and only one to stay to fight in a war that we all knew was lost the day the first shot was fired.

"I voted with you to come home. Hawk says you would not have come home if he had been there. Again he's wrong. I know that you all had a bellyful after two years—two years of starving and dirt and lice and fleas! And stupid generals! Two winters of ice and snow, standing guard without mittens or proper boots or underclothing to keep out the bitter winds. Two summers of corn meal in the midst of plenty, skulking in swamps to hide from British regulars, running twenty miles in the broiling sun so you wouldn't be captured! And why would you be captured? You know as well as I do, the same damned reason every time: first the militia runs, then the Line regiments run, then the colonels and the generals run, and pretty soon our ranger company stands there all alone, facing three thousand of the best troops in the world. So we run too. Count up the times! Remember how your legs ached and your lungs hurt and you had the taste of copper in your mouth—and you couldn't stop, because the British were right behind you.

"Hawk wants you to go back to it—he wants to take you. Just to clear your memories, let me list what you'd go back to: never a full belly unless you can steal a chicken or a goose; never enough clothes to keep your teeth from chattering; sick men all around you, and you hoping you can stay on your feet. Remember the smell of a hundred men with smallpox, all of 'em crying and moaning? A bullet or a bayonet is waiting for you sooner or later, or maybe a slash from the saber of one of Tarleton's dragoons—I don't have to go on.

"I can see by looking at your faces that you remember. You know we never beat them and never will, in spite of their stupid generals who had the chance a dozen times to wipe us out and didn't take it. But sometimes it seems that ours are twice as stupid."

A low hum went around the room, and some of the men shook their heads vigorously, glowering.

"All right," I cried. "We've got Arnold, and who else? Who else, by God, except the General? Name one for me that hasn't run, or shown himself to be a blockhead, or even worse, some of 'em, day-in-and-day-out drunkards? Name one! Who can do it?"

"Wayne," someone said, and there was a chorus of assent behind him.

"Wayne," I agreed. "Brigadier with a host of enemies because he wants to fight at the drop of a hat. How many major generals above him? I ask you—how many? Stirling, with his claims to nobility: and crazy Lee with his hounds underfoot: and loudmouth Putnam: and poor Montgomery who was a good one and is dead now: and Grandmother Gates: and Greene, who is maybe another good one besides Arnold. I could go on, but you know 'em as well as I do. Most of 'em couldn't hold commissions in any army but ours; most of 'em can't tell beans with the sack open."

I turned around quickly to glance at Hawk, but his pipe was on the table and he had his arms crossed on his chest. He nodded at me encouragingly. I knew what he was thinking: let the boy have his say, and then they'll do what I tell 'em to do.

"Never mind the generals and the cold and the food and the chance of getting killed!" I cried. "I wouldn't mind them at all, myself, not one bit would I mind 'em, if I thought there was a chance of winning. There's no chance, and you know it! Run, run, run, until you're caught! Mark you all what I say: one of these days the King is going to send a general to America, a real general, and that will be the end of it. One real general, that's all they need! Soldiers? They have thousands upon tens of thousands. Money? Equipment? Guns? What haven't they got? Not a single damned thing, except one good general, and he's coming. They can't be fools forever. Even the British wouldn't give away these colonies for the lack of one man. I tell you that we can't win, that it will only hurt us and our families for the rest of our lives to keep on with this idiotic war, that there is nothing but ruin ahead of us if we persist!"

I paused to run my tongue over my dry lips. Someone shoved a mug of flip at me, and I gulped it thirstily.

"You finished, Matt?" Hawk asked quietly.

"No, sir, I'm not! I've left the most important thing until last. You all know what it is. Harm Tallman and I got back today from a hunting trip. You know what happened to us. Senecas jumped us and stole our deer, our horses, our rifles, everything we had. What did they say? What did they promise us? They'll be back! Hundreds of 'em, painted!

"Where does Hawk tell you that you ought to be when they come? Here to defend your families, your houses and barns? Not by a long shot! He tells you that you ought to leave your people here to face the Indians by themselves, while you run up one turnpike and down

53

another, with Tarleton's bully boys yelling 'Tally-ho!' at your heels.

"One more point and then I'm through," I told them soberly. "Look back and see what two years of it has got us. Mean crops, and some of 'em lost entirely because the women and children couldn't take care of 'em, couldn't keep the deer out of 'em, or get 'em into the barns before the weather got to them. How many of you would have had a new house or another barn up in these two years? Another thing: how many of you have I heard complaining that the youngsters are running wild, that they don't behave, and don't have respect for their elders? Why don't they? Because their fathers are traipsing over the countryside, fighting a war that was started by New Englanders for New England's advantage. Finally, if you go, who among you will be the ones who do not return to the Deerkill Valley? Think of the ones who went to Boston with us. There was James King that we buried in Cambridge from the smallpox, and there was John Remsen that we left dead when we ran from the Hessians on Long Island, and there were the Palmer boys that got captured in the Jerseys. Where are they now? You know where: in the hulks in New York bay, starving and freezing. And how about Teunis Felter, who lost a leg at Brandywine and shot himself because he couldn't stand the pain?"

They were listening in silence, their eyes fixed on me. I'd talked long enough. If they had the good sense I'd always known them to have, they would follow my advice now.

"I tell you that you should stay home," I said wearily. "We couldn't win if we fought ten years. Stay here in the valley where we all belong."

I turned away. The silence in the big room held for a long moment. Then somebody said softly, "Matt Hill, have you turned Tory?"

I searched the faces to find the one who'd asked the question. It was Tobias Garrison, corporal and a good soldier.

I shook my head slowly. "I'm no Tory, and you know it, Toby. I fought alongside you too long for you to say that and believe it. But I never have been a Liberty Boy, either. I just think we can live our own lives here in this valley without interference from anybody. I don't like the British with their high-and-mighty ways any more than the rest of you do. All I said boils down to this: a bunch of farmers on three-months' muster, without discipline and training, cannot whip the finest troops in the world. You know it; I know it. Let's stay home and mind our own affairs for once."

They all stared at me silently. I couldn't read their faces. I looked at Youngblood, King, Tallman, Billy Bill. Tallman winked elaborately, as if to say that I had sounded fine.

Hawk tapped the table. He said quietly, "Well said, Matt. Are there any questions?"

Gerret Blauvelt raised his hand. "Hawk, you think the Injuns will come?"

"No," Hawk said firmly. "Not with so many targets so much closer to them. And not now, certainly, with heavy snows due any time."

Blauvelt kept his hand high. "One more question, Hawk. Matt said our side couldn't whip the British, not in ten years. You hold with that?"

"We'll whip 'em," Hawk said. "I believed it when I took you all to Boston, and I wouldn't take you back now if I didn't believe it. Look at the battle at Freeman's Farm or Bemis Heights, or whatever they call it—Saratoga. Burgoyne's whole army scooped up in the bag. There will be more like that. We will win when our farmers get a little of that discipline and training that Matt talked about. That day will come."

He waited, then asked, "Any more questions?"

There appeared to be none. I looked from man to man, knowing that the vote would come now. I didn't expect that my heated speech would sway them all from loyalty to Hawk's leadership, but I knew them to be sensible men and their women to be strong in the frontier cast. I would get enough of them on my side to ruin Hawk's plan. He had to take a whole company, more than thirty men, into whatever command he would serve with, in order to keep his unit on ranger service. I was sure that he would not consider taking them back to be incorporated into one of the New York regiments of the Continental Line.

Let him go alone, I thought. He's such an admirer of the General he'll get a staff position, while the rest of us stay home where we belong.

"Are you ready for the question?" Hawk asked.

Several voices chorused: "Question! Question!"

"All right," Hawk said. "A show of hands will decide unless the count be close, and then a paper ballot will be taken. The question: Shall this meeting order the immediate return of the Highland County Independent Company of Rangers, under command of Marion Hawk Hill, to service with the Continental Line, duration of such service to be the duration of current hostilities with the minions of the King of England? Those in favor raise their right hands."

I should have known what my neighbors would do; certainly I had full knowledge of my father's power with them. Yet I felt bitter disappointment—more than that, the flush of anger—when every single hand but mine went into the air.

Hawk said softly: "Those contrary-minded?"

I lifted my hand.

"You seem to be outvoted, Matt," my father said. "You want to make it a unanimous vote?"

"Nothing doing," I said with cold anger. "Mark it down that there was one vote in favor of common sense."

As I turned swiftly and made for the door, I heard Harm Tallman's laconic voice. "Looks as if I'll have to whip him a few more times before he says yes."

I went out into the night and walked home alone, bitterly telling myself that they were a pack of fools. My father said "Frog!" and every one of them hopped.

Hawk had been fair, though. I knew that. I'd had all the time I needed, with no interruptions. Upon reflection, I doubted that he'd even contemplated staging his pipe-lighting act.

Further than that, I knew that the vote reflected the men's thinking about the issues for which we fought. Under Hawk's tutelage, perhaps, but of their own will, they had all come to believe that no sacrifice was too great to free America from British bonds. After Germantown, they'd voted to come home for the rest, rather than because they were giving up the fight.

Now they'd voted just as easily to go back, asking Hawk only if he still believed as they did—that the British could be beaten.

How wrong they are, I told myself. How much they will suffer because of it.

Not I, I thought blackly. He will begin in the morning, trying to convince me. I won't be convinced. The next battle will be the last one, and I will not be there to see it—to see the militia run like rabbits, to see the Line regiments melt away again when the red ranks come at them. I won't be there when we stack our arms like whipped dogs, and then stand sick in ranks while they hang the General.

CHAPTER FOUR

I had some surprises in store the next morning. We all sat down together for breakfast at the big table in our kitchen (all but my mother, of course, who never in her life was able to take her place on time, what with more bread to toast and more eggs to fry, and bacon, ham or deer liver to be tossed into the pan when we were already surfeited).

"Good morning, all," my father said when he and Johnny came in from the barn. He nodded affably to me, as if this were a morning like any other. He wrapped his big hands around his white coffee mug and began to sip the brew, black and strong the way he liked it. My sister Abbie was chattering about the Christmas party that the minister's wife had promised the Scripture class, even though it was weeks away.

My brother John sat at his place with a hangdog look, so obviously sulking that I was sure Hawk had given Johnny's enlistment plans a knock in the head.

Harm Tallman came into the kitchen, still brushing bits of hay from his buckskins, indicating that he had slept in our barn all night instead of going to his cabin at the head of the valley. As he came close to me I was sure of it, catching the traces of the horse blankets that he'd rolled himself into. He greeted my mother with his usual deference, "Good morning, ma'am," and eagerly straddled the bench beside me when she nodded that he was to sit and eat. In addition to the scent of the horses, he carried a high redolence of the rum he'd taken the night before. He shuddered a bit when he swigged a mug of black coffee.

"So, Matt," my father said, as he loaded his plate with ham and eggs, "today we can go over most everything that I'll want done over the winter. There's not too much I'll have to show you, because Johnny'll know most of it. We'll want at least ten more acres of pasture next year, so you'll have a lot of fence-building to do. I've got it staked out; Johnny will show you. If you stick to that, he can handle most of the rest. Maybe between the two of you, over the winter, you can clear the heavy cedars off the slope behind the barn. I hate to do that; it will drive the partridge higher on the mountain. Getting so that a man has to walk a mile up to get a shot at a partridge or a mile down the creek to bag a woodcock."

Johnny clashed his knife and fork across his plate. "Pa, I want to go. You got no right to stop me."

Hawk shook his head amiably. "Not this year, nor next, either. You'll get your chance to soldier, son. It will last for a time."

"It won't look right to folks for both Matt and me to stay home."

"I'll tell you when the time comes for you to join up," Hawk told him, "but it's not now. That's enough, John. You've got to help Matt with all he has to do this winter."

So he had already drawn up all the plans for my time! While I'd expected him to urge me to return to the army, he'd been busy arranging my affairs in the Deerkill Valley. He had another think coming.

Harm beat me to speech. "You don't mean to say you believe Matt ain't coming, Hawk? We got a whole week to change his mind. Anyways, we need him. He's a good man when he gets his mind off thinking about how good the British are."

"It's not that simple," Hawk said quietly. "I don't want an officer in my command who doesn't believe in himself, in his men, in the army. I wouldn't take him, thinking the way he does. First thing you know, you'd all be voting again to come home." He said it gently, with a smile, but it hurt.

"I had nothing to do with that first vote!" I cried. "That was their own idea. Ask Harm. Ask any of 'em."

"I didn't say you put 'em up to it, son. But for two years you talked about how we couldn't win and were fools for trying. After I went home with the broken leg, I expect they listened to you a little more carefully."

"The way they listened last night? No, Hawk. They'll always do just what you say, and they can go right on doing it, for all of me. But I won't. There are things more important than your pasture and your cedar wood lot. I'll tell you what I'll be doing this winter: watching the northern trails for Indians. Somebody's got to do it."

Hawk nodded agreeably. "Fair enough, until the snow gets deep in the mountains. Then you can start on the winter's work. But, believe me, Matt, the Indians won't come. There's no danger now. I can tell you when they'll come: when we send an army against them to wipe out their villages, whether we send the army across the Mohawk or up the Susquehanna. Then they'll try to maneuver behind that army, and we'd be a likely target, for diversion and for supplies. But not until then."

My mother, who had so far been listening silently, brought the coffeepot to the table and set it on its brass trivet. "Now can I say something?" she asked quietly.

"Go ahead, Anne," Hawk told her.

"I agree with your father, Matt. There's not much danger from Indians. What's more, Johnny and I can make out fine with the work, just the way we have for the past two years. We can hire the Van Buskirk boys if we have to. You go back with the company, Matt. You belong there with your father."

I spoke more sharply than I ever had to my mother. "You heard him say he didn't want me unless I was one of those straw-chewing farmers who say that one American militiaman can lick five British regulars. I'm not going, and there's an end to it!"

She surprised me then. She started speaking French, which she rarely did when anyone present, like Harm, couldn't understand the language. Hawk had never mastered it either, although I always suspected he knew more of what my mother said in French than he let on. It had been her childhood language, in the home of her Huguenot parents in the village of New Paltz in Ulster County. She had drilled it into me and Johnny and Abbie.

"You will go, Matt," she said. "You believe in the cause of liberty as much as anyone does, almost as much as your father does. More, perhaps, because it makes you so sick at heart to be beaten and to run away. And there is another reason. I want you to go. I want you to watch over your father's health. You know that he will not take care of himself as he should."

I replied in French. "He's as strong as a horse and as healthy as any man in the company."

"No, he is not," she said, turning away and ending the conversation. "Excuse me," she said softly to Harm.

"That's all right, ma'am. Matt sure can rattle that stuff, can't he? I heard him at Brandywine speaking frog to the French Boy a mile a minute."

My conversation with the Marquis de Lafayette had been limited to telling him that the troops opposing us were Hessians and grenadiers in that part of the line. His remarks had been confined to thanks and a brief comment on his amazement that I could speak French with a flat York State accent.

I had had enough of their dealing with my future. I got up and left the table; my face was probably black and stormy as a summer thunderhead.

I dressed hastily but warmly in blanket coat and boots. I took a flask of small shot and one of powder and the only bird gun we had left, one of English make with an open choke—not of much use for reaching out for ducks, but a splendid piece for upland birds.

My old dog Porky saw me reach for the bird gun and went wild. He dashed frenziedly between me and the door, fearing that I would not notice that he was ready. He was called Porky from his first adventure in the wilds as a pup, when he had discovered, to the extent of more than one hundred quills in his mouth and tongue and dewlaps, that it was unwise to argue with a porcupine. He was curly-haired and ginger-colored, similar to the type that are bred so carefully in England and Scotland for flushing and retrieving game birds. I have shot over many a dog, but seldom one so fond of hunting as Porky, nor so aware that the partridge or woodcock that rises at fifty yards is beyond the range of most gunners.

I tramped with Porky to the northern slopes of the valley where the Deerkill speeds between the mountain shoulders. There would be partridge in plenty, and perhaps a bounty of the wing-whistling, secretive woodcock, if the migratory flights had not already passed to the south. To my mind, the dark breast meat of woodcock broiled over slow coals has ever been my prime delicacy, although most men take the plump partridge, the quail, or the black duck as first choice.

I went to the northern slopes, expecting to find the birds there in the thickets and tangled growths that flourished in the wake of blow-downs and ancient forest fires, but also because, if Indians were to cross the mountain barrier to our valley, they would come from the north.

I'd imposed a task upon myself in lieu of returning to the army; I might as well get at it. And in the woods I would be alone to ponder the universal foolishness of my family, my friends—indeed, of all those who identified themselves as patriots and whom I styled well-meaning dupes of the men who had to win the war or be hanged for starting it.

Before noon, in the chill whistling of an east wind, a heavy wet snow began to fall on the mountains. I suspected that in the valley it was rain. The hunting thus far had been frustrating, with the birds going up like gray ghosts far ahead of the dog and the gun, warned far too quickly by the rustling of dry leaves that we were coming. There were woodcock in the valley, however, and I had had two shots, with one plump bird from the northern flights tucked into the game sack.

With the advent of the snow, I took my bearings quickly, called Porky, and headed down-valley toward the ridges above Remsen's farm. There on a series of flat, rock-strewn plateaus, an ancient storm had cut a swath northward out of Pennsylvania, long before our valley had been settled. There were signs of old storm damage elsewhere, but on the ridges above Remsen's, it had struck with odd fury. Great trees had been tumbled like wheat at the touch of the scythe blade, and in their places had grown a tangle of black birch and twisted cedar.

For those who have no firsthand knowledge of the habits of that woods thunderbolt, the partridge, or ruffed grouse as some people wrongly call them, I would make haste to say that he may be stupid in some matters, such as holding thick cover until a dog is almost atop him to point him out to the gunner, or in holding a night roost until you are directly beneath him. However, he has brains enough to like his comfort as well as any creature. The partridge is not partial to bad weather. When it portends, he will head for the kind of cover that will shelter him from the wind and keep the rain and snow from his plumage. If you are hunting partridge in the face of a storm or during one, then seek you the clumps of cedar or other enveloping evergreens.

I entered the cedar scrub from the open pastures above the Remsen cabin. Porky went eagerly ahead of me, with his tail going at the great rate that always signaled game. The partridge were there, all right. Two went out before I'd taken ten steps, and I saw neither of them until they were out of gun range. They went down in the cedars again, evidently determined to stick to their storm refuge. The dog put up a woodcock from an alder thicket, and I tumbled it before it had climbed high enough to zigzag out of range. He brought the bird to me, then sat on command while I reloaded the gun. Since the partridge had kept themselves from my sight by the thickness of the cedars, Porky and I changed tactics. He was well trained to hand signals; he sat watching me while I advanced perhaps twenty yards into the cedars, then he circled on signal wide to the right or left so that he might flush the birds toward me.

For two hours we were busy in that fifty acres of cedars and birch. Porky flushed perhaps twenty-five partridge, only a few of them out of my sight or range. I downed five of them and one more woodcock. I doubted that either my brother Johnny or Harm Tallman, crack wing-shots both, could have done better.

The snow was now coming down heavily from a darkening sky, and was already so thick in the open spaces that I knew we would have a thick covering by nightfall. When our storms come out of the northeast in November, we can expect twelve inches of snow in as many hours. As the snow increased, I had more difficulty keeping the pan of the bird gun dry and ready to fire, so I gave up the hunting.

I walked down through the pastures toward the Remsen cabin, which, I will confess, I had probably intended to do all day. The weight of the birds in the game sack against the flat of my back brought to mind the memory of other days spent on these hillsides with John Remsen. We had left John with a Hessian ball in his brain, left him sprawled in the stagnant water of a Long Island bog that hot summer day when we had run from Howe's overwhelming force.

How many more will be left dead or dying, I thought angrily, before we give up the senseless struggle?

John Remsen's widow was down there in the cabin with a small child, holding to the house and land that was all he had left her—and the land mortgaged to Hawk. She was not a girl from the back country; she'd been raised in the town of Highland Landing. There were plenty to help her, including John Remsen's family, but in the little time I had spent home since Long Island, I had visited her to cheer her loneliness if I could. More than that, of course—she was a very handsome woman.

There were candles gleaming within the cabin against the darkness of the storm, although it was not yet late in the day. I could see shadows moving against the light as I approached the house. John's brother, Tom Remsen, answered the door to my knock, standing aside for me with a welcoming grin.

"I heard the shots," he said. "Wondered who it was fool enough to tromp the woods in a snowstorm."

"The birds were there in the cedars," I said. "Hello, Peggy."

"Welcome, Matt," she said, smiling warmly.

My dog Porky and the Remsen dog were stiffly exchanging scents at the door, until Porky, assuming guest privileges, walked to the hearth and settled down to sleep.

"I was just making tea for Tom and me before he goes home," Peggy said. "You'll have some?"

"It would go well in this weather. Where on earth did you get tea in these times?"

She laughed, busying herself at the great fireplace. "I had it from before the war. When I left home with John, my mother gave me three pounds in a lead cask, saying that I'd never find a tea leaf in the wilderness. John didn't care for it, so here it is. There must be well over a pound left."

She was a beautiful woman to any man's eyes, with flashing dark eyes and black hair that shone in the firelight. She carried herself trimly, without the hunching of shoulders and sloping of back so common to women who worked hard on the frontier. She wore her plain clothes with an elegant air, and in spite of four years in the Deerkill Valley she still bespoke the niceties of life as the daughter of a prosperous Highland Landing shipbuilder. John Remsen had gone to Highland Landing, as several of our young men did, to take a job building ships. The others had brought back money to buy land in the valley, but John had come home with his employer's daughter as wife and a cartload of house furnishings that rivaled my mother's in fashion and cost.

In the firelight on the far side of the hearth, their child, about three years old, crooned placidly to a rag doll that was bedded in a tiny cradle. She was a pretty little girl, a miniature of her mother.

Tom Remsen, then about twenty and a good farmer and steadfast soldier in the ranger company, tapped the game bag at my back. "You got a few with all that banging."

"They were in the cedars, sheltering from the snow," I said. "It was good shooting. I would have done better, Tom, with a partner or two. Lots of 'em went up out of sight on the right or left."

I unbuckled the bag from my belt, putting three partridge on the sideboard. "For you, Peggy," I said.

"Thank you, Matt. All you hunters are so kind to us. Tom has got a deer for me hanging in the woodshed, and Jared King will bring a haunch of bear meat soon as he butchers it down, and Father Remsen has been packing black ducks and mallards and geese, in fat to keep them, all fall."

She set delicate china cups of tea on the long walnut table, so incongruous with the chinked log walls of the cabin, and we all sat down. There were little cakes tasting of anise, and brown bread, and a slab of pumpkin pie.

"Tom has been coming every day to help with the work," she said. "We usually have tea before he goes home."

"You shouldn't be out here alone, Peggy," I said soberly for perhaps the fiftieth time. I did not want to mention Indians, but I was also unwilling to let Tom Remsen miss my meaning.

"We tell her, Matt," Tom said quickly, "and Pa says she should come down to the farm to live. We would keep John's place going. But she won't do it."

"You have no room for us," Peggy said. "We make out well right here, and here we'll stay until we can join my parents."

Tom looked uncomfortable. "Look here, Peggy. Pa and Ma both say they'll not breathe a word of politics or war or whatever, if you come."

She shook her head without answering.

"I don't think it's safe, Peggy," I told her. "Isn't there any place you can go in Highland Landing? I'd be glad to take you, and we'd use our big wagon to carry your things."

She looked at me wonderingly. "You think I'd go back there, after the way they treated my family?"

"You must have friends there."

Unhappiness clouded her face. "They wouldn't take me in, for fear of what the neighbors would say."

"It's not that bad, Peggy," I said quickly. "Tempers flared in the first year of the war, maybe, but people have to live with each other."

"Maybe you forget," she said, her voice rising. "The Liberty Boys came in the night to our house. In the night, like the weasels they are. Don't forget, Matt, they clubbed my father and cursed my mother. They set fire to the house, howling and guzzling my father's rum and applejack while they danced in the light of the flames. They wrecked the shipyard and gave my mother and my father one day to leave Highland Landing. All they took with them to New York were the clothes on their backs. Don't suggest to me that I go back to Highland Landing."

"There'd be no trouble for you, not now."

She stared at me levelly. "Yes there would be. I'd make trouble, the first time I saw one of them on the street. And they've got long memories too. They haven't forgotten that my father said publicly that he stood for the Crown, that he said no ship he built would be used against England. They haven't forgotten that their scandalous newspaper listed my father and my brother as the most evil Tories in the Hudson Valley."

Tom Remsen spoke up uncomfortably. "I guess I better get on home before the snow gets deeper. Anything else I can do, Peggy?"

"No, Tom. Thank you. Will I see you tomorrow?"

66

"Sure," he said. "Like always." He was gone almost before I could say good-by to him.

Peggy smiled briefly as the door banged behind him. "He doesn't like to hear about it. I'm afraid he thinks he's partly responsible for what the Sons of Liberty did in Highland Landing. And Father Remsen can't, or won't, understand my feelings. He believes, I suppose, that because the King's troops killed John, I should condemn all who stand for the King, including my own father. We quarreled bitterly about it, twice. I don't go to the Remsens' any more. Sometimes they come here, but we haven't talked about the war in a long time."

"Have you heard anything from your parents?"

"They're still living on the charity of my uncle in New York. My father is clerking in my uncle's warehouse. My brother is an officer in Colonel Simcoe's regiment. The last letter I had from them told me that my father is trying to be commissioned as quartermaster in the regiment. They may be in Philadelphia already. If I went anywhere from here, Matt, it would be to Philadelphia."

"About what happened to your parents, Peggy," I said. "I've heard of such things happening in New England and down in the Jerseys, but I didn't know it came so close to home. Of course, I've heard soldiers talk about what they did to loyalists in their home towns, but I thought a lot of it was brag."

"It's all been true enough, Matt. It happened to others in Highland Landing and in Kingston, and in Peekskill, too, I heard. And up on the Mohawk River all the King's people fled to Canada. The finest people in the country, ruined by this war. How I hate it, Matt! It ruined my father, killed my husband, and turned my brother into a vengeful and bitter man. I hate it, and I hate your Congress and your General for keeping it going."

"Don't call them my Congress and my General," I said softly. "I've spoken my piece against them, even if it had no effect."

"Tom told me," she said swiftly. "That took courage, Matt. To speak against Hawk Hill that way. Your own father. Maybe I hate him too, although he's been more than kind to me since John died. He even tried to give me back the mortgage on the land, but I wouldn't take it. Still, John wouldn't be dead if Hawk Hill hadn't said, 'Come on, boys, we'll go give the British a whipping.' And John and the rest of you followed like sheep, just because it was Hawk who said it."

"I don't know. I believed, at first, that we could win."

"Yes, but now you see how wrong it is. Maybe what you told them last night at the tavern will keep them from hallooing after Hawk Hill this time."

I shook my head with a rueful smile. "Not a man voted with me."

"I know that, but what you said had some effect. Tom told me you spoke very well, but that he had to do what Hawk said was best to do. Your father is a wizard, I think. He uses some secret power on their minds."

"No," I said, "it's just his undying belief in the General and the principles of independence. Besides that, they have prospered all their lives by following his leadership. They won't change."

She got up from the table and walked to the side of the hearth, where her daughter had fallen asleep with her head pillowed on the rag doll. Peggy picked the child up gently and tucked her into a trundle bed that she pulled from the curtained recess where a big bed stood.

"She's a dear," Peggy said softly. "She'll sleep now for an hour and then play all by herself again—no trouble at all. I wish she had playmates, Matt. I wish she had someone besides me."

"I have to say it again. You shouldn't stay here alone. I know what I'm talking about, Peggy. It isn't safe."

"Indians," she said, nodding. "Tom told me that too. But they won't come now, with the snow, will they? Besides, Matt, until I hear from my parents I have nowhere else to go. I was happy here before the war. And I'm not afraid to stay here."

"I'll come around often," I said. "As often as I can."

She looked quickly at me. "I hope you do, Matt. I'm afraid it is lonely, most of the time." She smiled suddenly. "And maybe we loyalists of the Deerkill Valley ought to stick together."

"I'm no Tory, Peggy. I just favor an end to the war."

She spoke surely. "Isn't it the same thing, Matt?"

"It couldn't be, because if it were then all the fighting I've done would be in vain. Remember, I believed in victory when we went to Boston. I want to quit now because I know we can't win."

68

"The fighting was in vain, Matt. Come, let's clean the partridge, and you will have supper with Nancy and me."

I stayed with her until there was nothing left of the birds but scraps to feed the dogs, until we had finished a pot of coffee and the pumpkin pie. I stayed for three reasons, I suppose: the first, because she was lonely; the second, because she was probably the sole person in the valley who thought my views more sensible than my father's; and, finally, because she was the loveliest woman for many a mile. I whistled on the long walk home, although the driving wind snatched away the sound.

Even with the heavy fall of snow—about eleven inches in the valley and deep drifts on the mountains—I thought it wise to start immediately on my patrols of the northern approaches. It was a bit like running a trap line as Harm and I had done until we went away to war: each morning I made the long circle of the upper valley, with special attention and caution for those passes and cloves that I knew the deer used. Where the deer came through, the Indians might. I saw nothing other than wildlife, of course, and probably admitted to my inner self that Hawk was right as usual—a raid on our valley could only be a diversion or a hit-and-run affair for stock and supplies—but I stubbornly held to the fact that people could be killed just as easily on such a raid as they could by a major effort against us.

After I had satisfied myself each day that all was well in the hills, I applied myself to the task of replenishing the supply of deer meat lost by Harm and me to the Senecas. This was still-hunting, or stalking, and more difficult than lying on a stand along the runs. The first day I had a shot, but missed, blaming my failure on my unfamiliarity with Hawk's rifle. The next day I took Johnny's, that had been my own, and downed two does in the windfalls above Peggy Remsen's cabin.

That was occasion enough for another visit, and I was inordinately pleased with her bright surprise when I trussed one doe high in her woodshed, out of the reach of rats and other predators.

"I'll be around to skin and butcher her later in the week," I said.

"She won't need much hanging. She's not really a doe at all, but an early spring fawn, for all her good size. She'll be tender as butter."

I found myself stopping at Peggy Remsen's place every day after that. In point of fact we had more snow, and the weather gave promise of a long, cold winter. My common sense told me that Hawk and the rest were right—the valley was safe from Indians surely until spring.

Yet each day I made my swing through the northern hills alone, although Harm, who was at loose ends until the day came to return to the army, offered to accompany me. I spent more and more time at Peggy's cabin. I butchered the doe and salted and smoked the meat; I stuck the three young pigs she had raised to give her enough pork for the winter. I did the job alone because she confessed unhappily that she had grown so fond of them that she could not bear to see them killed.

There were other chores, fence-mending and the like, that occupy a farmer once the frost has bitten deep into the land. I did them all with zest that I once would have sworn I could not feel; my brother Johnny was the farmer born, while I had always been attracted equally by such opposites as the wide world of forest and stream and the sedentary life of study. Hawk had once told my mother in my hearing that I would reach my destination in classroom or courtroom. Yet I was now twenty-four, and had made no move in either direction. In truth, just before we went to Boston, I was planning to read law in the offices of Elihu Bellnap, an old friend of Hawk's, in Highland Landing.

Here I was, however, suddenly spending most of my days at farming, and enjoying it. Why? I knew the answer, of course. Her eyes flashed delightedly at my witticisms; she laughed so gaily that some of our valley matrons would have frowned at such indecorous behavior; she was light and free and graceful. More than anything else, perhaps, she listened to my talk with intelligence and interest, and she shared my bitterness against the conflict that we both believed would be the full ruin of the colonies.

Hawk's week, given to the company to prepare for departure, was not half gone before Peggy Remsen and I knew that we loved each other.

It happened late of an evening when Tom Remsen had long since left us. Peggy had fixed a stew of deer meat that had simmered most of the afternoon on the crane above the fire. She had put carrots in it, and onions and turnips, along with a cup of tart fox-grape wine and a handful of the dried mushrooms that grew in such profusion in the hollows of the Drowned Lands. Most of our folks would have been horrified at the thought of eating "toadstools" as they called all kinds of fungi. Harm Tallman, however, had learned to choose the edible types, being schooled by the bandy-legged Canadian Frenchmen whom he met in the Indian country. He had in turn taught me and my mother their delicious use, and I had brought Peggy a sack.

The stew had been a wondrous success. The little girl, Nancy, had cleaned her platter and asked for more. Peggy and I had sat long over coffee and good conversation that coursed a dozen topics. We were startled by the thump and flare of the great fire log on the irons of the fireplace, as it burned through and the heavy ends tumbled with snapping sparks.

"I'll haul in a log for the night," I said, "and then I'll head for home."

I brought in a length of hickory that would burn slowly with excellent heat for the big room through the cold night. I rolled it onto the fire irons, causing a flight of sparks from the remnants of the other log. Unseen by me, one of the coals caught in the shoulder thrums of my buckskin shirt. It glowed instantly on the soft dry leather. I felt the heat and slapped at it. Peggy, too, tried to knock it away. When our hands became entwined, we laughed. The coal was gone, but she stood close to me, looking into my eyes. She came into my arms, and I held her tightly.

On the frontier, we live in a manifest extension of that rigid morality that has so long subdued the New England colonies, at least overtly. In the main, marriage vows lay rigid boundaries for our frontier conduct. Lacking the ceremony, however, be it for the absence of a preacher or other reason, our people are perhaps more realistic than their Puritan forebears would have them be. We are apt to recognize love for what it is and to accept its pleasures. Many a marriage is born of loneliness and need, with never a preacher to give it his blessing.

I stayed with Peggy until the eastern sky brightened at the "first dawn" of the duck hunter, and was home before sunup.

For the rest of that week, I made no pretense of how I spent my time. While Hawk was still home, he and Johnny could easily care for our place and the stock. He seemed to approve when I announced casually that I was doing my best to help John Remsen's widow.

My mother, I am sure, knew the situation exactly, and did not approve. She cast me sharp glances whenever I mentioned Peggy, and more than once I saw her frowning as I made ready to leave the house. By some mutual understanding beyond words, I gathered that while she was not going to protest heartily she had real doubts on the wisdom of my conduct. Once, at breakfast, apropos of practically nothing, she launched into a discussion of the hardships in store for women not born to the frontier, with somewhat obvious comments that pretty faces and soft voices are apt to attract strong backs and weak minds.

Harm Tallman, who had come in from hunting the night before, thought that was a hilarious remark. "What you told me, Matt, was that you're watching for Injuns in them hills. You seen any yet, or ain't you got time to look for 'em?"

A few minutes later, outside the house, Hawk spoke to me. "She's a pretty girl, Matt. Things serious between you two?"

"They are, Hawk. Maybe we'll get married soon."

He nodded. "If you do, bring her right home here. Your mother would want that, at least until I get back. Then what will it be, son? The law or farming? What? If a man takes a wife, he'd do well to give up woodsrunning as his occupation."

"I don't know, Hawk. It will take some thinking."

He was silent a long moment. Then he said softly, "I would have liked to dance at your wedding, Matt."

He had not said another word to me about my rejoining the company, and I was sure he had told my mother to withhold her arguments that I should go with him, because she'd not mentioned it either.

In the few ensuing days, as I went back and forth between Peggy's cabin and our house, there was plenty of evidence that the men were hastening their preparations. It was not surprising to see slaughtering in the barnyards in that season, but all the families killed pigs and lambs and calves seemingly on the same day. There were deer hanging too, alongside the domestic carcasses—dozens of them all over the valley. Rail-splitting was going on apace, so that fences could be easily repaired; the still air pulsed from dawn to dusk with the rhythmic tapping of the shingle shaver's mallet, the rapid hollow beat of hammer against nail on the roofs, and always the thunking of axes as that extra cord of wood was laid by in each woodshed. In winter camp or on campaign, the soldier's worry was that his family might be cold, hungry, or sick, all the while he endured these evils every day.

I viewed the heavy labors of my former comrades with a sour eye, since I must admit that my own decision to have nothing further to do with their war lay heavily in my mind. I suppose I felt a great deal like the militiaman who has run under heavy fire and must find reasons to convince himself that he is a man, after all. That's probably the reason that any militiaman is an expert on all the battles of the war, while a veteran of the Continental Line doesn't do much talking at all. (I fervently hope that the historians of the war do not take as gospel the accounts of the militia in writing their histories.)

At any rate, I told myself again and again that the Deerkill Valley men were fools to go crusading, that their women and children would suffer before springtime for their men's folly. No man could prepare a family for the winter's hardships in a week, no matter how hard he worked at it. (I am amused at the label that some of our more romantic orators use on Independence Day in describing our soldiers. They call them "minutemen" and explain that the name comes from the soldiers' aptitude in dropping everything and being ready to repel the British within a minute's passage. If they were to ask me, or any other veteran, I would tell them who the real "minutemen" were: those militiamen who could never stand for one minute before the advancing red regiments.)

Tommy Remsen was as busy as the rest on the big Remsen place, and I suppose he was glad to hand over to me his task of helping Peggy. I know that we were glad to be rid of him. In the happy presence of the little girl Nancy, I felt as if Peggy and I were already married. Yet there were a thousand things to remind us that only a day or two ago, she had been a lonely widow and I only an ex-soldier without purpose or direction. Neither of us yet knew the other's inner mind, habits, attitudes, customs. Each day we discovered each other anew.

For example: on our third evening together, we were having our meal at the table after Nancy was asleep. Suddenly Peggy stopped eating, watching me with a puzzled smile.

"What's the matter?" I asked.

"There's something wrong—different, I mean—about the way you eat. What is it?"

I flushed a bit, I guess. Perhaps I hadn't grown up in a Highland Landing manor house, but my mother had always jumped on bad table behavior. I didn't drip gravy, or eat with my knife except when I was in the woods, nor did I pour my coffee into the saucer.

"I eat as anyone else does," I said testily.

Suddenly she laughed. "I know! You're left-handed."

I grinned, taking delight in telling her that she was wrong; in point of fact, I had always been ambidextrous—could write with either hand, throw a ball as well with my left, and could shoot from either shoulder with equal skill. As far as eating went, I had long since dispensed with the genteel English habit of cutting with the knife in the right hand, putting it down, transferring the fork to the right, and then picking up the food. It occurs to me that our people have always aped too many English habits for our own good—yet perhaps that is better than aping French ones.

There were long and tender hours for Peggy and me to spend discovering one another. We talked about everything under the sun, but soon we were returning to the one topic most vital to us—how we would spend our days together.

Until the war was ended, we would probably stay in the Deerkill Valley. She agreed that upon our marriage we would live in the big house with my family. We were sure that the war would come to a sudden end with the next year's campaign, and then we would go to Highland Landing. She wouldn't mind it if I were with her. We might find it difficult to live without friction in the Deerkill Valley, since the beaten soldiers would surely resent my refusal to get whipped with them.

In Highland Landing, I would read law with Elihu Bellnap. It never occurred to me that Colonel Bellnap, commanding a New York regiment in the Continental Line, might not take kindly to the presence in his office of a ranger officer who had refused to fight the redcoats. My mistake, and Peggy's as well, was one that we held in common with most new lovers: there were many matters of import that did not occur to us.

We talked without restraint. She said that she liked and admired my mother very much, that my mother was a rare find on the frontier —a lady. She said she would be long in finding affection for Hawk. I say we talked freely, yet I did not care to tell her then that my mother was the one who took a dim view of our sudden attachment, while Hawk had already given us his blessing.

We spoke of John Remsen, whom it was easy to see she had loved. I was surprised to find that I held no hidden regret that another man had known and possessed her. Indeed, John Remsen came forward in my memory as a man of taste and judgment simply because he had chosen Peggy. I thought that I would be proud to raise his daughter as my own.

Then, of course, we had the nights of love.

The company had only one day left. On the next to last morning Hawk mustered the men on the acre green in front of the tavern. All the men of the rangers were there excepting William Leecraft, who was butchering pigs, and the Welch brothers, who sent word that they were taking advantage of an east wind to go still-hunting deer on the mountain behind the Welch place. James Welch was married, with four children; his family would need the meat. Hawk had always accepted any good excuse on muster days, just as he had been quick to impose stiff fines when the excuse was false.

The home guard assembled as well as the company, and Hawk's first detail of business in the blustering wind was to suggest to the men who would stay at home that they elect me captain. This they did immediately by acclamation. Hawk spoke a few more words to them about their responsibilities, not mentioning Indians, and then said that if any of them wished to come to the army in the spring or summer, there'd always be a place in the company for them.

When he finished, he nodded to me. I took my fifty-odd men to one side of the snow-packed green, while Hawk, looking every inch the expert commander that he had become in two years of grim war, went into the business of inspection. This was the most serious part of the muster because the men's health and comfort in winter camp would depend in no small measure on the contents of the packs they carried out of the Deerkill Valley in the morning.

I paid only halfhearted attention to the inspection of my own men, while my gaze wandered ever to the ranger company's ranks. One could not, I realized, have served so long and through so many hardships with a group of good soldiers without deep regret at leaving them or, rather, having them leave him. My mind kept telling me items for Hawk to insure during the inspection: he should see that Tim Halstead's shrewish wife had allowed him to take good warm blankets instead of the most threadbare in the house; that Justus Rider had not neglected to have his rifle rebored—it was leaded so badly as to be almost worthless; that Teunis Ekerson, a lugubrious spindleshanks who was fanatically devoted to the doctrines of John Wesley, had not filled his pack with the pamphlets and tracts that it was his pleasure to pass out to fellow soldiers (who more often than not, as I remember, put them to other purposes).

The inspections over, all the men made tracks for the tavern, where Wisner, as was his custom on muster day, had kettles of steaming flip ready to remove the bite of the cold wind.

I had never before, on muster day, passed up the opportunity to partake freely of Wisner's flip, not only because it was good flip, but because Wisner was a man of whom it was said that he had the first penny he ever made. Or, as an old friend of mine puts it when he comes to visit, and I offer him a noggin of rum, "I'll take it, because I'm not the one to check a generous impulse."

I left the common and walked at a good pace the length of the valley to Peggy Remsen's. The brisk walk cheered me, and I no longer felt so keenly about the imminent departure of the company. There were probably traces of my regret apparent, however, because Peggy seemed far more solicitous than was her easy, natural custom. She set a milking stool before the fire so that I could dry my moccasins, and she made a steaming jug of tea. She bustled around the big room at a dozen tasks, talking constantly about nothing at all. I watched her, amused.

"Something's bothering you," I said.

She nodded solemnly. "The Remsens," she said. "He was here yesterday to talk to me. Said that everybody in the valley knows you come to see me, Matt. He was kind, you understand. He said he knew I was lonely, and that you were one of the finest young men he knew. But he said that he thought I ought to know that everybody thinks it's wrong for us to be together."

I smiled. "All right, it's time to be married. I never believed in long courtships, anyway. I'll see Mr. Cornwall tomorrow, when the company leaves, and he'll read the banns on Sunday."

She came into my arms glowingly, to the delight of Nancy, who capered around us, chirping, "Now kiss me, Mother. I want a kiss too."

We both kissed her, laughing, and everybody demanded more kisses.

It was a happy day that followed. We made plans that had nothing to do with the war, nor in fact much to do with anything of reality. We all three had a good time, as if we adults had suddenly been reduced to Nancy's level of simple pleasure in almost everything.

There was one small note of discord. Peggy suggested that after we were married we could travel to Philadelphia to see her parents, perhaps to stay for a time, if we liked it. Her father would, she was sure, find me a place with a Philadelphia lawyer where I could get a start reading the law.

My surprise at such an outlandish thought must have showed on my face.

"You don't like the idea, Matt?" she asked.

"It's wild," I said. "How could I walk into a city held by the British Army? They'd throw me into gaol as soon as they saw me."

"What on earth for?"

"They'd think I was a spy."

"Oh, Matt! I thought you were finished with the war. You could go to Philadelphia just the same as any loyal subject of the King."

"I'm not a loyal subject of the King. You forget I've been fighting for two years. No, Peggy. After the fighting is over we'll see your family. They'll come back to Highland Landing."

"Think about Philadelphia, anyway. I want to go there if we can, Matt."

It was late afternoon when we heard the creaking wheels of a wagon outside the cabin. I went to the door, opened it, and faced my mother, who was getting down from the seat of the small spring wagon that Hawk had had built for her.

She nodded to me, then spoke pleasantly to Peggy. "I came to talk to Matt," she said. "This will be a better place for it than our house. And, Peggy, you should hear what I have to say."

"Come in, ma'am," Peggy said. "We'll have tea while you talk."

My mother smiled agreement, came into the house, and caressed Nancy's dark locks. "She is a lovely little girl."

"Thank you," Peggy said.

There was light talk between them for a few minutes, until Peggy poured the tea. I was on the point of telling my mother that Peggy and I were going to be married, but a man can get few words in among two women and a teapot.

My mother commented on the taste and quality of the tea, then looked at me. "Matt, I thought you would have changed your mind by this time."

"What about?"

"The army," she said. "Going with your father."

I shook my head, then laughed. "You're the first to know, Mother. Peggy and I will get married as soon as we can."

"Good," she said, rising to kiss Peggy on the cheek. "I'm happy to hear it. Although it has been no secret these past few days, the way Tommy Remsen has been spreading the word." She looked at Peggy. "He's a good man, my son. Like his father in many ways, even to his stubborn nature—and that is not always a bad thing. It has served Marion and the rest of us well through the years; had my husband not been muleheaded, this settlement might have been abandoned a dozen times in the early days." She paused, looking levelly at us. "And it's right to get married soon, once you've decided. It's the way of the back country here. Your father, Matt, met me and married me and brought me out here to live in a wagon bed while he built the first house, all in the space of ten days. I think you should be married quickly. As a matter of fact, you'll have to be. Marion will delay the departure and you can be married tomorrow. Mr. Cornwall will dispense with the banns for good reason."

"All right with me," I said, grinning. "So Hawk and the others can be at the wedding, is that why? What do you say, Peggy?"

She turned to me soberly. "Hear your mother out, Matt. I think there's more to this than a marriage tomorrow."

"Yes," my mother said. "You'll get married tomorrow, Matt, and you'll leave with the company the next day."

"How many times do I have to tell you? I'm not going back to the army." I refused to take her seriously. I laughed and shook my head. "You said I was stubborn. You're right. I'll stay put right here."

"You'll go, Matthias," said my mother slowly. "You will go because I tell you that you must."

"We've been through all this before. I'm not going to leave Peggy, and that's all there is to it."

"I drove out here to talk to you simply because I knew that here neither Marion nor the children would overhear me. Have you looked closely at your father, Matt? He's a sick man."

"His leg is fine," I said. "The limp will go with exercise. He can march twenty miles a day with no trouble at all. He's never been sick a day in his life. He's the first one to tell you that."

She nodded. "His pride—he wouldn't admit to being sick. He won't even admit it to me. He laughs. But I know, and the doctor knew too. Before you came home, Matt, your father and I went to Highland Landing. I took him to see Doctor Burton. He didn't want to go, said his leg was fine. Then he tried to bluff it through. Denied there was anything wrong with him. But the doctor talked to both of us, and then said I was right."

"Well, what is it, for God's sakes, Mother? It can't be very serious.

He looks just as fine as he always did. He's a young man—he hasn't even got a gray hair in his head."

"He's losing weight steadily," my mother said. "He tires easily. Haven't you noticed how often he says, 'Think I'll take a little nap'? He coughs all the time. What decided me to take him to the doctor was seeing blood when he coughed."

That was reason for alarm. "The doctor didn't say he has lung fever?"

She shook her head. "No, he doesn't think it's lung fever, at least the kind we know. Marion laughed at him and said it was nothing. But Doctor Burton studied in England, you know, and he talked of something he'd seen there—a growth in the lungs, one that won't heal and keeps getting worse. He took me aside and told me he didn't know what to do for it, that no doctor did. He said the pain would get bad later on. He said we should keep a big supply of opium for the pain. I have it, a lot of it. Marion hasn't needed it yet, or says he hasn't."

I stared at her almost in disbelief, my mind picturing my father, just as hearty as ever, so strong that, as he said, they ought to yoke him in with a team. It seemed so strange to think of him as ill, yet I could see the pain in my mother's eyes as she talked. It must be so.

"Then he can't go," I cried. "He'll stay home and you can nurse him until it gets better, whatever it is he's got."

"The doctor was honest with me, Matt. He doesn't think it will get better. He told me that he couldn't lie to me, just to put off the truth for a time. He said your father will probably die of this."

"No!" Peggy cried softly. "You keep him home, with rest and good food and care. He'll get better."

"You don't understand, my dear," my mother said gently. "You will when you've known Matt as many years as I've known his father. Marion Hill can't be kept from doing what he has set his mind on, no matter how sick he is. More than that; my husband has dedicated himself to, well, to liberty and independence, for want of better words. He will go back with his men. Don't you think I've tried? I've begged him to stay home with me. He laughs and says that doctors don't know beans with the sack open. He tells me the war will be over next year, and then he'll come home to stay. But he's going. I can't stop him."

"He can't go," Peggy cried. "He must know he's sick, and that he will get worse with the terrible conditions in the army."

"I'll leave it to Matt, who knows him well," my mother said. "Could we make him stay home, Matt?"

"No," I said in a low voice. "Probably the General himself couldn't."

My mother's next words were a simple statement of fact. "So you see, Matt, why I came out here to talk to you. You'll go with him and take care of him."

I nodded. "I will."

"No," Peggy said. "What of all our plans, Matt? I'm upset about your father, of course, but what about us? You can't leave now."

"I must, dearest," I said gently. "We can be married tomorrow, as Mother said. And it won't be long. You know that. The army can't hold together for another year."

"Another year? A year of loneliness here in the backwoods? A year of lying awake and wondering if you're safe? Or knowing, sometimes, just being sure that you're lying dead, the way I knew John was. I imagined it a hundred times before it really happened."

"No harm will come to me," I told her. "I'll come home to you."

"You mean you won't even try to keep Hawk home? You can do it. It's madness for him to go. He can understand that."

"He's going," my mother said. "Oh, he has promised that he'll come home if he can't manage. That's why Matt must go with him, to bring him back when the time comes."

"What about Tallman?" Peggy asked. "What about Sergeant King? They could take care of him."

"He's my father, Peggy," I said.

My mother wrapped her cloak about her, preparing to leave us. "I'm sorry, my dear," she said to Peggy. "I don't want my son to go to the war again. I know what it is to lie awake in fear, to dread the first rumor that there has been a battle somewhere, and then to wait for the letter from some friend in the company. Perhaps Matt is right, and it won't last long now. But he must go. You will come to live with us. We'll all try to make the waiting go quickly."

Peggy nodded through tears, turning away.

I went to her, telling my mother to wait for me. I took her gently in my arms, telling her not to cry. Nancy was crying too, in sympathy, clinging to Peggy's skirts.

"You go home, Matt," she whispered. "Let's not talk about it now."

"I'll come and get you later," I said. "You and Nancy can stay at our place tonight, and we'll have the wedding early tomorrow. Hawk will want to have a big wedding party."

"There won't be a wedding, Matt. I'll not marry you if you go away. I couldn't. I couldn't face it all again, especially when I don't believe in your war, just as you don't believe in it, either. The thing you have to do is convince Hawk to stay here. You go home now, Matt, and try to talk to him."

"You'll change your mind," I said gently. "I'll be back later and we'll talk it all out."

She shook her head, turning from me. "I will not marry you if you go to the army. I mean it, Matt." She walked to the door and held it for me. "You go with your mother now. Try to make him see some sense."

Hawk merely smiled. "Doctors and wives," he said. "Wives and doctors. Nothing they like better than a patient to talk wise about, and nod their heads in sympathy. Do I look sick, Matt?"

I told the truth. "You've lost weight, Hawk. And your color isn't what it used to be. But you don't look sick, no."

"I've been laid up with a broken leg," he grinned. "That accounts for the color. And this cold in my chest, or whatever it is, that your mother and the doctor are wailing about, has taken the edge off my appetite. That accounts for the weight. Otherwise, I'm the same man."

"Stay home, will you, Hawk?" I asked bluntly. "It means a lot to me. Not only your health—although you're right; you don't look bad for a sick man—but there's my marriage to Peggy that will go flying if I march off with you."

"If she really wants you for a husband, she'll wait for you. Or marry you tomorrow, as your mother suggests. That's a good idea— we can have a big party to celebrate. One way or the other, Matt, you can have Peggy, if you want each other. But I've got to go with my boys, Matt. You know I do."

"Then I'm going too," I said unhappily.

"I knew you would," he said. "I've always known it. In your heart, Matt, you believe in the cause as much as I do."

I shrugged. "It takes more than faith, Hawk. It takes an army that will stand and fight, and knows how to fight. We haven't got that, and never will have."

"Will we have a wedding tomorrow, Matt? That's the prime concern of the moment."

"Peggy says no, Hawk. I'll do my best to convince her."

"I hope you have more luck with her than you had with me."

Peggy continued to say no. That was all there was to it. In fact, she made up her mind overnight that, if I were going to leave her, she'd pack up and make her way with Nancy into New York and thence to Philadelphia. In spite of my protests and pleadings, she held to that plan.

I promised to come to find her in Philadelphia as soon as I was free of the army; she said she'd wait for me no matter how long the war lasted. We were both sure, however, that we'd be together before another summer went by.

We marched away from the Deerkill Valley on that day in early December, 1777, with Hawk Hill striding proudly at the head of our buckskinned ranks, with women and children and the men we were leaving behind all cheering us bravely. Some of them were crying; only a few were smiling.

We stepped out buoyantly, with packs full of warm winter clothing and supplies. We were the best company of partisan fighters in the General's army, not excepting Dan Morgan's bully boys in the rifle corps, and we knew it. We looked forward—I admit that I shared the anticipation—to seeing Wayne's Pennsylvania regiments again, with whom we had served before; we recalled the best moments of army service; we thrilled beforehand to the sight of the General's magnificent presence; we joked about General Lee and his hounds, and General Knox and his cannon—dogs and guns treated as well as spoiled children; admittedly, we felt our blood race as we looked ahead to seeing the great ranks of redcoats in the next campaign.

Had we known where we were going, and what the months ahead would bring, I doubt not that every single man, Hawk Hill as well, would have turned in his tracks and gone home.

CHAPTER FIVE

The road snaked through the Pennsylvania hills, a back-country road wide enough for a hayrick, but no wider. The crown was tufted with coarse grass, lifeless now in December. The men walked on the crown in a long straggling file, to avoid the ice-edged puddles in the tracks.

The road climbed steadily to a ridge where hemlocks grew thickly, shutting out the pale light of the December sun. On the crest of the ridge Hawk stopped and looked down into the valley below.

He was a step or two ahead of me. I turned as I reached him, holding up my hand to halt the column. When I looked at him he was staring at the gray clouds building above the horizon in the northeast, clouds the color of the slate outcroppings back home in the hills of Highland County.

"It looks to snow soon," he said quietly.

Harm Tallman and Walter Luckey joined us, their eyes searching the valley. Walter spoke first, slowly and carefully as always. His speech matched his heaviness of frame and his long-jawed face.

"There's a place, Hawk. There's another way off. They look good to me."

Hawk nodded. "I can see 'em."

"They say they're hungry," Walter said. "They say they're beat out, Hawk."

"So am I. We'll stop somewheres, one of those places."

Tallman laughed harshly, without humor.

His voice was hard. "Just pick a place, Hawk. It don't matter much."

"What doesn't matter, Harm?"

"Which place. I'll bet they're King's men, every whelp of 'em. Take from any of 'em! Sleep in any barn."

Hawk smiled, looking tired to my keen scrutiny. "I don't like 'em any more than you do, Harm. But you hold up on your thickness. We want no trouble now. That first place. Maybe they won't be Tories. They might even say welcome. Send somebody down to look, Matt."

I studied the men who leaned on their muskets until I saw two that looked less weary than the rest. "Billy Bill! Eben Lowry! Get down there and take a look. Be careful; there might be dragoons up this far. Don't shoot if you see any. We can sneak around them if we have to."

Harm grinned tightly. "We're good at that, ain't we, Matt? Like you say, we ain't much good at fighting, but we sure can sneak away."

He was baiting me; he said it did his heart good to have one argument a day. I didn't rise. I said mildly, "We've had good instructors—militia from New York, Connecticut, New Jersey, anywhere you want to name."

"Don't start on that again, you two," Hawk said. "It's a dead subject, anyway. There won't be any more running."

Harm couldn't resist. "Unless there's dragoons down there. You'll run too, Hawk."

"I might at that," Hawk agreed.

The men stood wearily in the center of the road, waiting for the scouts to return. Some lit pipes, others dug into their pockets to find some ration overlooked from the noon meal, a few sat on the frozen ground. Hawk went back to talk to them. Harm and Luckey and I stood silently, watching the valley.

While Hawk was gone, the scouts came into sight.

"Here they come," Luckey said. "They ain't running, so it must be all right."

The scouts told Hawk the valley was quiet. There were no signs that dragoons had been there, no sleek horses grazing at the first farm, no unusual amount of fresh horse droppings on the road.

"We'll go down," Hawk said, "but keep your eyes open. That bloody Tarleton might be anywhere out from Philadelphia. Sometimes I've thought his horses have wings. You know who Pegasus was, Harm?"

Harm nodded. "Run the smithy in Highland Landing, didn't he?"

"He may have," Hawk said easily. "Not when I heard about him. I'll do the talking down there. They might be the right kind of people, and if we ask them decently they'll treat us well."

"It ain't likely," Harm said bitterly. "Watch 'em bolt the doors and pull the shutters when they see us. Can't stand the sight of the lousy, stinkin', thievin' army. Can't stand to see a soldier's bare butt stickin' out of what used to be his breeches."

We laughed. My mother, since the wife of Harm's cousin Teunis had all she could do to provide for Teunis and his brother Woodhull, had outfitted Harm with a good blanket coat, new buckskins, and winter moccasins, as well as warm underclothing and shirts. We knew what he meant, however. We had too often seen how some of the populace treated our army, especially when the British were in strength nearby and we were in flight.

The men shouldered their muskets and rifles at Hawk's word, starting down the grade with a show of alacrity. There was food down there, and shelter from the storm that was promised in the sullen northeastern sky.

The farm buildings stood beside a swift brook that crossed the road at the foot of the ridge. The house was built so close to the foot of the slope that it seemed to be dug into the hillside. It was a white house with green trim, long and low. Looking at it, I could see that there were probably three rooms on the first floor and a gallery of three bedrooms on the second. The ceilings would be low; a really tall man would have to keep his head down to avoid hitting the beams. It was the kind of house that would look fine in our frontier valley, maybe when the war was over and people could turn their hands once again to making better lives for themselves. It was the kind of house I would want for Peggy and me, when the time came for us to build one. It was also, however, the kind of house that bespoke people of property and standing; unhappily, they would turn out to be King's people in all likelihood.

There were plenty of windows, I saw, to brighten the rooms, but there were also four great maples towering over the roof to shade the porch. A close stand of cedars faced the valley, furnishing snow fence and windbreak. Peggy would like it.

It was a house fairly typical of this part of Pennsylvania, not far from the Delaware and the Jerseys. Two or three generations had probably lived in it; it had furnished them comfort and ease; it spoke of a prosperous, long-settled land. Back home in the Deerkill Valley, the only structure to rival it was our house that Hawk had built, and that was raw and new.

To the right of the cedars were the outbuildings: a carriage house, woodshed, and a structure of similar size that was probably a granary and tool shed. They were painted bright red with a white trim. A root cellar built of fieldstone jutted from the hillside. Thirty yards to the left of the house was another small stone building; I supposed it to be the springhouse. The big barn and a pigpen were across the road.

The fields that stretched over the valley were handsomely fenced with high stone walls. In one pasture there were a few cows grazing; in another were five sheep. The spring lambs would have been butchered, I thought, and those sheep were breeders.

"They're not poor folks," Hawk said, his eyes sweeping in appraisal of the abundance in view.

The men grinned and called comments to one another. They straightened their backs. Their eyes were bright with the prospect of full bellies and soft hay to sleep on. We had brought provisions in good quantity with us from home, but Fred Youngblood was ever loath to "live on the principal" if we could forage. Since the summer of '76, when Fred was made quartermaster, he had become a fanatic about hoarding our staples. We had good reason, time and again, to thank him. On the march, when hungry troops surrounded us, we mostly managed to sit ourselves to a filling meal.

"A sheep and a pig, Hawk," Aaron Conklin called. "Maybe two sheep."

"And flour and turnips," Harm said. "That and the meat will see we don't starve, nor eat Youngblood out of house and home either."

Billy Bill called in his deep young voice. "Couple of gallons of milk. They sure got milk in that springhouse."

Somebody else said something about rum in pleading tones. They all laughed.

They began to crowd as Hawk turned into the lane that led to the house. He held up his hand; they stopped.

"I'll go alone," he said.

The lane wasn't long, thirty yards of blue flagstone bordering a wagon track that led to the outbuildings. Hawk was halfway when the farmhouse door opened. A slim-waisted boy stepped out, watching Hawk approach.

I could hear the voice, clear and level, without fear or surprise. "What do you want?"

"Food," Hawk said. "And lodging in the barn. To get out of the storm that's coming, if you please, ma'am."

I took a second look, surprised, and saw that it was indeed a woman, or a girl, rather. She was dressed in a tow-cloth shirt, open at the throat, and a pair of heavy wool breeches which were folded tightly to her legs by knee-length winter moccasins. I imagine I had taken her for a boy by the cut of her hair, which was very short and straight, without frizzing by hot irons.

"Which side are you stealing for?" her quick voice asked, "King or Congress?"

Hawk told her who we were, and that we had no intentions toward theft, but had hard coin to pay.

She moved a step forward from the darkness of the doorway. "Talk to my brother," she said, lifting her arm toward the barn. "He's coming."

A tall thin man with sloped shoulders crossed the road and pushed his way through us. His face was pleasant enough, lean and lined by weather. There was a sharp look to him, though, as he faced Hawk.

A King's man, I thought. He thinks to run us off.

Hawk would handle him. I glanced again at the girl, whose eyes were on her brother. She was young, for sure, not twenty yet. The short hair was deep yellow—almost the shade of wheat ready for reaping. Seeing women garbed in men's clothing was no novelty to me—it was easier so for women to work at haying and gathering; but this girl, for my taste, had carried things a shade too far. The second button on her shirt might best be fastened, I thought, and the breeches could use letting at the seams, if she were going to stand before a group of soldiers.

"What do ye want here?" the brother cried. His voice was shrill but controlled; he showed tension by the clenching of his hands at his sides. There seemed to be some foreign flavor to his words. Welsh, I decided. There were Welshmen in plenty in this part of Pennsylvania.

"They're for Congress, William," the girl said quickly.

The man relaxed instantly, nodding in welcome.

"Food and drink would go well," Hawk said to him. "A place to sleep the night. Some word on the road to the camp."

"All those we can give you," the man said. "My name is Lloyd. William Lloyd. That there is my sister. Can ye pay, or will it be a bill on the commissary?"

Hawk smiled. "Hard coin, Lloyd."

"That's good. I been selling to the Line and to milishy troops for two years, and all I got to show for it is a basketful of paper that says Congress owes me. I don't begrudge it, you understand. Them dirty brigands of Tarleton was here a month ago, took what they wanted, cursed me, treated us like dirt. They even fouled the spring, the green-coated pigs!"

"Can we use the barn?" Hawk asked. "The men won't smoke inside."

"Welcome to it," Lloyd said. "You get 'em settled, before the storm hits. Then come in the house, tell me what you want, and we'll get it out for you. We had good crops and good stock this past year, and I sure as hell can't sell it to Philadelphia no more. How many officers you got?"

"Four," Hawk answered, "counting myself."

Lloyd turned to the girl. "Fix supper for six of us. And bring out applejack. A jug for the men too."

I could see that she didn't like taking orders. She glared at him the way my brother Johnny would do when I told him to bring in firewood, as much to say, in the manner of youth, "What's the matter? Break your arm or something?"

Lloyd seemed to be a talking man, because he had already erupted into a new flow of words when there came a sudden stop.

Tallman shouted urgently from the road: "Hawk! Matt!" Another man yelled sharply, the word holding clear in the still air: "Dragoons!"

The company scattered in an instant, making for trees, rocks, and fences. They had experience with those hard-riding troopers. I ran for the road, looking up the hill we had traveled. They were there, pehaps fifteen of them in green jackets—Tarleton's big riders on their sleek horses.

I looked everywhere behind them and across the valley for the rest of the troop. They wouldn't be such fools as to charge thrice their number of dismounted veterans in cover. Of course they could not know us as veterans—they might think we were militia.

There were no more of them. I ran to the end of the lane, about twenty yards, where I crouched beside Tallman in the culvert where the lane crossed the road. The dragoons came swiftly, sabers flashing high. They were used to seeing rebels scatter before those sabers. I heard Hawk's ringing voice giving calm orders. He was standing on the flagstone walk, in the open, directing our men to form a half circle with our backs to the house and the hill.

The troopers were led by a young officer with a bright grinning face, who rode two lengths ahead of the nearest man. A silver gorget at his throat labeled him the leader.

Muskets cracked flatly as the men settled to cover. The officer's horse stumbled, recovered, and came on again, showing streaming blood at its neck.

A dragoon dropped his saber and slipped directly into the hoofs of the following horse. The officer still led, although his horse was faltering. The man yelled something to his men in a high boyish voice; perhaps it was some military equivalent of an English hunting cry.

Some of the dragoons reined their horses, sheathed their sabers, and pulled from saddle scabbards the short German rifles called carbines with which Tarleton armed his troopers.

Then the farmer William Lloyd was standing atop the ditch above Harm and me, armed with a long musket that had seen better days long ago. He pulled trigger with a shouted curse for the dragoons, and the pan of the weapon flashed but no report followed.

It came instantly to my mind that he'd had it standing loaded in some damp corner of a storeroom; at the same time I reached for his breeches' leg to pull him into the ditch. I was too late, for I felt his body jerk, then he fell sprawling into the ditch with us. Blood bubbled in his mouth, and he was dead of a ball taken in the middle of his chest.

The officer was still calling his hunting cry to his men. In contrast, Harm Tallman whispered an obscenity, as he would have done had he seen a wolf loping on the hills at home. He leveled his rifle on the officer, swung it in a brief arc to lead the faltering horse, squeezed the trigger.

With the shot, the young man jerked in the saddle. His grin disappeared. He cried out shrilly, the way a rabbit sometimes does upon the impact of a ball. His horse lunged on, passing us as we lay in the culvert. The rider rolled from the saddle and fell into the road a few steps from us.

That was the end of it. Two dragoons rode bravely but foolishly forward to try to rescue the officer, but musket shots dropped their horses. They scrambled to their feet and fled awkwardly on foot. The rest of the dragoons dismounted in the woods on the hillside and fired a few rounds from the German rifles.

I turned to see that Hawk was all right. He was. He hadn't moved. He was now yelling to Walter Luckey to take half the company forward into the woods. Behind him the door of the farmhouse stood open.

The firing had stopped now. The dragoons were evidently pulling foot up the hill.

We went back to look at the men in the road. One dragoon, the one who'd been shot and then trampled by the horse, was dead. The officer was alive. Harm bent over him to look at the wound.

"High in the shoulder," he said. "My grandmother could shoot better'n that when she had the ague."

"We'll get you into the house," I said to the officer. He was clenching his teeth in pain. His boyish, handsome face was pale. He looked uncommonly like my brother Johnny. This man was in his twenties, but his cheeks were smooth and his features had the gentleness of youth.

"Why'd you pile into us?" Tallman growled harshly. "Can't you count up to forty muskets when you see 'em?"

"Militia," the young man explained. "Always run from the sabers." We could scarcely hear his voice, but in it nevertheless was the familiar contempt for our quality as soldiers.

"We ain't militia," Harm said with savage anger. "I got a good mind to blow yer head off for being stupid." He swung the barrel of his musket, and even though he hadn't reloaded it, I grabbed his arm.

The officer wrinkled an eyebrow at Harm in distaste, as if discounting a bluff. That was one of their mistakes; they thought, the young arrogant ones and the older port-swigging ones, that we were some kind of peasants. Harm might have killed him for no more reason than the lifted eyebrow. Harm hated them all, from Billy Howe down to the file-closer in the rear ranks.

"Don't talk," I said curtly to the Britisher. "There's a woman in the house—maybe more than one—to take care of you. Get some men to carry him inside, Harm."

I took a long look at the hillside, where all was quiet now. I knew the dragoons hadn't gone far. They would watch us from a distance, some of them, while others went for help. I knew the officer wouldn't tell us how far his men would have to go to find more of Tarleton's troopers. There was a way to find out, though.

I crossed the road to the barnyard, where the dead dragoon's horse stood drinking at the horse trough outside the gate. The animal sucked up water greedily. I fingered the saddle blanket, which was soaked with sweat, and I looked carefully at the streaks in the dusty hide where the sweat had channeled. The mud had a reddish tinge, like the earth over in the Jerseys.

They came a long way today, I thought. That gives us time before they can bring back a troop, but not all night. They ride hard. We'd better make tracks in an hour.

Crossing the road again, I found the girl standing over the body of her brother. Her face was set, and her eyes were cold when she looked at me. "You stood there like a great fool and let them shoot him down," she said.

"You come inside," I said gently. "I'll see that he's taken care of."

"What care does he need now? Will your men dig a hole to put him in?"

"If we have time," I said, displeased at her callous tone. There wasn't a sign of a tear in her blue eyes.

"I'll show the men where to dig when they're ready."

She turned quickly and stepped away toward the house, walking like a boy without any motion of her hips. I dismissed her from my mind with the reflection that she might have shown sorrow. Her brother had seemed to be a nice sort, although talkative.

I reached Hawk at the porch, where he stood looking at the girl as she entered the house. "Too bad for her," he said softly. "She's taking it hard. Wonder if there's anyone else here. She'll have a bad time if there isn't."

"Taking it hard?" I said abruptly. "Looked to me as if she didn't give a damn, one way or the other."

He shook his head. "The shock of it," he said. "She loved him. It's written on her face."

"I told her we'd bury him if we had time."

He nodded. "Little enough for us to do. The ground has taken frost already. Better set some men to it right away. Put Tallman to gathering food. Get some others to cooking for us. You think we'll have time to eat?"

"I'm sure. They were long on the road before they found us. We'll be safe for a couple of hours, maybe longer."

"All right. Can't be more than a troop, anyway. We can hold 'em off until we get to the woods, if they do come. You do those things, Matt, and then come in here where the officer lies. We'll talk to him if he's able."

Harm came out of the house and joined me.

"Anybody else in there but the girl?"

"Not that I saw," he answered.

"How is the Britisher?"

"He ain't dead. The girl can look after him until they come back. We better be long gone then."

I set him to his tasks and the others to theirs, then I went back into the house. Billy Bill was lounging in the hall. He told me Hawk had posted him there, to give warning in case the dragoons came back sooner than we expected.

"That's some pretty girl, Matt," Billy said wistfully. "We ain't got 'em like that to home."

I laughed. His standards at eighteen could scarcely be those of a man grown. To think that girl attractive, when he knew Peggy Remsen, seemed youthful foolishness to me.

"She was a-crying her eyes out, till Hawk got her to help him with that Tarleton boy. Poor thing, her brother dead and all, and her helpless."

Helpless, indeed! She'd looked the picture of independence and competence to me. But she had cried, Billy had said. That was a mark in her favor.

I went inside. The dragoon officer was lying on a couch in the front room. By lamplight (it was getting dark now, and the storm clouds were overhead) the girl was dressing the wound. If she'd been crying, she seemed to have recovered quickly enough. The dragoon was talking softly to her, while Hawk stood across the room looking at them.

"All right," he said when I came in. "Young man, I want to ask you some questions."

The officer looked at him with a faint smile touching his pale lips. The girl stilled her hands for an instant, then continued with the bandaging.

"Ask away," the dragoon said. "I won't answer."

"You will," Hawk told him harshly. "It will pay you to answer. If you don't, we'll take you with us. You know what it is to be our prisoner? We don't usually have food for ourselves, nor quarters to sleep in. You ever met any of our doctors? I say it, that maybe shouldn't, but most of 'em couldn't take a sliver out of your finger, let alone a ball out of your shoulder. They lose more patients than they cure."

"The ball went through," the girl said quietly. "It's a good wound."

"None of 'em are good," Hawk said, "but some aren't as bad as others."

The wound was bound now. The girl tried to straighten the dragoon's fine linen shirt.

"Stand away, Missy," Hawk said. "He's all right now."

She stepped to one side. Hawk took her place, looking down at the pale, handsome boy.

"First question. Where is the General with our army, sir?"

"It doesn't matter where he is at the moment. He'll soon be dancing from the end of a rope."

"That's enough of that. Where's the army?"

"You mean those few thieves and cutthroats he has left?"

"You say cutthroats," Hawk said evenly. "I have a few with me. One word from me and your throat is wide open. Now answer me, sir. Where is the General?"

The thin lips curled. "I don't frighten that easily. But I see no reason for silence. He left Whitemarsh with his ragamuffins, marching on the road to Lancaster and York. We were out riding wide to pick up deserters. We hear hundreds leave him every day."

Hawk nodded agreement. "Winter's coming on. The weak ones leave in the winter. Where will we find him, most likely?"

"I told you. This side of Philadelphia, looking for a place to stay the winter, if Sir William doesn't drive him."

"Billy Howe is incapable of driving himself, let alone anyone else. Good enough. I thank you. Will your own people come back for you?"

"Soon," the officer agreed. "They'll catch you and cut you down for a pack of rascals."

"No," Hawk said. "We've played hare and hounds with you Tarleton boys before. You think you're chasing a fat rabbit, and suddenly find yourselves being clawed by a painter."

"A painter? What might a painter be?"

"Catamount. Panther. Mountain lion. Don't hunt 'em, boy, until you learn their habits."

While they talked I looked casually at the girl. She was looking too, but at nothing—at the wall, where hung a painting of birches bordering a blue lake—staring, but not seeing anything.

She was slim and not very tall; she would pass under my outstretched arm, for certain. Her face was long, and her cheekbones were broad and prominent, falling away to hollows along her jaw. I supposed a boy like Billy Bill would find her attractive, especially if he came from a frontier village where girls her age were long married, with children. Come to think of it, Billy had spent two years in the army among troops for whom any woman, no matter what her age and status, was a target of admiration at the least.

My mind turned to Peggy, and I wondered how long it would be before the dragoon's prediction came true, before the General danced on that rope they had waiting for him, and I could join Peggy once more.

"One thing more," Hawk said. "You want us to bury your brother, young lady?"

"If you can. If your men can get through the frost. If not, I can get neighbors to help me."

"We'll do it," Hawk said. "You'll not come to any harm after we leave." He looked at the British officer. "Is that correct, sir?"

The dragoon nodded. "I'm grateful to her. I'll see that my men don't annoy her."

We left the house then. The men were busy packing food, tending fires, and cooking. The meal was ready when the storm came on us ten minutes later. It was a cold freezing rain instead of snow. The wind blew savagely for a little time, dashing the sleet against our faces. We took shelter in the barn, eating the greasy bacon and smoked cheese that Youngblood had foraged, drinking cold milk with it.

Soon enough the rain changed to a heavy wet snow. The men stared morosely into the darkening world, muttering bitterly about the chance that was forcing them out of their dry barn at night in a snowstorm. We went out, officers and a few men, to bury Lloyd in the orchard on the hillside where several gravestones stood in rows. It was done quickly, with Hawk praying for the spirit of the man. The girl, without bidding, crumpled a bit of frosty earth in her hand and threw it down into the grave where the body lay wrapped in a white sheet. Then she left us, her head bowed. Hawk followed her, to give what comfort he might.

When he came back into the barn he nodded to me. "Let's get 'em on their feet. It's time."

They came out of the shelter with hunched shoulders, forming

97

wearily in the road. There was no word of command. Hawk stepped out, with me beside him, and the rest followed.

"How long and how far, Hawk?" Tallman asked.

"Maybe tomorrow. Maybe the next day. I'm not just sure how far it is. He's moving, and Howe is likely after him, if Howe's got any brains at all. It's been said he hasn't by better men than I. An army isn't hard to find. We'll find him."

"No," said Harm, laughing shortly. "An army ain't hard to find. Not that one. If it's the same as it was when we left it in the fall, we'll smell it ten miles away."

We laughed with him and then fell silent as we bowed our heads to take the driving snow on our shoulders. I looked back once, seeing a small patch of yellow light where the house stood.

I heard Billy Bill talking to Gilbert Hutchings. "I don't even know her name," he said. "I ought to of found out. I'll bet it's a pretty one."

"Her name's Lloyd," Hutchings said shortly.

"I mean her first name. She sure was pretty."

"Yeh," Hutchings said. "And rich now, if she ain't got folks."

"Maybe I'll come back here and marry her," Billy Bill said.

"The hell you will," Hutchings growled, and that closed the conversation.

The snow fell heavily. It grew colder as the night wore on, but we couldn't stop. We marched on toward the war and the ragtag army, and the General, wherever they might be.

CHAPTER SIX

We were two days getting there, although in normal weather it would have been just a fair day's march. The snow lay heavily on the ridge roads we traveled, where we figured dragoon horses would have even more difficulty than we did.

Some of the men had old and worn boots. These fell apart in the everlastingly wet footing. The worst of it was that several of these men had neglected to bring extra footgear. Hawk scored them roundly, but he and I both gave away our spare pairs of winter moccasins, with lacings above the ankle, the whole lined with fur.

There was no sign of pursuit in the two days that we kept to the woods, avoiding the villages and isolated farms that dotted the hill slopes.

At midmorning of Friday, December 19, we heard a rifle shot in the middle distance. We were moving at the time along a timber road that crossed a ridge above the Schuylkill. The trees were mixed —mostly huge white oaks, tall and straight hickories, with groves of chestnuts here and there. There were cedars and other evergreens, although not as many as we had at home in the Deerkill Valley.

Hawk sent me and Teunis Polhemus ahead to find the rifleman, a natural precaution in spite of the fact that the shot had been from a light rifle instead of a musket, indicating a hunter rather than a soldier.

We found him, a boy of fifteen or so, who had a sack of dead squirrels and rabbits slung over his back.

He handled a handsome Pennsylvania rifle that looked to be twice as long as he was. It took a ball the size of a large pea. His name, he told me, was Sam Baronson, and he lived at the Valley Forge on the Schuylkill.

"Do you know where the General is with the army, Sam?"

"Not rightly, no," he answered with countryman's deliberation. "You mean where is he, or where is the army?"

"He's not with the army?" I asked, astonished.

"He is and he ain't," the boy said. "He's with some of 'em. They're all spread out, like, between Gulph Mills and the Valley Forge. They ain't very spry. Some of 'em has got bare feet, and they're tracking red in the snow."

"Where is the Valley Forge?" I asked him.

"Just over the hills there," he said, seeming surprised that I shouldn't know a fact so fundamental. "Some folks call it Dewees', account of he owns it. The British burnt it in September, you know. Them damned British."

He paused, then added, "Them officers that been there since yesterday say it's to be the wintering place. My ma says if that's so, she'll send my sister Jane to the Jerseys to my aunt's so she won't be around the damned soldiers all winter. Like to end up with a turkey in the oven, my ma says."

I sent Polhemus back to tell Hawk, who then ordered Polhemus and Billy Bill to rejoin me. We were to look over the place and try to find the Pennsylvania regiments for us to share bivouacs. (We had long since discovered that it was wise for us to shy away from York Staters. Every colonel of every undermanned regiment, and they were all so, tried to take us into his ranks as soon as he found out we were an independent York State company. On the other hand, Pennsylvania's General Wayne had welcomed us to march and fight with him without seeking to destroy our independence. Further, Wayne was a fighter, and Hawk admired him.)

The boy led us along a timber road bordered by fine forest, as we had come through all morning. Teunis Polhemus, a practical man and a good farmer—albeit somewhat morose of feature and sullen of eye, perhaps because at thirty years of age he already had ten children and a wife without a tooth in her head, which in turn probably accounted for his enlistment in the company—marked each stand of

pine and cedar and other trees on a grimy slip of paper, using a sliver
of lead for a pencil, his notes reading something like this:

> On ridge—red cedar—200—scrub
> North slope—big hemlocks
> Yellow pine in clove

"You drawing a map, Teunis?" Billy asked him, when we were
forced to stop while he counted the trunks in a chestnut grove.

"You might say," Teunis answered. "A tree map."

Billy thought he knew why. "For squirrel hunting?"

"Hell no, boy. We winter just over the hills, wasn't that what the
young lad said? What's the first order going to be?"

Billy looked puzzled. I was amused. If you asked Billy what a tree
was good for, he'd likely give you one of two answers: "It's a thing
you shoot squirrels out of," or "It's a thing you stand behind to
shoot a deer from."

"Shelter," I said.

"Right," Teunis said. "And what will every mother's son in that
army be doing soon as the order is given?"

Billy grinned. "Hiding from the officers, same as usual."

"No, they won't," I said. "They'll be fighting over the last scrawny
tree that doesn't have to be dragged more than a hundred yards."

"Right again," Teunis said. "We'll come a little farther and get the
best, even do we have to hitch ourselves to trace chains."

"Good man, Teunis," I said. We waited while he finished his notes,
although I would have wagered that Hawk had already taken shelter
into account and was marking stands of trees with his mind's eye,
which was probably more accurate than Polhemus' lead point.

We came out of the heavy trees on the shoulder of a big hill. Below us lay the valley of the Schuylkill.

To our left, at the junction of the creek and the river, were a few
scattered houses and the blackened ruins of the forge that gave the
place its name. Here and there on the flat land were houses, looking
snug and prosperous in this snow-laden world. There was no sound
and no motion in the valley, except for the distant steady barking
of a dog chained at one of the houses in the hamlet.

Billy Bill spoke to our guide with a veteran's condescension. "You said the army would be down there, sonny. Where's it at?"

"I told you they was coming slow. Some of 'em can't hardly walk. I been over to the Gulph Mills and seen 'em. Yesterday I traded ten squirrels and six rabbits to some men said they was from around Boston. They wanted to give me that paper money of theirs in trade, but my pa warned me ahead of time. He said no good ever come out of Boston, counting this here war too. So I looked at the money, but I made 'em give me powder and lead. They was so hungry, looked like they'd eat the critters without cooking 'em. I never seen such scarecrows. I seen British too, in September when they come here. They was big and fat and had nice clothes to their backs."

While the boy spoke my ears caught an old familiar sound, the steady marching beat of a drum, and beyond it, like an echo, the distant rattling of another. The snow that had been driving on the keen wind earlier in the day was now swirling again in ragged clouds across the valley. The sound of the drums faded as the wind rose.

The boy pulled Billy's arm. "There they come! See 'em?"

He was right. In the shifting curtain of snow, far down the valley, I saw the column moving, two files of small dark figures moving lurchingly, crookedly over the gray-white ground. There was only a brigade or less, but I could picture the rest of them, marching that way in double file, strung out for miles. I wondered whether Howe was chasing them, or whether he was taking his comfort in Philadelphia.

"God, Lieutenant," Billy said, "it don't look like they're even picking up their feet. I never seen 'em move so slow."

"I told you they was anything but prime," Sam Baronson said. "Come on. Let's get down there and see 'em."

I shook my head, smiling. "We'll stay here awhile. You go ahead. Much obliged for your help."

He went quickly, half-sliding and half-running, and soon vanished among the trees. Billy and I and Polhemus watched the distant troops for a few minutes without speaking, while we rested from the rough trail and the swift pace that the boy had set for us. Finally I spoke to Polhemus, sending him back to Hawk with the word that we'd found the army.

"All right, Billy," I said. "Let's go down and take a look."

"Yessir, Matt—I mean, Lieutenant." For a few days, Billy would be military, while the return to the army was new and fresh. Then he would lapse into the easy ways of the rest of the company. We had never needed discipline of the usual kind; early in the game Hawk had ended the custom of saluting officers by saying that it was silly when we'd all known each other most of our lives. Anyway, Hawk said, it was a British fashion, and we were done with those.

Billy gave me a quick grin as we started down the slope. "One thing about this place," he said, "we ain't going to want for wood and water."

"The wood is green and the water is frozen," I said. "It's going to be a long winter."

We reached the open ground where the wind and driving snow had free play. I could feel the biting cold through the layers of good winter clothing I had brought from home.

The men of the first brigade were already scattering as we approached, slowly as if they had no will for the work, to gather firewood and draw water. I stared at them as we came up, a slow sickening creeping through me. I could see by the tattered remnants of uniforms among them that they were North Carolinians. They paid us no heed. They were bearded, dirty, smoke-grimed, gaunt. Some of them bore festered sores. In truth, as the boy had told us, a few were without shoes, and the ragged cloths that covered their feet left red spots where they touched the snow.

We had never had enough of anything in two years: clothing, weapons, powder and ball, food, medicine, transport—whatever one can name that is vital to an army, we had always lacked.

Yet never had I seen soldiers of the Line in such straits.

I hailed one of their officers, who sat a gaunt horse in a faded blue cloak, his back hunched to the wind.

"Your pardon, sir," I said, standing close, where I could see that the flapping sole of his right boot was tied with several bits of cord. "Can you tell me where Wayne's division is positioned in the march?"

He stared at me with dull eyes, seeming not to have heard me. He stroked a silky beard, a week's growth, with a grimy hand. I was about to repeat the request, when he nodded his head across his shoulder. "Yonder," he said harshly. "Somewheres," he added. He suddenly shook himself as if to come alert after dreaming. His eyes flickered with sudden interest as he looked me up and down. "Trade you," he said swiftly, the words running together. "The horse for that coat. You can eat the horse."

"Sorry," I said, shaking my head.

"Horse meat is good," he said quickly. "You boil it up with a couple onions, if you got 'em, and it's real tasty."

I shrugged my shoulders, somehow momentarily ashamed of the weight and warmth of the blanket coat wrapped around me. I thought bitterly that if all the thousands to come were so badly off as this southerner and his men, then surely it was a great crime to pretend that there was hope.

The officer's eyes grew dull again. He slumped further in his saddle. I thought he was finished talking, but then he said wearily: "First there's us, and then McDougall, and then the Boy, and then Wayne, somewheres back there."

I thanked him and returned to Billy. "All right, you can go back and bring the company down here. Wayne is beyond the French Boy's troops. I'll have a bivouac picked when you get here."

"Sure, Lieutenant. Watch for us. It'll be dark when we come up maybe. My God, they sure are a sight, ain't they?"

They were a sight indeed. As I walked among these poor ragged creatures who were supposed to be soldiers of the Continental Line, I remembered them as I had seen them in every imaginable situation since the beginning of the rebellion:

At Boston, they had caroused, rioted at times, and generally viewed the fighting as a lark.

Then they crouched on Breed's Hill and found out what war is, when they saw the dead and wounded stretched in bloody windrows before them.

I had seen them panic, whimpering like children, as they scurried through the marshes on Long Island, with the redcoats and the Hessians moving calmly forward to the slaughter.

I had seen them on better days, when they had flinched and cowered under the terrible thunder of British volleys, but then had stood when the drums had rattled and the fearsome red ranks advanced steadily.

I had known them to spruce themselves and their camps, in their amateurish attempts to have the name as well as the game of soldiering.

Now I saw them ragged and despairing as they had never been since the General had taken command of them. This is the end, I thought. They are done, finished, whipped. Most of them look as if they're dying.

The beards they wore, in an army where the shaven face was the rule, were grown simply from the lack of will as much as from the lack of hot water. Their jaws were slack and their eyes were dull.

Even in the open valley, as more brigades came into sight, a fetid smell came down the wind. It was not, it seemed to me, only the odor of men who have abandoned all pretense to personal cleanliness, not alone the smell of soiled clothes and unwashed bodies. It was acrid, bitter, vulpine, as if the entire army had spent the last several nights in some gigantic fox den.

It was Hawk who later defined that effluvium for me: "They don't care any more. They've quit. They're like animals, faced with survival alone. They'll claw each other for a bit of dry wood, a scrap of rotten meat. They've come down to animal level, so they smell like animals. It's going to take some powerful doing to bring 'em back to what they were."

They were not all like that, of course. Almost all were ragged and threadbare; a great part of them were gaunt and sick—the sound of hundreds of men coughing was an incessant rattle above the whining of the wind. Here and there among them, however, was a sergeant who drove a squad with whipping words to prepare a bivouac; I saw officers offering cheering words, quick commands, as if they really believed in the promise of better days ahead.

Passing beyond the North Carolinians, I saw Jersey men, Virginians, a Connecticut regiment of less than fifty soldiers, all spreading across the hillside in the dusk.

The artillery of the Virginia Line screeched along on ungreased axles, four six-pounders and two coehorns drawn by four gaunt horses and thirty stumbling men. A gun slid into a ditch. The horses stopped and the men stopped. An officer started to bawl toneless commands. A dozen scarecrows bowed their shoulders to the ropes, and the gun inched back to the road. Many of the men who were forced to wait instantly fell asleep on their feet. Two or three tumbled while they waited and had to push themselves unaided out of the snow.

I moved on, passing among Lafayette's troops. I saw the French Boy himself, mounted on a good horse, with a great blue cloak wrapped around him. His youthful face twisted in the raw wind. He looked as if he were about to cry in pity for his men.

Then I found the Pennsylvanians. Hawk's wisdom in choosing them as neighbors was immediately apparent.

They were in better shape than any troops I'd seen. Most were ragged and dirty, of course, but man for man they were adequately protected against the weather. Few of them were helpless. Regiment by regiment across the slope, they prepared to bivouac with some semblance of order.

Their officers were alert, instead of huddling near the fires that were already burning. Their sergeants told the men off in squads for woodcutting, cooking, and building temporary shelters. Only the sick men and those without shoes were allowed to crouch by the fires. The men in other commands for the most part milled listlessly while the strongest among them did the work. Many of them wandered back and forth in droves as if searching for some protected spot or some warmer fire. The Pennsylvanians, on the other hand, looked for all the world, in the half-light of the failing day, like an army of great black ants scurrying for forage.

In retrospect, I know two reasons for their ordered activity:

The first of these was their command, in the hands of Brigadier General Anthony Wayne—reckless, headstrong, capricious, to be sure, but a commander whose first two concerns were fighting as hard as he could and the welfare of his men. He might bully them on occasion; he might expect them to stand against hopeless odds and then rage at them when they wisely pulled foot, but he took care of them.

If there was food to be had in the army, Wayne's men got their share. Shirts, shoes, breeches, hats—Wayne screamed for them in a constant flood of messages until the commissaries of the Commonwealth of Pennsylvania in York were said to flee from any mud-spattered orderly on an exhausted horse.

The second reason for the Pennsylvanians' comparative well-being could be found, I thought, in the men themselves. Almost half of the soldiers of the Pennsylvania Line were "stumpjumpers" as people back in Highland County (or that part of the county that bordered the Hudson) were wont to call those of us who lived back in the hills. A city man, born and bred, is likely to be more alert and quick to see advantage in a situation than is his country cousin. But put both men into an army in the field, and you will see which one makes the best mark in adversity.

These Pennsylvanians had lived on the frontier, traded or trapped along it and beyond it, hunted its timbered hills, worked for dozens of the surveying parties that constantly traveled the wilderness beyond the Susquehanna. Their officers and non-commissioned officers and many of the private soldiers were old enough to have fought in the old French War, in which Pennsylvania militia had been kept so busy. They were woodsmen, or at least hardy farmers, and they were used to hardship.

Hawk had often said to me, and I agreed with him, that the people of our Deerkill Valley were more akin to our neighbors in Pennsylvania than to the townfolk of Highland County beyond our barrier of hills. The wide swift Delaware and long stretches of wilderness separated us from Pennsylvanians, but we all came of the same stock.

In the quarter hour or so that I waited for Hawk and the company, the Pennsylvanians were as settled as they could be without tents or other shelter. Everywhere I looked their bright fires flamed in orderly rows, and beside the fires the dark bulk of evergreen lean-tos seemed to spring bodily from the ground, far outnumbering the few ragged tents that some companies had. These shelters, flimsy as they were, made at least the pattern of a military camp, with their backs to the biting wind.

The company, led by Billy Bill, finally came through the scattered regiments. Our Highland County men were staring about them in astonishment, unable to understand that these wrecks of men were the Continentals they had fought with at Brandywine and Germantown a few months before.

They were viewed with equal wonder by the scarecrows. Resentment and covetousness were also in the surveillance, as shivering men saw blanket coats and heavy boots and thick wool mittens.

"Pick a campsite that will drain," Hawk said to me, eyeing the hillside carefully. "We may be on the same one all winter. Leave us room to breathe, and caution the men not to leave anything untended that isn't red-hot or nailed down. Looks to me as if there's not a thing in the world that these poor fellows don't need."

"All right," I said. "You look tired, Hawk. Go pick a fire to sit by. Maybe Youngblood will loosen up with some rum in celebration of the way Congress takes care of its heroes. I'll see to everything."

"I'm not tired," he said. "I'll go find somebody to report to. Wayne, if I can find him. It won't do to wait. Sooner or later we'll be found by a York State colonel, and I'd hate to have to depend on the bounty of New York commissaries. A man can't thrive on air and promises."

Sergeant Jared King joined us in time to hear Hawk's remark. King, as husky as a standing bear and with strength to match, spoke wonderingly. "These fellers around us could do with some air and promises, Hawk, and maybe some salt to season 'em with. What they got ain't much more."

"Tell Youngblood to watch the supplies," Hawk said.

"I already done that. He's sitting on 'em. Hawk, I just seen them nearest men of Wayne's fixing their supper. I thought they was making some soup broth to start a nice chowder with. First the feller doing the cooking puts two gallons of water to boil. Then he chops up some green beef, real green; the wind shifted and I had to hold my nose. He drops in the beef, one good handful of it. Then he chopped six pertaters and put 'em in, skins and all. They were black from being froze. Then he stuck in two carrots no bigger than my thumb, and after that one white turnip about as big as an onion. Make a good stock for soup, could you stand the smell. But there was seven or eight of them fellers watching him like a parcel of foxes ready to jump on a rabbit. Then one of them says, I swear to God, he says, 'George, how long is that stew going to take?' Stew! My God, Hawk, we got to eat better'n that."

"We brought enough food to last us for a time," Hawk said. "Meantime, we'll get on the commissary list. You won't starve, Jared. Those fellows probably got ahead of their commissary."

"About a week ahead of him, looks like," King said.

"You get the company settled, Matt," Hawk said. "I'll go look for General Wayne."

He didn't get a chance to leave. While we were talking, a ring of gaunt Pennsylvanians gathered silently around our company. To our men, veterans though they were, these tatterdemalions looked desperate enough to rush us for our clothes and knapsacks. Some of our men nervously lifted their muskets and held them self-consciously at the ready.

"Where'd you fellers come from?" a husky voice asked us. "Wherever it is, I'll go back with you when you leave in the morning."

"What makes you think we're leaving?" Sergeant Dutcher asked.

"You tooken a look at us, ain't you? You're crazy if you ain't leaving."

"We're from Highland County, York State," Hawk said. "We've served with you before. The Deerkill Independent Rangers. Where can I find General Wayne?"

They ignored the question, but one of them, a tall cadaverous fellow with an air of authority whom I reckoned to be a sergeant, stepped forward and offered to shake hands with Hawk. "Name's Palmer," he said. "Jed Palmer. Seventh Pennsylvania Line. I remember you. You were with us all last summer, wasn't you? And then you went home?"

"That's right," Hawk said.

Palmer spoke in a flat tone. "What the hell did you come back for? I never heard such a damn fool thing. Some of you ain't going to leave this place, same as some of us. We're in a bad way, Captain."

Hawk took the somber words easily. "They got a levy back home. If you hang around, they put you in the militia. Even you boys are better company than militia. Where can I find General Wayne?"

"Dunno," Palmer said. "He's around. You'll hear him before you see him. He's lost some weight, like the rest of us, but he hollers just as loud. He's a roaring son of a bitch, he is," Palmer said in obvious pride. His lips curled over crooked yellow teeth in a friendly grin. There were low chuckles from some of the other Pennsylvanians.

"Tell them about the pig, Palmer," one of his comrades called.

Palmer grinned. "Sure. Maybe you know Wayne has got a big farm over them hills just a few miles. Well, the other day, over to Whitemarsh, where we camped before we came here, Wayne was in his headquarters yelling his head off about one thing or another. You could hear him all over camp. And there was a farmer outside making a trade for a big pig with Wayne's cook.

"Just then, up rides the General, with Colonel Hamilton and Colonel Laurens and them other aides of his. The General listened to Wayne a-yelling, and frowned the way he does when he ain't pleased. Wayne was using some words that is looked down upon by some folks. Then the general spoke to one of the aides, Tilghman I think it was, never showing a smile. Tilghman got down off his horse, led the pig to the door by twisting its tail, and booted it right inside where Wayne was.

"Out comes Wayne, a-boiling, cursing that pig and the fellow who put it through the door. The General nods to him as pleasant as could be when Wayne pulls up short. But the General didn't laugh or nothing. 'Well, General Wayne,' he says, 'I used to think we Virginians were the world's best hog-callers, but you just let out a few bellows and your pig came all the way from Waynesboro.'

"Wayne got as red as a Britisher's coat, but he never said a word. He's been almost quiet ever since. The General paid the farmer for the pig out of his own pocket, and give it to us, and we et it all but the squeal."

From the crowd came a sound like a pig waiting to be fed, and Palmer nodded. "Somebody must of et the squeal too."

I had noticed that while he was talking, the ring of soldiers had drawn ever closer to our men. It was a circumstance far from pleasing to the nose. Close up, you could see the crusted dirt on their flesh, the greasy, grayish-black grime of woodsmoke, and the filth of their clothing.

Who could blame them? It takes more courage than most of us have to wash one's body in an icy stream, to launder in the stream the few rags that keep the bitter wind from bare skin.

I noticed that the greater part of them were scratching themselves, unconsciously, as if they were doing it not so much for relief as from habit. I wondered how long it would be, even on a fresh campsite, before the vermin moved in with us. It is possible, even in a close-quartered army, to stay free of lice and fleas, but it requires so much daily attention to person and clothing that most men give up the struggle.

The Pennsylvanians began to crowd our men, with the men in the rear pushing the front ranks forward. They weren't begging, but they were asking for tobacco, food, old shoes, anything at all, and offering labor in return. They wanted to draw water for us, build fires, put up lean-tos, and asked only a share of the wealth so evident to their paupers' eyes. I began to get uneasy. There was friendliness now, but a shove or a careless word or a wrinkled nose might lead to a fight. I'd seen it happen before.

Hawk didn't like it either. "Pull your men back, Sergeant," he told Palmer. "Matt, you tell our boys off in squads for shelters and wood and water."

"Yes, sir," I said, looking around for our non-commissioned officers.

Mordecai Mott, a few paces away, stripped off his red-and-white striped mittens and thrust them into his side pocket. Then he reached into his shirt for a stick of chewing tobacco. He always had a wad in his mouth, and you could follow his progress everywhere by the brown-stained trail he left. In a battle or skirmish, Mott would spit, aim, fire, chew rapidly while he reloaded, and then spit, aim, fire, and chew again. He offered the stick to a couple of Pennsylvanians, who seized it, split it, and stuffed it into their mouths.

I moved forward quickly as my eyes caught a third Pennsylvanian slip behind Mott's back and deftly ease the mittens from his pocket.

"You man, hold it!" I called.

The thief started to run, but Mott's big arm shot out and grabbed his collar. "You oughtn't steal from a friend," Mordecai rumbled.

The ragged coat tore completely away at the shoulders and flapped in Mott's hand. The man turned instantly and grabbed for the piece of his coat, more important to him than his physical safety under Mott's anger. Mott's musket butt came up and plowed into the man's stomach, doubling him in agony. As Mott reached to retrieve his mittens, the tobacco-chewers jumped him.

In ten seconds there was a full-sized brawl under way, with all the yelling and cursing of a tavern fight. I saw Harm Tallman's gleeful face as he pounded forward with big fists thumping. The Deerkill men could handle three times their number of the weak Pennsylvania troops, but others were rallying by the score. Worse, not all of these were intent on fighting. Here and there in the tangled mass of brawlers, a ragged man would grab mittens or hat or scarf or even knapsack, and race for safety with his treasure.

There were some who tried to stop the fight. They didn't make much headway. I took a blow in the eye from a bony fist that set lights flashing brilliantly in my brain. A pair of wrestling men reeled into me and knocked me sprawling.

Beside me on the ground Teunis Ekerson tried to stanch a bloody nose with his finger, at the same time roaring in anger, "*Vengeance is mine, I will repay, saith the Lord.*"

Then he yelled, "*Let him that thinketh he standeth take heed lest he fall.*"

He got to his feet, still crying Scripture: "*Resist the devil, and he will flee from you.*" Then he went down again, under an avalanche of Pennsylvania devils.

Above all the noise I could hear Hawk shouting orders.

A new sound pervaded the fracas: a thick angry roar that had the effect of a sudden clap of thunder.

"What in hell is going on here?"

The thunderclap came from a big man in a blue uniform with a blue cloak lined with scarlet. He was astride a chestnut horse. The animal reared and pranced at the edge of the riot. The newcomer's broad face was twisted, seeming black and ugly with rage. We all knew him, of course: Anthony Wayne.

His appearance stopped the brawl almost instantly, and quelled the sound, excepting Ekerson's mournful: "*Is there no balm in Gilead? Is there no physician there?*" The blood poured down Ekerson's face.

The two parties drew apart, leaving the general and his horse in the center of the fighting arena. A young aide rode to the general's side, frowning down with spinsterish distaste upon the rude men.

Wayne flicked a big hand at Sergeant Palmer. "Start talking, Palmer. You're all half dead already, yet you try to kill each other."

" 'Twasn't nawthin, Gen'ral. Just a sort of argument, you might say."

"You might say it, but you can do better. I'm minded of the time you thought the Rhode Islanders were British spies."

"Aw, we never did, sir. This was just an argument among friends."

"Argument, hell! Look at the blood on the snow. Look at this man's eye," he yelled, pointing to me. "It looks like a boiled onion. Who are these people?"

"York Staters, sir."

Wayne transferred his anger instantly. He singled out Hawk as the leader. "Double-damn you, what are you doing helling around my men? You don't belong here. Get the devil along to——" He paused, leaning forward in the saddle to see better. His voice changed as if he had closed one valve and opened another. "Captain Hill. Welcome back. You picked a poor time to arrive. What brought you back? I thought you took all your traps and went home."

"The men decided they'd made a mistake, sir," Hawk said easily. "We're ready to sign on again, sir."

"How long this time? Be damned if I'll have militia souring my troops. How long will you stay?"

Hawk said it simply. "Until we win."

Wayne's eyes narrowed. He stared down at Hawk, not saying anything for a time. Then, abruptly, he swung down from his horse and thrust out his hand. "Until we win, Captain Hill." Wayne's sudden smile made his broad face handsome. "There are only a few of us left who say that, Captain. The General is one, and I'm one, and I'm happy to find another." He nodded. "We're glad to have you back. I'll use your company as division rangers, same as before."

"Yes, sir," Hawk said. "We wanted to be with you."

"Well, I'm damned," Wayne said mildly. "We've had 'em going away from the army every day, but you're the first ones who have come in since the frost hit the pumpkins. Now, one thing more. How did this fight start?"

Palmer spoke up readily. "We jumped them, General. Some of our boys tried to reach for what wasn't theirs, and first thing you know, a ruckus."

Wayne laughed shortly. "These fellows have enough equipment for a regiment. Captain Hill, I'll have your company attached to my command tomorrow, and you can start to draw rations then, if there are any." He eyed the Deerkill men speculatively, a flash of humor in his eyes. "Nice warm clothes. Mittens and scarves. Shoes without holes. Captain, you draw the guard tonight. I'll tell the officer of the day to give you your orders. It's fair. Your men are the only ones who won't stand in danger of freezing tonight."

The young aide spoke a troubled question. "But, sir, orders insist on regular Line troops for guard detail."

"Lieutenant," Wayne growled, "who issued that order?"

"You did, sir."

"Then I hereby rescind it. Make a note of that, Lieutenant."

"Yes, sir."

The lieutenant blushed when we laughed. He would have to learn to watch for the bite of Wayne's tongue. The general rode off into the snow. Most of his soldiers left us to our own affairs.

A few of them stayed on, however, talking amiably as if not a man of them had raised a fist to us. Palmer was among them, saying that he was sorry his comrades had stolen things, but making no offer to try to get them back. Our men hadn't lost much in the fracas, but I nursed my swelling eye and a grievance against Pennsylvanians.

The grim landscape and the ugly camp took on more pleasant aspects when the fires were burning and kettles swinging above them. Youngblood apportioned the meat from a spring lamb, giving each man fair portions of rib meat and such less choice pieces as shoulder and neck. Along with the lamb, every man received three potatoes and three onions, with corn for journey cakes. Sergeant Palmer

114

watched the distribution hungrily, agreeing that it was probably wise to be so free with the food, lest it be stolen during the night.

Eben Lowry, a solemn-faced, slow-minded fellow whose only skills, so far as anyone knew, were plowing a straight furrow and cooking, set to work on supper for the officers' mess, consisting of Hawk and me, Harm Tallman, Walter Luckey, Youngblood, and of course Eben.

Sergeant Palmer spent about twenty minutes being helpful in various ways: he showed us where the Seventh Pennsylvania was drawing water; he provided steel wedges for splitting a storm-felled ash and a few hickories on the hillside; he dispatched a team of horses with trace chains to drag the firewood down the hill. Then he stood fearfully close to the fire, smoking some of Hawk's tobacco in a charred corncob pipe.

By degrees he edged even closer to the fire and the aromatic stew that Lowry fussed over. Once Lowry said mildly, "Sergeant, don't smell all the good out of it."

A half dozen times Palmer suggested that he'd better be getting back to his men, but it was no sooner said than he had another topic to talk about while he watched the stew.

Eventually Hawk winked at the rest of us and said, "There's too much in that pot for us to eat, Sergeant. Could you sit down with us to the meal, when it's ready?"

"That's kind of you, Captain," Palmer said, his face twisting. "Right kind and neighborly. I could eat a bit, I guess, long as you got too much. It smells kinda like stew ought to smell. Seems to me there's only one thing missing from it. A real stew for sticking to your ribs ought to have turnips in it, oughtn't it? Just so. And I got five or six turnips in my rucksack right now, if some thief ain't stole 'em. Lemme get 'em."

He went off in a shambling run for the nearby bivouac of his regiment. Hawk smiled wearily after him.

"I never put turnips in my stew, Hawk," Lowry said aggrievedly. "Turnips don't mix good with lamb."

"You put 'em in," Hawk said. "You know, he was bringing his pride down to the point where he would have asked. He couldn't have stood here much longer without asking. So we saved his pride for another day." He held out his big hands to the glow of the fire, rubbing them as if washing them in the heat.

"Turnips," Lowry muttered.

Palmer came back with five shriveled objects the size of duck eggs. He cut them each in half with his hunting knife and plunked them into the kettle before Lowry could restrain him.

"You didn't peel them!" Lowry cried.

"Peel 'em? Peel 'em? Why that would be downright foolish. Don't you know there's more good in turnip skins," said Palmer, "than almost anything you can eat? They're full of more nourishment than, say, an egg or maybe a big slice of bread with a slab of butter on it. Doctors will tell you that."

"What doctors?" asked Lowry.

"Why, any doctor at all. Especially one that's been with this army the last month. We ain't had nothing but turnip skins at all this last month. Fine good turnip skins, that's what we been eating. And look at us. We're still on our feet, ain't we? Why, I reckon I couldn't rightly eat anything any more without it being seasoned with turnip skins. It wouldn't taste right, and besides, I'd fear for my health."

Lowry looked speculatively at the pot, thought for a minute, then shrugged. He wandered over to the sergeants' mess after a while, and faintly I could hear him telling Sergeant Curran that there was nothing like turnip skins to keep up a man's health. Doctors all said so.

It was a splendid meal—although in that army a soldier was likely, in times of plenty, to get almighty tired of stews of one kind or another, since that was the easiest way to cook meat and vegetables when we had them. We all ate well, but poor Palmer stuffed himself, with frequent apologies, to the point of pain.

Shortly after we finished we heard a cry of anger from Lowry at the fire. "Sergeant, you don't have to steal it!"

We looked to find Palmer bent shamefacedly over the kettle, filling a pannikin with leftover stew.

He stood up and turned to Hawk. His face was red, but he looked levelly at Hawk. "Captain, we got a real sick boy in our company. He's had nothing but fire cakes and dishwater soup for two days.

I was going to take a little nourishment to him. This wasn't for me, Captain."

"Take it all and welcome," Hawk said.

"Thanks, Captain. He's a sick boy."

"If you don't get enough rations of the right kind, we can spare something for him every day for a while," Hawk told him. "See Fred Youngblood here about what the boy needs."

"We won't forget, Captain. Thank you. And, whatever you give, there won't be a crumb of it et by a man who's still on his feet."

With Palmer gone, we smoked pipes by the fire.

Harm Tallman spoke to me. "Say, Matt, what did that boy today say the name of this place was?"

"The Valley Forge."

"It has a good sound to it," said Walter Luckey.

"Has it?" I asked grimly. "Just you listen to the sound of it."

Caught by my seriousness, they all listened. Hawk cupped his hand behind his ear, as he was wont to do when trying to catch a distant sound.

The wind whined through the trees and hissed across the snow.

Axes thudded unevenly in the darkness, lacking the rhythmic ring of woodsmen's blows.

Weary voices droned orders the words of which were lost on the wind, but which kept a fitful hum of despair.

Here and there men cursed shrilly, weariedly, at horses, tools, or at other men.

Above all, in incessant punctuation of the noises of an army making camp, rose the rattling, strangling, pain-filled coughs of hundreds of sick men.

CHAPTER SEVEN

The Deerkill company had done guard duty under worse conditions, and not a man of us really resented being chosen arbitrarily by Wayne to stand sentry that night. We were well-clothed and fed, and we could walk in the snow and freezing slush without fear of frostbitten feet.

Nonetheless, because of the storm, Hawk ordered that the sentries be relieved every two hours, and each man had four hours to sleep by the fire, if he could, when he came off duty.

In point of fact, no sentries were needed to guard against British surprises. Howe's regiments were snug and well-fed in Philadelphia. Further, a large part of Morgan's rifle corps was camped between the army and any British line of march. The enemy would not get close to the woodsrunners without being discovered. We needed sentries to keep men inside the guard ring, rather than outside it.

In the best of times, that army had been plagued by desertions. Men not trained to a lifetime of soldiering thought it no crime to take French leave when their reasons for going outweighed, in their opinions, the stringencies of the Articles of War.

A wife might be sick, a hired man might have quit, a barn might have burned. There were hundreds of reasons for pulling foot, including the basic one of having had a bellyful of fighting. Now, facing the bitterness of these bleak hillsides, and a long winter stretching ahead, it was to be expected that hundreds of men might try to sneak away.

They tried that night.

Woodhull Tallman chased a dark ghost that drifted across the hillside from the camp of the Seventh Pennsylvania. The man vanished among the trees.

"Whyn't you take a shot at him, Woody?" Harm Tallman asked his cousin, when he and I came running to the post to investigate the noise.

"I yelled and run after him," Woodhull said, "but hell, Harm, you wouldn't of shot him neither. Poor feller." Woodhull pointed to footprints in the snow. The track of the right foot was tipped at every step with a blotch of blood. "I hope he makes it home."

"He's worse off out there than he would be here," I told him. I looked into the distance, where the trail disappeared in the timber. "I'll send some men after him. Try to stop the next one, Woody."

"By shooting him, Matt?"

I hesitated. Were these poor fellows any more wrong than we had been when we'd voted to go home? Yet a sentry's duty was specific. "You always hit everything you shoot at, Woody?"

"Pretty much," he said, "but I'll try to run the next one down."

There were others.

Isaac Bogert, who later said that the wind was whipping the snow so much that he couldn't see the end of his musket, was jumped by three men who throttled his cries and quickly stripped him of coat, hat, scarf, mittens, shoes, stockings and musket.

Walter Luckey and I took six men along the deserters' trail into the forest, but we lost the tracks on the ridge, where prints were covered by the wind in a matter of minutes.

Toward dawn, while Hawk was making the rounds, he turned back a sick man who was burning with fever. The fellow fought wildly to continue his journey. He was bound for Easton, he screamed. He insisted that the town was just three miles the other side of the ridge. Only three miles! He could be home for breakfast.

The hours went by slowly. The snow stopped sometime after midnight, and then the wind grew colder and more piercing.

The night was strange; there was some quality in it that seemed to breed isolation and loneliness in the midst of thousands of men. Perhaps it was the view of the clustered bivouacs dotting the white slope, a view that added a dimension to the knowledge of how small and inadequate this army was; perhaps it was the wind that twisted and whined, separating from each other all men who were abroad in its chilling grip.

I made my rounds; I spoke to the sentries; I drank the hot bitter tea that Fred Youngblood had brewed for the guard detail; every so often I wrapped myself in a blanket to catch an hour's sleep. But I felt alone in the raw night, disheartened and despairing.

We should not have come back, I told myself. We should have stayed in the Deerkill Valley where the war was a remote phenomenon, played by phantoms against a backdrop of fantasy—where names like Philadelphia and New York and Boston were in another world, where Franklin and Hancock and Jefferson were only names in the rare newspaper that reached us.

In the valley the great concerns were plowing and sowing and harvesting. The war had nothing to do with hunting and fishing, with barn-raisings, with birth and marriage and death. At home, I thought, there would have been militia musters once a month, and maybe Matt Hill would raise an Indian scare whenever a Six Nations war party was reported beyond Oghwaga on the Susquehanna. We would not have been expected to respond to militia calls from the Hudson's River forts, not while the Indians menaced the frontier.

There would have been Peggy Remsen.

If we were home, the war would run out its time, its inevitable course affected not in the least by our absence. I was certain that this pitiful excuse for an army would be crushed in the spring campaign. Life would then resume the pleasant, rewarding pattern of the days before the men in Philadelphia had signed their names to the document that said: *When in the course of human events.* . . .

Who but Hawk Hill had faith in victory? A few, perhaps, like Wayne, among the generals. A scattering of others down through the ranks, hotheads who were also as stubborn as my father. And the General. He believed in victory. He had to. They'd hang him high if he lost the war. He was one of the few who had actually staked— what were the words from the document?—his life, his fortune, and his sacred honor.

The best troops in the world, proved on a hundred European fields, waited patiently, in warm comfort, only twenty miles away in Philadelphia. They'd have their rum and beer and their doxies to cheer their winter. When the time came, when death and desertion had reduced our ragged regiments to a handful, the British and the

Hessians would come marching out in measured pace. They would pound out the miles to the rattle of confident drumming. And that would be the end of it.

I wondered what the General was thinking in these wind-swept hours of a cold winter's night. Was it possible that he could not see ahead to that final day? He had been abroad in this miserable camp this night. I had seen him striding, his cloak flying in the wind. Hadn't he given up hope at the sight? Was he listening now to the laments of the sick men; was he brooding on the disaster to come?

I could picture the last day of this army. It was an easy scene for my mind to draw.

On the one hand, the thin lines of scarecrows, waiting. Their pinched faces would show their fear. They would look behind them from time to time, to verify that there was an escape route. The officers would be with them, some drinking to build up their courage, others bawling incomprehensible and contradictory orders with a view to hiding their incompetence with noise.

There would be a few steady, calm, quiet ones among them, men like Hawk and Harm Tallman, eyeing speculatively the red legions across whatever field—it might be this very slope.

The militia would be there, that rabble that came so reluctantly when called for an impending battle. The militia would ebb and flow nervously, watching the distant crimson waves that would soon begin to roll forward. Even the least reliable of the Line regiments would eye the militia with contempt.

Then the drums, the stirring of the red ranks, and sudden silence would fall across the field as the faraway voices shrilled the commands. They would come slowly, ponderously, in perfect formation in spite of rocks, trees, brush.

A few militia muskets would bang far too soon, and wild-eyed colonels, who the day before had been horsetraders or barbers, would scream orders to hold fire.

They would be closer, now, ever closer, until you could see the chin-straps bobbing with each step and the dark sweat patches staining the armpits of the red jackets.

The first volley from us; a few of them would tumble. Their comrades would step aside and around them and the ranks would come on in massive perfection. The second volley; this would be returned in a vast roll of smoke and thunder. The first militia regiment would turn tail and run. Another would follow, streaming every which way like chickens when a weasel is in the henyard. Then all the militia would run.

The third volley; now you could see the sweat beading on the close-shaven faces, you could hear the sergeants barking, "Close up! Close up!" Now the red lines broke into the charge, route step, bayonets gleaming terribly in the sun. Heavy-soled boots thudded like distant thunder. On the flanks, Tarleton's troopers started to cut down the running men.

That would be the moment, that would be the end. The few hundreds of these miserable men who faced those bayonets, these gaunt beggars of the Continental Line, would give ground. It would be slowly at first, pausing to thump home powder and ball for one more shot, but moving as they did so. Perhaps they would halt for three minutes at a stone wall or brush-lined rail fence, but for only three minutes, three more shots.

They would keep running, shame and fear mixed on their thin faces.

The General and those few with him who preferred death to awakening from the forlorn dream of victory, would be alone to face the gallows. I could see Lee's saturnine face as he worried about his hounds; I could imagine the French Boy's shrug as he handed over his sword, saying, "Ça va," and I could see Wayne's countenance black with anger and despair.

I shivered, although I was warm enough beside the glowing hickory logs of the sentry-post fire. Under an evergreen lean-to that caught the warmth of the flames, Harm Tallman and Hawk were sleeping. My father's face twisted with pain as he coughed hackingly. He didn't wake up.

I left the fire, feeling the wind bite deeply as I climbed the slope toward the line of sentries. I could see Walter Luckey and Sergeant James Dutcher making the rounds. I heard a sentry challenge them, heard the parole and countersign pass between them.

I stopped walking short of the sentries, standing on bare earth in the shelter of a great hemlock whose lower branches had been stripped by soldiers for beds and kindling. Before me stretched the camp with its hundreds of fires winking brightly on the white slope.

We should not have come, I thought once again. He should not have brought us back.

He holds to hope, I told myself. Not only hope, but faith, so strongly that he almost has you believing it as well. Witness the conversation we'd had just a couple of hours before, over tea at the fire.

Matt Hill: "It isn't a war, Hawk, and it never has been. You can't call it war, not when all we've ever done is run away."

Hawk Hill: "We've got lots of room to run in. Maybe they'll get sick of chasing us. And sometime, when they think we're running, we'll turn on 'em in the right place at the right time. We've been on many a coon hunt together, Matt. How many hounds does it take to kill a coon?"

Matt Hill: "Only one, if he's a good dog."

Hawk Hill: "Right. But tell me what happens when the coon gets to a creek and stops on a rock in the middle."

Matt Hill: "You've got a point. The dog had better look out."

Walter Luckey: "Yes. If the dog is fool enough to swim near the coon, the coon will drown him. Hold his head under the water until he drowns."

Hawk Hill: "Just so. We've all heard that the General hunts foxes down in Virginia, when he's to home. I'll wager, though, that they have coons in Virginia, and I'll say he's been on many a coon hunt. He knows a smart coon has to run until he finds his place to turn and fight."

Matt Hill: "It doesn't do him any good against a big pack of hounds."

The chance, I thought, is so small that it can scarcely be said to exist.

I stood on the frozen hillside, looking at the fires of a desperate army. He can't be right, I told myself.

The keen wind sighed in the branches of the hemlock. I bowed my shoulders and stepped out of the shelter to make the rounds of the sentries once more.

CHAPTER EIGHT

Seeing the camp for the first time in daylight, I remembered the others I had seen since '75, and the comparison was painful. An army of eight or nine thousand men should be raucous, bustling, mobile. In this camp a few hundred soldiers plodded here and there in the snow, a few axes tapped monotonously, an occasional shout lifted mournfully in the brittle air, and the only constant sound was the low uneven rattle of sick men coughing.

Yet I had to grin in spite of myself when Hawk came to stand beside me. He saw a different picture.

"Old soldiers," Hawk said softly. "Not a man of 'em will stir on a frosty morning without a sergeant to root 'em from under the blankets.

"They've come a long way since we saw 'em first in Boston, son. They're all beat out now, and some are sick, but they're hard. They're mean. They know that it will take all that England's got, and then some, to whip 'em."

I shook my head, smiling. "The way they look this morning, one troop of Tarleton's legion could do it."

"Never you mind Tarleton, or the redcoats, or the Dutchmen they've brought to do their fighting. They're giving us time, Matt, while they glut themselves with Philadelphia food and Philadelphia drink, all at good Philadelphia prices, I trust. All we need is time to get ready for next year."

"I've heard that before, Hawk. Next year has been a long time coming."

"All the better when it comes, son. And you'll know when we're ready. I can't say how, but you'll know—the way you know that fall has come from the feel of the air on a September morning; the way you sense the light coming over the Drowned Lands before dawn, making you bring your gun up and look to the sky for the first sight of the ducks coming in; the way you look at a man and know right off if he's telling the truth or lying. You'll know all right when we're ready for them."

"I know what we're ready for now. Some food. How about it?"

The men hadn't finished breakfast when the orders for permanent winter quarters passed swiftly down from the General's staff to divisions, then to brigades, then to regiments. Sergeant Palmer brought a copy for the use of the Deerkill company.

As we understood it, one of the young Frenchmen who had been flitting among us for months in almost-clean lace and almost-neat cambric, this one an engineer named Duportail, had planned the camp.

Engineers for each division were to lay out the campground and superintend construction of the quarters. While the men were gathered around Hawk and Palmer for their instructions, the engineers' work parties were already making the hillside ring with the sound of hammers driving stakes into the frost-hardened ground.

We were to live in huts, the orders said, which were to be built in files of three, with four huts to a file, each five yards asunder. The huts were to be eighteen feet by sixteen feet in external dimensions, with six feet from the base to the eaves. They would have roofs of the best material available (the General offered a prize of one hundred dollars to the man who contributed the best idea for roofing, since the sawmill in the hamlet had been destroyed by the British). Officers' huts were to be built in the rear of each grouping of cabins, with officers of two companies sharing one hut.

Commissary wagons rolled through the camp distributing tools. Working parties of twelve men each began to move slowly into the timber. They were reluctant to begin the heavy labor of felling trees and cutting them up to the proper dimensions. They had to argue first about the selection of trees, the proper ax techniques, and the distribution of labor. To have started without a good sound quarrel or two, some blustering, and assorted sneers would have violated all concepts of good soldierly conduct in any Line regiment.

The first few parties enjoyed the bickering, but before a half-hour had gone by, each working party was actually running for the woods as soon as the men received their tools, because the most suitable trees closest to the camp area were already claimed by the first parties.

One tactic that quickly developed was to split a party in two while they waited. Six men went to mark and hold enough trees for a hut, while the other six clamored for tools.

Hawk Hill read the orders to the men, made sure that they understood them, then asked Palmer a single question: "We have no horses, Palmer. Can we use yours?"

Palmer grinned benignly. "Can't let you have any horses, Captain, less'n I come along to see they ain't misused or overworked. We got to eat them horses before long, and we don't want 'em run down to bone and muscle. So while I'm keeping an eye on the horses, guess I'll have to take my meals with you fellers until you get all your logs hauled."

"In other words," Harm Tallman said, "all we got to do to use your horses is keep your belly full?"

"I wouldn't put it that way," Palmer said.

Hawk nodded. "Fair exchange is no robbery."

"Done," Palmer said happily. "I'll get two teams and a few of them turnips that turned out so fine in your stew last night. I wouldn't think of sharing them stews and soups and such without furnishing my share of their innards."

Behind me, I heard Eben Lowry mutter to Justus Rider: "Best thing in the world for what ails you is turnip skins. The head doctor of this here army told that to Palmer."

The Highland County company was among the last to be furnished with tools, and so had to trail far on the ridges to find good timber. The men grumbled when Hawk took them past the most distant working parties, passing stands of hickory and ash and chestnut until he stopped in a windfall clearing that had been marked on Teunis

Polhemus's tree map. The clearing was fronted by a grove of good white pines.

"All right, boys, get to work," Hawk said. "Don't crowd each other and make sure your felling lanes are clear before you drop a tree. I want to hear you yell your heads off when you've got one ready to drop, and I don't want any man to take an extra lick with his ax after he hears the yell."

Jed Palmer found a convenient log in the windfall, seated himself comfortably, then prepared to argue. "White pine won't do, Captain. Spark gets into it after it dries a bit and you ain't got no cabin in ten minutes. Maybe the men inside are sick of smallpox or something and can't even get out. I wouldn't pick pine, white or yellow. Our boys are all cutting maple right close to our bivouac."

Hawk sat down beside him, offered tobacco, then spoke pleasantly. "Maple is good wood to build with. You take a dozen men who want to build a fine cabin that will last a lifetime, and put 'em to work with sharp axes and plenty of time and good nourishing meals to keep their strength up, and you'll have the best cabin you can build in a week or so. Matter of fact, Sergeant, after we get all our cabins up tomorrow and finish the floors and chimneys and bunks the next day, we'll come over and watch you. I wouldn't be at all surprised if you were living in your fine maple cabins by the first of the year, anyway."

"Maple holds the heat inside," Palmer said doggedly. "Keeps the cold out too. Nice solid wood, maple. You take a pine log, it will soak up cold just like a pig sucks in swill."

"You're absolutely right," Hawk said. "Maple is a good solid wood. You take an eighteen-foot log of maple, the kind the General's order specifies, a foot thick, say, and I'd guess that six strong men can hoist it into place. The bark peels right off too, after the log has dried a few months. Of course, if you don't let it dry, that bark doesn't come off so fast. You going to peel your logs, Palmer?"

"I don't favor pine, Captain. I can't say that I like pine at all."

Harm Tallman grunted derisively. "You don't favor pine because you didn't think to come up here where the pine is. Listen here, Palmer. Any fool knows pine is best for a quick cabin. It's soft, so even a dull ax can notch a corner neat as a pin. And it's light enough so a team can pull two logs instead of one of maple or chestnut or hickory. And it smells good too. Nice and clean and fresh. But to give you the main reason, Hawk said pine, so pine it is."

Palmer rubbed his long nose with a grimy finger. "That's all as may be, but I can't say as I would favor pine for a cabin. For some things, yes, but not for a cabin."

"Let's get to work," Hawk said, laughing. "Harm, you see that stand of cedars yonder on the ridge? Take two men from each work party and start cutting cedar. Get it all cut today and keep a guard on it. Tomorrow they'll all be looking for cedar, and there's not much of it on these hills."

"Roofing, eh?" Palmer said sadly, but with obvious eagerness to get his say in. He shook his head. "You don't want to fool with cedar shakes. There's bark for roofs, and turf, and straw. What do you want to bother with cedar for?"

"So you lazy Pennsylvanians can come in and get dry the first time it rains or snows," Harm Tallman said. "I'll take a team when one is free, Hawk, and I'll haul the cedar down here. That way nobody will jump the guard and sneak away with it."

"Nobody wants cedar, so it will be safe enough," Palmer said. "You take a good roof of elm bark, or even birch if you got good trees, and it beats cedar every time. Easier to put on too."

"You eating with us, Palmer?" Harm said harshly.

Palmer's sad face brightened. His tongue touched his lips. "Already? You fellers ain't had breakfast but an hour ago. I guess I could eat a bit right now, if I had to. What did you have in mind?"

"We'll eat at noon, but you won't eat with us if you don't shut up with what you favor and what you don't favor. Now get your lazy butt off that log and let's move those half-dead horses of yours. We'll get that cedar like Hawk said."

The work moved with astonishing speed. The logs were down and cut to the proper lengths before noon. Palmer's teams snaked them, three at a time, across the snowy slope to the site marked by the engineers for the Pennsylvanians' huts. This was on the ridge along the southeastern slope of Mount Joy. The ranger company was to share a grouping with Palmer's regiment.

Harm Tallman's men had built a rough sled to bring the cedar, which was cut into twelve-foot lengths. Walter Luckey and I supervised the building of the huts, but all the Deerkill Valley men were old hands at putting up log houses. In each squad of twelve, two men peeled the logs, six skilled axmen cut saddles near each end of a log, and the remaining four were charged with positioning the logs on the walls of the hut. The cutting of the saddles required good judgment. If a saddle or notch was just half as deep as the diameter of the log, and if the next log to be fitted had a saddle of the same depth, width, and angled slopes, the two formed a perfect right angle when they were laid in place.

Walter Luckey had a craftsman's sure eye for the ax-work. His swift hand measurements saved the axmen a lot of trimming as the afternoon passed. I gave a hand with the hoisting of the logs, kept good fires going with the scrap wood, and doled out hot tea to the workmen from Youngblood's diminishing supply. When I wasn't busy with these tasks, I split lengths of pine into triangular wedges for chinking. No matter how true our logs and how fine our saddles, the completed huts would be only as draft-free as their chinking permitted. In spite of how much care we put into the original chinking, the men would be adding to it, day and night, for weeks, as new drafts poked their fingers between the logs every time the wind changed direction.

All along the ridge from the Schuylkill to Mount Joy, on the slopes and in the flat lands, squads of men were doing their best to get their huts built. For many regiments, their best was poor indeed.

There is a real knack to building a log cabin, and few units had a core of frontiersmen to supervise the work. There were hundreds of town-bred soldiers, grouped in companies of various regiments, who had never had any reason to look closely at a log hut. These men were unable to follow the written directions issued by their brigade commanders. While many of them might have been artisans skilled in a particular craft and the uses of its customary tools, their problem now was to take an ax and build a dwelling with it. It was too much to ask of them. Given time to learn, and a couple of failures to sharpen their practice, they would have done well. But they had no time, and the hut they built would be the one they would live in all winter.

Some of the squads were youngsters who had grouped together. If they were all city boys, they usually plunged into an immediate variety of difficulties. They dropped trees one atop another, ruining good logs and doubling their labor; they were unable to hew the saddles with regular accuracy; they failed to allow for contour level and time and again had to undo the frameworks of their huts.

They could learn quickly, however, and their adaptability had been proved in a half-dozen campaigns. The need to teach them was apparent before the hut-building project was many hours along.

In the early afternoon, General Wayne came riding along the files of his division's building site, accompanied by an aide and the brigade engineering officer. Here and there he reined in his horse and his heavy voice pounded at squads that worked ineptly or lazily. From time to time during his inspection, a group of men would gather tools and leave huts that were well under way, going to other locations in the division position where men or boys were hacking at logs without effect.

Finally, Wayne reached our company, where the walls of five huts were already rising log by log, with the promise that the men would roll in their blankets within four walls that night.

Wayne nodded to Hawk Hill's greeting and salute, lifting his hand casually to his hat brim. His hard eyes stayed on the men who worked without seeming effort or painstaking care.

"They know what they're doing," Wayne said to the engineer. The general pointed with a gloved hand to the rows of pine logs ready for hewing by the axmen.

The officer nodded, squirting tobacco juice from the corner of his mouth as he did so. The general's prim young aide looked frowningly at the ugly brown stain in the snow, then glanced at Wayne, as if expecting to hear a reprimand for the engineer.

"Nice easy-chopping pine," the engineer muttered, speaking around the chew that puffed his jaw. "Like I said this morning, only none of them stumpjumpers and appleknockers of ours would listen to me. If I'd of said hickory, they'd of been out in the woods cutting pine like fools, just to do different from what I said."

"You'll learn," Wayne said, grinning and winking at Hawk. "For three campaigns now, whenever I really wanted 'em to do something I'd let the word slip around that I actually had the opposite thing in mind. Then, when the orders are posted, they're sure they've brought me around to their way of thinking."

The officer nodded. He spoke lazily to Hawk. "What about roofs, Captain? I suppose you're going to cut you some turf and lay it across poles so that the rain water will be nice and dirty when it drips through."

"Shingled roofs," Hawk said. "Cedar." He indicated the far side of our building site. There the Welch brothers, William and James, were upending eighteen-inch log sections on massive chopping blocks and trimming them. When one of them had a section trimmed, he picked up his frow, made of a sharpened bayonet, and one of the wooden mallets the brothers had made that morning. Then he would rive half-inch shingles as fast as his arms could move. They were using mostly raw wood, but their speed was still remarkable.

"Only one good stand of cedar on the ridge," the engineer said morosely, "and I had it marked. Time I got to it at noon, these York State thieves had every good tree cut and hauled. They even cleaned up the chips."

"That's right," Hawk said equably. "We'll have more than enough chips by the time those boys get through shaving shingles. I'll give you a sackful, sir."

"I'll take 'em," the engineer said, spitting again.

Wayne looked puzzled. "What good are the chips? Do they make a better fire, or what?"

"That just goes to show you," said the engineer, who was obviously a backwoodsman and stood in little awe of a brigadier general, "how much a general officer has got to learn about armies. You ever had fleas, General?"

Wayne laughed and removed a glove with one quick motion, showing reddish scabs on his wrist, as if he'd been pawing his way through a brier patch. "You know anybody in this army who isn't flea-bitten, Major?"

"That's a good collection," the major said judiciously. "More than I got, but then I'm only a staff officer and I don't get to sleep in the kind of places you do. I won't be flea-bitten long, though, nor these fellers here. You take and build you a bunk of fresh cedar, and fill it with cedar shavings, and cover your floor, if you got one, with cedar sawdust or chips, and you won't keep a self-respecting flea in the place."

"It's the oil in the wood, General," Hawk said. "They apparently won't breed in cedar or stay in it any longer than it takes 'em to jump out of it."

Wayne nodded. "My men at home bed the dog kennels with cedar shavings."

"A man gets a little pungent sleeping in cedar," Hawk said, "but he sleeps. It helps some with lice, but not so much. Let yourself get lousy and you'll stay lousy."

Wayne's gaze, while they talked, had been fixed on the Welch brothers. He spoke now in open admiration. "Those boys are artists, Captain. I've seen shingle shavers before, but never any so fast and so true."

"Their father taught them," Hawk said. "He can rive and shave six hundred shingles a day. I've yet to see his equal. They're good, but not as good as their father."

Wayne pursed his lips in momentary wonder, then looked sharply at Hawk. "How are you going to fasten the shingles, Captain? We haven't got a nail in the division outside of a few pounds of horse-shoe nails in the farriers' kits."

"We'll manage one way or another, sir."

"How? I want to know exactly."

"We might bind them down, or peg 'em," Hawk said.

The major spoke up. "You might as well tell him, Captain," he said mildly. "I wouldn't be surprised does he already know. And if he don't, he'll find out. I seen lots of generals in this here war so far, but this one is the nosiest I run acrost."

"Major!" the young aide cried, speaking for the first time, in great distress at the irreverence.

"He is nosy," the major said calmly, "because if he wasn't, he'd let these York Staters nail down their shingles any way they figgered to do it, without asking too close."

"That's more than enough, Major," Wayne barked. He kept his eyes fixed sternly on Hawk. "You have nails, Captain Hill?"

"A few," Hawk admitted.

Wayne nodded. "Let's see them. Bring 'em out of wherever you have 'em hidden."

Hawk hesitated, shrugged, and called to Billy Bill, who was peeling logs nearby. "Billy, roll out those nail kegs."

"Yessir, Captain," Billy answered brightly, eager to please. "You want the fire plates too?"

"No, damn it, I don't!" Hawk shouted.

The general and his two companions watched with interest as Billy threw aside a pile of cedar boughs, revealing two wooden kegs, blackened by fire, which stood upon a stack of rectangular iron sheets of uniform size.

"All right, sir," Hawk said unhappily, "I'll have a squad take 'em back."

Wayne seemed not to be listening. He turned to his aide, who was gazing disapprovingly from the kegs to Hawk and back again. "Make a note for headquarters, Lieutenant," Wayne said. "Tell them that we checked the division and that we found no evidence that Pennsylvania troops under my command stole nails or fire plates from the ruins of Colonel Dewees' forge, as complained by the colonel this morning."

"But, sir!" the lieutenant cried. "Those kegs! Look at the scorch marks on them. That's what headquarters said——"

"Get the language right in that report," Wayne interrupted. "'. . . no evidence that Pennsylvania troops under my command stole nails or fire plates . . .' Furthermore, Lieutenant, you will add that, in response to the accusation of Colonel Dewees' brother-in-law that three Pennsylvania soldiers stole a sheep from his barnyard this morning just before dawn, the general commanding the Pennsylvania division has found no mutton among the stores in his command, what there is of them."

"The reason he didn't find any," said the tall major soberly to

Hawk, "was that he made the search after breakfast. When I come to headquarters, him and the lieutenant here was having mutton chops. Fresh ones."

"Those chops were donated by a corporal from York who was home on furlough," declared the lieutenant excitedly.

"Of course," Wayne said equably. "That's what the corporal told the lieutenant, and I believed him. So, we have disposed of the matter of nails and fire plates."

"Don't forget the mutton, General," the major remarked. "You disposed of that too."

Wayne fixed his hard stare on the major. "One thing, Major. This is a relaxed command, in a manner of speaking, but it is not as relaxed as you appear to think. I am willing to allow an officer who has served with Dan Morgan, who went to Quebec with Arnold, a certain amount of freedom of speech in my presence. You have taken more than your share today. Understood?"

"Yessir," the major smiled. "I know what you mean. I picked up some bad habits from Old Dan. Got some good ones too, along the way. Like hating the redcoats and loving a fight."

Wayne nodded. He turned again to Hawk. "Captain Hill, I'm pleased to see that your men are expert, and, shall we say, resourceful in preparing huts for their winter's shelter. So expert and so resourceful that I will relieve you of half of them to help companies in the division who are not so skilled."

Hawk started to protest. I suppose he was going to ask that our men be allowed to finish their own huts before helping others. Wayne cut him off.

The general's heavy voice lost the bantering note that it had held during the byplay concerning the nails. "You know the penalty, Captain, of being good at your job. People keep you busy. Now you've seen some of these fellows of ours, and you know how they're fixed. They must build their own shelters, but I intend to see that they have the best they can possibly get. Your men are best fitted to help the ones who badly need help. So get to it. The major here will tell you where to send them."

Wayne rode off with the aide, leaving the tall major, who dismounted and tied his horse to a sapling beside the first hut. He turned to shake hands with Hawk. "My name's Williams," he said. "Joe Williams, from Fishing Creek on the Susquehanna."

"I know," Hawk said. "I remember when you left Boston with Arnold."

Major Williams beamed. "I got frostbit in the jail that the British stuck us into in Quebec. I couldn't hump it with the rifle corps no more. So Wayne got me a promotion and called me an engineer. Hell, I never done much in that line but run some survey parties back home. This is a good bunch of men you got, Hill."

"They are," Hawk said simply.

"They could make a rifle company," Williams said, as if that were the highest praise he could give. "You can spare half these boys and still finish your huts before most others can even get a good start. Pick 'em out and I'll take 'em along."

Hawk shook his head unhappily. "They won't like it. They know how fast they are at building, and they figured the first squad to finish a hut would get the General's prize of twelve dollars."

"Nope," Williams said. "That don't matter. Wayne said take 'em, and you know Wayne. He meant it. Besides, they shouldn't pay any mind to that twelve dollars. First place, you ain't in a regiment, and that prize is twelve dollars per regiment. Second place, that money is Continental, and it ain't worth twelve pennies in hard coin. Third place, what in hell would they spend it on, if they got it?"

Hawk shrugged. "At least the company can share the hundred-dollar prize for the best kind of roof."

Williams clucked his tongue. "Mister Hill, I know you got better brains than to show up at headquarters and claim a prize for *nailed* cedar shingles! First thing one of them fancy colonels like Laurens or Hamilton would ask you is where did you get the nails. Then you'd say, being an honest man, that some of your men crawled into Dewees' forge and stole 'em, wouldn't you?"

"No, I guess maybe I wouldn't," Hawk answered.

"See, you got better brains than you allowed. By the way, Hill, you got an officer's hut going up and how many officers to go in it?"

"Four," Hawk said.

"That's agin the rules, Mister Hill. Got to be officers from two companies share a hut. That's the rule. Now, I'm a field-grade officer, a staff officer to boot, and I got the right to take quarters in a stone house in that village with the crazy name, King of Prussia, or in Paoli, or at the Gulph Mills. I can do that because Congress has said that I'm a better-grade person than you are, you being a low-down captain. All the brigadier generals and colonels was fighting over them houses this morning. All the majors was lined up by date of their commissions to get what was left. If I'd of got into line, I'd of been last man, because I only got to be a major last Thursday. Course, if I did get into line, there'd be a pantry or something left for me to sleep in, and I would get to eat with folks who, by order of Congress, are my equals or not much more. Majors and lieutenant colonels and colonels. A man ought to be proud of having a chance like that, oughtn't he?"

"Just so," Hawk said.

Williams spat a jet of brown juice to the ground. "Tell you what, Captain. I'm willing to give up that honor. One major, by order of Congress, ought to be worth a company's roster of ordinary mill-run officers like captains and lieutenants. Ain't that right?"

"Just so."

"Then I'll declare myself a company's roster of officers and move in with you. Then you'll be following the rule."

"Glad to have you, Major. Why pick us, however? You must have plenty of friends among the officers in the rifle corps."

"They're off in the Gulph Mills, and Wayne can't get along without me to advise him on engineering problems. Anyways, I figger to make out fine with a bunch that can steal a stand of cedar from under my nose, and build huts that sure ain't going to be drafty like a real fancy pantry in a stone house, and are axmen and shingle shavers like we got home, and can steal nails, and all the rest you fellers seem able to do. You didn't steal that sheep, did you?"

"No, we didn't."

"Too bad. I thought you might have a chop or two left. What have you got that I can eat with both hands?"

"Why both hands?"

"All I et lately I could use only one hand. Had to hold my nose with the other."

"We've got some lamb we brought from up the line. Enough to put a taste in a stew."

"I'll move right in. This will be fine fixings. Lamb that hasn't been stole, and dry cabins, and no fleas. I'll get my traps and be back in time for supper."

"We'll be pleased to have you, Major."

"Call me Joe. And you won't be half as pleased as I will. You ever had to live with majors and colonels and such?"

"Not yet."

"Don't ever do it," Williams said, turning to his horse. "Seems a good man gets promoted to field grade and right away he has to start being an idiot, and a nincompoop, and a bragger, and a fathead. The only colonel I ever knew was worth anything is Dan Morgan, and he don't count, because they ought to have made him a general instead of a colonel. Now where's the men I can have?"

"I'll tell 'em off in squads," Hawk said. "My son Matt—Lieutenant Hill—will go with you."

"Don't give me the culls," Williams said. "I want your best."

"They're all good," Hawk said quietly.

Williams wasn't gone long before returning with his tired-looking horse, a bed roll, a sack of bolts and nuts for linking the fire plates to make usable ovens, a bundle of fireplace cranes on each of which a keen eye could read *DEWEES* stamped in the metal, and a fine Pennsylvania long rifle, mounted with German silver and bound in brass. The rifle was cased in doeskin, on which was lettered in fading colors the old blazon of the rifle companies: LIBERTY OR DEATH.

"I'll live to see one before I see the other," Williams said when he was replacing his rifle in its sheath after showing it to Hawk and me.

"There are some who don't think so," Hawk said quietly. "There are men who say we are whipped now. We should ask the King to take us back. They say we could go home, and the British would just hang a few, like the General and some of the Congress. They wouldn't hang many, as I've heard it said, just a few to teach the rest of us rebels a lesson."

Williams looked at him coldly. "If that's what you think, Captain, I'll get the hell out of here right now."

Hawk laughed at him. "Hold on, Major! I'll see the last shot fired before I go home, God willing. And it will be fired at a redcoat running for the boats."

"All right then," Williams said. "I'm pleased to bunk in with you and Matt here. I can't stand these fellers that go around saying it's just a question of time before they whip us."

I turned away to warm my hands at the fire.

CHAPTER NINE

There were many inept building squads in the Pennsylvania division. Our working party from the ranger company covered a lot of ground.

The task of instruction was easier than I thought it would be, because there was scarcely a squad that did not include several skilled workmen who needed only to be shown the few tricks of cabin-building before they could proceed without help.

We found that the working parties most in need of help were those in which several men might be too sick to stand, let alone wield an ax or lift logs. I filled out these groups with Deerkill Valley men whose instructions were to stay at the job until the four walls of a hut were finished, which, with a makeshift roof, would at least provide shelter from the cutting wind until the hut could be properly finished.

With Major Williams, I spent the late afternoon of December 20 and the following day searching for trouble spots and transferring my men to them as soon as the men were available.

It was impossible for me and Williams to limit our help to Wayne's division, because many working parties in the neighboring brigades— Scott's, Woodford's, Poor's, Glover's, and Knox's artillery—were making a hash of their attempts to put up cabins. Soldiers from other units, moving on one errand or another across the ridge, would join the ring of Pennsylvanians watching me saddle a log or split chinking or strip elm bark for roofing.

Sooner or later, when I'd finished the demonstration and instruction, the outsider would say, "Can you spare a minute, sir, to come to Glover's? We ain't getting them notches to fit right, and the goddam thing looks like a corncrib that's been hit by a windstorm."

Or another would say, "Lieutenant, can you come to Poor's brigade and show four of us some of them tricks? We ain't but four now. Seven are down sick and one took French leave last night. Ain't one of the four of us ever done much with an ax but split kindling."

I have heard and read descriptions, by those who were not there, of our Continental village at the Valley Forge. Always it is pictured as row upon row of neat log huts, uniformly made to the General's specifications. Even on the second day of building it was apparent that we were to have a hodgepodge of every type of building construction known in the thirteen colonies and all the countries of Europe.

Before the second day had passed, other commanders had copied Wayne's action in assigning roving parties to help the inept or the sick. I could more or less confine my work to the Pennsylvania huts. Williams was supervising the building of a hospital hut, a commissary hut, and sanitary trenches for every company.

In that day, however, I saw fully for the first time the terrible condition of this army, and I was filled with horror and disgust and pity. Fully a third of the men I worked with had no shoes. They used instead flannel wrappings, makeshift moccasins, and rough pieces of new hide cut and sewn into shapeless brogans.

I saw scores of men without coats or shirts, wearing threadbare blankets with holes cut for head and arms and belted at the waist. I spent an hour with some New Hampshire men who had to work time and time about on the hut they were building because they had only six shirts and six coats among them.

Shocking to see was a burial party of the New Jersey Line, six men in the remnants of their once neat brown-and-white regimentals. They carried the body on poles. The dead man was going to his grave as starkly naked as he had come into life. They had stripped his wasted body of every stitch he possessed.

For the first time that day, I heard the chant that was to become so familiar to us all: the staccato beat to which men timed their ax-strokes: "NO MEAT! NO MEAT!"

They told me that this was true in each brigade. There had been no issue of meat for two days and no bread for three days. These soldiers were doing heavy manual labor on a diet of corn journey cakes and a broth made of a few frost-blackened vegetables.

How could it be called an army?

"Is Congress composed of madmen or fools?" I cried to Joe Williams, ashamed that we were sitting to a lunch of boiled tongue and cabbage with fine wheat biscuits, from the diminishing supplies that Fred Youngblood had made us carry from home.

"A dab or two of both, I reckon," Williams answered. "Maybe with a sprinkling of good men, or Congress wouldn't have lasted this long. But these fellers ain't so bad off, Matt, one way of looking at it. On the way to Quebec, we didn't have a damn thing to eat for days. Course, we had that bantam cock Arnold to convince us that we didn't have to eat. Only wasted time, he said."

"This entire camp will starve to death!"

"Nope," he said quietly. "Some will freeze before they starve. But you hold on, boy. It won't stay this way. Things will get better, soon as the commissaries can start buying. There's enough food in Pennsylvania to feed five armies this size."

"They'd better get it here, and get it here fast," I said. "I've never seen anything like this, not in the worst of the past two years. Not anywhere near as bad."

"I'll tell you, Matt. There ain't one single damned thing that you and I can do about it, except to do our best to see that they are halfways warm while they wait for something to eat." He pushed himself to his feet. "So let's get to it."

In midmorning of the third day, I was working with the Seventh Regiment of the Pennsylvania Line, First Brigade. This was a first-rate regiment, with the men in good shape, but many of them were mere boys who had flocked together in mess groups, and some of them had cheerfully embarked on building projects not even remotely similar to those called for in the general order. If left alone, those youngsters would have found themselves shivering in the open on the first blustery night, while their weirdly contrived shelters went sailing in the wind.

My attention was called from directing the lining of a wooden chimney with eighteen inches of clay. The voice that addressed me sounded sad, mild, and yet marked with authority.

"Would you be Lieutenant Hill?"

I looked up to find a spectacled man peering down to where I lay on the earthen hearth. He was of medium height, thin and seeming frail, a most active man in small nervous gestures. Before I got to my feet, he adjusted his tiny spectacles, wrapped a muffler more securely about his throat, scratched his ear with a thin forefinger, and blinked his eyes several times.

"I'm Matt Hill. What can I do for you?"

"Surgeon Walden," he introduced himself. "Connecticut. Place called New Haven. Big town, New Haven is. Don't believe I ever looked twice at a log cabin before I came to the army. Albion Walden, doctor from Connecticut. So I used to think, anyway. Not so sure, now. Doctor ought to know what a man is sick from, shouldn't he? That's not easy, in this army. How are you, sir?"

All this was said pleasantly, but in jerks and starts, as if he tested each phrase in his mind before letting it out to the foreign ear. While he talked, his hands were busy again: adjusting a button, brushing invisible dust, checking the time on a great silver watch that he had to probe for in the vast side pocket of his ragged coat.

I nodded and said again, "What can I do for you?"

He reached into the pocket again, pulling out what seemed to be a grimy ragged copy of the general order on huts. He took off his spectacles, peered hopelessly at the paper, put them back on, peered again.

"Hospital hut," he said. "I can fit a wooden leg, but I don't know how to drive a nail. Don't even know where it should be driven. They said you were the man to see."

As might be expected, I had become irritable with those who made constant demands on my limited services. I spoke harshly to him. "Good God, man! Can't your own men help you? I've got a dozen tasks lined up. Get somebody else, sir. When I get a chance, I'll send a man to check the job. That's the best I can do. Tell me where you're located, and one of my men may get there tomorrow or the next day."

He nodded, as if helplessly. "I see. I hate to insist. Six men with camp fever, you see. At least that's six I know what's wrong with. A dozen others in poor condition. General Wayne told me you'd be available."

"You went to Wayne?"

"First thing. Heard about your work. I told him my men would die without shelter. They will, too. So he gave me an order." He pulled out another piece of paper, this time from the opposite pocket. "Says 'immediately,' Lieutenant. That means now, I guess. Can I help carry your tools? I've got a cart here."

He held out the order, but I spurned it with an angry snort. "All right. Two hours to get your men started. That ought to be enough. You have logs?"

He said he did. He picked up my ax and sledge and went out with surprising speed, his thin shoulders bowed under their weight. I followed, with the rest of my tools, to find him already seated on the single board that served as seat of a dilapidated flat-bed wagon. An old horse that drooped in every muscle was harnessed between the shafts. I jumped in; the horse was off with a shambling gait that seemed to grow ever faster, as if once thrown into motion he couldn't slow down or stop until he fell down dead.

"Take it slow," I said. "You'll kill the horse."

"I wouldn't be surprised if he was dead already," Surgeon Walden said. "Just hasn't dropped yet."

"How'd you get the order from Wayne?" I asked, still put out about the affair.

"Asked him," he said mildly. "Known him sometime now. Point of fact, I treated a festered finger he had last summer. He had put spider webs on a cut."

"Good way to heal it," I said offhandedly.

"Good way to lose a finger," he said. It was a moment before I realized that he had corrected me.

"What's wrong with spider webs?" I asked. "Anybody knows they stop bleeding and heal cuts."

"Ever look at one when the spider was living in it? Nice fresh dead flies on it? Butterflies fluttering? Flies and butterflies are partial to dung heaps, ain't they? Would you stick a cut finger in a dung heap?"

"Can't say I would," I admitted.

"I try to keep dirt and such out of cuts and wounds. When I see a dirty wound, I figure it will fester as sure as God made green apples. Wayne's doctor—said he was a doctor, anyway—was about to cut off the finger. So was I, come to think of it. Glad I didn't. Got *you* out of it, and you'll give me a hospital."

He'd somehow stopped the wagon with the final words, and was halfway to the ground, while the horse proceeded to sag and droop into a travesty of equine posture.

That was quite a day. Surgeon Walden on first impression was simply a putterer and a potterer (as my mother used to call ineffectual people) but that idea soon went glimmering. (Have we not all known men or women who seem to be at wit's end constantly, yet in the upshot are remarkably efficient and capable? Walden was surely such a man.)

I sketched his hospital for him in half an hour, and in five minutes of fumbling and scratching, he'd changed my entire idea and had incorporated more bunks with more breathing space for the sick men than I had thought possible, as well as a folding operating table for himself and shelves for his instruments, medicines, and nostrums. He had windows where he wanted them, and he produced oiled paper to cover them. I'd even promised him a doorway twice as wide as I would have considered necessary, because he would not have sick men on stretchers tilted or dropped as they were carried through.

He produced men by the dozen to work for me, all of whom affectionately called him "Doc" and bragged to me interminably that he was the best physician in America. This opinion seemed to be based on his manner of treatment, rather than any concrete results that I could see.

First of all, strangely enough, he asked a man what he thought was wrong with him, and *listened* to the answer. Most doctors I had known or heard of seemed to make a practice of having you tell them your symptoms in English, then telling them back to you in Latin or Greek, adding the fee for the consultation.

Secondly, he evidently never said that he could cure anything, but that he'd like to give it a try. Further, while he was quietly and mildly insulting to every one of his patients in respect to their physical and moral habits, he was *kind* to all of them.

He treated a dozen men while I was with him that day, seemingly annoyed with them for interfering with him in his interference with me. But while he puttered and probed and poked at his man, his questions and the answers they elicited went to the heart of the matter every time.

One gaunt, slack-jawed fellow came into the "dispensary," as Walden was calling it before the first logs of the walls were into place. This man was crying before he started to talk.

"The boys say I been tooken by a demon, Doc," he sobbed.

Walden nodded sympathetically. (This was one patient he did not rasp mildly with his tongue.) "Let's see where you got that knock with the musket at Brandywine," he said.

The man bared a long raw scar on the side of his head.

"There may be demons," Walden said, "although I've never seen one myself. How does it affect you, Timson?"

"Times it all gets black, and I fall down and grind my teeth. The boys force my jaws apart and put sticks in so's I won't crack my teeth, but I bite right through 'em, Doc. They say it's a demon, for sure."

Timson didn't hear the doctor's reply, but I did: "It is a demon, my boy." He fumbled at a jar and took a handful of white pills from it, rolling them into a paper twist. "Take one of these every morning," he said. "And, Timson, I think we'll send you home for the winter. Home is the best place to chase demons or any other trouble you can think of."

"I signed on for the end, Doc. I'd liefer stay than go home."

"Come back in the spring if you're better. I'll put word into headquarters to give you four months' furlough."

After Timson shambled out, I looked accusingly at Walden, who had returned to scratching with a piece of lead at the hospital plan. "Doc," I said, "what the hell was that about demons?"

"Good a name for it as any. The falling sickness. Have you ever seen it?"

I nodded. Back home we always said a person who had it "took fits." A good many of our people thought also that the devil had hold of a body who had it.

"A demon is something I can't whip. He won't be back in the spring. I'll write to his folks. It was that knock with a musket butt that did it, I'll be bound it was."

"Now wait a minute, Doc," I said. "You gave him a handful of those white pills. That's what you gave to the fellow with the headache, and the one with the bellyache, and the one who said he couldn't sleep at night."

Walden nodded. "I've got pink ones and blue ones too. I'm thinking of getting a color for every day in the week. They don't do no harm." He paused. "They don't do much good, either. The boys like to get something, though. The fellow with the headache has his bowels bound up from poor food. The fellow with the pain in his belly is probably the same thing, although maybe it's something in the water he's been drinking lately. The man who couldn't sleep at night is lonely and homesick. Those pills won't hurt 'em."

"Haven't you got any medicine that will do any good?"

He peered at me across the tops of the spectacles. "That ain't even medicine in the pills, unless you call sugar medicine. Maybe it is, with the food we're getting. Medicine! Where in hell would I get medicine, Lieutenant? Just where in hell do you think I'd get it?"

I nodded. "I see, Doc."

"Let's get on with the building," he said, "so my sick men can die in comfort."

"Why don't we all go home, Doctor, and live in comfort?"

"That's a good question," he said softly. "I dunno the answer, but I'll think about it. I will surely think about it."

A half-hour later, as he held a log steady while I saddled it, he said: "I guess we wouldn't live in comfort, knowing we'd been whipped."

I didn't answer him.

As dusk was falling, I asked him to come to our area for supper. I had it in mind that you can never get too many medical opinions. He would look at Hawk and tell me what he thought.

146

It wasn't a long trek to our huts, but it was colder than ever, and I set a good pace. Surgeon Walden walked as he seemed to do everything else, awkwardly or clumsily, but he kept with my long-legged stride without apparent difficulty.

"He'll laugh at you if you want to examine him, Doc," I said. "So you'll have to go on what you see and what I tell you."

"I'm pretty nearsighted," he said sadly. "I'll get as close as I can without knocking him down. What do you think is wrong with him?"

I told him what my mother had told me, plus my own observations about his coughing and that he tired much more easily than ever before, that sometimes he grimaced as in pain.

"Uh-huh," he said. "Your mother told you he spit blood, eh?"

"That's right, Doc."

"Uh-huh." That seemed to end it. I was disappointed when he said no more, though I waited a full minute.

"What do you think?"

"Wait until I see him, Lieutenant."

Another twenty yards of silence, and he spoke again, going back to my question earlier in the day.

"Maybe here's another answer to what you said about going home. I saw two boys meet yesterday in that freezing rain we had, one going off guard and the other going on. Said the boy going on, 'Good morning, brother soldier. How are ye today?' Said the other, 'All wet, I thank ye. Hope you are soon the same, you bastard.' They both winked at me and went on. Give 'em food and rum, Lieutenant, and clothes to cover their backs, and they'll storm Tophet itself. And take it, I believe."

Surgeon Walden found instant favor with our mess. After introductions, he stepped up to the glowing cooking fire, spread his thin, blue-veined hands to the warmth, and remarked pensively, "I do believe it may turn off cold tonight."

Harm Tallman almost choked with laughter; even sober Walter Luckey grinned. Perhaps it wasn't the funniest remark they'd ever heard, but it hit the spot, spoken as it was into the teeth of that rattling wind.

147

Joe Williams exchanged light banter with Walden for a few minutes, being bested every time; the mild voice and soft words made mincemeat of Williams' coarse backwoods baiting.

"Being you're a doctor," Williams said, winking at the rest of us, "could you take a look at my horse later? Seems to me there's something wrong with him, Doc."

I knew that one. When Walden asked what seemed to be the trouble, Williams would say that everything the horse ate turned to manure. Walden knew it too.

He peered sadly at Williams, shaking his head. "My father was a veterinary, Major."

"That's all right, Doc. I'm a veteran myself. I been to Quebec with Arnold and Morgan."

"No, Major. A veterinary is an animal doctor. I'm not skilled enough for that. I can only treat humans."

"So? A human is more complicated to treat than a horse, ain't he?"

"Not at all, Major. You come to see me, and I ask you what seems to be the trouble. Then you tell me, and I give you some pills or some elixir of one kind or another, and you pay me, and you go off quite satisfied. But a horse, Major, can't tell me what's wrong with him, and I'm lost. That's why there are more doctors for humans than there are for horses. It takes a smart man to be a horse doctor."

Amid the laughter, Hawk spoke to me. "A fine fellow, your Surgeon Walden, Matt. Did you bring him to look me over? I'll be like the horse; I won't tell him the symptoms."

"Damn it, Hawk! Let him look at you."

"He can look all he wants. I like him."

Walden did look. He and my father went aside after we had all eaten and the rest were sitting around smoking and discussing the day's work. The doctor poked and pushed at Hawk with his slim fingers, put his ear to my father's bared chest, had Hawk cough for him, and asked a few seemingly aimless questions.

"Lost about twenty pounds, haven't you?" he asked.

Hawk shrugged. "Burn up my fat in the winter. Like a bear does. How'd you guess so close?"

Walden picked with forefinger and thumb at the slack flesh on

148

my father's neck. "I'm a good guesser," he said. "All right, Captain. Button up your shirt."

"So I'm a healthy man, Doc?"

The pale eyes behind the spectacles looked into Hawk's face. "As healthy as you ever will be, Captain."

He stayed awhile longer, drinking hot rum and water with us. When he said he had to leave, I walked along with him.

"Well, Doc?"

"I think your other doctor was close to the mark. It's either lung fever or a growth in the lungs. Take him home, boy. Your mother will want him there."

"He won't go, Doc."

"I expect he won't."

"Is there anything we can do for him? Anything we can give him?"

"Your love and respect, Matt. That's enough for now."

CHAPTER TEN

During the two nights preceding Christmas Eve, the desertion rate in the Pennsylvania division rose like the flight of a mortar shell. Who could blame the poor fellows? Some of them were only twenty or thirty miles from home.

In our own company, two men were missing at morning parade on the twenty-third of December. Garret Perry was one of them; he had married during our stay at home that fall. The other was Aaron Conklin, a steady man of sober mien, who had left his wife and four children in the household of his mother, an old rip if there ever was one.

Hawk went after them with four men. They were back before noon, with Perry and Conklin. They'd met them on their way back, each packing half of a doe that had spooked before them as they'd started to cross a pasture in the dawn's first light. They'd stalked the deer, and Perry had shot it. When they were butchering the deer, Perry said, Conklin had touched his arm, saying simply, "Let's go back with this meat."

One deer does not go far among a company of men. When it was gone, that same day, we were out of provisions, although the prospect did not alarm us. The real bite of hunger comes, I have found, when a man has been on short rations so long that he has to hunch his shoulders against the gnawing in his stomach. I would as lief do without food entirely for two days than go on a diet of soup and bread for a week.

Youngblood drew from the Pennsylvania division several buckets of wheat flour, a few sacks of black potatoes, and one hundred pounds of ancient salt beef packed in butter firkins.

Now we had a taste of the fare that ten thousand men were receiving, whenever there was enough to distribute.

Perhaps half the encampment was housed in huts of one kind or another before Christmas, but the rest were in nondescript tents and lean-tos. The once-forested slopes above the Schuylkill were now a maze of stumps through which crooked wagon tracks and pathways wound.

I call to mind easily the discomforts, the misfortunes, the outright horrors of that Christmas season, which were tempered only by the everlasting hope that the food—stacked in warehouses, stalled God knew where in wagon trains, held jealously by stupid commissaries in a dozen cities and towns—would soon be coming. Not only food, but clothing and medicine—how long would it be before they arrived to alleviate the miseries of the starving, the naked and the sick?

Always the soldiers' plaints were marked by that leaven of mockery that perhaps did more than anything else to make their troubles bearable. I saw a sign displayed before the huts of a New York regiment: REGIMENTAL LAUNDRESS NEEDED. ONLY 26 DIRTY SHIRTS LEFT.

There was little or no straw or other bedding. A man without a blanket huddled by the fire to get what sleep he could. Of a morning, passing the crude huts, one did not know which was the stronger emotion: pity at the sight of the fevered cheeks, at sound of the wretched coughing, at view of open sores, or revulsion at the stench of filthy clothing and unwashed bodies.

There were New Hampshire men of Poor's brigade not far from us. I heartily wished that some of those unfeeling and unseeing men who decorated the Congress with their vain oratory were there with us to witness the changing of the guard for New Hampshire. One soldier from each hut would have drawn the guard duty. Draped with all he owned himself, he'd stand and call his needs: "Mittens." A pair would be handed over. "Stockings." He'd get the remnants of ragged wool that some wife had flashed busy neddles into many months before. "Shoes." They might or might not be forthcoming. And so on, until he was ready as could be to go forth, leaving the donors of his clothing to shiver by the fire.

The memory that epitomizes those December days for me, however, is the one that I have had brought back to me by the paintings of artists who have tried faithfully to depict the bitterness and misery of our winter of discontent. I tell nothing but the truth when I say that men on guard stood with their feet in their hats to keep the bandages that they wore in lieu of shoes out of the snow.

One third of the army was on "sick, present" listings in the daily returns of the regiments, not because all of them were sick, but because they had not clothes to cover them.

I have often cursed those shortsighted, economy-minded and downright criminal men in government who so frequently failed our citizen-soldier, as they did at the Valley Forge. In the length and breadth of the thirteen colonies at that time, there were goods and stores in abundance to equip and clothe and feed ten times our ten thousand.

I add this: thus far in this narrative I have made it clear that I truly believed we could not hold together until victory. I was right in believing that. There is no man who was at the Valley Forge in December who would not honestly admit that if Billy Howe had marched his warm, comfortable legions over those twenty-odd miles that separated us, we would have been whipped and scattered to the four winds.

But General Sir William Howe had his good reasons for not moving. As the ballad has it:

> *Sir William he, snug as a flea,*
> *Lay all the time a-snoring,*
> *Nor dreamed of harm as he lay warm*
> *In bed with Mrs. Loring.*

Withal, we had a Christmas dinner that must have rivaled any in the stone houses where the generals had their quarters.

Early on December 24, Hawk called for a foraging detail. Many men stepped forward, but with a smile he picked Garret Perry and Aaron Conklin, the two men who had pulled foot the day before. They were to be accompanied by one corporal, Peter van Houten.

Hawk handed them a pass from camp, a blank receipt form with a strip of lead to write with, and these instructions:

"We all want a good meal on Christmas. You won't get it within fifteen miles. Every farmer and his brother has his musket loaded to repel foragers unless they show the color of hard coin. You men go north and east. Farther north than east, and watch for dragoons. We don't want patriots to skimp on Christmas because of us. So when you get far enough away, sound out the folks. Approach the house you pick, and if they welcome you have a meal and go on. If they run you and curse you, then come back later and see what they can spare. You know what will make a good dinner. Once you've made your—ah—selection, then sit you down, Van Houten, and fill out the receipt. Something like this: 'I, the undersigned, have this day accepted a due bill on the Highland County Company of Independent Rangers, Continental Army of the United States, to be paid on demand by commissary of said company, for the following listed items:'

"Then, Aaron, you sign it for the King's man you got the stuff from. Sign it—let's see—sign it 'Banastre Tarleton.' You understand?"

"Don't know how to spell that, Hawk," Conklin answered dubiously. "Can't you make it something simpler?"

"All right. Sign it 'William Howe.' And be careful, boys. When you get close to camp again, you'll have to show that receipt to the provost guard, likely. If you don't have it, they'll confiscate everything you've got. And be sure to list everything."

They returned at midmorning of Christmas Day. We all turned out when shouts greeted their arrival. They were an astonishing sight. The three of them, who had trudged away through the snow on the rutted road to the northeast, returned perched on the cushioned front seat of a handsome black sleigh with yellow runners. The horse that pulled them was nearly blown; he stood with heaving sides and hanging head, but he was a handsome young animal, almost coal-black to match the sleigh.

"Reportin' for duty, Captain," Peter van Houten said with a huge grin. "Foraging detail completed."

"I'll be goddamned," Hawk said.

Garret Perry slid into the body of the sleigh and began singing out cargo.

"One sheep," he cried, holding a limp woolly head above the sideboard.

"Right, one sheep," Aaron Conklin said solemnly, making a show at checking his receipt.

They went through their act, enumerating turnips and cabbages and beets, four hams, six sides of bacon, a bushel of squash, a sack of onions, a few other items.

"And one sleigh and one horse," Garret Perry chortled triumphantly.

"One sleigh and one horse," Conklin said, handing the receipt to Hawk.

My father eyed the equipage with misgiving. "You'd better tell me the story fast," he said. "We'll have to get rid of that rig and horse right away."

"No we don't, Captain," Van Houten said. "That's all been blamed on the British."

Van Houten told the story:

They'd traveled a long way before they found farm country that wasn't already up in arms against foragers from both sides. Finally, they'd scouted a prosperous farm from a hillside, deciding it was a good place to start. They worked their way up through an orchard to take a better look, when a troop of dragoons came clattering down the road. Our three men took cover behind a stone wall close to the stable. They heard the ensuing argument between the farmer and the captain of dragoons.

"He was a Tory, all right," Van Houten said. "One of the tightest, most cantankerous I ever heard. The British officer was throwed by his horse and hurt his leg and shoulder. Horse broke its leg and they had to shoot it. So the captain didn't want to ride, he hurt so much, and wanted to buy this sleigh and this here horse. The old Tory says nothing doing, without cash on the barrelhead."

"Kept saying over and over," Perry interposed, "that he was loyal to his King and had two sons serving in the Royal Americans, beating the devil out of the filthy rebels. But he wasn't going to give up his property for no slip of paper."

"So, anyways," continued Van Houten, "the dragoons rode away after a while, sore as boils. We stayed by the barn until night come, then we crawled up to the house when the light went out in the kitchen. We was under the bedroom window and the Tory and his woman come in to go to bed. We could see 'em by the candle on the table. Not her, Captain. She went behind the door to put on her nightdress. You know what that old cusser took off? Two sets of wool long drawers and shirts! Two sets! Then he opened the window a mite and blew out the candle. We waited until they was both snoring. Then we reached in the window." Van Houten pulled aside his coat, pulled up his shirttail and proudly displayed thick woolen underclothes.

"So we went out to the barn, hitched up the horse, and then we filled the sleigh from the smokehouse, the root cellar, and the ice-house. Didn't even have to kill the sheep. It was hanging in the icehouse. The old fellow had hisself a watch dog—we made friends with it while we was watching the house, and it was with us all the time we was filling the sleigh, nice and friendly."

"Then I wrote him out a note," Conklin said. "Spelled it out real good, too, Hawk. I wedged it in the stable door where he'd sure see it this morning. Said: 'Every subject of His Majesty should give aid and comfort to the army. You can get your money at headquarters in Philadelphia.'"

"So then we let this nag fly," Van Houten said, "and here we are. Merry Christmas!"

"I'll be goddamned," Hawk said.

Perhaps this narrative seems to dwell inordinately on food, both its abundance and its lack in somewhat equal proportions.

This is not unnatural, I would aver, since during that winter the cold fact of our starvation diet vied for dominance with our dreams, or nightmares, if the truth were said, of tables laden with all the delicacies the mind could conjure.

In the time that has passed since our encampment on the cold hills at the Valley Forge, I have fought the hidden fear, ever lurking in the inner reaches of my mind, that one day I would be hungry again. I have of course gone without food time and again, on campaign or on hunting trips, but always I knew that a few hours or at most a day would see me filled and content. Perhaps it is that secret fear that leads me to seek, wherever I may be, the good food of the fine inn or tavern.

Suffice it to say that our Christmas dinner on the bleak Pennsylvania hills was enough to make that a memorable day. Of course, forty-odd men and those few ragged and thin-faced guests whom we did not have the heart to turn away, made short work of the lamb and ham and vegetables our three wonderful scoundrels had brought us.

Wonder of wonders, there was enough applejack to give all of us the glow of Christmas. The officers' mess had guests: Surgeon Walden and Sergeant Jed Palmer, the latter claiming he had scented roast mutton at five hundred yards—his nose was so good, he said, that his father had always used him for flushing woodcock and partridge in the field in place of a dog, principally because he admitted that he was smart enough to know he would get whipped if he took to running rabbits.

Our log hut glowed with a cheerful fire to add to the warmth of the applejack. We were all content, but Albion Walden was perhaps more so than the rest of us. His sad smile flickered across his face like waves rolling on a shore, never did he look at any of us through the lenses of his spectacles, but rather over them, a sign that I ever took to be keen interest in the speaker's words. When he spoke himself, his soft voice held us firmly.

"Where did that haunch of mutton come from?" he asked Hawk, while we all chewed on crackling bits of skin—the remnants of the meat.

"I can't tell you exactly," Hawk started to explain.

"Ah—then it came from Providence," Walden smiled. "My good mother used to say, Providence will provide, and I have found her words true at times in this army. Providence usually acts at night when all good folk are sleeping."

"I wouldn't wager we'll see more," Joe Williams said. "The countryside around here is already up in arms about what you call Providence. I seen two Providencers yesterday on the parade, getting thirty-nine licks on their backs for one chicken apiece. How many would headquarters give for a whole sheep?"

"Did they get to eat the chickens?" Walden asked.

"All but the feathers."

"They shouldn't complain overmuch if payment is exacted for Providence," said Walden. "Now things are a little different at our mess. We don't have any problems of chickens and sheep and such. I come out, ready for a new day in pleasant surroundings, and I say to the cook, 'What's for breakfast, lad?' He smiles like a good, well-brought-up boy, and says, 'Fire cakes and water, sir.' Then, about suppertime, I see him going to his work with vim and vigor, my mouth waters, and I say, 'And what is the meal this evening, my boy?' He makes prompt reply, with the joy of youth. 'Water and fire cakes, sir.' Now, you see, Major, there's no problem. Solid food and liquids, sir, to keep a man trim and fit. I have only one wish in respect to them. I believe that men ought to be apprised of the results of their work. I just wish that the General would send our Commissaries of Purchases around to take meals with us."

"Until their guts turn to pasteboard, like mine!" cried Williams. He smiled then. "Tell you what, Doc. You come around and take meals with us. Hawk, how long will this here fine food last you?"

Hawk looked enquiringly at Fred Youngblood, who shook his head unhappily. "This is the end of it," he said.

Walden went back to pick up Williams' words. "Are you having trouble with your innards, Major? I've got just the thing. Dried persimmons stewed with a generous quantity of oil of castor bean. I'll fix you a good mess of it."

"The hell you will! I druther be sick all the time than dying for a whole day."

Youngblood spoke sadly. "I don't know where I'm going to get anything around here for the men to eat, besides what we're issued. This is the worst damn place I ever saw. How come they picked here to spend the winter, when we could have gone on to York or Lancaster?"

"Congress is in York," Williams cried. "You wouldn't want to be where Congress is, would you? You'd never get nothing to eat, if you was there."

"I dunno," said the doctor. "My dear Youngblood, this location has its excellent points. Firstly, there is plenty of wood and plenty of water. That's about all you can see in any direction you look.

Secondly, there are but few families for the soldiery to steal from, though far be it from a soldier to steal. We agreed previously that Providence provides. Again, there are the warm sides of these hills to erect huts upon. Being in a place like this, being swallowed up as it were, will put them in a Heavenly frame of mind, like Jonah in the whale. Once more, they will not become homesick, as young fellows are apt to be when allowed into the open world of people. They will think noble thoughts here on their quiet hillsides. They will have ample time for the reflections that will fill their spiritual and moral knapsacks for the journey to another Home. No, Mister Youngblood, taken all in all, this is a capital place, sir. A capital place. I can think of no better location that would lead to a full and vigorous practice of my profession during the coming months."

"The only thing it needs, Doc," Williams said, "is Congress members to live in the huts with us, to make speeches whenever we get to thinking things ain't what they ought to be."

Harm Tallman said sleepily, "Hawk, you send me out with hunting parties. I'll bring back plenty of food."

"For four dozen men?" Hawk asked. "No, gentlemen, we'll make out just fine as soon as the wagons full of food start rolling in."

"When do you think that will be?" Harm asked.

"About the same time," said Doc Walden, "as the chests of medicine I ordered before the battle of Brandywine. They're in the same warehouses with the clothing that is coming. It's just that nobody has been able to find out just exactly where those warehouses are. Let us sing in celebration of this day, gentlemen."

He held up a directing forefinger, waggled it ludicrously in time, as he hummed "*Adeste Fideles*," and we all joined him in the hymn. We were not good, but we were loud enough. Even Walter Luckey awakened from his applejack sleep and sang with slurred syllables.

We finished the jug of applejack and fell happily into our bunks, reeking of good food, alcohol, and cedar shavings.

CHAPTER ELEVEN

"Say, Matt," said Billy Bill excitedly. "Ain't this the same place? Just over that dip in the road? Where the pretty girl is?"

I nodded shortly, thinking that he should have recognized the country miles back. They all should have, but they seemed surprised that we were here.

"I dunno, Matt," Sergeant King said. "You think it's wise to come back to a place where we found dragoons once? I'd of said something if I'd of known you were headed here."

"It's out of the way," I said, "and it's too far out for any foraging parties to have reached yet. And they can't mostly be Tories, or that Lloyd fellow that was killed wouldn't have been so prosperous. Take a small valley, with eight or ten farms in it, the people have to think generally along the same lines, or they don't stay together."

Why was I bothering to explain to them? Wasn't I in command? When Hawk sent us out, with Wayne's orders, as a regular foraging party, I'd picked the place as likely to furnish good provender. It was a good piece from the encampment, but for that very reason prices would be lower and supplies more abundant.

"How long we going to stay, Matt?" Billy asked.

"As long as it takes," I said shortly.

"Goddam," he said happily, "I got two questions to ask that girl. First one: What's your first name, Miss Lloyd? Second one: Will you marry me, Miss Lloyd?"

They all laughed, but I put a quick end to the horseplay. I didn't want them to think it was a pleasure jaunt we were on—I wanted quiet, alert men when we moved into that valley.

"Stop that foolishness and get back in ranks, Billy!"

He sounded aggrieved, mocking me. "How in hell can we have ranks, Lieutenant, when there ain't but six of us? And you think it's foolishness to want to wed a pretty little girl like that?"

"Shut up," I said. "Now, you people stay up here on the hill. I'll go down to see if it's all right. If I don't come back in an hour, or if you hear shots, leave the oxen and the horse and take to the woods."

"We should of gone somewheres else," King said nervously. "Six of us can't stand off nobody."

I didn't reply. Maybe I was nervous myself. Where dragoons had been once, they could be again. I watched the men climb into the flat bed of the first wagon, putting their blankets around their shoulders. The oxen yoked to the second wagon stood motionless on the road, the steam of their breathing puffing from frost-rimmed muzzles.

"Can we light us a fire to warm up?" King asked. "It's almighty damn cold, Matt."

"No fire," I said. "I'll be back as soon as I can."

I started down the hill, keeping to the road. The snow on the wooded slopes was too deep to allow me to take the safer way through the trees. Besides, there was no sign that the road had been used other than the marks of the heavy runners of a farm sleigh drawn by a team of calk-shoed horses. I saw chips of wood and bits of bark along the track. One of the farmers had been drawing firewood or fence rails.

It was late afternoon of a cold gray day. Just like the other time we were here, I thought.

I studied the dark house at the bottom of the slope as I walked. I took short sliding steps to keep my feet under me on the grade.

There were matters of duty to consider: I wondered if the oxen and the horse would get enough purchase in the snow to pull a loaded wagon back up the hill. There were ways, of course; I could borrow another yoke of oxen in the valley, or set the men to clearing the track of snow, or we could winch the load up the steepest part of the grade with ropes.

But these things left my mind as I considered the true reason why

I had brought the men back here on our foraging trip. There were hamlets and farm settlements many miles closer to Valley Forge where we could have procured the supplies we needed, but I confessed to myself that the Lloyd house had intrigued me. I wanted to see it again.

As a matter of fact, I had picked Derrick Archer as one of the six men for the foraging detail simply because he possessed a splendid talent for sketching. While the rest of us worked, Derrick would devote his time to making me a charcoal sketch of the house in its setting against the hillside (appropriate enough, because back home a man might have been pressed to find a building site that was not on a hillside and did not flood in springtime if it were not), and I wanted Derrick also to do exterior and interior plans.

Peggy would see the beauty of the house, its graceful lines, and would smile happily at the thought of a big house like that—three bedrooms arranged in gallery on the second floor. Only the house that Hawk had built was bigger in all the Deerkill Valley.

I smiled to think that I, never having cared one whit about any house in all my life save as shelter, had, one might say, fallen in love with a dwelling. Because, I told myself, all men do when they think of marriage and family.

The house was dark. The shutters were all closed, but in the fading light I saw smoke billowing from one of the chimneys. With the house in full sight, I saw a glow of light faintly through the shutters where the kitchen would be.

I stopped at the edge of the cleared land, looking alternately at the house and the outbuildings. Nothing moved. There was a small chance, I decided, that the British officer's wound had been worse than it looked. They might not yet have moved him to Philadelphia. What had it been? Ten days, eleven days? If the officer was still here, there'd be a squad of troopers with him. I waited, watching and listening.

No dragoons, I decided, after three or four minutes of standing motionless among the trees. The only sounds I'd heard were the bawl of a calf from the stables, the treading of one horse's hoofs on the puncheon floor of its stall, the far-drawn scream of a wildcat deep in the forest.

If there had been troopers, their horses would have moved during these minutes, sounding their presence by thudding on the floors of the stalls, or on the barn floor where they would be stabled through lack of enough stalls in the horse barn. I was sure there was no infantry. The British would not send foot soldiers in a small party this far from Philadelphia, through a countryside that swarmed with rebel foraging parties, most of which were much larger than the one I commanded. It had to be dragoons or nothing.

So the girl was alone, unless she had managed to find someone to help her, or unless some neighbor or relative had come to stay with her. I had the sudden thought that maybe she wasn't there at all. She might have gone off and left the farm in care of some neighbor, who was now in the kitchen. I'd have to be careful in my approach in either case.

I left the shelter of the trees and moved along the road toward the lane that led to the house. At the head of the lane, I found all the signs I needed to tell me that the British were long gone. Here were the traces of many horses, shod with the distinctive craftsmanship of British farriers. There were mounds of horse droppings at least a week old. I saw twin ribbon trails of a light sleigh, going into the lane and coming out many days ago. That would be the equipage they'd brought from Philadelphia to transport the wounded officer. I found a path worn by small narrow boots, from the house to the barn and back, many times.

She's probably alone in the house, I thought.

I moved along a path that had been shoveled in the heavy snow. All the windows were shuttered, evidently against the wind. I rapped with my mittened knuckles on the heavy door. There was no answering sound for perhaps the slow count of five. I could imagine her inside, standing at the hearth, looking at the door with startled eyes, her hand to her throat in the way that women have when they hear a strange noise.

I rapped again and then heard movement near the door.

"James?" her voice called, muffled by the thick door; I could detect neither fear nor alarm.

What answer should I give? My name? Would she remember? I didn't think so. Who was James?

"Continental soldiers," I called. "Those who were here the day your——" I stopped, realizing that was a crude way of reminding her that her brother was dead. "Those who were here on December seventeenth," I amended.

There was silence for a long moment. Then: "What do you want here? Who is talking?" She was right, I thought, to keep the door barred until she was certain; deserters might have come here as a place they knew would be easy to pillage.

"The lieutenant," I called. "Second in command. The captain was my father. I talked to you that day."

"What's your first name, Mr. Hill?" she asked.

"Matt."

"Not enough," she said after another pause. "Your true first name."

"Matthias," I said.

I heard a bolt slide back, then a bar withdrew with a grating sound. The door swung open. A heavy-barreled musket thrust forward in line with my chest.

"It is you," she said simply, lowering the weapon. "Come in, Lieutenant."

"Not yet, miss," I said. "I left six men on the ridge. We would shelter in your barn tonight."

"You are welcome," she said. "I'll start food and coffee."

"We can care for ourselves," I said quickly. "We wouldn't want to cause you trouble."

"No trouble. I will enjoy your company. Have your men stow their gear in the barn, then bring them into the house."

"Thank you," I said. I didn't step back immediately; it seemed an occasion for more friendliness and less matter-of-fact speech. I saw that she was dressed as before, in the breeches and man's shirt that slimmed her to unwomanly proportions and yet left not the least doubt that she was a woman.

"How did you know my name?" I asked for want of something more to say. "My first name?"

She laughed coolly, in so superior a manner that I bristled. "I asked your father, of course."

"Why? What difference could my name mean to you?"

"None," she said levelly. "I just wanted names of witnesses to my brother's murder by the British. I will file a claim against them when they are beaten."

"And when will that be, miss?" It was my turn to be superior.

"You answered me that you were Continental soldiers," she said. "And that's a good answer for you—the British will be beaten when you really become an army for the whole country, instead of New Yorkers and Rhode Islanders and Pennsylvanians. Now go and get your men. I don't want to heat the outdoors."

I was about to ask her how she qualified as an authority on the army, but the door swung to, and I turned on my heel and made my way back toward the ridge.

King and the others came quickly when I reappeared on the grade.

"She down there, Matt?" Billy Bill asked eagerly.

I nodded and looked sourly at him. He was beginning to irritate me. I'd have to see that he stayed away from that girl. Or better, let her take that sharp tongue to him. He might as well start learning about women.

It was bitterly cold in the wind, and the men wanted to get to a fire and food and shelter.

"Is it all right down there?" King asked.

"The girl seems to be there alone," I told him. "There's no sign of Tarleton's boys, or anybody else."

The oxen refused to be hurried on the grade, and we let the animals make the pace, the men keeping their usual loud drovers' cries to themselves.

We settled the animals, stowed our blankets and other gear, and then I led the men to the house. She opened the door quickly at my knock.

"Wipe your feet," she said. "I don't want my kitchen tracked up."

"Evening, ma'am," Billy said with a wide smile. "Nice to see you again. You're looking well, real fine."

"Thank you," she said, just as sweet as one of my mother's steamed puddings. "It's fine to see you again too, soldier."

"William Bill, ma'am," he beamed. "Call me Billy."

"It's an easy name to remember, Billy. Come in so I can close the door."

There was a jug of applejack on the table; she told us to help ourselves. I noticed that the kitchen was small with all of us crowded into it. I saw the reason: a wall-to-wall pantry. I would tell Derrick to open that up in his plans; a pantry could always be built as a lean-to.

Six of us sat down; Billy perched himself on a stool by the hearth, where she was wielding long-handled pots and pans.

"I know your last name is Lloyd," Billy said. "I heard that when we was here before. What's your first name, ma'am?"

She smiled at him. "It's Glennis. That's a Welsh name."

"That's real pretty, ma'am. Like you. It fits you fine." Billy turned to us with a broad grin. "Well, I asked her my first question."

"You have more questions for me?" she asked.

"Not right now, ma'am. A little later, when I get to know you better."

"That's enough, Billy," I said sharply. "Mistress Lloyd, can you tell us if there have been other foraging parties in the neighborhood?"

"British," she said. "They pay in hard cash. You're offering bills on the commissary?"

"That's right."

"You'll not get much, and that at high prices. People here are for Congress, mostly, but they don't take much stock in the Congress' promises to pay."

"We'll take what we need and be damned to 'em!" King growled.

"You'd best be fast, if that's what you'll do," the girl said. "I told you the British have been here, as you well know. My neighbors have fully developed the art of hiding all their provender and stock at short notice."

"We'll deal fairly," I said, "or not at all."

"If you mean that," she said, "I can help you, maybe. The farmer who has the most to sell, being the biggest landholder and stock breeder, will come here tonight." She paused. "He drives a hard bargain."

There seemed to be a note of resignation, perhaps regret, in her voice. I looked inquiringly at her.

"He's buying this place from me," she said quietly.

"You have no one?" I asked.

She shook her head and turned back to the cooking.

165

"If we can help——" I offered. "We will be staying a couple of days."

"We can pick him up by the heels," Billy told her, "and shake the coin from his breeches if he don't deal right with you."

"Thank you, Billy," she smiled. "It will be all right. He's not an easy man to deal with, but he's fair enough. I'm pleased to sell at his price."

"What will you do?" I asked.

"I don't know," she said simply.

"I know what I'd do if I were you," Billy said softly.

"What's that?"

"That's the second question, and I ain't ready yet to ask it."

It was a fine meal that she put before us: fried eggs and potatoes, slabs of smoked ham, hot biscuits, peach preserves, and coffee. We plied our cutlery with a vengeance, without talking overmuch other than to praise her cooking. I noticed, however, that over the faces of my companions, even as they wolfed the food, came expressions of contemplative sadness. Evidently they were thinking, as I was, that such a meal should be set before every starving man at the Valley Forge this night.

When the meal was finished the men thanked her, and all but Billy got up to go out to the barn. Billy was having his third cup of coffee. Sergeant King, Gerret Blauvelt, and the Secord brothers, Andrew and William, went out of the house, but I asked Derrick Archer to tarry.

I spoke to Glennis Lloyd. "Archer here is a craftsman with charcoal pencil and paper. Would you mind if he measured and sketched your house, inside and out?"

"Whatever for?" she asked.

"I have it in mind to build one exactly like it at home. I admired it the first day I saw it, and I've been thinking about it ever since. The idea came to me that I should duplicate it for myself."

"Mr. Archer is welcome to draw all the sketches he wishes," she answered, then paused a moment. "You're married, Lieutenant?"

"Not yet."

"He's courting the prettiest widow woman in New York State," Billy said cheerfully. "Almost as pretty as you, Mistress Lloyd."

"Finish your coffee, Billy, and get along with the others," I told him sharply.

"I figgered to stay and talk a little, Matt."

"You can stay, Billy," the girl said evenly, eyeing me. "I choose the guests in this house, and I don't often have visitors who pay such pleasant compliments. What does she look like, this widow woman that plans to marry the Lieutenant and live in a house like mine? What color hair does she have? What's her name? Where does she live?"

"I druther talk about you," Billy said, and then proceeded to talk about himself. I started to give him a direct order to go to the barn, but hadn't opened my mouth to speak before the girl withered me with a glance and then beamed upon Billy. So I shut up.

Archer already had his few materials laid out on the table and was starting to sketch the kitchen with its heavy locust beams, puncheon floor, and massive fireplace.

I wasn't bidden to stay, but neither was I invited by look or gesture to go. I sat there like a stick, searching for something to say, while Billy rattled nonsense to her and she smiled charmingly at him.

Finally I had a chance to get a word in. "Miss Lloyd, what did you mean when you told me before that we'd beat the British when we really became an army? We're an army, all right. Not much of one, I'll admit."

She shook her head severely. "My brother William was wounded in the fighting on Long Island. I went to nurse him. I was with you for better than a month before I brought him home. I watched the brawling and the stealing that went on between regiments from different colonies. I saw that you had no respect for your officers, that you would as soon put down a leader and elect a ruffian in his place as you would take a day or a week from duty to go gallivanting wherever you pleased. Continentals! You're proud of the name, but as far as I could see you were little better than raw militia, and I don't imagine you've improved. When the day comes that you can say, man for man, that you're better soldiers than the British and the Hessians, you've beaten them."

That opinion was pretty close to my own, but I had to disagree that our bobtail crew could ever improve. I was about to say so, but a knock at the door, peremptory and heavy, forestalled my words.

Billy dashed for the corner where our rifles were leaning against the wall. Derrick Archer jumped up to join him. I also was on my feet in an instant.

Glennis Lloyd smiled at us, motioning us with her hands to be at ease. "Is that you, James?" she called.

A muffled voice answered. "It's me, all right. Who'd you think it was?"

She went to the door, opened it. A tall thick man stood there, muffled to the throat against the cold. The light from the kitchen showed his face, heavy-jowled and dark-browed, having a look that seemed sullen, maybe sour, to me.

"What's all this?" he rumbled, looking at Billy and Archer with their rifles.

"Soldiers, James," she told him. "Come inside."

"Why are soldiers here?" he asked. "They don't look like soldiers to me. They look like woodsrunners."

I called past the man into the darkness beyond the door. "All right, boys. Go back to the barn."

He turned and stared into the night. "Did you have men behind me? Were they going to shoot me?"

I laughed. "Not unless you wore a red coat."

"Why are you here? We have naught to do with your war."

"Foraging," I answered shortly, turning away from him to go back to the table.

"I sell for cash," he said. That seemed to settle his interest in our presence. He spoke to the girl. "I have all the papers ready here in my pocket, and a draft on my bankers in Philadelphia."

"I sell for cash, James," she said, her eyes flashing.

"Who has so much hard money in these times?" he asked harshly, not seeming to remember what he'd just told us. "This draft I'm going to give you is convertible to hard money on demand. When you can get into Philadelphia, that is."

"And when will that be, James?"

"Soon as these scarecrow soldiers is whipped, which ought to be in the springtime."

"I can go to Philadelphia now," she said. "They do not bar civilians on business."

"My bankers are in York," he said glumly. "Only their money is in Philadelphia. Damn fools sided with Congress."

"So do we, don't we, James?"

"Far as it goes, we do," he answered. In his complete arrogance, he talked as if Billy and Derrick and I weren't even there. "It was a mistake. I can see that now, but I got to hope. I hold too much Congress paper to change sides now."

He seated himself heavily at the table; he was a big man, tall and broad and heavy. The chair creaked when he lowered himself to it. "You got coffee, Glennis?"

"It's all gone," Billy Bill said coldly.

The big man looked at him, grinning. "You a soldier, sonny? They must be hard put for men."

Billy's lips split in a tight grin. "Now, mister man, you had no call to say that. Let's you and me step out into the snow. First I'll chop you down to even with me, and then I'll show you who is a man."

"Billy," I said. "You'd best to go to the barn and bed down for the night."

The big man laughed. "Let him be. My business won't take long." He eased a sheaf of papers from his pocket. "I'll show you right where you sign, Glennis."

Billy subsided, staring coldly at the stranger; Derrick went back to his sketching; I watched the girl read through the papers hastily. Then she brought quill and inkpot, scrawled her name in several places, accepted copies of the documents, and returned writing materials and papers to the cherry breakfront that held the household china.

"Lock, stock, and barrel," she said evenly. "It's yours, James. Use it well, or the ghosts of my father and my grandfather will haunt you all the days of your life."

"Should you not have a lawyer, Miss?" I asked.

The fat man turned red and glowered at me. She smiled coolly. "We have. Each the same one. He prepared the papers."

"Your draft, Glennis." The man handed her a parchmentlike sheet. "When will you be gone?"

"Don't rush her," Billy said softly. "Maybe she wants to stay awhile."

She smiled warmly at Billy. "A few days, perhaps, James. I have not decided."

"And where?" James asked.

"Maybe to York, to find your bankers. Maybe to Philadelphia, to wait for your bankers to find me." She smiled again at Billy. "Maybe to the army. I have a bale of bills on the commissaries. My brother Will took Congress receipts from everybody, even New Jersey militia. Some of them may be good, although many of them are signed with a big X in place of a signature."

"Come to the army," Billy said eagerly. "We'd look out for you real fine, Miss."

The heavy man looked pointedly at us, then back at the girl. I thought that he should have made an effort to hide the manner in which he looked at her, so eagerly did his gaze travel over the slim charms revealed by the man's clothing she wore. "I'd like a few words alone, Glennis."

She nodded. "Come into the front room if you don't mind the chill. I've had no fire there."

They were gone some time. I could hear his voice rumble softly, hear her answer in alternately bantering and chiding tones. I took advantage of her absence to call Billy down for speaking out of turn several times that evening.

He accepted the rebuke, but grinned in reply. "Hell, Matt, I wasn't fooling, what I said. I'm going to ask her to marry me."

"A girl you've seen twice in your life?"

"Sure, Matt. I only seen her twice, but I never seen one better. Hell, she won't have me, but I'm bound to ask. 'Ask, and it shall be given you; seek, and ye shall find; knock, and it shall be opened unto you.' Ain't that one of Teunis Ekerson's favorite Bible quotings, Matt?"

"And I'll tell you another," I said angrily. "'A continual dropping in a very rainy day and a contentious woman are alike.' She's got a sharp tongue, Billy. How will you feel when she laughs at you and mocks you for asking her?"

"It won't make no mind to me," Billy said. "I'd liefer take my chance at it than not. Won't do no harm to try, Matt."

"You're only a lad, Billy! Eighteen. She's not a year more herself, I'll be bound."

Derrick Archer looked up mildly, speaking softly. "Ain't often, Matt, I speak up against you. But I will add to the Scriptures, long as you two started: 'Whoso findeth a wife findeth a good thing.' Go ahead and ask, Billy."

"First chance I get," Billy agreed.

"If you want to be a pure fool," I said, "I won't stop you."

The girl and the man James came back to the kitchen. She was flushed, angry-looking; he was red-faced. He stepped heavily toward the door. "When you change your mind, Glennis," he said ungraciously, "you send for me. I'll be waiting."

"Don't hang until I do!" she cried after him. She went to the hearth and began to bang pots and pans around.

"Should I go after him and give him a trimming, Miss Glennis?" Billy was on his feet, ready to start.

"Sit down, Billy, and have another cup of coffee." Her voice was normal again; she smiled so sweetly at him that I grew alarmed for the two of them—just children, after all.

"Billy and Derrick, join the men in the barn," I said. "I want to talk to Mistress Lloyd about the provender we want."

"Put in a good word for me, Matt," Billy whispered hoarsely as he passed. "Tell her I'd be good to my mother if I had one."

When they were gone, she sat across from me, regarding me with head cocked to one side, her eyes merry. "Did you guess what James wanted to talk to me about, Lieutenant?"

"I noticed how he looked at you," I said, trying to bring disapproval to my eyes of the open-throated shirt. I succeeded only in flushing when she stared levelly at me.

"He wanted me to marry him," she said. "That's about the fiftieth time he's asked me. Wouldn't you think he'd get tired?"

"He's not near your age," I said for want of something else to say. "Do you have someone else?"

"I'd better have, sometime. I wouldn't marry James Kettrick if he were the last man on earth."

"He didn't seem pleasant."

"He's a dull money-grubber."

She leaned on the table, chin cupped in her hands, and elbows akimbo on the cloth. The lapels of the shirt gaped disconcertingly. "Tell me about the girl you will marry, Lieutenant Hill? She must be pretty. Billy said she was a widow. That's sad. Tell me all about her."

I thought it was most friendly and hospitable of her to show concern for the close affairs of a near stranger. I told her about Peggy: how her hair would shine in the firelight, how she could fix herself to look a lady of fashion with a few scraps of this and a few bits of that, how graceful she was even at common chores which she had never had to do when she had been a Highland Landing belle, how cruelly she felt our separation, how happy we would be once this foolish war was ended.

She eyed me oddly when I stopped talking. I was aware that I was running on to embarrassing length. Suddenly she laughed like a hoyden; I stared in amazement and some irritation.

"La, Mister Hill! I doubt very much that I would care for your lady Peggy. Nor she for me, for that matter. I can just see her nose curl, should she have the chance to look me over."

"That's not so! She would treat you kindly and well."

"Don't you want to know why I wouldn't like her?"

"Not particularly."

"I'll tell you anyway, Mister Hill. From what you tell me, she doesn't get along with her in-laws; she almost kept you from your duty with your father; she has your life and future work all planned; her farewell to you was a threat to go find her Tory parents. If you marry her, Mister Hill, I'd wager that in ten years you'd be reduced to two words in your own house: 'Yes, dear.'"

She laughed again, to add to the stinging words.

"That's enough," I said harshly. "Let's get to the matter of supplies. I'll tell you what I have in mind, you tell me where I'm likely to get it."

"I only said what I thought," she said contritely. "I'm sorry if it made you angry. It's a bad habit of mine."

"Miss, I care not at all what you think. Let's get to this work at hand."

"That Billy," she said abruptly, with that disconcerting way of changing the subject in an instant. "He's a fine young man."

"He's only a boy."

"He's as old as I am. He's soldiered a long time. He was at Boston, wasn't he?"

"Look, Miss," I said sharply. "I'll tell you something about Billy. He has a silly idea in his head about you. I want no trouble from it. Understand me?"

"I might, if I knew his idea."

"The young fool wants to marry you. I'd appreciate it if you'd put a quick end to it. I'm responsible for him."

"So he's a young fool because he wants to marry me?"

"I didn't mean that, not at all."

"He's a handsome man, Billy is."

"He's eighteen years old! He doesn't know his own mind. What's more, he scarcely knows you."

"How long did you know your lady Peggy before you asked her to marry you? Or did she ask you?"

"Mistress Lloyd, I don't want to wrangle with you. All I want is for you to give him a quick answer. That will finish it. He tells me he's bound he's going to ask you."

"All right," she said demurely. "I'll give him the answer as soon as he asks. Will that please you, Mister Hill?"

"Of course."

"Now what supplies did you want and how much are you willing to pay?"

We were up early next morning, as a beautiful dawn was pushing the dark sky over the hills, but Glennis Lloyd was before us. The two Secords set about fixing a fire and readying our breakfast, while the rest of the men, excepting Derrick Archer, tended our horse and the oxen and did all the chores that faced the girl. I sent Derrick to catch the exterior of the house in the dawn light.

He came back quickly with word that she had our breakfast prepared and on the table. It was a most pleasant meal at the big table in the bright kitchen. We had hot cakes and bacon and eggs and a dish that was strange to us: a sausagelike mixture of minced pork and herbs and corn that the girl called scrapple. She also put on the table a platter piled high with popovers, and I vow they were as good as my mother's.

The men were unstinting in their praise of her cooking. I thanked her as well, then took five minutes to quiz her on the suggestions she'd made about purchasing supplies. I had a list of names, a crude map with the farms in the valley marked as to location, and notes on how I should deal with each man I was to meet.

"They'll all be fine," she said, "except James Kettrick. As I told you, he drives a hard bargain."

I nodded. "The one who wants you and your farm both."

"Don't let him think you easy," she said. "Go to the others first and establish the prices you think are fair to pay. When you get to James, hold to your own price. He'll come around after a while, although it may take hours. The day after my brother was killed, James made his first offer for this place. Day before yesterday, we finally agreed. I got my price. Just don't show your need to do business with him, and you'll not get skinned."

"And there are no Tories in the lot?"

She shook her head slowly. "I wouldn't say so, although it's really hard to say. Some of these people think little of either side. Lieutenant, maybe you can help me?"

"Anything," I said cheerfully, thinking of her hospitality and her cooking. "What is it?"

"James Kettrick bought me out entirely, you know, but there are many things of my own here—family things and such. James said I can store them all in the barn until I have need of them and can send for them. Could you spare one of your men to help me pack and store them?"

"Sure," I said. "Archer can stay here with you to help out, and make improved sketches of the house at the same time."

She frowned. "He's a silent man, Mister Hill. He'd not be so pleasant to work beside. Anyway, I'm not so sure I want you to copy my house for your Peggy."

It was my turn to show displeasure.

"I was thinking of Billy," she said quickly, smiling placatingly. "Billy it is, then," I told her. "But remember what's in his mind. He's apt to pester you if you don't cut him short."

She laughed in that exasperating fashion that made me feel like a sobersided parson. "Billy and I will get along fine," she said, leaving me to wonder.

Foraging for a field force is never so easy as it may sound, and our task in that valley was multiplied in difficulty by the reluctance of the farmers to accept commissary bills as payment. It might be months, a year, or even two, before the bills would be honored, if they ever were, and who could say what the value of Continental money might be at any time in the future? Congress seemed to print it at whim; so did the counterfeit money-makers (and their product was often of better quality than the official paper money); it was backed by no coin whatsoever; it might well be worthless if the British overwhelmed us in the spring. The farmers knew all this; who could blame them for backing away from the promise to pay sometime in the future?

Furthermore, we were an official foraging party of the Pennsylvania division. This complicated our task by forcing us to plan for supplying the wants not only of the four dozen men of the Deerkill company, but of the company and the Seventh Pennsylvania Line as well. Whatever we brought back in our two carts would be sufficient for only a few days, and we had to buy provender that would provide the most nourishment for the least money.

The matter of rations can be examined by taking the Deerkill company alone. Now, in those days, each man's ration daily was supposed to consist of one and one-half pounds of either flour or bread, together with one pound of meat or fish—if the ration was pork, three-quarters of a pound. If peas or other vegetables were available, each man got half a pint, plus one-half pound of pork or bacon. To every man each day was supposed to go a gill of rum or whisky or other spirits.

Assuming that the best of conditions prevailed, and we were eating spring lamb as our meat ration: a good spring lamb dresses out to fifty pounds. The four dozen men of our company would therefore eat one lamb a day. Suppose we had fresh pork: an average pork carcass would yield one hundred pounds of meat, or little better than two days' meat ration. It is well to remember then, that wherever in this narrative I speak of one lamb or one pig or one deer, I am talking about meat for our company for no more than three days on slim rations.

We split the task of visiting the farms in the valley for that day. I sent Jared King with two men and the horse and cart to the head of the valley, while I took the oxen and the Secord Brothers to the second farm distant from the Lloyd place.

Suffice it to say that we worked it that way, round and about, throughout the first day of our stay. We made haste very slowly, as the saying goes. Those farmers were slow talkers, and each of them was a man who fancied himself as a bargainer. We spent twice as much time over coffee or applejack, talking about every conceivable subject but the final bargain, as we did in selecting, picking, and loading the food we bought.

Sunset caught us midway down the valley, with King and Archer and Gerret Blauvelt at the next farm. Both families were pleased to have us stay the night, sleeping in the barns, and we were glad to do so. All of us were feeling the effects of the quantity of spirits we had taken on during our visits, and we looked forward to sleeping. There was no reason to return that night to the Lloyd place, although I remember fretting at the idea that Billy might not be behaving himself.

The Secords and I, however, didn't burrow into the hay in the barn loft before we were treated to a delicious supper by the family who were our hosts, quiet and pleasant people named Thomason. Mistress Thomason served us a meal that had us filling our platters three times—soft thick biscuits with fresh butter, that salad known to Pennsylvanians as slaw, and made of shredded cabbage, carrots, and perhaps a trace of onion, and a work of art as a main course—the finest venison stew I have ever tasted. I fancy myself a good man at the kettle with game of any kind, but the exact duplication of Mrs. Thomason's stew has danced beyond my abilities ever since.

We worked our way down the valley the next morning, having a long and exasperating session with the hulking James Kettrick, who it turned out was the proprietor of one of the finest farms I had ever seen in the back country, although there were plenty to match it in abundance and style along the banks of Hudson's River back home. Kettrick maintained he had little to sell us, and the prices he named for what he had set my blood a-boiling. However, after much haggling that did little to soothe my temper, we bought parched corn and peas and onions and salted beef from him at scarcely higher prices than we paid the other farmers.

Jared King, Archer, and Blauvelt met us at Kettrick's place a little after midday, and we then set off to pick up Billy Bill at Lloyd's and be on our way. I thought that by traveling until dark set upon us, we would make a good portion of the journey back to camp, perhaps arriving there by sunset of the next day.

We turned in Lloyd's lane, noting a drab black sleigh standing at the hitching post. I hesitated only a moment; whoever it was boded no ill for us, since such an equipage must be part of the countryside rather than the traveling vehicle of any British officer.

It turned out that the owner was a minister named Pedersen from some Swedish settlement nearby; he was in the kitchen with Glennis Lloyd and Billy, and there were two women with him, introduced as his wife and daughter. I shook hands with him abstractedly, frowning at Billy, who had obviously been tilting the jug of applejack that sat on the table, together with cold meats and bread and relishes and sugar cakes, all arranged festively.

"I knew you'd be back in time for the celebration," Billy said with boisterous abandon. "I told Glennis to wait, Matt, and here you all are. Have a drink."

I stared at him. "What celebration is that? What are you talking about?"

The girl eyed me speculatively as she called to the rest of the men to come in and help themselves to food and drink.

"The wedding celebration," Billy yelled, then took a gulp of applejack. "I told you I'd ask her, and by Judas, she said 'Yes'!"

I turned swiftly to the girl, who now stared boldly at me with a curl to her lip. I glared from her to Billy. "You're not marrying anybody. Pull yourself together and get your rifle. We're leaving right now."

"Too late, Matt," he chortled. "It's all done. The knot is tied."

Mr. Pedersen spoke nervously. "I married these young people, sir. Against my judgment, I must say. So young and no banns read beforehand. I ought to insist on banns. I ought to."

"You're joking!" I cried. "Why, he's little more than a child. You couldn't have married them!"

"It's done," he said uncomfortably. "He came early this morning and got me. My wife and daughter came as witnesses. It's all done. I'll be going."

"Took some talking to get him here, Matt," Billy cried. "But he done a nice job, with prayers and all. Thanks, Reverend."

The minister and his family beat a hasty retreat as I started in on Billy. I called him all kinds of a young fool, told him that if he had a brain it would rattle in his head like a dried pea in a gourd, told him that the marriage was null and void because he didn't seek my permission. Then I turned to the girl and flayed her with words as well; all the while she looked me full in the eye and curled her lip at me in that exasperating manner she fancied.

The men were crowding Billy, drinking from the jug as fast as they could pour, eating like wolves, paying me no mind whatsoever.

I halted for lack of further words.

"We're married," the girl said levelly. "There's nothing you can do about it, Lieutenant, and if you say any more harsh things about my husband or me, I won't stand still for 'em."

"Why in God's name did you do such a crazy thing?"

She held my gaze. "We wanted to," she said in her infuriatingly cool voice.

"And what do you expect to do now," I asked, "with Billy in the army and you without a place to live?"

"I'll live with my husband," she said.

"I just said he's in the army. He can't have a wife."

"He's got one. And I'm going where he goes."

"I'll be hanged if you will!" I shouted. "There's no place for a woman, a girl like you, at the Valley Forge."

"Lots of women there, Matt," Jared King interposed.

"Not like this one," I said angrily.

"How am I different, Mister Hill?"

"You're—you're delicate——"

She burst into laughter.

"Lots of soldiers' wives," Jared King said easily. "As well as the others. We'll fix a place for Mistress Bill. No trouble, Matt."

"Hawk won't stand for it," I said.

"Sure he will, Matt," Billy grinned. "He told me hisself he thought Glennis was one of the prettiest girls he ever seen. Right after we left here that other time. Told me he believed she'd make some lucky fellow a good wife some day. I'm the lucky fellow, Matt."

"Lieutenant," said Billy's wife, "why don't you have something to eat and drink to celebrate with us? What's done is done, and all your talk can have no effect."

"You told me you would turn him down!" I growled.

"I said no such thing. You asked me to give him a quick answer, and I did. He asked me, and I said 'Yes.'"

"I almost dropped in a dead faint," Billy cried. "Says, 'Glennis, I got another question for you.' She says: 'Ask away.' I says, 'Will you do me the honor to become my wife?' Nice and fancy, like that. She says, 'Yes, Billy.' My God, I almost fell down dead. Drink up, men!"

I turned away from them, still angry, still thinking them foolish children. What kind of marriage would this be? Whatever would a gently reared girl like that do among the thousands of men and the few slatternly women at the Valley Forge? Why in hell had she married him? It was beyond me. Yet I looked at them—he stood straight and slim, a veteran if any man was; and I had to admit that everyone else was right: she was radiantly pretty as she smiled gaily.

An hour later we poured Billy to repose on top of the potato sacks in the cart drawn by the oxen, we stowed her luggage around him, closed up her house for her, sent Kettrick word by Andrew Secord that his new farm was waiting for him but that his proposed wife was gone, then struck for the long pull up to the ridge.

At first I walked grimly by myself, seething at the foolishness of it all, but I could not remain dour in her happy presence. The other men were in the best of spirits, mostly induced by spirits of another order. I feared that if we ran afoul of Tarleton's riders, my boys would be apt to grin at them, telling them to come and have a drink in honor of the bride and groom.

"Close up!" I yelled to them. "Close up! Pick up your feet; we've got a long way to go."

Glennis Bill was standing in the road, looking back briefly at the home she was leaving.

Soon enough she was walking near me, humming a lilting tune in low tones, while her young husband snored drunkenly in the cart behind us.

CHAPTER TWELVE

We came into camp after sundown the following day. We'd halted only for sleeping and eating, and our time had been measured by the pace of the oxen.

The watch fires flickered in the darkness on the cold slopes of Valley Forge, but a stranger would not have imagined that thousands of men were huddled there in their shelters until he was well among them. Close up there was no mistaking the presence of the army.

The rank smell struck our nostrils in waves. The place truly stank of sickness and filth. There was a new odor that my woodsman's sense picked out from the others. Green wood threw its choking smoke over the entire encampment. I have often debated with myself the creature discomforts that most plagued us during that winter: hunger, sickness, bitter cold, slashing rain, drifted snow, lack of clothing, and the hundred-odd others I could name. Of them all, perhaps the acrid choking smoke of green wood was the most constant and irritating.

As we moved through the regimental streets we could have timed our rough route step to the coughing that rattled from every hut. We could hear, too, the groaning and moaning of sick men, a sound that must have doubled in volume since Christmas Day.

Above all, however, rising over the ordinary sound of a great encampment and over the coughing and crying of the sick, was one insistent wailing chant—a sound with a peculiar whining rhythm that was evidently formed by a thousand voices, yet seemed to be coming from a single throat. It went on and on, seemingly formed by a series of words, although we could not distinguish them. We cocked our ears, glancing puzzledly at each other.

"What is it they're yelling, Matt?" King asked.

"I don't know. I can't make it out."

Then we came upon six or seven men standing in and about the doorway of a hut. Their mouths were open in the mournful chant. Now we could understand it, as it came clearly and despairingly:

"NO BREAD! NO MEAT! NO SOLDIER!
"NO BREAD! NO MEAT! NO SOLDIER!"

We could hear it on the far slopes and in the valley; we heard it sadly echo; we could have touched some of the men who sang it mournfully.

Though I gave no command, my men moved close to the carts in protection. We moved through the streets of Woodford's and Scott's brigades, and we attracted followers. Gaunt tatterdemalions emerged from shadowy huts, cluttering like flotsam in the wake of the carts. Some of them pressed forward silently, and thin fingers plucked at the canvas coverings on the wagonloads, unmindful of King's harsh directions to stand away.

"What you got? What'll you swap?" Their importunities flowed against us in waves of whining words. We could only keep them away and go on without answer.

We thought several times in ten minutes that these sad-faced scarecrows were awaiting only a word to flow forward and overwhelm us. Our men marched close upon the wagons, facing half outward and half backward to the strangers, who trailed us like a school of minnows after an oversized bait drawn through the shallows.

Glennis Bill was riding on the ox-cart, staring at our unwanted escort with pain, surprise, and perhaps fear showing on her face. As I looked at her, she suddenly shivered and buried her face in the collar of her cloak.

I seem to hear them still, plaintive, pitiable: "NO BREAD! NO MEAT! NO SOLDIER!"

My God, I thought, we are coming to the end, but I did not think it would come this way, that we should find disaster in starvation.

We had been gone but a few days, not enough to have allowed any significant changes in our company's camp conditions, but sufficient time to haze my former view of Hawk's appearance. Now, when he came to greet us, the light of a campfire flickered brightly across his face, and I was struck with painful apprehension.

He looked tired and drawn, but more: he was thinner than I had ever seen him. The Deerkill company thus far had had only a few days of short rations; it was not our plight at Valley Forge that was taking toll from my father. The doctors, that man in Highland Landing and Surgeon Walden, were surely right; he was a sick man. Even as I stepped forward to greet him, I resolved that he must go home, where in God's mercy and with my mother's tender care, he might well recover.

"It went well, Matt?" he asked.

"We brought all we could carry of wholesome filling food," I told him. "It won't go far."

"There have been other parties out—enough to keep the men's belt buckles from tickling their backbones. I see we have company." He smiled at Glennis Bill, who still perched on the ox-cart while Billy strutted like a peacock before her.

I shook my head. "Not company, Hawk. A permanent addition. That young fool Billy married her. Married her, the idiot!"

"Married her, eh? And you call him an idiot? Seems to me he's pretty damn wise for one so young, to have picked himself a flower so pretty."

"Good God, Hawk! What will we do with a woman here? Not even a woman—a child really, although she has a tongue like an old rip and dresses herself like a man."

"I must have missed somewhere along the line in raising you, son," he said mildly. "Or else there's not so much in the idea of heredity as folks claim there is. Because surer'n hell you've not picked up my eye for a pretty face. Or maybe you have, and don't know it. Whatever made you think of going back to that valley where she lived?"

"Hawk, you're across the mountain and far away! The only reason I went there was because I remembered the good-looking farm land and was pretty sure it wasn't owned by Tories. I certainly didn't go to catch another sight of a sassy girl without too many brains. Marrying Billy Bill! Can you tell me why she did that, Hawk?"

"I could make a pretty good guess," he said without further explanation. He went forward to greet Mistress Bill, who curtsied to him for all the world like a proper lady and smiled happily at whatever he said to her. Hawk shook hands with the beaming bridegroom. I spat into the snow disgustedly and moved forward to supervise the off-loading of the carts.

Wayne himself came to oversee the distribution of the rations. He stood to one side, big and heavy-seeming in his blue cloak, his eyes pouched with smoke-grimed circles, his thick lips peeling away from his teeth every few seconds, as if he were trying to smile but some hidden pain prohibited it.

Ringed around our hut area, visible as a sea of thin white faces, were the men of the Seventh Pennsylvania, a silent circle of wolfish eyes and appetites, watching the apportioning of supplies. As time went by, the ring grew thinner; a few men melted away each time the non-commissioned officer of a mess group drew the share of his mess.

Finally it was finished; Youngblood had doled out the last of the potatoes, corn, other staples, and had fished the last piece of salt beef from the final cask.

Wayne came forward. "A good job, Lieutenant," he said to me. Then he spoke to Hawk. "Captain Hill, what do you intend to do with that pretty little girl your son brought back?"

Hawk grinned. "Not up to me, sir. She married one of my men. They'll make out fine. We'll fix 'em quarters."

Wayne nodded. "You'd better. I don't want a situation like the one Woodford faces. Every drab in Virginia, seems like, is living in the huts of his troops. Seems to average one to a hut. Two of them were whipped this morning for inciting to desertion. You heard that?"

"Yes, sir."

"See that she sticks to her husband, then, like a proper wife, or she'll get a touch of the cat too. You understand me, Lieutenant Hill?"

"Yes, sir," I said, flushing. "She's only a girl, sir. A young girl. She'll be fine, but I'll keep an eye on her myself."

"That's what I'm afraid of," Wayne said dryly. "She keeps an eye pretty well on you. Just keep it in mind. Any woman living with my command must be three things: married, sober, and respectable. Otherwise she'll be whipped and drummed out of camp."

"This is a nice young lady, General," Hawk said softly. "We'll have no trouble."

"That's just what I said," Wayne answered him. "We'll have no trouble." He grinned bleakly at us and rode off.

"Who was he," cried an angry voice at my elbow, "talking about whipping and drumming?"

"That, my dear," said Hawk to Glennis Bill, "was Brigadier General Anthony Wayne. His word is law around here."

"He's got a nasty tongue," she said.

"Look, girl," I said. "This is an army. Everybody has to toe the line. He meant what he said. You stick to Billy and you start wearing female clothes in this camp!"

"La, Lieutenant! Suppose I haven't got any of what you call female clothes?"

"Then get you some, and get 'em quick."

She smiled at Hawk. "Is that an order the Lieutenant is giving me, Captain?"

He shrugged. "He certainly doesn't get it from his mother, and I don't think he gets it from me. Maybe somewhere in the line one of our ladies knew Oliver Cromwell. But you'd better make a try, missy. We'll see what we can do for you in the way of quarters and clothes, as soon as we eat."

"By rights, Hawk," I said stiffly, "we ought to pack her off home. Billy could take her and be back inside a week. She could stay with Mother and Peggy and the youngsters. She'd be a help to Peggy, taking care of little Nancy."

She stamped her foot like a child, poking her pert face forward and upward until I had to lean back to escape her. "A help to Peggy, is it! Let me tell you, Matthias Hill, that if I left here, I'd go to Billy's folks and not to yours. Not that I'm leaving here. And especially I wouldn't go to your Peggy, no matter how much you think she needs a servant."

"Billy hasn't got any folks," I answered. "Didn't you know that?"

"Well, he's got folks now! I'm his folks, and I'm staying right here with him, no matter what your General Wayne or you or anybody else says."

"Calm down, missy," Hawk told her, laughing. "We'll fix you up fine for as long as you want to stay. Later on, if you wish, we'll send you home with Billy. We'll see how it works out."

I turned away, having had more than enough of her sharp tongue. Joe Williams and Harm Tallman were standing not far away, laughing as if we had put on a comic show for their entertainment.

"Sour grapes, Matt," Williams said, "not that I blame you. But tell me, how come you let that fuzzy-faced boy beat you out?"

"You go to hell," I said sourly. I stalked away into the night, to visit Albion Walden, to whom I could talk pleasantly without being ridiculed for not recognizing that a snip of a girl with no maidenly qualities whatsoever was actually a fine lady who deserved courtesy and consideration. Further, I wanted to plan with Doc Walden some way to convince my father that he ought to go home. If we succeeded, perhaps we could send the high-and-mighty Mistress Bill with him. As long as she was with us, we'd have trouble with her. I had no doubt of that.

Doc Walden treated me to supper: bits of fat raccoon meat floating in thin gruel spotted with an onion or so and a trace of carrot. Then he invited me to his hospital to test the medical brandy to see if it had turned sour or bitter or sweet or some other undesirable condition. This, he said, was one of the requirements of his position. He was always willing to have some help in making his decision on the quality of the brandy.

Actually, of course, he poked and puttered among the nine or ten sick men who lay groaning in the bunks of the hut, seeming ineffectual in whatever he was doing, but by some magic touch easing their mental or physical tortures.

We had our tots of brandy, but before we could get well into any conversation, sick men began drifting in to see him. Soon there was a line of five, six, or seven at a time. There were the usual complaints: toothache, or aches of stomach, head, and throat; several men who sought some specific against the flux, which had them weak as kittens, and one man who said his heart kept fluttering at a great rate and he wanted to go home to Connecticut, where it had never fluttered. Doc said he'd look into the matter of medical furlough and sent the man back to duty.

"The universal disease," he said to me. "Homesickness."

There was another complaint that threatened to become universal. It wasn't new, but it was swiftly spreading through the entire army. Many of the men who came to see Doc had it: the itch. It attacked them first on exposed skin, then slowly progressed over the entire body. They were in constant torment, and their scratching only made the ailment worse.

One after another, they received salve in small pannikins from Walden, with the instructions that they were to use it morning, noon, and night for three days, then report back to be examined for improvement. The salve was yellowish tan and had a bad smell.

"What good is salve, Doc?" I asked when the last of them had vanished into the darkness. "The itch is in the blood. Folks back home say you get it for seven years."

He grunted. "The folks back home would make as good doctors as some of the ones I've seen in this camp, who say the same thing. The itch is in the blood. It is like hell! You know what causes that? Next one that comes in, I'll take a quizzing glass and show you. It's a tiny insect burrowing. Makes a tunnel, lays its eggs, gives you a nice itchy festering spot. Doctors have known it for three hundred years—everybody ought to know it. But the folks back home and some doctors in this camp say it's in the blood and lasts for seven years. But it's a bug so small you can't see it with the eye unless you pick it out and examine it under a quizzing glass."

"And what's the ointment good for?"

"It ain't no damn good for the itch, I'll tell you that," he said owlishly. "It kills the burrowing insect, though, and the eggs, and then you don't get any more itch. The rest of the doctors around here, they treat the itch, but not the cause. I feel like going home to New Haven, where folks don't pass the itch on to each other. The

187

whole town might stink of sulphur ointment, but they don't have the itch very long." He shook his head. "I been a doctor so long I'm beginning to lose my faith in doctors."

"Why don't you tell the others you use sulphur ointment?"

"That's the surest way to get 'em to prescribe something else. Now if I had some way to disguise the smell of that stuff, and had them men going around to show the other doctors that I never used sulphur ointment, they'd all take it up. As it is, I bet the itch goes through this army like a brush fire. If you get it, come over, and I'll give you some sulphur ointment."

He looked at me soberly, pausing for a long moment. "'Course, I can't be sure about all the doctors. I met one the other day was sure that the itch comes from flea poison injected into the blood. He's bleeding men with the itch, on the theory that the flea poison will come out first, since it was the last thing that went in. Now that makes sense, don't it?"

"Not a hell of a lot," I said, "because it was the first thing that went through my mind. A doctor ought to be able to do better than that."

He shook his head. "You ought to set up as a doctor. There you had a first thought, and it agreed with the first thought of a real doctor. You'd make a good doctor then. Every bit as good as that feller that's bleeding for the itch."

"No, thanks. I'll come to you. And that's what I'm doing tonight. I'd like to talk about my father."

"What about Hawk?"

"It's pretty clear that he's not getting any better, Doc. Isn't there some way we can get him to go home? Can you think of anything? Maybe get Wayne or somebody to certify him as unfit for field duty?"

"Pretty hard to do. He still looks as healthy as any of these heaps of skin and bones. He hasn't complained, has he?"

"Hawk? Complain? He never will, Doc." I looked down unhappily. "I have seen him shudder a couple of times, as if pain hit him hard. I've heard him moan at night. You have plenty of opium, Doc?"

"I have enough."

"Give me some, then. I'll get him to take it when the pain comes on him. That will be some help. My mother had some for him, but I don't know if he brought it."

Doc Walden shook his head, the spectacles wobbling on the bridge of his thin nose. "Nothing doing, Matt. Not now."

"Why not, Doc? If it would help him—— You said you had enough."

"First place, it would make him sick to his stomach, time to time."

"I thought it put you to sleep."

"It does, you take enough. A man has a little pain, Matt, and he takes a little opium. Pain goes away. Man has a bigger pain, takes a bit more opium. Pain goes away. The pain gets bigger, the man takes more and more. He needs it. The more he uses, the more he needs. We'll wait, Matt."

"Wait until when, for God's sakes?"

He spoke softly. "Until he wakes up screaming, maybe. You'll know when. I'll know. Hawk will know, and he'll tell us."

CHAPTER THIRTEEN

Billy and his wife had a hut to themselves for a day or so, while he and his messmates built them one to use exclusively. It would have been possible to get her quarters at one of the farmhouses in the area, but she balked at that. She would stay with her husband, she said—an attitude that seemed to me typical of her contrariness.

She was underfoot most of the time, in my view, but no one shared my opinion. You'd think they'd never seen a woman before, the way they bowed and scraped before her, attended her slightest whim, and submitted to her attacks on their housekeeping. I admitted to Hawk that within three days we had what was probably the neatest and cleanest set of huts in the encampment, but at the cost of our free-and-easy irregular way of life. At any time of day one could hear her shrilling orders to the men to air their huts, to bury refuse (how she expected that with a foot of frost in the ground, I could not comprehend) and eternally she was telling them to wash themselves and their clothing. All good procedure, mind you, such as I would have been foolish to have objected to; it was the air of command that she assumed that annoyed me.

Doc Walden viewed her efforts benignly. "Every unit in camp ought to have a Mistress Bill," he told me. "Got more sick men that are sick because they were dirty beforehand than for any other reason."

"This is no place for a woman," I said aggrievedly.

"Ain't no place for a man, either," said he.

Then, for a time, I had no reason to find her too much in the offing. Early in January I was relieved of all regular duties by General

Wayne's order, together with Major Joe Williams, to sit on the general court that was formed by orders from headquarters.

This was my first experience with courts-martial. Since I was, by a considerable number of lieutenant colonels, majors, and captains, very much the junior member of the court, I found that I would have had little to say had I had the inclination to say anything.

Our military justice was, to my mind, exceptionally severe, yet in service on that court and on later ones, I came slowly to realize that the very nature of an army requires hard control of offenders, particularly in wartime.

Joe Williams was bound by no sense of low standing in rank during his service on that court; he held the independent frontiersman's concept of courts and lawyers in general—he was contemptuous of them, cantankerous with them, and inclined ever to disagree vociferously with the majority.

Joe's comments, asides, fulminations, and orations—punctuated with ribaldry and backwoods philosophy—made the dry proceedings of that court so lively that it was sometimes a question whether we were hearing a case or hearing Joe Williams discourse on the war and the army and the military life.

Although none of the cases that came before us have any bearing on this narrative or the fortunes of the Deerkill company, summaries of some of them may well serve to illustrate the soldier's life and problems during that winter:

Ensign Wilkins, —th Virginia Regiment of the Line; charges: sodomy and perjury; finding: guilty; sentence: cashiered, drummed from camp before his division, never to serve these United States henceforth. Joe Williams' comment: "So that's the right name for it, sodomy. I got to vote not guilty because the feller ought never to have been let into the army in the first place. I got to vote guilty on the perjury, though. He oughtn't to of lied about it, but took his whipping like a man. Maybe he ain't really a man, though. They say that's the trouble with them fellers."

Anne Johnstone, follower, —th Maryland Regiment of the Line; charges: prostitution and inciting to desertion to the enemy; finding: guilty; sentence: 100 lashes on the bare back before the division assembled. Joe Williams' comment: "I got to vote not guilty on the whoring. A woman's got to get paid to be rated as a whore, and them Marylanders ain't got no more money than I got. On inciting to deserting, I ought to vote not guilty, too. One look at her face would incite anybody to desert; it ain't her fault."

Daniel Williamson, civilian teamster, Chester County, Penna.; charges: seeking to aid and abet the enemy by selling provender to said enemy; finding: guilty; sentence: 250 lashes on the bare back. Joe Williams' comment: "Who got to eat the sheep? This here court ought to get a chop or two. I bet the attorney for the accused has got a good bellyful of mutton."

Wilkins Freeman, quartermaster, ___th Rhode Island Infantry of the Line; charges: stealing rations from the men of his regiment; finding: guilty; sentence: 100 lashes on the bare back, to be then mounted backwards on a horse, his coat turned inside out, drummed from camp before his division, never to serve the United States henceforth. Joe Williams' comment: "Hang the son of a bitch."

Robert Gest, drummer boy, Lamb's Artillery of the New York Line; charges: attempting to desert to the enemy; finding: guilty; sentence: because of his youth, 50 lashes on the bare back. Joe Williams' comment: "Let the poor shaver off. Go back inside there and take a look at him. He'd ought to be home with his mother. How can you say a boy like that should get the whip? He don't need a cat laid to his skin; he needs somebody to comfort him and feed him and put clothes on his skinny back. You put him to the whip, and I'll go to the General, by God, to beg him off."

He went to the General. Robert Gest's sentence was suspended.

Through the best part of January, we sat daily on the court, held in the front room of one of the stone farmhouses in the hamlet. My memories are mixed on that duty: perhaps half the cases that came before us were those of scoundrels, rascals, and thieves of all descriptions; and the other half were conditioned by the times, by the exigencies of war and the hardships of our bleak existence. I tried to be fair and impartial in my judgments (little as they counted among the ranking officers who flanked me) but I remember that my heart turned to stone in those cases where a man stood before us on clear evidence that he had committed crimes against his fellow soldiers. I remember my voice ringing "Guilty!" when the verdict was asked against the Rhode Island quartermaster. Here was a man who stole from his sick and starving comrades, and then sniveled before us that they deserved it because they called him names for doing it.

As can be imagined, I saw little of the Deerkill company; Joe and I usually returned after dark, having taken our suppers with the members of the court. Their food was little better than that of the soldiery, though graced with wine and followed by brandy. Taking our rations from headquarters, however, allowed the men of the company to have two extra rations per day—little enough, but sorely needed.

It was in January that I expected mutiny. Hawk scoffed at me, saying the vast majority of the men were steadfast, that the weaklings had already deserted or were so few that their voices could have little effect on the good soldiers. He was right, as far as that went, since there was no mutiny. But desertions increased by leaps and bounds. I believe that one third of the troops posted on returns for December and January became temporary or permanent deserters in the course of that winter.

What else could have been expected? There were days when the only rations were black potatoes. In early January, we went six days in a row without a bread ration for the Pennsylvania division under Wayne; in that period we had shriveled carrots, frozen potatoes, and three pounds of sour salt beef per man: the kind of food that our good country housewives throw into the garbage heap during their midwinter inventories of the root cellars and the pantries.

The sick had long since crowded the limited hospital facilities; they were jammed into the meetinghouses of the Quakers and the Baptists in the community, and a full thousand overflowed to the Moravian meetinghouse and adjacent buildings at Bethlehem. In all these sanctuaries they died by the scores. They were buried in un-marked graves for the most part; some were laid head to feet in shallow trenches.

The itch, that most cursed of plagues, swept the army with its fiendish discomfort. Take a man who is suffering from a heavy chest cold, give him frostbitten extremities, allow his flea bites to fester, reduce his food to the point where scurvy sores are blossoming, and then give him the itch! He may not die, but he will wish that he could.

In the midst of this universal misery, our bridegroom and his bride seemed the most contented of humans. It fairly sickened me at times to hear Billy say fatuously, "Glennis says——" and "My wife thinks——" on every possible subject, even including the mounting of the guard.

Still believing that the middle of a vast military encampment was the least suitable place for any woman to be, let alone a slip of a girl, I asked Hawk what measures he would take to see that she went home to the Deerkill Valley, where at least she would be of some use to somebody and least likely to suffer from her foolishness in having married Billy.

"Good Lord, Matt," he answered, "that girl is heaven-sent to this company. I wouldn't send her off for all the beef in Billy Howe's mess kitchens. She makes the men toe the mark in keeping themselves and their huts clean, as I never could if I stood over them with a whip. And could we have had a finer nurse for Pete House and Tom Babcock and William Knapp, before Doc sent 'em off to Bethlehem?"

"I've had no chance to see much of her," I said. "Is she behaving herself? Has she been dressing herself properly in female clothes?"

Hawk gave me an odd look. "I'd thought I'd raised you to have some sense, Matt. But there must have been a lot of things I took for granted."

I felt the need to explain. "Hold on, Hawk. I'm only thinking of what could happen. Every day at the court we have cases having to do with the women in this encampment. They seem to cause half the trouble."

"And the other half is caused by damn fools," he said shortly. "That girl is no camp follower, Matt. Good Lord, she's the best possible thing that could have happened to young Billy. She'll make a good man of him."

I shrugged. It seemed to me that Hawk and my mother and the other people at home who had raised Billy Bill had started him on the way to being a good man. I didn't see how a youthful and foolish marriage would help him.

The men had built Billy and his wife a tiny hut within a grove of hemlocks that had been left standing at the rear of our camp area. There were times when we could hear them laughing together, or if Billy were posted to the guard we could listen to her singing as she did whatever household chores the small cabin gave her. I had to admit that the sound of happiness added a touch of pleasure to our gray days.

Following one of the worst weeks of the winter, during which the snow whistled out of the northeast on all days save one and the nights were crackling cold, a bounty came to the Deerkill company that we gratefully accepted, wishing only that the other troops from distant parts of the country could have shared it: my brother Johnny, accompanied by Will van Houten, arrived at Valley Forge, the two of them leading pack horses laden with food and clothing.

It is true that the food borne on the backs of two horses did not go far when apportioned to four dozen victims of slow starvation, but it brought heart to men close to despair. Indeed, having even so small a part of home brought to them at that time, I am sure, kept a few of them from making tracks some moonless night. The clothing that the boys brought was sorely needed by this time. Hawk parceled it according to need, many of our men being already without shirts and stockings and wearing their footgear in the last stages of dissolution.

Perhaps more important to most of us were the letters the boys brought. My mother must have labored many an hour in preparing them—fully half the letters were penned in her careful hand, since the large part of our valley people could do little with quill and ink.

As has ever been the case with troops in the field, the distribution of mail from home sent the soldiers wandering off to such privacy as they could find for the reading of it. I, for one, was immediately disappointed. There was only one letter for me, from my mother; there was no letter from Peggy. I found a quiet place, a stump beside the officers' hut, where I could read what my mother had written:

My dear Son:
I trust that you are in good Health and Spirit, and that the Lord will keep you so. May the same be true for your Father, although I look forward with Misgiving to the Tidings that you will send to me with your Brother, John.

See to it that your Father, so careful of the Well-Being of others, takes for himself the fine wool Stockings topped by red Knitting. Tell him that they were made for him by your Sister. It is true, although she made such slow Time with the Needles that I had to take hold with the Finishing of them.

Take Loving Care of him, Matthias, and I pray you, Delay Not when he needs me.

Mistress Remsen is not with us. She prepared for her Journey some time since, and now News from her has come to the Remsens from Philadelphia. She bids them sell her Land and other Property and bids them take its small Value for themselves. Her Father is Commissioned as Commissary in a Loyalist Regiment, I think the Queen's Rangers. She tells the Remsens she will not Return to our Valley ever, and she wishes to Forget now and always any Ties she made there. She said that the Remsens were to tell that to Mistress Hill, who was to know that any Understanding she might have had with any Person should not be looked upon as Binding. It grieves me to pass this Information to you, Matthias, as it is evident that she considers there are no Ties between you. It is because you saw your Duty differently, I am sure.

The News that comes to us about the Army through traders and Travelers is Heart-Rending to be sure, yet I discount much of what we hear. You cannot be in such Sore Straits as is said. It must be Tory Gossip, fitted to cause us to lose Hope in our Cause.

Write to me, sending the Letter with your Brother, telling me all that passes with your Father. Keep yourself well and stand not in Draughts for Fear of Cold and Fever.

Your devoted, affectionate Mother,
ANNE LeFEVRE HILL

In spite of the crushing news of Peggy and what she was supposed to have written to the Remsens, I could not keep from smiling for an instant at the ending of my mother's letter. Draughts, indeed! This vast hillside was one continual draught, doubling and redoubling every time the wind shifted. And I could wish nothing more dearly than to keep myself from it!

Little more than twenty miles across the landscape, Peggy was supposed to have put quill to paper and scratched me from her life. I didn't believe it. It was impossible that two people who had meant so much to each other so little time ago could now be parted by the misinterpretation of a letter.

Peggy in Philadelphia.

I climbed the ridge quickly, thirty or forty yards to its crest, where I could look east by southeast to the point where the horizon mixed gray sky and white landscape. Beyond that point was the city. She knew I was here. I wondered if she had not perhaps asked someone to show her in which direction lay the Valley Forge, if she had not climbed some hill in the city, if hills there were, and looked into the distance as I was doing. Surely she had. And whatever the Remsens had told my mother was tosh and balderdash! Peggy would wait for me until the war was ended, and then I would go to Philadelphia to find her.

A quiet voice interrupted me. "Your mother must be a wondrous kind woman, Lieutenant."

I turned to face Glennis Bill. She smiled at me so pleasantly, not at all in her usual fashion, that I could not tell her that I wished to be alone to stare toward a Philadelphia that I could not have seen on the clearest summer's day.

"She is, indeed," I answered. "Why did you say that?"

"Your brother brought letters to all the men of the company. It's said that she wrote many of them for their wives and mothers who couldn't write themselves."

I nodded. "That's been her practice since we first went to the army at Boston."

"She wrote one to Billy," she said softly. "He's the only one without family at home, and she remembered, with all she had to do, to write him a long letter. I left him alone to read it over again. It was a kind letter, Lieutenant."

"She's always been fond of Billy."

"When you write to her, will you thank her for me for writing to Billy?"

"You can thank her yourself. I think you should. Go home with my brother Johnny. My mother would welcome you."

Her expression changed, as the saying goes, quick as a cat can wink its eye. "Mercy, Lieutenant, that would be fine! Then I could be maid to your lady Peggy."

I shook my head. "My lady, as you call her, isn't there at all. Matter of fact, she's yonder." I pointed toward the city. "She went to Philadelphia to join her family."

She looked at me solemnly, but I could swear that she was about to laugh. "Such a pity, Lieutenant. All that separates you from her is Billy Howe's army."

"That won't be for long," I said.

"Are you going in after her, or is she coming out to you?"

"Your husband would do well to put a curb on your tongue."

She laughed outrageously, so that I might have boxed her ears had I been able to reach her, but she ran off, leaving me to take such comfort as I might in standing there like a fool staring at what I could not see.

Whatever it was that Peggy had written to the Remsens, it was not that there was no understanding between us. Rather, there was the greatest of bonds.

Only Billy Howe's army stood between us. Only Billy Howe's army . . .

CHAPTER FOURTEEN

    In spite of the varied miseries that we had in
quantity to liven our days, life at the Valley Forge was as humdrum as
could be imagined in any winter quarters. There were only so many
ways to spend one's days: fretting about the itch, attacking lice and
fleas, cutting firewood for weeks ahead in the hope that when it
came to burn it would be cured enough so that we would not suffo-
cate with the smoke, bargaining with the sutlers for any kind of
nourishment or sweet, trading in the various public markets set up
in the encampment where the local people charged high prices for
poor goods.

 Desertions continued to mount; the sick were carried off to hospital
in ever-increasing numbers—many of them never to return; courts-
martial kept busy with almost every crime that violated the Articles
of War.

 William Knapp, a walking skeleton, came back from Bethlehem
cured of the camp fever, or at least recovered from it. He brought
the sad news that Peter House and Thomas Babcock had died of it
within twelve hours of each other. He did not even know, he told
us, where they had been buried. They had been good steadfast men,
and our huts were gloomy in the days that followed. Harm's cousin
Woodhull put a musket ball into his foot while on picket duty; we
had Doc Walden attend him, which probably saved Woody's foot,
but Teunis Tallman took him home on a horse borrowed from the
Seventh Pennsylvania. It seemed likely, Doc said, that Woody would
hobble for the rest of his life.

 Several times we stood to arms briefly, for one or another of the
wild rumors that flashed through the encampment—the entire British

Army had left Philadelphia—they were at the Gulph Mills—their front ranks were already forming for the charge on our redoubts. Some of us suspected that the General himself engineered a rumor or two, just to snap us into an alert.

Anthony Wayne was not content to let his division stagnate. Scouting and foraging parties were always on the go from the Pennsylvania brigades. We understood by camp rumor that Wayne himself was a nuisance to the high-and-mighty headquarters staff, with his demands for everything in the military lexicon, action and supplies in particular.

During one of the alerts, Wayne would be astride his horse, eagerness to fight somebody showing in every strained muscle as he dashed about the redoubts and entrenchments. When I remember the tribe of washerwomen in the guise of major generals that strutted in and out of headquarters all day long, I remember too that Wayne, commanding a full division and spoiling for a fight always, was but a brigadier. It seemed to be policy with Congress to promote nincompoops and ignore fighting leaders.

It was no secret to us that Wayne wanted to harrass the British supply lines into Philadelphia, and that for many weeks his pleas for action were ignored. He didn't fail entirely, however, and one of his efforts brought Hawk and me and Major Joe Williams to his headquarters. We cooled our heels for a while until Wayne finished writing letters to practically every Pennsylvanian of note; apparently oblivious to our presence, he raged and ranted between sentences, saying that if these begging letters failed to produce food and clothing, he would ride through York and Lancaster with his sword flashing. He could cut down every damned pettifogging pipsqueak who had the least to do with holding warehouses jammed with uniforms simply because they lacked buttons of the proper color.

"I would, by God, strangle him with my bare hands," he cried at one point, "if I had him in front of me. 'The soldiery must be selling shirts for rum,'" he quoted thickly from a letter that he slammed to his desk. "Good God, let him come here to see them standing naked in the wind! Hell no! Travel on the winter roads from Lancaster to here? Impossible, sir! The Commonwealth's business demands my presence in Lancaster. Surely you can understand that,

General Wayne? Well, I'll be damned if I can understand it! How can one single man be so stupid, mean, ignorant, niggardly, and downright rotten, all at one time?"

He stopped shouting suddenly, the dark fury left his features, and he looked pleasantly at us. "Major Williams," he said, "how is the engineering?"

"Dammed if I know, General," Williams said affably. "I set up a redoubt, and the boys get her dug, and then that frog general comes along and starts a-chattering away in French or whatever it is he talks, and the boys have to dig her up and do her over again. But we're getting along, General. How you doing?"

Wayne laughed. "General Duportail's English leaves something to be desired. How do you know what he's saying?"

Williams flicked his thumb toward me. "Matt speaks frog pretty good. At least he says he does. It sounds all right to me."

Wayne's eyes flashed to me. "You speak French, Lieutenant? How'd you learn that in the backwoods?"

"My mother, sir. Her parents were French Huguenots who lived in a place called New Paltz, in Ulster County. She taught me and my brother and sister."

Wayne nodded. "The way all the Penn Dutch young ones spout German around the house. You speak it also, Captain?"

Hawk shook his head. "A few words, General. I courted her in English and married her in English, and it worked out fine. As the boys say when they play cards, I quit when I was ahead."

"I'm not really proficient, sir," I interposed. "General Duportail and his aide are inclined to hide smiles when they listen to me."

"Hah!" Wayne snorted. "Hide smiles, do they? Listen to me, Lieutenant. You speak English perfectly, and French well enough to be understood. How many languages do they speak? Only one, right? Or they wouldn't need you to interpret for them. And they smile at you. Smile right back, Lieutenant Hill. Laugh out loud if you want."

"My accent's pretty bad, sir. My mother says I speak French like a Maine man with a cold in his head trying to sound as if he came from Virginia."

"I'll remember you can speak French," Wayne said. "If Congress hands out any more major generals' commissions to Frenchmen, I may end up with one as my aide." He looked at each of us in turn. "Got something for you to do. Real nice job. Keep you busy for a few days."

"Fine," Williams said. "Long as it ain't building more redoubts. I been diggin 'em in my sleep lately."

"I'm going to send you into the Jerseys," the general said. "I'm going myself as soon as His Excellency gives me permission. For cattle and whatever else we can nab. A big raid on these penny-pinchers that supply the British in Philadelphia. Williams, you'll be in charge of foraging on this little raid of yours. Take two squads of men from the Seventh and bring back enough food for two regiments for a week. That's to make headquarters think your trip is worthwhile. Captain Hill, I want you to go mostly for scouting. I want to know as much as I can about all the countryside lying here and here and here." His big thumb jabbed at a map of the Jerseys that lay on his desk. "Below Trenton and in that semicircle on the far side of Philadelphia. New Salem and Mount Holly and this country here. You know the kind of information I want: the big herds of cattle and sheep, the richest Tories—by God, I think there are more Tories in that area under my thumb than there are in all of Pennsylvania. I want to know the roads and their condition. I want to know where wagons won't go, and where guns might bog down in case of a thaw in the next few weeks, and I want to know for sure how often the British come into that country and in what force, and what the inhabitants think of them. Get me all that, and check this map. If there are any mistakes on it, I want to know now, before I take troops in there. Come back with any other information that we can use to sweep in there and clean 'em out of everything they have that we can eat."

"My, my," Williams said. "When this army gets done with the country around here, the folks will wish they'd been visited by a plague of locusts instead."

"You understand what I want, Captain?" Wayne asked.

"Yes, sir," Hawk said. "My boys have done this kind of job before. But it's a long hike, sir. They might cut us off. Wouldn't it be better to send horse?"

"Hell, no! First place, you know damned well I haven't any horse. I'd have to borrow Harry Lee. And this is a Pennsylvania operation. Let Virginia take care of her own."

"Pennsylvania operation," Williams repeated. "That's why he's sending York Staters."

"Williams, some day I'm going to make a file closer out of you," Wayne said. "Hill, I don't want you to engage the enemy, no matter how few or how many. Try to keep your command looking like an ordinary foraging expedition. Be sure that whoever you talk to in gathering information is the right kind of person. I know for a fact that the British plan to move into that country to clean it out before the winter's over. I want to beat 'em to it, and I don't want anybody to know I'm coming."

"We'll do what you want done, sir," Hawk said.

"I'll write the orders," Wayne said. "Thank you, gentlemen."

"From an engineer to a cattle drover in five minutes," Williams said. "You keep the boys at them redoubts while I'm gone, General. I may come back with the whole British Army at my heels, and I want some protection when I get here."

We sat with our backs to a stone wall, lounging comfortably although the air was chill. We did not risk a fire, for there was always the chance of a British patrol, even at a country crossroads where both roads seemed to lead from nowhere to nowhere.

We were high on a birch-topped knoll, once cultivated but allowed for some reason over the past ten years to go to thin birch saplings that stood black and white against the gray sky—come to think of it, we saw little but gray sky through all that winter. The background made good cover for us; it would take a pair of keen eyes, watching for danger, to distinguish us atop the knoll. We had a good view of the crossroads and the wagon tracks in three of the four directions.

There were five of us: Williams, King, Gilbert Hutchings, Teunis Ekerson, and myself. Hawk, with our company and the two squads of Pennsylvanians, was deep in a marsh about a mile to our rear. All tracks and marks of carts where they had pushed their way into the recesses of the marsh were well hidden. Such caution was wise, but perhaps unnecessary, because our British cousins and their Hessian allies were well-nigh incapable of following a trail from quarters to regimental sinks and back again. Loyalist troops, Americans like ourselves, were another question. They could snuff out our hideaway.

There were enemy troops in the vicinity, we had been told by such patriots as dared talk to us. We'd had word that they were hunting us. Let them, was our view. As I say, the only danger lay in the chance of their being Loyalists. They were good soldiers and some few of them woodsmen, those Americans who served the King.

Hawk had set us and several other patrols at likely spots around the marsh, while within its fastness the men rested the draught horses and repaired the carts for the dash to the Delaware and cross-country to Valley Forge. They would slaughter and dress the cattle and sheep as well. We were too small a raiding party to chance a forced march limited by the speed of a drove of animals.

It was midmorning. The work in the marsh would take most of the day. We'd break out and run for the Delaware at dawn. Meantime, those of us with the patrol relished lazily the task set to us.

Williams talked interminably in that drawling buzz of his, so that we might have dozed off if he hadn't poked one or another of us from time to time to emphasize a point.

". . . why, I wouldn't even eat a trout that's over a foot long," Williams argued. "Take a trout that big, what's he been eating? Fish, that's what. He just lies under a rock and waits for one of his little brothers and gobbles him up. Two, three fingerlings a day and he's had his fill. So what's he taste like? Fish, that's what, same as I'd taste like salt pork if somebody was to bite into me. There ain't nothing less tasty than a fish that tastes like a fish. Now you take a trout, say nine or ten inches, and what's he been eating? Bugs, that's what. You may not be partial to bugs, mind you, but inside a fish they add flavor. A good diet of bugs makes anything taste good. You like woodcock, Matt?"

I nodded lazily. "About as well as anything."

"And what's he eat? Worms and bugs, don't he? There you are. *Hup!*" The exclamation was sharp and sudden. Williams grabbed my arm.

We all looked toward the crossroads. Coming into sight were two men seated on a cart drawn by a heavy white horse. Country people, for sure, I thought.

As the cart came closer, we heard a curious sound that none of us seemed to place immediately. Rather it was a chorus of sounds, rising and falling. All I could think of was school children playing at recess, their voices shrilling.

Teunis Ekerson looked at me dolefully. "*A bird of the air*," he whispered, "*shall carry the voice, and that which hath wings shall tell the matter.*" Then his Adam's apple rose and fell, the sound that was puzzling us came clearly from his mouth. "Turkeys," he said solemnly.

Indeed, they were. A dozen crates of them, two to a crate.

We were on the two men before they knew we were there. They didn't take kindly to coming down from their cart. One cursed us fluently and vividly until Ekerson jabbed the barrel of his musket into the man's ribs. "*Ye are fallen from grace*," Teunis said as the fellow gasped for breath.

The other man called us thieves and brigands and told us he would turn us in to the high sheriff.

"Where were you taking the turkeys?" I asked.

The second man shrugged. "Where else? Philadelphia. They're on order. They pay good hard money for 'em."

"Who ordered them?"

"Mr. Holden," he said sourly. "Commissary for the Queen's Rangers. You fellers take 'em, you got to pay hard money for 'em."

I was startled by the name. That was Peggy's father. These were his turkeys—indeed, Peggy would have been dining on one tomorrow night, likely, had we not intercepted them.

"How do you get into Philadelphia?" I asked.

"We got passes from the provost."

"Let's see 'em," I said, holding forth my hand.

Each of them put a grimy slip of paper in my palm. The passes stated that William Smithson and Harold Smithson were duly authorized to pass the guards with produce for sale to his Britannic Majesty's forces in North America.

I think the scheme was in my mind as soon as they said they had passes. I motioned Williams to step aside. "Joe, let's go into the city with these turkeys."

"You gone mad? They'd hang us for spies."

"Hell, they won't catch us. We'll be out again sometime tonight and back here before Hawk is ready to leave."

He shook his head. "I ain't much of a soldier, but I do what my commanding officer wants, Matt. Wayne would have a fit if we tried it."

"I'm going, Joe. Just think of it. We'll see the troops, what condition they're in, any signs of activity against us—Wayne would say go, if he knew about it. Come on."

"If Hawk says you can go, I'll go with you. Otherwise, nothing doing."

"I wouldn't ask Hawk," I argued. "First place, there isn't enough time to go back in the marsh and ask him. Second, he'd say it was too risky."

"That's what I say, Matt."

I turned impatiently from him. "Who wants to go into the city with me, with these passes?"

The men were silent.

"All right, I'll go alone. Tie those two up and keep 'em safe until tomorrow morning. First, give me a coat and a hat and a pair of those farmers' boots."

"You're a blamed fool, Matt," Teunis Ekerson said. "I'll go with you, to bring you back safe."

I grinned at him, strong words from Teunis, to call a fellow human a fool.

We were rattling down the road in another minute or two, a dozen turkeys in the crates behind us, the other dozen, with their necks stretched, laid in a line on the stone wall. Beside me on the wagon seat, Ekerson quoted Scripture in a mumbling voice, mostly passages having the word "fool" somewhere in their context.

I felt like singing. We had been in the Jerseys for four days—twenty, thirty, thirty-five miles from Philadelphia, but seeming much closer than at Valley Forge because this was country that the British normally controlled. All the while I thought of Peggy, so near. As Glennis Bill had said, only Billy Howe's army between us——

And now I would go through that army without the least bit of trouble. I was sure of it. Not only that, but I could go right to Peggy's father, once in the city. Where he was, she was sure to be. I thought that I would see her within hours, if the old white nag would keep his ground-covering pace.

It seemed the most likely thing in the world that I would easily find her. Why not? Philadelphia, although I had never been inside the city proper, had not looked so great a place viewed from its environs. Find the Queen's Rangers, ask for their commissary, deliver the turkeys to his dwelling. There Peggy would be.

"*They brought Daniel*," quoth Teunis, "*and cast him into the den of lions.*"

"Cheer up, Teunis," I said happily. "You know spies from our camp go in and out of the city all the time, the same way we have British spies at the Valley Forge."

"*His hand will be against every man, and every man's hand against him.* Let's be careful, Matt."

Getting into Sir William Howe's stronghold was so simple a feat that briefly I feared we were somehow being tolled into a trap. A ferry operated by an artillery battalion took us across the Delaware through the floating islands of ice. The sergeant who operated the boat did not even look at our passes. He and his men were most affable, although we could scarce understand their Yorkshire tongue.

They set us down at a slip well north of the main part of the city. Immediately we were challenged by a provost's guard—three soldiers and a corporal. They glanced at our passes, admired the turkeys, and waved us onward.

I drove the white horse at a sedate pace, warning Teunis not to gawk at the sights, lest some Britisher smarter than most pick us out as strangers rather than farmers from the nearby Jerseys. I had the feeling that every eye was upon us, and that we would be nabbed as soon as we were far enough within the guard lines to make escape impossible. Were it not for the exciting prospect of seeing Peggy, I would have thought with Teunis that I was a fool.

We traveled a pleasant avenue lined with handsome houses. There were officers, both British and Hessian, riding or walking along the street, and with them were many well-dressed civilians. I wished to ask no directions of any officer, but this was obviously not a billet area, and the only soldiers we saw were engaged in driving rigs for their superiors. I wished I could keep the turkeys quiet; their gobbling brought curious glances upon us.

We kept going until we came to cross streets, where I guided the horse left toward the river, then right again toward the heart of the city. Now we were passing inns and taverns, and the streets were dotted with red coats as well as Hessian blues and greens. The pavements were scattered with refuse thrown by the soldiery; I thought the city remarkably filthy for one that I had always heard reputed as a neat place.

We turned so many corners that I had no idea how far we had come from the ferry. I told Teunis to keep his mind on the direction that would take us to the river in case we had to run for it.

I decided we had come far enough. I pulled in the horse and stepped down from the cart to the street. I started to ask sauntering soldiers where I could find the billets of the Queen's Rangers. After two or three minutes of this, I despaired of getting any proper answer. All I had for my pains were two vague stares, a flow of Scot's burr that I couldn't make head nor tail of, and a couple of curses along with the information that the cursing one didn't know where the so-and-so Americans were, and cared a hell of a lot less.

I finally had my answer from a hostler at a busy tavern, who told me to go three squares ahead, then one square left, and another right, and there I would be.

And there I was, indeed—right in front of a big warehouse-type building, in and out of which were passing dozens of men in the handsome green uniforms of Simcoe's Queen's Rangers. There were others lounging at the entrance to the building, all of them seeming to stare fixedly at me and Ekerson. I had told Teunis on the way into the city why I intended to carry out the delivery of the turkeys. He didn't favor the idea at all, not wishing to risk his neck so that I might see Peggy. I didn't blame him, but certainly we'd be doing our own cause a good turn by observing carefully everything we saw. Just being in the city was danger; seeing Peggy wouldn't add to it. Her father didn't know me from Adam.

"They don't look hospitable," I said softly to Teunis.

"Let's get out of here," he said dolorously. "*Whoso diggeth a pit shall fall therein.*"

I stepped down to the street and spoke to one of the soldiers. "Your servant, sir. Could you tell me where I might find Mr. Holden?"

He looked coldly at me, up and down. "Why should I? Them turkeys is for officers, ain't they?"

"Tell him, Joe," said another man. "We'll get soup from the bones, anyways."

The soldier jerked a thumb in the direction of a brick house at the end of the street. "He's to home. I seen him go there about ten minutes ago."

"I thank you," I said as politely as I could. I climbed back on the cart and urged the horse swiftly along.

My heart pounded as I mounted the red stone steps of the house. At the cart, Teunis was busying himself with the ropes that bound the turkey crates. His bemused air reassured me when I looked back. No one would take us for more than a couple of stumpjumpers come into the city to deliver provender.

Peggy is inside, I told myself. She'll see that we're left alone, and then I can take her in my arms.

I tugged at the bellpull and heard the bell jangle within the house. After a few moments, the door opened suddenly and a sharp-faced woman glared at me. "Deliveries at the rear," she said harshly, then slammed the door.

I went to the back of the house, where she waited for me. "Put the turkeys in the shed," she said, pointing to a woodshed set against the back wall of the garden. "Took you long enough. Mr. Holden said you was to be here this morning. It's a good day's work for us here in the kitchen to clean and pluck two dozen turkeys. I got other things to do, you know. Put 'em in the shed. They better be young birds."

"I'll have to see Mr. Holden," I said.

"I got your money," she snapped. "I'll give it to you. Mr. Holden ain't to be bothered. He's got company."

"I'd better see him. There's but one dozen birds."

"One dozen! Good Lord, he'll be fit to be tied! He promised one dozen to Colonel Simcoe. He'll have your head, fellow!"

"You had better call him," I said. "I'll explain."

Her eyes narrowed. "What is this? You aren't Smithson. Who are you, anyway?"

"I'm a neighbor. Smithson's sick. He couldn't come. Call Mr. Holden, will you?"

She vanished within the house, and I directed Teunis to start lugging the turkey crates to the woodshed.

I heard a heavy step, then a cold voice said: "Come in here, my man, and explain this outrage. Smithson pledged two dozen of his best birds. Colonel Simcoe is having a dinner tomorrow evening, and Sir William will attend. He ordered a dozen turkeys; I ordered a dozen. By thunder, I want 'em! Step in here."

I moved into a sparkling white kitchen where the sharp-faced woman stared vindictively at me. "He's so late I'll never get the dozen cleaned and plucked, let alone what we're ever going to do about the other dozen."

"We should know better than to depend upon bumpkins," Holden said sourly. I didn't like him at all, but he was Peggy's father. I smiled in friendly fashion.

He was a tall spare man, with straight black hair and a prominent nose, hooked above a strong jaw. I could, however, see Peggy's soft features in the lines of his face.

"You'll get the rest of the turkeys, Mr. Holden," I said cheerfully. "Smithson's cousin is bringing them in. He ought to be here in another hour. I'm a neighbor who offered to help."

"You don't get paid but for one dozen until I see the other twelve," he said coldly. "If I gave you the money, the other birds would never arrive."

"That's all right, Mr. Holden. I'm glad to do Smithson a favor, but he can handle his own money matters. I asked to see you for a different reason, sir. You see, I happen to know your daughter, Mistress Remsen."

"Damnation, fellow! You have your gall right with you, I see. I'll have Smithson on the carpet for this. How would my daughter get to know the likes of you?"

If this was Holden's usual manner with tradesmen and others he might consider inferior to him, then the less I saw of him after he became my father-in-law the better I would like it.

"Before I moved to the Jerseys," I said, "I lived in the Deerkill Valley in New York. Right next to Mistress Remsen, matter of fact. I knew her right well."

"She's well out of that nest of rebels, and so are you, my man."

"Yes, sir," I smiled. "You might say I was the only man in the whole valley who thought the British would win."

"Good for you! What did you say your name is? I'll tell my daughter you send your good wishes."

"I'd like to see her, sir, if you don't mind. She'd be glad to speak a few words with me."

"She has guests. I'll take a message. What is your name?"

My name wouldn't do. I wouldn't trust this fellow Holden farther than I could throw him, and of a certainty Peggy had told him that I was a lieutenant in the army at Valley Forge. Any other Deerkill name would serve, however.

"My name is Harm Tallman, Mr. Holden. You tell her that, and tell her that I saw a friend of hers, Matt Hill, not too long ago."

He glared at me for a moment, then seemed to decide that it might be best to go along with my irritating whim. Maybe he thought that by humoring me he'd insure the delivery of his other twelve turkeys.

"Come along, then," he barked.

He took me into a hall, then into a small room that seemed to be a study. Across the hall, I heard voices and laughter through a closed door.

"Wait here," Holden said. "I'll see if my daughter wants to see you." He swung the study door closed as he left.

He was gone for perhaps three or four minutes. I glanced through the window several times; Teunis Ekerson was carrying turkey crates as if that were the most important matter of his existence.

The door flew open and Peggy came into the room. I made a quick motion with my finger to my lips to enjoin her silence. Her eyes widened in alarm and she put her hand to her mouth, as if dismayed to see me. After all, she had expected to see Harm Tallman, if her father had given her the name.

"Hello, Peggy," I said. "It's a surprise, isn't it, to see an old friend with a message from Matt Hill?"

"Matt, are you mad?" she whispered. "To come here?"

I smiled. "Your old friend Harm Tallman, Peggy. You surprised?"

Her father entered the room behind her, shutting the door again. "Sit down, sir," he said pleasantly enough.

Peggy turned to her father, speaking quickly. "Father, I was wrong. This is a cousin of the man I mentioned——"

He smiled, but I thought I saw a note of warning pass from him to her. I began to get uneasy. Was he going to stay here? Why didn't she get rid of him?

"That's all right, my dear," he said. "You go right ahead and talk. Mr. Tallman says he has a message from somebody named Hill. What is it, my man? My daughter's guests are waiting."

Peggy stared at me without speaking, her eyes wide and troubled. Suddenly she started to cry. I moved quickly to her.

"Take your hands off my daughter, sir!"

I hadn't anticipated this turn of events. Then I was in further trouble. The door behind Holden opened softly. Little Nancy came into the room, saw me, and came running with a glad cry. "Kiss me, Matt!" she said happily.

Peggy pulled the little girl away from me. Holden started angrily toward me.

There was a hubbub outside. I heard shouts, then a musket banged just outside the window.

We were discovered. I took two steps toward the door, but I was too late. Heavy boots pounded in the hall, then bayonets bristled in the doorway. Four of the Queen's Rangers stood at the ready. A young captain passed among them, entering the room. His sword was drawn.

"Good work, sir," he said to Holden. "I feared this one would make tracks through the back of the house. The other one got away over the woodshed and the wall behind it. My men are after him. They'll bring him in."

The shock was so great that I could say nothing, although I remember lifting my hands to Peggy in a gesture almost of supplication. She was still weeping.

"Thank you, Captain Armstrong," said Holden, nodding. "You did well to act so quickly and decisively. I suppose you had better take this fellow away."

"Peggy," I said, almost whispering, "did you know he called them?"

"Of course she knew," her father said coldly. "Captain Armstrong was with us when you arrived. He left by the front door to get his men when I ushered you in here."

"Come along," said Armstrong gruffly.

"Matt!" Peggy cried. "Father said it was Harm Tallman. That's what you told him. I wouldn't have said anything if you'd given your right name."

"What did you say, exactly?"

"That Tallman is a rebel officer—that he is with the rebel army—that if he's here, he's a spy. I didn't know it was you, Matt!"

"You would have turned Harm in?" I asked incredulously. "When you knew they would hang him for a spy? Just as they will hang me?"

"Don't be a fool, man," Holden said to me. "You'll go to prison where you belong, but we are not barbarians. I explained all this to my daughter."

"Just the name should have been enough," I said to Peggy slowly. "Harm was a friend of yours. Yet you heard the name and said 'rebel officer' in the next breath."

"It's the best thing, Matt," Peggy said in a whisper. "My father will see that you are well treated, and when they let you out he will find a place for you here. They won't think you a traitor or a spy, Matt. Don't you see? You'll be all right. Colonel Simcoe will free you when he knows you just came to see me, won't he, Captain Armstrong?"

Armstrong smiled frostily. "I haven't the Colonel's ear, ma'am, but I do know that he always does the right thing."

I could not believe it, but I was slowly turning sick as I watched her. Armstrong plucked at my arm impatiently. I shook him off.

"Your father said, 'Harm Tallman' and you said, 'He's a rebel. Grab him!' You would do a thing like that."

213

"Oh, Matt, please! It's all been so difficult for me. You can't know how it's been."

"I suppose not. All I can know is that you'd turn a friend over to be hanged. Suppose it had been Tallman—you wouldn't have cared if they hanged him, would you?"

"Don't say that, Matt! We don't hang people. They'll treat you well. You'll see."

"You've turned me over to the enemy," I said bitterly.

"Enemy, indeed," Armstrong snapped. "You have it wrong, friend. Mistress Remsen simply did her duty, giving over a rebel and a traitor to justice."

He took my arm again.

"My father will look after you, Matt," Peggy said, weeping again. "Just be patient."

I laughed shortly, harshly, then left the room with Armstrong. I didn't even look back as we went through the doorway to the street. I felt nauseated. I hoped I wouldn't be sick before the crowd of curious who had gathered.

The gaol was a small brick building of one story, evidently used formerly as carriage house and stable, if one could judge by the lingering odor of horses. It was on a street backing the big building in which the Queen's Rangers were quartered. Beside it, separated by a wall and garden, was a roomy house in which the officers of the Rangers were probably quartered. At least I thought that was so, since from the single barred window at eye-level, I could see officers going in and out of the big house all day long.

For three days following my capture, I might have vanished from the face of the earth. No one paid me any mind but the guards who supplied food and water twice daily. I was entirely free to brood upon the end of my happiness and the approaching end of my life. She had betrayed me—thinking I was Harm Tallman, true, but I would not have thought her capable of betraying anyone. Now I spent my time cursing myself for being all kinds of fool, as Teunis had said, when I wasn't brooding on Peggy's faithlessness or my imminent neck-stretching. I had no doubt that they would hang me; I'd been in civilian clothes—not even wearing the hunting shirt and buckskin breeches that they would have recognized as a uniform of sorts.

It was cold in that small gaol. I spent many long hours of each day and night curled in the single blanket on the cot that was the only furniture. Lying there, I tried to reach into Peggy Remsen's mind. Surely she had loved me, back home. I could not have been mistaken about that. And I thought I knew her well, as well as one person can know another.

She had betrayed me. That fact drummed at me from morning until night. Even believing that the man in the study was Harm Tallman, she had turned him over for execution.

For perhaps thirty-six long hours that bitter fact made me care little what they did with me. I didn't want to hang any more than any man would, but for a time I accepted the belief that I would.

Then, gradually, a change came over me. I thought less of Peggy Remsen and more about what would happen to me. I gave it clear thought. There was a slight chance that instead of hanging me they would send me to the hulks in New York harbor. From what I'd heard of the foul conditions in those prison ships, I might be better off swinging on a gallows.

At least Teunis Ekerson seemed to have escaped my fate. I asked the guards each time they opened the big front door if my companion had been captured. They sometimes did not reply, but I took their silence as negative. One of them told me that Teunis had evidently got away clean, otherwise he'd be in gaol with me.

On the third day I spent the daylight hours in the faint light that filtered through the small windows set high in the wall, hunting for a way to get out of there. I found it impossible, after examining every brick, every line of mortar, every bar in each window. There wasn't any way out without tools. There were no odd pieces of metal or even wood that I could use for tools.

The guard changed that day, and another company of Simcoe's Rangers took over the duty. One of my guards was a husky boy of nineteen or twenty who seemed overly interested in me. He often looked through the barred window in the door, smiling in friendly fashion. He started to talk to me from time to time.

His name was Ben Parker, he said, and he came from White Plains in Westchester County. The third or fourth time he talked at length to me he volunteered in a whisper that he never wanted to be a Ranger. His folks were King's people, but he was not and never was. His uncles joined loyalist regiments, and his cousins did, so his father said he had to join. It wouldn't last long, his father said, and when the rebels were beaten, people would know that the Parker family had been loyal to the King.

The next time he spoke to me he said he would be a rebel if he ever had a good chance to desert.

I asked him how it happened that he was for Congress while his family stood for the King.

"I went a year to Yale College in New Haven. We had meetings most every day, to talk about the war and liberty and independence. A man couldn't hold with loyalist thinking once he learned the truth. Then my father pulled me out and sent me to Colonel Simcoe's regiment. Don't, for God's sake, tell any of the others, but I've hated every minute of it. Down with tyranny, that's what I say."

I smiled in the darkness, amused at his youthful fervor. For a moment I wondered if he would have been so ardent a patriot had he heard the soldiery chanting into the bitter wind: "NO BREAD! NO MEAT! NO SOLDIER!"

"When do you think they'll put me up for trial?" I asked. "Did you hear anything about it?"

"Yes, I did, Lieutenant. I heard Captain Armstrong say they'd deal with you tomorrow. He's been appointed prosecutor for the court. They'll try you tomorrow, and the next day——"

"You think they'll hang me, don't you?"

"They won't be easy on you," he answered quietly.

He was silent a moment. "How'd they ever catch you, sir? I heard it had something to do with Mr. Holden."

"You know his daughter?"

"The one that's going to marry Captain Armstrong? The widow with the little girl?"

"Marry Armstrong?" I said, finding it hard to believe. "Who told you that?"

"That's what the men said in barracks."

"Little more than a month," I said softly, bitterly.

"What was that you said, sir?"

"Nothing, Ben. Well, she's the reason I'm in here. I came to see her, and she turned me over to Armstrong. Now I'm in here, and I wish to hell there was some way to get out."

I said that musingly, but Parker heard it.

"I'd like to help you, but they'd hang me too." Suddenly he grinned, winked at me in seemingly high good humor, and said, "But I'm bringing you your supper tonight. I'm on duty alone until midnight."

Then he was gone from the window.

What he'd said made no sense to me at first. What did it matter to me which of them brought me the food? I thought about it, dismissed it and the memory of his grin, then came back to thinking about it again. A wild idea occurred to me, but I cast it aside. It came back and I examined it carefully. What harm in trying?

He made it simple for me. He unlocked the door sometime after dark, swung it open, then came in with his musket in one hand and a pan of food in the other. He set the musket against the wall, turned his back to it, and reached to set the food on my cot.

I grabbed the musket, set the muzzle against his back, said softly, "Don't cry out, Ben."

"I won't," he said. "You'd shoot me if I did, wouldn't you?"

"Yes," I lied.

"All right. What do you want me to do?"

"I hate to leave you in the cold, but take off your uniform and wrap yourself in the blanket on the cot."

He quickly did as I told him. I could scarcely see him in the darkness, but I had the idea that he was grinning.

He lay on the cot, and I bound him to it with his stockings and belt. Then I hurriedly dressed in his uniform, a pretty fair fit.

"Lock the door after you," he whispered. "That way they won't know you're gone until they can't find me on post. Good luck to you. Maybe I'll come over if I get the chance. Things will be hard for me now."

"What will they do to you?"

"Not too much. I'll lose some pay, maybe three months, and get sinks detail until they forget about it. I'm not in Armstrong's company, and he's the one will be up in the air about it."

"Good-by, Ben, and thanks."

"You better gag me, sir. It will look better for me."

I did as he said, tapped his shoulder in thanks, rolled my own clothing under my arm, and stepped through the doorway into the street.

In two hours' time I was picking my way along stone walls and through wood lots outside the city, without having been challenged once nor set upon by a single barking dog.

Once well free of the city and its encircling pickets, I changed clothes and set out with long stride for the Valley Forge.

I looked back once at the lights of the city, thinking of Peggy Remsen. For some reason, there suddenly sprang into my mind the words of Glennis Bill. "If you marry her, Mister Hill, I'd wager that in ten years you'd be reduced to two words in your own house: 'Yes, dear.'"

Maybe I'm lucky in more things than escaping a hanging, I thought.

The first person I saw when I reached the Deerkill huts was Teunis Ekerson, who smiled broadly for one of the few times in his life, and cried resoundingly, *"I am escaped with the skin of my teeth."*

Hawk took me up the scale and then he took me down again. I was all kinds of blinking young idiot; I'd risked Teunis' life for my own foolish fancy; I'd disobeyed orders by leaving my post; if a British court had missed hanging me, an American court, by all rights, ought to have the next chance.

I took it in silence. I merited every word of it. He went on at great length, every word a blazer.

"So," he said finally, "I've had to take it up with General Wayne. He was fit to be tied. He'll not put you before a court, but he approved my suggestion. We'll have our own court. Right now. Mr. Luckey," he called to Walter, "assemble the company."

When they were all there, Hawk stepped before them.

"Men, you know what Lieutenant Hill has done. As your commanding officer, I look at it as a foolish prank, unbecoming an officer and dangerous to himself and the man who went with him. I believe that Lieutenant Hill has demonstrated that he is not fitted for command of troops.

"You men know how this company is regulated. I am the officer in command, and you are bound by the Articles of War, as you duly subscribed to them. Yet we have always attempted to run our affairs with attention to those principles for which we are fighting this war. I mean that you have rights, that you are free men, and equal to all men or any man. You have always elected your officers; you always will.

"I say that Lieutenant Hill has destroyed his own effectiveness as an officer of this company. I believe that he should be reduced to ranks. You have a right to agree or disagree. Do any of you wish to speak?"

Not a man said a word.

"Then does any man disagree with my decision to reduce Lieutenant Hill to the rank of private soldier? If so, let him raise his hand."

Not a man lifted a hand.

CHAPTER FIFTEEN

Billy Bill had been shunted, as my mother used to say, from pillar to post all through his childhood. Now, given a wife who made a home for him in an eight-by-ten log hut, who cared for him lovingly, he was probably the happiest young man in the thirteen colonies.

The bitter weather and the choking smoke from green wood bothered Billy not at all. When he caught the itch, he just laughed and rubbed Doc's sulphur ointment on the raw flesh. When the flux gripped his innards, he made jokes about it. He sang and whistled at every dreary task. He belonged to somebody, and somebody belonged to him. This had never happened to him before. The world could not have been brighter.

There was one worry for him, a great one. His wife, afflicted as all of us but Billy were with the human trait of complaining about our living conditions, often turned up her pert nose at the rations. She had no idea that it turned Billy's heart to see her hold her nose when she cut a slab of ancient salt fish into chowder portions. She didn't know that every word tossed sneeringly at frozen potatoes cut Billy to the quick.

She really thought that he loved to hunt so much that he could scarcely bear to let a day go by without trekking after squirrel or rabbit. He set snares and deadfalls far from camp; he placed bait for raccoons and then would sit most of the frigid night through waiting for an animal to come into the sights of his rifle. He set tip-ups in the Schuylkill, cutting laboriously through the ice, then shivered in the wind for hours as he waited for a flag to tip under the pull of a ten-inch perch. (If he had to leave his lines, there was many a hungry Continental who kept an anticipatory eye on those flags.)

Billy managed somehow to have something good for his wife to eat almost every day. Hawk and Harm and Walter Luckey knew his concern for Glennis' palate; they put him on every foraging detail, where he could snare something special for his wife; they always sent him to the commissary when rations were to be drawn, because Billy could always wheedle an apple or a handful of prunes or a jar of mustard pickles from the clerks.

Although he himself was satisfied with the ration issue, Billy became an expert at the niceties of foraging. He came to know all the tricks of the Pennsylvania farmers. He could dig unerringly into a hayloft and bring out a bushel of squash; he could pick his way through a jungle of marsh grass and alders and come upon the hidden pen where a brace of fat pigs rooted.

There were many other men equally talented. The people of the Schuylkill countryside had to hide their surplus food and grain and animals, or they would have been stripped clean. Some of them wanted normal trading in civilian markets; others were determined to sell to the British in Philadelphia; all of them viewed payment in Continental paper as giving away their produce.

One day at breakfast, Glennis got to talking about milk. How good a big mug of milk would taste. What fine fish chowders could be made with milk. Whenever they had coffee, how wonderful to splash some milk into it. Billy nodded, smiling. He would bring her milk.

On the march, campaigning, there was always a farmhouse here and another there, where a fellow could get permission from Sergeant King or Sergeant Dutcher to fall out and get a bucketful of milk. Most farmers' wives were glad to give it to a handsome, fresh-faced boy who looked so thirsty and asked for it so politely.

Here where so many thousands sought any opportunity to get out of camp to roam the countryside, begging or stealing, it was increasingly difficult to set foot on a farmer's land without having him threaten to call the provost guard. If the farmers or their wives did consent to bargain, the prices they asked were outrageous.

Billy solved the problem of milk for Glennis in short time. Hawk had given him some hard coin and sent him to the farm of an old

Dutchman a mile beyond King of Prussia to buy applejack for the company. The farmer sold the applejack at prices below those charged by the sutlers and the public markets.

He kept the applejack in the feedroom in the stable. He took Billy there when Billy showed him the color of his money. While the farmer was filling the jugs, Billy looked around. Two of the milled boards that formed the outside wall of the feedroom were moving slightly in the probing wind. Billy saw that the nails that held them to the frame timbers were loose.

As a matter of course, Billy asked the farmer to let him have some milk. The farmer said no, he saved his milk to sell at a good price to the families of colonels and generals.

That night at supper Glennis mentioned milk again.

"You'll have it," Billy said. "I'll get some tonight."

"We have no money, Billy."

"Don't need any. A nice old farmer is going to give me some milk."

It was no trick for an agile young man to slip past the pickets. Going down the Gulph Road in the darkness, Billy tried to remember whether the old man had a dog. He hadn't seen one, he was sure.

No dog sounded the alarm as Billy approached the barn. Just a pull or two now, and the boards would swing free. He could hear the cows moving inside. He pulled the boards aside and started through with his wooden bucket ahead of him.

Then he was blinded by light. He didn't know it was a bull's-eye lantern aimed at the loose boards.

The old farmer shouted, "Stop, or I shoot you!"

Billy started to back out. Damnation, he thought, I wasn't the first to notice them boards.

A flash of orange stabbed at him. The explosion sounded louder than any gun ever made. The blow that smashed into his middle knocked Billy backward to the ground. He couldn't breathe, yet he thought he was screaming. His chest felt as if Jared King had him in a bear hug and was squeezing with all his mighty strength.

"*Gott helfe mir!*" he heard a voice say from afar. "I haf killed vun."

You ain't killed me, Billy thought. All I got to do is get up and run. Run back to Glennis.

He got up. It seemed to take a long time to get standing straight. Then he ran, or thought he did. He could feel the blood hot on his chest, but it was cold by the time it reached his belly.

He staggered into the officers' hut and stood for a moment, holding to a bunk frame. "Didn't get the milk," he said brokenly. "He was behind them loose boards with a gun."

He fell to the floor. Joe Williams and Hawk took charge, stripping his coat, shirt, and breeches from him. They put him in the bunk that I had vacated when I was reduced to ranks. Harm came out and bawled for me to run to get Doc Walden. He'd get the nearest Pennsylvania doctor, he yelled, but Hawk said to be sure to get Doc Walden.

The two doctors and Hawk were in there with him almost an hour. Glennis stood just outside the hut, crying softly all the while. Several of us tried to comfort her, but she paid us no mind. Every few minutes she went inside but came out quickly again.

The doctors came out. The Pennsylvania man shook his head to an offer of coffee, went striding solemnly into the night. Doc Walden sipped at a mug of strong coffee, standing close to the watch fire.

"Goddamit, say something!" Harm cried angrily.

Doc looked mildly over his spectacles, steamed by the hot liquid. "What do you want me to say, Harm?"

"He's gonna be all right, ain't he?"

"No, he's not, Harm. He's dying."

"Goddam you then! Get in there and do something. What the hell you standing here for? Get in there!"

Doc shook his head, sipped his coffee. "Nothing I can do. His wife is there. Hawk is there. He said he wanted to talk to them."

Harm stepped closer to Walden. His voice was low. "Nothing you can do, Doc? Not a thing?"

"Nothing."

We all stood silently. Doc poured himself another cup of coffee.

Glennis came out of the hut. She came over to us, looking at the ground. "He wants to see you, Matt," she whispered.

I went inside. Hawk stood by the bunk, holding Billy's hand. He nodded to me, then left.

Billy smiled weakly. "No more hunting, Matt, you and me."

I tried to hold back my tears, but they poured down my cheeks.

"I been a good soldier, ain't I, Matt?"

"The best, Billy."

"Two things I have in mind, Matt." He seemed to talk easily enough, although weakly. "First, when Hawk knocked you down to private soldier. I was gonna speak. I started to raise my hand when Hawk said it. But Glennis held me from it. She said you needed sense knocked into you. I was gonna tell Hawk that, barring him, you was the best officer in this here army. I just told him now to put you back to lieutenant. He said he would."

He paused, for breath or strength.

"Second thing, Matt. You take care of my wife. Will you do that?"

"Sure I will, Billy."

"She's like me. Got no family. I only hope you look out for her the way Hawk and your ma looked out for me."

"Don't you fret, Billy."

"Thanks, Matt. It hurts now. Call my wife. And one thing more. Call Teunis Ekerson."

I told Glennis to go inside. Hawk and Doc Walden went with her. I motioned Teunis Ekerson to come from the silent group of soldiers ringing the watch fire. We went into the hut.

Hawk had a Bible in his hand. He handed it to Teunis.

"Open the book, Teunis," Billy said weakly, his eyes fixed on his wife. "Read me that one that's so pretty for a man that's dying."

Ekerson stared at me in dumb agony. "I can't read, Matt," he whispered. "I got 'em all in my head."

"Open the book," I said, "and say it from memory. You know what he wants."

Ekerson's voice was soft, gentle: *"The Lord is my shepherd. . . ."*

BOOK TWO

Though others may choose as they please, I would not exchange the variety of seasons in our northern climate for all the warm sunny days in the midst of winter that I have heard southerners boast of on any and every occasion.

It may mark me as odd, but I actually enjoy the shivering in a duckblind on the Drowned Lands of a November dawn, when the water is fast freezing around the decoys.

I have been far from home in fall and spring, when it has suddenly occurred to me that with the changing season, the woodcock flights were whistling into our alder covers in the Deerkill Valley. At those times, whatever my surroundings, I wish to be home tramping the woods and marshes.

To return to the subject of our northern weather, I must be frank to admit that one of its worst features is the thaw of late winter, while the frost is thick in the ground. Given a sunny day and a warm wind quartering south, or perhaps a day's rain followed by sun, and what happens? Every footpath, every wagon track, every lane, every road—they soften into the frost layer below and we must move in thick mud.

We had such days at Valley Forge that winter, particularly in February and March, when the whole encampment would, by midmorning, be swimming in a vast sea of mud that turned stickier and more slippery as the day wore on.

The twenty-seventh of February was such a day, when a man was more likely tempted to plead himself sick and lie in his bunk at the tender mercies of the fleas, than venture forth on a day's duty in the mud. It is a curious fact that there were more deserters posted by the provost on a night following a thaw than on the bitter days when all was frozen and the wind blew strong and keen.

On that Friday in late February, I had to go forth into the mud with a party of men, on pass to a farm beyond Paoli, where Joe Williams had negotiated the purchase of some milled boards for an engineering project. My suggestion to Williams was that he take some Pennsylvanians and go get them himself, but he said that the farmer had included several bales of straw in the agreement, and our men needed fresh bedding. Hawk said go, so I went. Even in February, when supplies were coming to us at a rate that at least seemed to stave off mass starvation, straw was a scarce commodity.

It would be a miserable journey, even on the way out, when our carts were unladen. Paoli was a hamlet not far from the encampment, and fairly near to Wayne's home. It was at Paoli that Wayne and his Pennsylvanians had been sorely hit by a night surprise attack the previous fall. That was the night when Sir Charles Grey had made himself the name of "No Flint" Grey, when he ordered his men to remove the flints from their muskets so that none might fire an alarming shot.

I was already irritated by the prospect of sloshing through the mire to Paoli; further to my discomfort was the appearance of Glennis Bill in the company street, announcing that she would go with us.

"You will not," I said flatly. It was bad enough to have her as the only woman in constant view of our company and the Seventh Pennsylvania; I did not want her assuming that she could interfere with work details.

"Doctor's orders," she said, smiling as if I were in the best of tempers. "Doc Walden says that Hawk has to have a heavy quilt on him at night when the fires go down, and Doc has to have some medicine that I can get from a doctor at Paoli. Doc says this other doctor's wife will sell me a quilt too."

"What kind of medicine?" I asked. "Tell me, and I'll get it and the quilt."

"You could get the medicine," she said, "but I have to pick out the quilt. You wouldn't know a good quilt if you saw one."

"Listen to me," I said savagely, but in a low voice. "Don't talk that way to me before the men. Now give me the order for the medicine, and I'll get whatever it is. You'll stay here, out of trouble."

Doc Walden came up behind her, interrupting me. "It's a couple of crocks of sulphur ointment, Matt. And a few papers of opium. Let the girl go with you. It'll do her good."

"Please, Matt," she said quickly, changing to her most pleasant tone, which she could assume instantly when she wished. "I want to see something besides this dreary camp."

I didn't give up easily. "If you'd do what Hawk and I tell you to do, and go home to stay with my mother, you'd be out of this dreary camp for good."

She looked at me oddly, as if undecided whether to plead again or to speak flippantly, as she was more used to do. "Don't you think what I do for Hawk is reason enough for me to stay, Matt? If you don't, I'll go tomorrow."

I could but agree, however reluctantly. She was a wonder in her care for my father. He had failed badly in the past month. Now he was but a gaunt shade of his former strong self. I knew that the pain struck him frequently, and that Doc Walden had started dosages of opium to let Hawk sleep. In point of fact, however, Hawk still maintained the fiction that he suffered only from the privations of the winter as all the rest of us did, and I suppose some of our men believed it.

Glennis and Doc Walden were the only ones who knew the extent of his suffering from his own lips. Doc managed almost daily visits to us, in spite of his heavy duties with the Connecticut troops. Usually he claimed that it was Eben Lowry's cooking that brought him. He would have long talks with Glennis about what could be done for Hawk, and would issue nursing instructions for her, which she would carry out as inconspicuously as possible.

The three of them managed so well to pretend that they were treating nothing worse than a severe and lingering chest congestion, that I once heard unimaginative Walter Luckey tell Hawk that he'd be fit as a fiddle come the first warmth of spring. Hawk smilingly agreed. I pleaded with him to go home, to let me take him, but he would only say quietly that it wasn't time yet. Leave him to Glennis and Doc, he said; he'd be all right with them.

Now my irritation faded almost away when Glennis reminded me of the care she gave Hawk. Not entirely, however—she was so persistent in forever annoying me with mockery and general hoydenish behavior that I couldn't resist a final barb. "If you come with me, you come as a female. You can't walk the camp streets in those clothes."

She was wearing a blanket coat over her usual breeches and shirt. "How could I move in all this mud, Lieutenant, with a dress to drag in it? Would you like me to hold up the dress above my knees so it wouldn't get muddy?"

"I don't care what you do," I said, resigning the game. "Just don't interfere or make any trouble on this detail."

"That would be the last thing I'd think of," she said smartly with an infuriating tip of her head. I expected next she'd make some remark about my going into Philadelphia to see Peggy; it was her custom to remind me of that at least once a day.

"Don't come back without the medicine, Matt," Doc said. "I'm almost out of it."

"Doc, while I'm talking to you—can't you persuade Hawk to let me take him home?"

"You know what he says. He'll stay until his boys are through the winter. He'll make it, Matt. He wants two things, and I'm thinking he'll get them both. First, to leave the company in the best possible condition for the new campaign, and second, to see that Deerkill Valley of yours again. He'll make it."

I nodded doubtfully, then gave the order to march. Our party straggled down the division street, looking more like vagabonds and less like soldiers than any body of men ever assembled in the entire world's military history, unless it were another detail from this same encampment. ". . . leave the company in the best possible condition for the new campaign . . ." The company couldn't get much worse; possibly it could improve. I thought of the disciplined soldierly British regulars I had seen on my fool's errand into Philadelphia —these ragamuffins would have to face them, come spring.

I left Aaron Conklin with Glennis at the doctor's house while we went on for the lumber and straw. We loaded the carts at the farm beyond Paoli and came back on the York Road.

Not a quarter mile of the way passed without one or the other of the carts sliding off the crown of the road into the ditch. Then we put our shoulders to it and shoved it onto the crown again. In the process we were coated with mud every time. Often enough, the wagon was really mired—then we dismantled the nearest rail fence, set a bed of rails into the mud, took others for levers, and managed to get clear. Each time we had to halt to rebuild the rail fence, ever mindful of the General's proper strictures against further devastations of the countryside around the encampment.

We strained and we pulled and we cursed. Once we almost launched ourselves into a brawl with a patrol of the rifle corps, who halted to watch with great glee our attempts to get the heavier cart rolling out of a culvert into which it had slipped. We were on the point of dropping prying-bars and going for the riflemen, when they suddenly stopped guffawing and jumped into the culvert to help. They never were bad fellows, those men of Morgan's.

After we were through Paoli, with Glennis perched on the smaller cart, we went into another ditch. This one was at the edge of a patch of marsh. When we put our shoulders to the wagon, we were almost knee-deep in chilling water. The cart wouldn't move, although the team of horses and our eight men strained mightily. Swearing beneath my breath, I looked around for another rail fence.

There was a sound of horses' hoofs splashing through the mud, several of them, and the squealing of cart wheels that needed greasing. A dog barked sharply, as if taking the right to challenge any fools that would stand in icy water. I didn't even look up, trying to figure some easier way to get us free.

The cart went by, following the horses, and I heard Glennis cry angrily, "Why don't you take care?"

I looked up at her, readying a swift reprimand, thinking that she was talking about me and the mired cart. Instead, I saw her glaring at the party that had just gone by.

She was holding up Hawk's new patchwork quilt, over which the passing horses had spattered globs of mud.

I glanced incuriously at the group of horsemen that had preceded the cart. There were four of them, all of whom had reined in at Glennis' cry. Now they were turning their horses to come back. My disinterest in Glennis' problem dropped away. One look at the strangers was enough to tell me that we might have trouble on our hands.

They were important personages, obviously—at least their leader was. He wore a great glittering badge of some kind on his left breast, along with other medals of the sort we then used to associate with European officers. All four riders wore spanking new uniforms with shining jackboots. The uniforms, although blue and buff like those that were still left to some of our high-ranking officers, had less of a homely air—less so even than those worn by Colonel Hamilton. Put in another way, they looked fancy and foreign, and therefore I assumed immediately that we had to deal with another set of fancy foreigners. Of these we had had more than enough. Let me explain that, always excepting the French Boy and a couple of others, our troops in the Line had little use for the swarm of self-seeking Europeans who rushed to our shores to seek the highest rate Congress would pay for their swords.

I knew I was right when I heard the man with the flashing star speak to one of the others, a youngster who looked scarce older than my brother Johnny, in French that was heavily laced with a Teutonic accent. "Ask the boy on the cart why he is angry, Duponceau."

The youngster replied, "I think it is not a boy, but a woman, Monsieur le Baron."

I moved forward, thinking: a German baron who talks French but not English, and a parcel of Frenchmen in lace all willing to become major generals before they're twenty. Good Lord, if we get any more of 'em, we'll have to teach French to the troops and have a daily detail for catching frogs in the marshes.

Glennis let them have what-for before I reached the group: "Why didn't you look what you were doing? How do you expect me to get the mud off this quilt? Who do you think you are, with your high-and-mightiness?"

The leader, a man heavier than most, but solid in his saddle, with a full mouth and thick jowls, nodded smilingly. "Ah, Duponceau!

You are right, my boy, it is a woman. And a handsome one at that. If she be any sample of the countryside, you and DePontière and De L'Enfant will have yourselves a gay time here in this wilderness. If she has a mother, I might myself. What is it that she says?"

The one addressed as Duponceau swept his hat from his head, and smiled winningly at Glennis. "What is it, madame, that we have done? Monsieur le Baron asks to know."

"Your horses muddied this quilt, that's what! Matt, they ought to pay for a new one."

The youngster looked at me, as if she'd spoken too fast for him. "You speak French, monsieur, maybe?"

I was about to say that I did, but some contrary notion possessed me; perhaps I was so annoyed with mud and slush that I set my mind against speaking their language just to force them to use mine. I simply stared vacantly at him in the manner of our country people when they mistrust strangers.

"He doesn't speak French, Your Excellency, nor do any of them, I expect." The youngster shrugged in distaste. "What barbarity."

"What does the woman say? She's only a girl. Duponceau, look at DePontière. See his eyes light at her anger! She has fire, that one. This will be a fine billet for you young men, if there are many camp followers like that one."

I felt the blood rushing to my face, and I clenched my hands. Just like the rest of them, I thought. Calling her a camp follower! Come over here to see what they can get with their lace shirts and fancy manners!

"It's something to do with that rug she has," the young man said. "I believe we splashed mud upon it, Your Excellency. And upon her, too, if one judges from the spot on her nose. I will apologize for us, monsieur, and then we will ride on."

"No, no, Duponceau," said one of the other young men. "Do not let so graceful a pigeon escape from us on our first day. Find out her name, and who she is, and tell her I would like to see much of her as soon as Congress gives me some money."

"You spattered the quilt," I said thickly. "It's fair you should make amends."

"We apologize much, monsieur," said Duponceau. "His Excel-

233

lency's man will clean the rug for madame." He called to the man driving the cart, who began rummaging in the baggage behind him. On the seat of the cart with the driver sat one of the most ridiculous dogs I have ever seen, skinny as a rail and near as long—I came to know that he was an Italian greyhound named Azor and that he was a fine pleasant fellow, although of no working use whatsoever. This dog was barking madly all the time at our ragged crew, who had stopped all work and were watching this show with grinning faces.

"This muddy fellow is a soldier, Duponceau?" asked the Baron. "*Sacre!* What is it we have brought ourselves to, if this be a soldier? And the others, they are soldiers also? They look to me for all the world like the beggars of Paris."

Now I became really angry, although I must admit that this stranger's words were spoken more in pity than in scorn, and that were I not so furious at their levity concerning Glennis I would have noted that his speech was kind, that his words were ill-chosen only because he could not know that I understood them.

"Tell your master, whoever he is," I said icily to Duponceau, "that there is only one man in this encampment who can be called 'His Excellency.' If you want to get along with us, and get to be a colonel inside two weeks, you'd better watch that kind of nonsense."

"I do not understand, monsieur," he said puzzledly, his face reddening. "Why are you angry with us, other than the business of the rug? We have given you apology, and the Baron's servant is cleaning. Yes?"

"I don't think you'll ever understand, like all the rest of you people we have hanging on," I told him. "That's why maybe we'd all be better off if you and all the lace-trimmed generals and colonels caught the next ship back to France."

"You touch my honor! You are not officer, so I do not ask you to defend yourself. But give me your name. Tell me your officer's name. I will report that you have insult given to me and to these gentlemen and to Monsieur le Baron!"

Speaking slowly, so that my French would not be ludicrous, I answered him in his own language. "To whom do I report that Monsieur le Baron has insulted this lady and my men? I am an officer, sir, although I may look—" and I glared straight at the Baron, "—

like one of the beggars of Paris, as Monsieur so politely put it. As to satisfaction for my insult to you, sir, I am at your service."

"That's telling him, Matt!" said Jared King darkly, although he could not have had the faintest idea of what I said.

Duponceau started to speak, but the Baron interrupted him. "Enough, Duponceau!" He spoke to me—I must say most pleasantly —with a smile. "My unfortunate words, monsieur, were chosen in my belief that you spoke no French. I apologize to you and the lady, for myself and my staff."

"It is nothing, monsieur," I said with a stiff nod.

"Allow me to introduce myself," he said, slipping from the saddle with surprising grace for one so heavy. His handsome jackboots were up to the calves in thick mud. He was not so tall as he looked a-horseback. His bow was grace itself. "I am Frederick William Augustus Henry, Baron von Steuben, late in the service of His Majesty, the King of Prussia. These gentlemen are my secretary and my aides, Monsieur Duponceau and Messieurs DePontière and De L'Enfant."

I was somewhat flustered by the string of names he gave himself, but not greatly impressed—we had several barons and counts and such underfoot all the time. It seemed preposterous to respond to such a formal introduction when one was almost knee-deep in the mud of a back-country road. "Matt Hill," I said, "Lieutenant of the Highland County Independent Company."

His gentlemen bowed stiffly to me. The dog still barked; the servant handed the quilt back up to Glennis, and my men stood around with their jaws agape at all the "frog talk." They looked as if they had never seen a baron before, with or without a great star on his chest.

"You men hop to it," I said gruffly. "Get some rails down and get that cart back on the road."

The Baron started forward. "If we may, monsieur, let us put our several shoulders to the cart before we continue on our way to meet His Excellency."

If I was rude, it was simply because I didn't believe he meant it. I looked him up and down, openly showing that I damn well knew he'd never soil that brilliant uniform on our mud-spattered cart.

What's more, the last thing I thought any baron or marquis would want to do would be to soil his hands at hard work.

"You can go on your way, monsieur," I said coldly. "You might get a little mud on you, or tear that fine uniform. We wouldn't want the General to think that you were one of the beggars of Paris."

Duponceau and the other two Frenchmen started at me with cries of anger, but the Baron lifted his big hand to them in a halting gesture.

He nodded stiffly to me. "As you say, monsieur. It would appear that our first meeting leaves much to be desired. Perhaps our second will be more friendly. *Au revoir, monsieur, madame.*"

I nodded, turned my back, and went to help the men.

We could hear the dog barking wildly long after they were out of sight.

"Matt Hill, I don't understand you," Glennis said when the cart was back on the road again and we were trudging along. "That big foreign man was nice enough about the quilt. Yet you took on as if he'd insulted you and all your family. What was it that you all were jabbering about in French? I was watching your face—you were getting real thick there for a while."

"Never mind," I said.

"What was it, Matt? He looked important. You ought to have been careful what you said, whatever it was."

"If you hadn't yelped about the quilt, they'd have gone on and we wouldn't have been bothered."

"What did you talk about?"

"If you must know," I said testily, "they made remarks about you."

"La!" she cried, putting up her hands to smooth her straw-colored hair, and not looking at all like a woman recently widowed. "And what did they say, pray tell?"

"It wouldn't bear repeating."

"Did they say I was pretty, Matt? Did they?"

"That, and more," I said, watching her fingers play at her collar and again at her hair. I wondered what those Frenchmen, who were supposed to be connoisseurs of female beauty, saw so startling in this slip of a farm girl. Well, I thought, they've been long at sea and on the road.

"One of 'em called you a pigeon," I said.

"Is that all? Still, when a Frenchman calls you a pigeon, it must mean something. Do you know what he meant, Matt?"

"They thought you were a camp follower," I said harshly.

"Well, I am, I guess." She nodded, then suddenly flushed. "Oh. I see. Oh."

She was silent for a time, then said quietly: "What more did they say, Matt? It must have been interesting, because your face got so dark."

"They talked a lot, the way foreigners do. Now let be about the Baron von Steuben, or whatever his name is. I wouldn't care to see any more of him and his French popinjays."

"I would, Matt. So handsome, they were."

She looked sidewise at me, grinning.

A shout from Jared King stilled my answer. "Here we go again, Matt!"

I looked back. The big cart was in the ditch again.

Life was so unchanging, so dismal, at the encampment that a new topic of conversation always bid fair to be wrung dry of all interest whatever before it was cast aside.

At mess that night, the topic was Baron von Steuben, or Baron de Steuben, as it seemed he was generally called. We were eating inside the officers' hut—pork and beans and cornbread, a delicious meal proving the worth of the combined talents of Eben Lowry and Glennis, who now took her meals with the officers and shared Eben's housekeeping duties. There was plenty of food to go around, for officers and men, although I would venture that no kettleful was so tasty as ours. A full meal, in those last February days, was still a circumstance so unusual as to be attacked in ravenous silence. (There was generally some little pork to be had, but beans were a rarity that winter; why this was so I cannot say, since I had seen the day in that army when beans and more beans were all we had to eat.)

Little talking was done, therefore, until we had all sopped up the last of the juice of our first helpings with wedges of cornbread. I then debated taking another full helping or just a half portion. If I were not to think of my own belly, I could walk one hundred yards, find Jed Palmer among the men of the Seventh Pennsylvania, and invite him to have some beans.

The question was resolved by the appearance of Palmer's head in the doorway, and his apologetic voice. "Why, I thought you'd be through eating by this time, or I wouldn't of come over. Beans, ain't it? With pork. Seems I can smell a bit of onion in them beans, can't I? Don't remember when it was last I had pork and beans, *with onion*. It ain't the same thing at all. Onion is the making of 'em, my mother always said." He was in the hut and seated on a bunk beside Harm Tallman by this time. Harm was cleaning his bowl with cornbread. "Eben, I just wonder," continued Palmer, "I just wonder if you cooked them beans with the right amount of onion. If you don't get it just right——"

"There's plenty left, Jed," I told him. "Help yourself."

In about fifteen seconds he was back at Harm's side with a heaping platter, smacking his lips with each mouthful and nodding happily over the proportion of onion. He seemed to enjoy the beans so much that I decided to have some more.

Hawk, who ate little these days and that only when Glennis stood over him, was sipping a cup of coffee. His breathing was labored, and when he coughed it was rarely without the shadow of pain on his face.

He was the one who started the talk about the German. "Jed, did you hear anything about this new man who arrived today?"

"Yep," Parker said between mouthfuls. "He's a high mucky-muck over in Europe. Run a whole army by hisself over there. Feller told me he's the highest ranker we got, outside the General. Said he's a lieutenant general."

"That ain't high," Harm said. "Major general is higher, and we got lots of them. I'd say we got about a dozen more than we need."

"You don't know nothing about armies," Jed Palmer said disdainfully. "This Dutchman was highest man for the King of Prussia. Lieutenant general is lots higher than major general. Anybody that's been in the army knows that."

"I don't," Harm said doggedly. "I know that major is higher'n lieutenant, so a major general has got to rank a lieutenant general."

Palmer had his mouth full of beans, so he couldn't reply.

"Who's right, Hawk?" Harm asked.

"Jed is right on the rank, as far as that goes. But we haven't any rank that high, but for the General."

"This Dutchman ain't nothing, what I heard," Joe Williams chimed in. "He come over here from Ben Franklin in Paris, saying he'd be a volunteer. Good God! That makes him about equal to me. I'm a volunteer too. Imagine that. All this time I let these furriners act as if I wouldn't never be equal to them, by order of Congress, and here's one that says he's only a volunteer. There ain't one of them others that didn't ask for major general soon as he come off the ship."

"Matt met him on the road today," Hawk said. "Tell us what you think of him, Matt."

I hesitated. "I don't want to be unfair, but you know what I think of most of these foreigners, Hawk. I had harsh words with him, as I told you, and I didn't like the young Frenchmen he had with him. Like all of 'em, they make too free with their tongues. He put on a good show, Hawk. There was one thing puzzled me." I told them about the Baron's offer to put his shoulders to the bogged cart. "Doesn't seem to me," I said, "that a baron would do that, any baron. But I think he meant it, Hawk, and there was no call for me to turn him down the way I did." I explained the remarks about the beggars of Paris.

"That was real bad, Matt," Williams said dolefully. "You hadn't ought to pass insults to a real honest-to-God volunteer, even if he does turn out to be a major general. You might of got into trouble, real trouble."

"He might have too," I said mildly. "He might have been tossed into that ditch had he said another word about the appearance of the men."

"You can excuse him that, Matt," Hawk said. "You were the first of us he'd seen."

I nodded. "And we were coated with mud."

It was Walter Luckey who surprisingly furnished the most information about the German. As usual, he'd been content to listen, but now he spoke up. "Baron von Stoobin, that's his name. I was down to headquarters when he come into camp. Colonel Laurens grabbed every officer there and give us swords to strap on. I looked pretty good in that sword, if I do say so. We went outside where the General was waiting for him. I heard the whole thing, at least the English part of it. The young feller that talks English for him made a big speech about this baron coming here to offer his services, free for nothing. I heard Laurens and Hamilton talking about he ain't even going to ask to be a general. Just do what he can to help. Colonel Hamilton said that now maybe this army would get some training. Said this feller was supposed to be the cream of the Prussian Army."

Hawk immediately perked up at the mention of the word "training" and asked a multitude of questions of Luckey and me.

The most important query, I thought, that Hawk put to Walter was this: "How did the General seem to take to him?"

Luckey shrugged. "I seen that look on his face. You know, when he's rode up into the line and sits there looking at the nearest militia regiment? Like we say, he's wondering how long they'll hold under fire. That ain't rightly it, though. I wouldn't say he was cold, or even a shade chilly with that German—but he wasn't no more than lukewarm."

Hawk nodded. "He's got a right to be wary. Congress has sure sent us a lot of 'em, and there ain't many that's worth the powder to blow 'em back to Europe. Except the French Boy."

We nodded. Joe Williams said, "Except the French Boy."

Lying in my bunk that night, I couldn't sleep. Across the room I could hear Hawk's troubled breathing, and then a bad fit of coughing. He was silent for a while, then I heard a whispered cry of pain.

I wanted to get up, but he must have known I was listening.

"Lie still, son," he said softly. There was a pause as he caught his breath. "I'll take some of Doc Walden's magic remedy."

He stirred about, preparing the opium solution. Then he went back to his bunk. "This will put me to a heavy sleep, Matt," he whispered. "You take the company in the morning."

"Sure, Hawk. Good night."

"Good night, son. Tomorrow you find out more about that German. I want to know about him."

"All right, Hawk."

Soon he was sleeping. I hoped it was without pain.

I didn't think about Steuben as I lay there. Instead I reached the determination to go to General Wayne the next day and insist that he use his influence with my father to persuade him to go home.

I believe that a man thinks clearly when he lies wide awake in the darkness. He's not bothered by the intrusion of the eye upon the mind. I knew certainly now that my father had not long to go. Doc Walden kept putting me off and putting me off, saying, "There's time, Matt. He'll say himself, when he's ready." But it had to be soon. I'd ask Wayne to order it. There surely was no place in the army for a man as sick as Hawk.

I'd take Glennis along when we went. She had to have a home until she could negotiate the draft the farmer Kettrick had given her. Who could say? The British might be in Philadelphia until the end of the war, maybe next year or even, at the outside, the year after. She'd be all right once she had Kettrick's money, even if she couldn't expect to collect the money that Congress owed her for all the receipts her brother had taken for produce. When she had the money from the farm, she could go where she wished, but in the meantime my mother would welcome her. Billy had asked me to take care of her; that was the best way.

Philadelphia, I thought. Peggy. These were the times when I remembered, in the silence of the night. What did I remember? Curiously, in the beginning it had been the hurt and the loss. Slowly now, however, I was starting to reflect without any sense of pain; indeed, when I thought of Peggy, it was difficult to bring back the scenes in the Deerkill Valley. All the image I could seem to summon was the startled look on her face when she came into the study in Philadelphia and saw me instead of Harm Tallman, whom she had just betrayed. The image never stayed—dancing before it would come the slight figure of Glennis, eyes mocking me as she poked fun at me for my Philadelphia foolishness.

I was recovering more quickly than I had expected. Indeed, it was becoming increasingly difficult to summon Peggy's image in the darkness. I would some day like to see her again, I told myself, because it's just possible that she is not as beautiful as I have always thought.

There was no need to seek an appointment with General Wayne. Just after breakfast one of his orderlies came up and spoke to me. "General Wayne's compliments, Lieutenant, and he wants to see you right away."

I turned the company duties over to Harm and walked to Wayne's headquarters. I wondered what he wanted with me—a foraging expedition, perhaps. Yet he had just returned from a raid into the Jerseys, bringing a few days' beef rations for the army. The Deerkill company had stayed in camp; perhaps if he had detailed us to accompany him his success might have been greater. I had heard from Pennsylvanians that where Wayne had expected to find hundreds of fat cattle there were only a few score here and there. The rest were hidden in marshes and woods. Our men, I believed, would have found the hiding places. They were good at that kind of thing.

So perhaps he had orders to start out again. This time he would take us with him.

A disinterested orderly nodded to me when I arrived, pointing with a quill toward the inner room. I heard Wayne's voice rumbling in anger. There were two colonels with him, commanders of regiments in the division: Lt. Colonel William Butler, also commanding the Second Brigade, and Colonel Dan Brodhead.

Wayne was on the subject of clothing and supplies again. "They got 'em in Lancaster, they got 'em in York, and they got 'em in Easton! Enough shoes for this whole division, enough coats for every man to have two—one for every day and one for Sunday! They got 'em, and I'll get 'em, if I have to take a brigade to put the fear of God into those people. You gentlemen tell your men I'm doing my best. So far that hasn't been good enough, but by God, something will come of it. I promise you and I promise the men. Tell 'em that. Good morning, gentlemen."

They filed past me on their way out; Butler looked at me curiously, lifting his eyebrows and shaking his head slightly, as if warning me of something.

Wayne paid me no mind, drumming his fingers on the table before him and flipping various papers about. I thought he hadn't noticed me come in.

"Lieutenant Hill, sir," I said.

"I know damned well who you are," he barked suddenly without looking up. "You give me good cause to know. I'll be with you in a minute."

I reddened, clenching my jaws. He continued to slide papers from one place to another, his face dark in the dim light. Then he slammed his hand flat on the table.

"Hill, I've got a good mind to send you packing. What kind of officer are you? You could be before a court tomorrow morning if I say the word."

"What's the matter, sir?" I asked tightly. "What is it you think I've done?"

"Hell's fire, Lieutenant! Don't act innocent. Good God, do you mean to say you don't know you insulted the Baron de Steuben yesterday? Do you deny that one of his aides challenged you to a duel? Will you admit that you acted like a surly dog? Hah, answer me!"

"If the general will let me explain, sir."

"You'd damn well better explain!"

"Yes, sir," I said, putting tight control on my urge to flare back at him. "Well, in the first place, this baron, as I understand it, isn't even an officer——"

"Don't first-place me, and don't tell me what you understand or don't understand! Did you insult him and his aides, or didn't you? Now answer that, yes or no!"

"I suppose——"

"Yes or no, Hill!"

"Yes, sir."

"All right. Proceed."

I told the whole story in about three minutes, repeating the actual conversation as closely as I was able. I told how the baron had spoken of Glennis as a camp follower, and how he'd said my men looked like the beggars of Paris.

"He didn't know you could speak French, eh?"

"No, sir. Maybe I had no call to flare at him, but I was boiling, and covered with mud and trying to get a wagon out of the ditch."

"All right, Hill. One more question. What were you angry at: the remark about your men, or the one about that girl, whatever her name is?"

"What he said about the men, sir. You know yourself that they're as good, man for man, as any soldiers in this army, and they can't help it if they're ragged and dirty like everybody else in this camp. As far as the girl goes, if a woman stays with an army, she's got a right to expect talk."

He nodded. "All right, Hill. That answer will take you off charges." He paused, rubbing his full face with his big hands. Then he looked up at me darkly. "Close that door behind you, Hill."

When I had done so, he resumed.

"Now you listen to me, Lieutenant. You have all the earmarks of a good officer. Your father says you are one, and I haven't had reason to doubt his judgment. But you've never shown that he's right this winter, or after Germantown, either. You took that company home when we needed every man."

"Sir, the men voted——"

"Shut up and listen to me! First you sneak into the city to see some Tory female and take a good man with you.

"What's more," he continued, "I understand that you spend half your time talking about now the British are going to whip us."

"Sir——"

"I'm doing the talking, Hill! If it weren't for your father, I'd have transferred you to a New York regiment long ago. I don't want men in my command who think we can be beaten, who believe that we're going to be beaten. I'd rather have you go over to Philadelphia to your Tory lady.

"Now, yesterday you open your big mouth to a most important stranger. He came straight from Congress, Hill. And before that, straight from Mr. Franklin and Mr. Deane in Paris. So, what happens? I'm called to headquarters to meet him, and I arrive right in the middle of a fine tale about one of my officers insulting him and his party. I was never so damned mortified since I've been in this army!"

He stopped talking for a moment, rubbing his face again.

"I have trouble enough, Hill. Now it's not the Dutchman that's important, but it's the fact that the bunch at headquarters have got something else to blame on Wayne. You know I'm down there every other day, saying: send out raiding parties, cut off their supplies, send the light horse and my division into the outskirts of the city, do this and do that, but let's not sit here on our tails any longer while they're warm and well-fed. The General listens to me, but he has a damned council of midwives——" He broke off, and looked sharply at me. "What I say is in confidence, Hill."

"Yes, sir."

"Then I walk in yesterday and listen to Laurens and young Hamilton talking to that French secretary of the baron's, and what is it about? You, Hill. Nobody but you. Last month I kept you out of a court for your Philadelphia trip; first thing Hamilton said to me yesterday was, 'Will you bring the man up on charges, General Wayne?' Damn it, Lieutenant, if you're an officer, you have to act like one!"

"Yes, sir."

"And one more thing! The Frenchman was telling all of us about the girl you had with you on that detail. Is that the widow that lives with your company?"

"Yes, sir."

"Get rid of her, Hill. Any way you like, but I won't have unattached women in this command. They do nothing but cause trouble."

"She's of good character, sir. She causes no trouble with the men."

"Well, why don't you marry her? She's pretty enough for any man, and if you had a wife maybe you'd settle down and forget about Tories in Philadelphia."

I stared at him, forgetting my anger.

He shrugged, saying, "Well, somebody's got to marry her, if she stays. Just thought I'd give you first chance. Get her married, or get her out."

"Nothing would please me more, sir, than to send her home, but she's a pretty good nurse for my father. I wanted to speak to you about him."

He nodded. "I have a note here from Surgeon Walden. Your father refused to go home, but he'll have to go soon. You know how sick he is?"

"Yes, sir."

"Too bad. I like your father. All right, let the girl stay until Captain Hill goes home. She goes with him, unless somebody marries her first. Understand me?"

"Yes, sir."

"Go along then. I'll not turn you over to a court, but you haven't heard the last of this, Lieutenant. Not by a long shot. Toe the mark from here on."

"Yes, sir."

"You had reason, I suppose, to flare at Steuben, but I don't like the way you talk about defeat. Stop that, Hill, or you leave my command."

"Yes, sir. General, couldn't you issue an order to send my father home?"

He shook his head. "Not yet. He wants to see his company through the winter, and I'm going to let him do it. Walden says a few weeks more. He knows better than we do."

Word went around quickly, presumably spread by the orderly, how Wayne had ripped me up and down and crosswise. It didn't bother me to take the ribbing, because I knew I deserved it. I made up my mind to stick to the job of being a good company officer and keep my opinions about the war to myself.

I flared only when Glennis joined the jokesters. She followed me out of the hut after our night meal, coming to where I stood by the watch fire. "I hear that Wayne gave you the devil for your Philadelphia trip, Matt. Is it true that he said you were mixed up with a female Tory spy?"

"There were things that he said, after the door was closed, that the orderly didn't hear and couldn't repeat."

"And what were they, pray tell?"

"For one thing, he said that you were to get out of this camp as fast as I could send you!"

"Oh, Matt! He didn't, did he?"

"Why should I lie to you? He said he wouldn't have unattached females in his command. He said I'd have to get rid of you or marry you, one."

She gasped, but said not another word. I turned from looking into the fire. She was gazing steadily at me.

246

"What did you say, Matt?"

"I told him you were essential in seeing to Hawk's comfort. He says you can stay as long as Hawk does."

"What did you say when he said you should marry me?"

"What did I say? Nothing. What would you expect me to say?"

She was silent again for a long moment. Then she said softly, "Nothing. Thank you, Matt, for getting him to agree that I should stay with Hawk. And, Matt——?"

"Yes?"

"Let's not fight any more. I don't take any pleasure in it, except to see your face get red."

"There's never been a need for us to fight, if you'd watch your tongue."

"All right," she said, meekly enough. "I'll watch my tongue."

Soldiers are for all the world like village women who gather at market, or in a sewing circle, or outside church after services—they love to gossip and speculate and make up wild stories about the doings of others in their community.

My interview with Wayne was a twenty-four-hour sensation in our area, but was soon exhausted as a topic. The Baron von Steuben and his activities crowded my troubles right off the stage.

No clear idea as to his role in the army filtered down to us from the exalted heights where decisions in an army are taken.

Rumors, however, flocked to the subject like crows to a new-sown field. I was told that Hamilton had been heard saying the Baron was to be the General's second-in-command; others insisted that he was a spy for Congress, who had come to insure that Gates would replace the General; there was insistence that the Hessians in Philadelphia were all about to desert—when they came over, the Baron would command them. (Why the Hessians were expected to leave warm billets in the dead of winter for our bleak hillsides was never explained.)

The glittering star that Steuben wore on his chest (the Star of the Order of Fidelity of Baden, as I later learned) came in for long discussion. Surprisingly, in a republican army, there were few who objected to such ostentation. It had its effect, as I suppose was intended. Most of our country fellows speculated on how long it took the Baron's German servant to shine the thing, how much it was worth in hard cash, and how long it would be before some Jerseyite or Connecticuter stole it.

Mainly, I suppose, the advent of a striking new personality in such a dreary season accounted for the men's interest in Steuben. The oft-repeated statement that he was only a volunteer added sauce to the platter. Our soldiers had long been accustomed to foreigners of the Conway or Du Coudray or De Woedtke stamp (among others equally incompetent and boastful). Now we had a professional from Europe who did not ask to be commissioned a major general —*mirabile dictu!*

We had no clear idea of what he was doing, or what he was supposed to do. For several days he was everywhere in camp, from dawn to dusk. He and his retinue, in their bright new uniforms, with that big skinny hound frisking about them, would arrive at a brigade head-quarters and pass a few words with the brigade commander. Then, disregarding mud and snow and slush and ice, they'd walk up and down the company streets.

The Baron's behavior was odd for a man so obviously a dignitary of high order. He'd kneel in the snow to look at a guard's miserable footgear, most likely grotesque lumps of wrapped felt. He'd hold out his hand for a man's musket and examine it lock, stock, and barrel. Evidently he was not so fastidious as other foreigners of his station —he inspected the sinks; he would spend a half-hour in one of the fetid hospitals, with young Duponceau translating questions and answers. Wherever a squad or company had enough men on the duty list to make drilling worthwhile, he would stand and stare at them, pulling on his full lips and muttering to his aides.

We saw him nearby one day, in the area of the Seventh Pennsylvania, peering closely at the construction of one of their huts. He examined the corner saddles of the logs, poked at the chinking with a fat forefinger, mounted a stump to get a better view of the roof.

"What the hell's he looking for?" Harm Tallman asked.

Joe Williams grinned. "Tell you one thing he's going to be looking for, if he ain't careful. That big dog, and he ain't going to find him.

Jed Palmer will have him in a stew with a few turnip skins to flavor him."

"I wonder," Hawk said quietly. "I just wonder. Matt, you been able to find out anything more about him?"

"No, sir," I said. "Just what's got around. That he was a lieutenant general for the King of Prussia, and fought the Russians and the French and the Austrians. I hear that everybody at headquarters thinks highly of him, but that the General hasn't committed himself at all."

"Say," Harm said suddenly, "looks as if he's coming this way."

It wasn't odd that he chose to visit us. He'd been all over the camp; he had to hit us sooner or later.

"Maybe I ought to pull foot," I said. "His aides made an almighty fuss about me at headquarters."

"Might as well face him," Hawk said mildly. "He don't look as if he bites."

Williams licked his lips. "That's a young dog, Harm. Tell you what —you toll him around in back of one of the huts and I'll get me a tommyhawk——"

"Let be," Hawk said. "Somebody was to hear you, and that dog did disappear, you'd have some tall talking to do."

"Dog meat ain't bad at all, Hawk, when you're hungry. On the way to Quebec, in them Canadian swamps, there was some dogs——"

Joe lapsed into silence as Steuben and the three young Frenchmen came striding into our area. The dog raced up to us and we all fondled him, Williams perhaps a shade lingeringly.

"Good morning, gentlemen," Duponceau said as they came up. "The Baron von Steuben wishes to visit with you and observe your huts and facilities."

"We got huts, friend," Williams said, smiling vacantly, "but I ain't so sure about them facilities. What are they, anyways?"

"Let be, Joe," Hawk said. "Good morning to you, sir. The Baron is welcome."

"Do any of you speak German or French?" Duponceau asked. "The Baron has no English."

They all looked at me, whereupon Steuben and his officers did also. I thought that the young men's faces chilled a bit, but the Baron's mouth stretched into a delighted grin.

"Aha, the young Lieutenant Hill, who was first to greet me upon my arrival," he said in his heavy French. To my surprise, he stepped forward and pumped my hand vigorously but awkwardly, as if this were a new American habit that he intended to waste no time learning.

"I am happy to see you again, Lieutenant," he said.

"Yes, sir. Thank you, sir."

I introduced him and the other gentlemen, whose names I somehow remembered, to Hawk and Harm and Joe.

"I was told," the Baron said, "by the men of the neighboring regiment that this company of—what do you say? yes, rangers—that your company led in the construction of the huts in this area. May I look at them, please?"

"Go right ahead," Hawk said, when I translated. "Tell him, Matt, to poke anywhere he wants to."

My father was then struck with a heavy coughing attack, such as were coming on him these days with increasing force. He turned his back to us, bending his shoulders. I stepped forward, but he motioned me away. Steuben stared at him with troubled eyes, then looked inquiringly at me.

"Your father, sir, is a sick man. Why does he stay here in this stark camp? He should be at home with loving care."

"He understands French, sir," I said quickly in a low voice. "He will not go home until we are through the winter."

Steuben nodded gravely, then spoke aside to Duponceau. He turned again to me and spoke so Hawk could not hear him. "I just told Duponceau, monsieur, to make note in his journal—another example of the amazing spirit I find here. In all my military operations never have I seen so many men so faithful in their service to a cause. It is a wonderful thing to view such devotion with these tired eyes."

Hawk turned back to us, looking pale, but not otherwise in distress. "Ask him what he wants to see, Matt," he whispered, "and we'll do our best to show him."

It turned out that Steuben wanted to see everything, especially when he viewed our men in their hunting shirts, moccasins, and leather leggings. He had heard, he said, of Morgan's corps of riflemen, but had not yet had the chance to see them, encamped as they were at the Gulph Mills. I assured him that our company, although perhaps more sober of mien in the general run of things, could easily take its place in the rough-and-tumble rifle corps.

He looked at several rifles fashioned by the master smiths of Pennsylvania, telling us that such weapons were furnished to a few regiments of the King of Prussia's army, although the German weapon was much shorter in the barrel.

"Why do you have the long barrel, Lieutenant?" he asked. "Surely in the forest it is not so easy to handle as the shorter one?"

"For greater accuracy, sir. The lands in the barrel are so much longer they give the shot a stronger twisting motion. They carry true much farther, enabling a man to knock a deer or other game at range that would be impossible with an ordinary piece."

"True," he said. "I have seen rifle marksmen in Europe hit a circle the size of a dinner platter at one hundred yards."

I grinned broadly, translating this into English for the others. Harm snorted, and Joe Williams spat. Hawk smiled briefly, saying, "Give him a show, Matt. Let's see—call Teunis Ekerson and Pete van Houten. They'll do. Too bad your brother Johnny isn't here."

I hailed Ekerson and Van Houten from their labors at chunking firewood, telling them to bring their rifles.

The Baron smiled warmly when I told him he was to see an exhibition of the excellence of the Pennsylvania long rifles. He eyed the doleful Teunis and long-legged Van Houten critically.

"These are your best marksmen, eh?"

"Why, no sir," I said. "Just about any of us can do the same, given the weapon to do it. They may shoot a little better than most of us, because they have fine rifles."

I spoke to Ekerson and Van Houten. "You don't mind, do you, boys, if you show the Baron von Steuben a little Deerkill Valley shooting?"

"Good shooting, or just ordinary, Matt?" Van Houten asked.

"Make it good. You've got to do better than to hit a dinner plate at a hundred yards. That's what they do in Europe."

Van Houten guffawed, and Ekerson slackened his sad face into the semblance of a smile.

Steuben interrupted Duponceau, who was translating rapidly in a low voice. "Lieutenant Hill, tell me one thing. Am I to understand that these are private soldiers?"

"Yes, sir."

"And also do I understand that you *asked* them if they would *object* to shooting?"

"Yes, sir. They might not be willing to—" I paused, trying to think of the French phrase for "show off" but failing, "—they might not wish to perform as in a circus, sir."

He shook his head wonderingly. "I have a lot to learn, Lieutenant, about your independent people. You, an officer, do not just order a man to do something, you ask him if he will object to doing it."

It seems to me that we take a perverse pleasure in defending before strangers those very institutions that we sometimes strongly criticize ourselves. (You can criticize your school and your schoolmaster who teaches the children all the wrong things, or does not teach them at all, but let some stranger come to your town and turn up his nose at the school; you will set upon him violently.) So it was with me. I had argued for the better part of two years against what seemed to me the intemperate language of the Declaration of the Congress, and further, that it could not be implemented in our society.

Now I quoted it quietly to Baron de Steuben: ". . . We hold these truths to be self-evident, that all men are created equal . . ."

He nodded enthusiastically. "That is what I mean, Lieutenant Hill. You believe it, you say it, and you put it into effect."

I don't know if my face turned red, but evidently Hawk understood a lot more French than he'd ever let on—when I glanced at him he had his tongue pouched in his cheek to check his smile and his eyes were flashing laughter at me. "You do believe that, don't you, son?"

I spoke to Ekerson and Van Houten. "All right, boys, go to it, and make it good."

A few stunted pines had been left on the ridge to the right of our encampment, about eighty yards away. There were no huts in that direction, nor any soldiers at work or drill in the area. A few words of consultation among the two marksmen and Harm Tallman sent

Harm walking up to the pines. There he busied himself searching the ground beneath them, then cutting some long thrums from his hunting shirt. He tied five pine cones to the thrums and finally tied the thrums to a branch of a pine, in line with the bole of another tree that would stop the balls.

Van Houten held up his arm, watching the slight wind stir the thrums on his shirt. Then he eyed the waggling of a few leaves left on the shrubs around us. Finally he put his forefinger in his mouth, then held it in the air. He shook his head.

"It keeps shifting, Matt. Three out of five do?"

I nodded.

They both loaded their rifles, measuring the powder carefully into the barrel. They selected balls from their shot bags by rolling them between thumb and forefinger, then viewing them critically for imperfections. They pouched them in greased linen patches and drove them carefully home with the ramrods. They primed their pans with fine powder, and were ready to shoot. Teunis nodded to Van Houten.

Pete raised the long rifle in seeming careless fashion, took an even breath, held steady and squeezed off. He missed.

"Goddam," he said softly.

Teunis Ekerson stepped to the line. *"He putteth down one and setteth up another,"* he said.

The three young Frenchmen were talking eagerly among themselves. Duponceau stepped forward. "Does anyone wish to wager, Monsieur Hill?" he asked me.

"We have no money," I said.

"I have a few coins," Hawk said. "What will the bet be?"

"That your marksmen," said Duponceau, "do not hit one of the targets in five shots."

"Done," Hawk said. They matched coins for value, the wager coming to perhaps fifty dollars Continental (the worth of a gallon of applejack). Then Hawk nodded to Ekerson.

The rifle cracked. One pine cone disappeared.

In rapid succession, the two men stepped to the line. Neither missed again.

"Marvelous!" Steuben said. "Never have I seen such shooting. I would not have believed it had I not witnessed it."

"You tell him, Matt," Van Houten said, "how come I missed the first time. I didn't spit on the ball."

I laughed, translating. Steuben nodded delightedly. "The same in fishing. One spits on the bait for good fortune."

When Steuben had looked over our encampment to his satisfaction, Hawk asked him and his aides to stay for the noon meal. The best Eben and Glennis could manage was a thin stew, but there was plenty of cornbread, which the Europeans had never tasted before. They marveled about that as they did about so many things that were commonplace to us: the saddles in the logs, the chinking qualities of clay, the utility of buckskin clothing for field purposes, and each and every outlandish tale that Williams and Tallman told them. Hawk had to intervene several times, seeing that our visitors were taking in as gospel all that Joe and Harm said. (In point of fact, we discovered later that the only two matters in which they took no stock were just about the only truths that Williams and Tallman told: that one can catch trout in the hand by tickling them on the belly, and that the raccoon carefully washes his food before eating it.)

At length Steuben said that he and his staff must get on with their survey of the camp. There was not time enough, he said, for all they had to do.

"Ask him, Matt," Hawk said, "just what it is he will do here."

Steuben laughed. "How many times have I already been asked that question? Let me say it this way: I know what it is I must do, but the decision to do it must come from His Excellency, the General."

"That's no answer," Hawk said, smiling as I translated. "Ask him again."

The Baron nodded amiably. "I was not evading an answer. It is not simply stated, but I will try. I must make an army of soldiers of you. You are already veterans of much fierce fighting, but you are not soldiers. If the General permits, I will institute a program of drill and training and discipline as we knew in the armies of the great Frederick of Prussia, so that in the spring campaign, when you go forth to face the army of Sir William Howe, you will stand equal to them. There is not much time, but it can be done."

I translated that as closely to his phrasing as possible, and I tried

254

not to let my lip curl as I did so, but the Baron must have sensed, from either my face or my voice, that I thought his plan was visionary.

"Aha, Monsieur Hill, you do not believe I can do it?"

I shrugged, forgetting Wayne's recent order that I was not to talk of defeat. "You've been here several days, sir. You've seen these few thousands—one third of them sick, one third without enough clothing to cover them, all of them down to skin and bones because there's no food to put strength and health in them. Hundreds are buried in shallow trenches—they died like flies in January. Come spring, sir, the British will come out after us. Ten, twelve, fifteen thousand of them. We'll stand to them—for about twenty minutes. Then we'll run. We always run, sooner or later. No, sir, I don't believe you or any man can do it."

"What are you telling him, Matt?" Hawk asked. "You're going too fast for me to understand."

"Telling him what I believe, Hawk—that it won't work."

"Then tell him what I believe. That's only fair. Tell him I know he's just what we've always needed. Tell him not to worry about how little time he has. Tell him he will find that our boys learn faster than any soldiers he's ever seen, in Europe or anyplace else. Tell him that I know he will succeed."

I did as my father asked, adding that he and I had never agreed about the war, that I knew it was almost over now, but that Hawk still thought we could win.

"Almost over," the Baron laughed. "No, no, my young friend. Do not say that. It would mean I made that long and terrible ocean voyage for nothing. Your clever Monsieur Franklin in Paris did not send me all this way for a lost cause. I know what I can do, Lieutenant Hill. You will see how I do it. You will see a miracle."

"We need one," I said.

"And perhaps you will help perform this miracle, if you will. Ask your father if he will detach you to my staff. I need your services badly. You will help me to save the time that we need so badly to get this miracle accomplished."

I was astounded. "Sir, I know nothing of drills and military maneuvers. I couldn't help you at all. There are many officers in camp who served in European armies. Any of them could help you more than I."

"Pah! Drills I teach you in five minutes. I don't want you for drills. For drills I will soon have scores of men. Listen to me, my friend Hill. You are—how do you say it?—a man of the frontier, the back country? Correct?"

I nodded, puzzled at his meaning.

"So, how many men of the frontier are in this army? A thousand, maybe? Maybe more, maybe less. And these woodsmen, how do they act when the Baron von Steuben might want them to do something? How did you act when I met you in the road the other day? Aha, you see? They open the mouth, they stare with wide eyes, they do not understand a word. All the time, behind the open mouth and the wide eyes, they laugh at me. They do not like strangers, foreigners, and especially they do not like foreign barons with magnificent stars gleaming on the chest. Correct?"

I could not help smiling, as I thought of Conklin and Ekerson and Blauvelt and the Welch brothers, if they were to line up before this baron. They'd be slack-jawed, as he said, and just about the most stupid human beings you could imagine, and all the while, as Steuben said, they'd be rocking with inner laughter.

"No, my dear Hill, I do not mind being laughed at. I am getting old and getting fat and I speak no more than a few words of English. Goddam, eh? So they laugh. Now laughing wastes time, and we have no time to waste. You are just the man for these men of the frontier. I have other Americans in mind to help me, but not of the frontier. My three gentlemen here have as much to learn of your independent soldiery as I do. So I need you, Lieutenant Hill. I need you to tell me when they are laughing at me, so I can laugh with them, get it done with, and get on with the task. Agreed?"

Hawk had apparently been following most of the conversation. "He's asking you to help, Matt?"

"That's right, Hawk."

"You do it, son. I know a good man when I see one, and this one is all right." Hawk's voice dropped. "Maybe he struts a little like a turkey cock, and maybe that star is a bit too shiny for our taste, but I like him, Matt. You join up with him."

"What about you and the company, Hawk?"

"Good Lord, we can make out fine. You get in at the start of this training routine of his and learn all you can. That will help this company more than you could if you stayed here to run the wood and water details. I can do that, Harm can do it, Walter Luckey can do it. You take on with this baron."

"I dunno," I said unhappily. "His Frenchmen and I didn't hit it off well the other day."

"You can get along with anybody you want to," he said, smiling, "even Glennis. You do it, Matt. I have it in mind that this is what we've been waiting for."

"Is it an order, Hawk?"

"No, Matt. Not this far along the road. It will be your company soon. I wouldn't give you orders now."

"But you're sure I ought to do it?"

He smiled again. "I'm not wrong too often, am I, Matt?"

I nodded, turning to the Baron. "All right, sir. When do you want me to report to you?"

He grinned, reaching out to pump my hand with that awkward excess of energy. "At dawn tomorrow, Lieutenant. Hard work every day for months, dawn to sunset. And we make soldiers of them, eh?"

He shook hands with Hawk and the rest, then he and his young Frenchmen and the dog were off again on their whirlwind rounds.

I wondered if I had done the right thing in accepting. Happenstance had led Steuben to me, his request that I serve him was on the spur of the moment. I wondered how much help I could be to him. I thought of Hawk—should I leave him all day, every day? At this point, I was beginning to wish that my mother had spoken only English in our house. If I couldn't speak French, I'd never have found myself in this fix, if fix it was.

Since we were serving with the Pennsylvania division, Hawk thought it proper that headquarters be notified that I was to be on detached service. I walked there to have the order put on record. While I was talking to the orderly, General Wayne came stomping in, in a hurry as usual. He brushed by me, then stopped suddenly and looked back.

"What do you want, Hill?" he asked, frowning, as if whatever it was would mean trouble.

I explained that Steuben had asked for my services.

He stared at me as if I were a damned liar, his face clouded, then he shook his head puzzledly. Finally his mouth twitched, then he roared with laughter.

"You didn't like those Frenchies, and now you'll be surrounded by 'em all day long! That's rich, that is."

He stopped grinning, looking at me soberly, nodding his head. "I know what he's going to try to do, and I like it, Hill. You know me, and you know that I never stop trying to make better soldiers of my men. They're the best division in the army now, but they can be much better. You learn everything that German teaches, Hill, and then learn what he doesn't teach. Every damn single thing that will make a man a better soldier I want you to learn! And when you've learned 'em, you bring 'em back and teach my boys. If I find another division learning more and learning it faster, I'll have your head."

"Yes, sir. I'll do my best."

"Of course you will," he said, turning instantly to good humor again. He began to chuckle. "Watch those Frenchmen, Hill. Before we know it, you'll be eating frogs and snails and saying they're better than deer meat."

CHAPTER SEVENTEEN

"You learn everything that German teaches," Wayne had told me.

It wasn't as simple as that. To serve under Steuben, a man had to discover so many new talents that he never knew he possessed that half the time his brain would be a-whirl trying to keep up with the Baron.

He was older by two years than the General, but he had the energy and stamina of a boy of twenty. He was invariably up before dawn, had shaved and dressed and breakfasted before the rest of the encampment came to life. I never arrived early enough to find him not already working. We pitched in with him, his three Frenchmen and myself, and sometimes Colonels Hamilton and Laurens. We kept at it until darkness stopped us.

What did we do? We did a thousand things actually, and some of them seemed to have little or nothing to do with each other, but, put all together, we fashioned a provisional training program for the army in a shade under two weeks.

Not such a difficult task for a professional soldier? Perhaps not, although we had dozens of professionals ranging from major generals down to smooth-cheeked French lieutenants, and we'd never had a shadow of a training regimen before.

We had one now, after two weeks of what I can only call a modern Tower of Babel.

Day after day, we plunged into paperwork—most of it a drill manual. Steuben wrote furiously on upon dozens of pages of foolscap, mostly in German since that was his military language, so to speak. Then Duponceau translated it by some roundabout method of his own, arriving eventually at English, or what he thought was English. I translated his translation, if you will, into American speech that could be understood and acted upon by a sergeant like Jared King.

Our never-ending problem was a confusion of terms. Duponceau or De L'Enfant would keep repeating a word or phrase to me in French, Duponceau would try it in English, and neither word would mean a thing to me, all the while Steuben was telling us the word in German, French and, I believe, in either Polish or Russian. Sometimes we had to finish with Colonel Hamilton to decide what we were all talking about. Usually I found the answer to be some simple American word or expression as familiar to me as my hunting knife, quite lost in the slippery business of translation.

"No time," Steuben would say. "We have no time."

Translating for the manual, however, was not enough. The sheets had to be copied many times by a dozen clerks, who had to supply fourteen brigades with copies for every company. Then, all day long, we were writing reports for Steuben: all kinds of reports flowed from that quick pen of his, and they contained dozens of suggestions for improving the camp conditions and the health and welfare of the men. We made flying inspection trips a half-dozen times a day. You had only to mention something in the encampment with which he was not familiar, and the Baron had to run to look at it. General Sullivan's bridge across the Schuylkill, the rifle corps in a sham battle, an arriving drove of beef cattle for the commissaries, a court-martial of an officer who stole his men's rations—a hundred other things he observed, noted, made suggestions concerning, and tucked away into his memory.

Every day at the noon meal we had our English lesson. "Goddam, Matt," the Baron would say, "speak de English to me."

"Goddam" was his favorite word, and it was difficult to tell him that the General's lady and Mrs. Greene and Lady Stirling would not appreciate its use at dinner. He learned the soldiers' other rough phrases as time went by and sprinkled most of his conversations with them.

It seemed to me that he learned to understand English quite rapidly, but his speaking of it was a horse in a different barn. He said outrageously funny things most solemnly, with involute constructions and the right words in all the wrong places. He never got angry, though, when Duponceau and I laughed at him. He would just grin with us and listen attentively when we corrected him.

There was a certain stiffness among the three Frenchmen and myself for a day or two, but I soon found out that they were all splendid fellows, that each combined intelligence with efficiency.

All four of us were soon joined in admiration and respect for Baron von Steuben. No matter how hard he drove us with his muttering about "no time, no time," we worked unshirkingly to get the preparations made for the grand opening of the training program.

Every man in camp, I suppose, came to understand that the Baron was going to make drastic changes in the army. I was badgered with questions from all sides, but I had to answer truthfully that I knew little about what he intended to do, since I'd never had much military training myself. I would be a recruit as raw as the rest of them when the time came.

Steuben was still a volunteer, although we on his staff knew by this time that he craved the appointment as inspector general of the army, in place of the worthless Conway. We understood that the General was prepared to ask Congress to make the appointment. This would give the Baron, in effect, the rank and pay of a major general, but would not give him a command in the Continental Line. None of the brigadier generals could thus be angered by a Congressional appointment of yet another foreigner to rank higher than their own.

He smiled shrewdly when he spoke to me of the post of inspector general. "Your wise old man Franklin said to me in Paris: 'My dear Baron, if you ask to be commissioned a major general, you'll cause every brigadier general in the army to pack up and go home. So you say again and again you are only a volunteer, and Congress will be so happy to find a selfless man they'll finish by making you a major general anyway.' That dear Franklin. A very wise man. But alarming! My God, the number of plots that chase one another through his brain!"

He didn't tell me what other plots Franklin had made known to him, but one I thought I could put my finger on. I will dispose of it now, and have done with it, and henceforth in this narrative he will simply be and remain "Baron von Steuben" or "Baron de Steuben." He used both German and French spellings. Begin with the title: "Lieutenant General in the service of the King of Prussia." I knew by this time that he was no more a lieutenant general than I was. In preparing some of the vast number of presentations that he made to the General and to the Congress, I examined his documents and personal records. His actual highest rank in the service of Frederick the Great had been *Quartiermeister General Leutnant*, which in any other army might have ranked him as a somewhat glorified drill captain. It is, at least, somewhat startlingly different from being a lieutenant general. I have always been convinced that the shining star on his chest, and the words dropped here and there about exalted rank and great estates in Europe, as well as the insistence that he was nothing but a volunteer—all were products of two able brains in Paris, his and Franklin's, plotting together to make his arrival in America most spectacular.

Was he a baron? Did he leave estates and fortunes in Europe to cast his lot with us? Or was he a half-pay captain, a penniless adventurer, who sold his sword? I know the answers, but I care not for them. I say only that he was a man I respected.

He worked us so hard that I scarcely saw my father, Glennis, or the rest of the Deerkill people. Indeed, I rarely thought of them during the long busy days. Hawk seemed about the same when I saw him by firelight, although his coughing had become almost incessant. He asked searching questions about my work with Steuben, and seemed inordinately pleased at my answers. I had a wait-and-see attitude toward what the Baron planned to do. I could scarcely believe that he could work the miracle that he had predicted.

How unlikely was it? Well, the British would surely come out after us as soon as the frost came out of the ground and the resulting mud had dried into a surface that could carry artillery and wagons. May 1, that could be the target date. Here we were well into March, and not a man trained yet, even if one believed that training at this point would do any good at all.

Suddenly—you might say before we on Steuben's staff realized we were ready—the great day came.

We were to start with one hundred picked men, to be added to the General's guard. They were selected for intelligence and leadership, from each brigade of the army. Since I had something to do with the orders for their assembly, I included Jared King of our company on the list.

The plan was this: each brigade had a new officer's rank, brigade inspector, who would be responsible for training his brigade. As Steuben put the model company—the one hundred, as we came quickly to call them—through its drill routine, the brigade inspectors would learn by demonstration and take the lesson back to their brigades. The one hundred men would always be five or six drills ahead of the rest of the army, ready to show skill in any portion of the drill that the rest were learning. Each day, brigade inspectors and other officers without specific duties were to attend drills on the Grand Parade.

On Thursday, March 19, there was a snap in the morning air and the wind picked the smoke from hut chimneys and whisked it away with a low moan. I felt well, however; as I stepped from our hut in the dawn, I heard a pair of phoebes calling in the distance near the river: "Phee-bee! Phee-bee!" The phoebe's complaint is for me one of the sure signs of spring, rather than the appearance of the robin, who as every hunter knows, has been in numbers in the deep woods all winter, anyway.

On the Grand Parade the hundred men were assembled waiting for us.

It is necessary to explain one of the great problems in our project. If our army had had a drill system in the first place, it would have been modeled on the British system, with competent drill sergeants to train the men. We had neither capable officers to put the system into effect nor drillmasters to execute it, but whatever the men knew about drilling was done in clumsy imitation of British regulars. We had to eliminate all that imitation. The Baron's system was the Prussian drill, reduced to fundamentals. We had to start from scratch, from the top down and the bottom up.

Had we not been so serious and so intent on the job at hand, had not the General's orders underlined the importance of this program, I have no doubt that we would all have collapsed with laughter that first day, and that might have been the end of the drill system and the end of Steuben's American adventure.

The Baron alone was as good as an entire team of traveling clowns.

The first thing he did was to point a pudgy forefinger at eight men, motioning them to step forward from the ranks. Then he assumed himself the "position of a soldier" with a borrowed musket. He directed the men by pantomime to imitate him. Then he moved along the front, correcting each soldier's posture and bearing. Back went the shoulders and in went the bellies to escape the jabbing of his fingers.

The first laughter came when he tapped a man's chin to close his gaping mouth. Having painstakingly memorized the English commands of the simple drill, the Baron began to use them. His "dress right" and "dress left" produced only wondering stares from his recruits.

"Goddam, Matt," he cried. "Explain dem."

While I told them what he wanted them to do, he did an exaggerated pantomime with Duponceau and DePontière. When the men moved to comply, the Baron hopped up and down the line like some gigantic flea, poking elbows and kicking at misplaced feet, straightening muskets. The poor fellows shuffled and tangled themselves; one dropped his musket into the sticky mud, and the Baron lashed him unmercifully in harsh German, punctuating the sentence with "Goddam."

The rest of the hundred were enjoying wonderfully the trials of their comrades; all the spectators were laughing. I watched the Baron narrowly, expecting him to take quick-tempered offense to the raillery. He did not. He seemed to pay no attention, but went into a display of the slow step forward. He stepped off with his left leg a dozen times, tapping it with his hand as he did so, shouting "left" and "vun" alternately. Then he motioned them forward, singing the cadence in his thick voice: "VUN—Two—Tree—Four—VUN—Two—Tree—Four."

They hadn't moved five yards before they were all out of step, stumbling to regain it. The Baron shouted, "Halt!" He unleashed a short stream of German, then French, asking them what was the matter, then shouted in English, "Vot? Vot?"

One tall Virginian in the first rank spread a broken-toothed grin. "Smith has got two left feet, Your Lordship."

The watching crowd laughed, and I translated what the man had said.

Instead of a reprimand, the Baron grinned back at the man. "I tink so. You vas Schmidt, nein?"

The drill continued to be a comedy for a few more minutes, as they tried marching again, the about face, the march to the rear. Then they had left face and right face.

The Baron finally gave this squad the command to halt. He looked at me, then back to the hundred men, ignoring the spectators. "Explain dem, Matt," he said in English, then began to speak authoritatively in French, halting at the end of each sentence so that I might translate.

"We all laugh at ourselves, and that is good. But you men who have been drilling are the only ones who have the right to laugh now. You know more than any man here at this moment about being a practiced soldier. Soon you will all know. We had good cause for humor, these fifteen or twenty minutes. It is ended now. We will get serious. Next squad, forward."

Before two hours had gone by, the entire draft was divided into squads. The Baron went from one group to another, watching their efforts like a suspicious schoolmaster, poking and pushing them into place, singing out the cadence here and there, tossing explosive "Goddams" at errors.

I was busy, as was Duponceau. We traveled among the squads, explaining commands and striving to execute them with the benefit of our limited practice in the Baron's quarters. I suppose it might have been eleven by the position of the pale March sun when I noticed that the atmosphere of the Grand Parade had changed.

There was little laughter at the awkward squads. In place of merriment was an air of excitement. Where there had been forty or fifty officers watching us in the hour after dawn, now there were perhaps two hundred. At least a brigade of soldiers followed the action on the Parade with sharp eyes. They were ranged in quiet groups around the muddy field, very few of them pointing and guffawing.

There were general officers among them, staring keenly at the portly Baron, who scampered like a schoolboy. There were field officers, dozens of regimental commanders, some of them talking earnestly but never taking their eyes from the drill squads.

Standing away from other officers, I saw my father, Glennis by his side. He was leaning forward on a hickory staff that Eben Lowry had cut for him. His sunken eyes were fixed on me; when he knew that I had seen him, he raised one hand in a curious gesture of encouragement, as if he had to tell me to get forward with what I was doing. Glennis smiled and waved.

Turning back to the squad that I was drilling for the moment, I hoped that I appeared to be proficient, even though I was learning as the men were.

At this point, the Baron thought that each squad had mastered its first few lessons. He formed them into a company and took command himself.

Here was a result of his long days of planning, of his muttering, "No time! We have no time!" There would be a shortening of the usual procedure for drilling recruits in the regiments of Frederick the Great: so many days for the squad, so many for the platoon, so many for the company. The Baron was determined that each day's lesson would begin with the squad and end with the company assembled. So we finished the morning with marching and countermarching in formation, trying again and again the few simple drill procedures that the hundred men had learned.

Steuben took them through this company drill himself. There was no laughter now when his voice roared, "VUN—Two—Tree—Four, VUN—Two—Tree—Four. Left! Left! Goddam, mit der left!"

Freed of responsibility for the moment, I walked to Hawk and Glennis.

"A wonder," Hawk said softly to me. "A man like that—a lieutenant general from Europe—a nobleman like those that Billy Howe has—a man with that star on his chest so proudly, and he's down in the mud with the private soldiers. He's drilling 'em the way a sergeant would, if he had a sergeant as good a soldier as he is. It's a wonder, Matt."

I smiled. "They learn fast," I said.

He waved his hand abruptly. "That's not it. That's not it, a-tall, Matt. It's Steuben. We got him to do it. Those soldiers could learn anything they had to, so long as there's a man to teach 'em. I'm glad we got him."

"Tell Matt about the colonels, Hawk," Glennis said swiftly.

He smiled, started to speak, then coughed at length, painfully. "Colonels," he said finally. "Yes. Ten minutes ago. We were standing near a few of 'em. Young Burr that was with Arnold to Quebec. Van Cortlandt from New York. Dick Butler from our division. Some others. One of 'em says, 'Look at him. It's not good for the men to have a high officer teaching them drill.' Another says, 'Good Lord! Look at him! He's touching them with his hands.' Then Dick Butler speaks up, not loud, you know, but so everybody could hear him, 'I sure to God wish that I was soldier enough to go out there in the mud to help him.' Look at the generals watching, Matt. This is a big thing, I tell you."

"Let's hope so, Hawk," I said, unable as always to gain his enthusiasm. "We're about done now, so why don't you go back to the hut? You must be tired."

"Ha! I'll go back, all right, and take a good rest, because I'm coming back here this afternoon, and tomorrow morning, and every day from here on. I don't want to miss a thing."

I looked at him worriedly, knowing that it was too much to expect him to summon the strength to stand for long periods without rest.

Glennis spoke up. "The Welch boys will make us a bench, Matt. They'll bring it down each morning and take it back each night, so nobody will steal it for firewood. We'll make out fine, Matt. It will do Hawk good to be in the sun and fresh air. That's what Doc Walden said. Sun and fresh air."

In the afternoon the guard company assembled again on the Grand Parade. First we reviewed the morning's drill, then Steuben gave them wheel to the right and wheel to the left until all the squads had it to precision. Finally, in double ranks, they went through the full list of movements they had been taught through the day.

On Friday morning we started all over again and, as a schoolmaster might surmise, there were some who had lost their mastery of yesterday's lesson overnight. Steuben advanced the step, gave each squad new commands as soon as he thought they were ready. All day long we were at it, dawn to dusk. The Baron was by turns demanding, dominating, speechless with exasperation, blasphemous in three languages, stern, and tireless. Withal, he was kind and human and patient. Perhaps he swore at length with a slow learner before him, but the man knew he was not being cursed with malice. The men grinned at Steuben, made their sly back-country jokes even though he couldn't understand them, and they growled at the pace he set for them.

One could not have served in the army for two years without learning to read these soldiers' minds through their eyes and voices. It became quickly apparent to me, before the second day was through, that this middle-aged, portly stranger whom Franklin had sent us, be he lieutenant general or half-pay captain, would soon be second to only one man in the hearts of the Continental Line.

CHAPTER EIGHTEEN

Every unnecessary detail and maneuver had been eliminated from the Prussian drill system to render to our efforts more speed and more effectiveness in a short time.

Day after day we went on, passing from soldier's drill to musket instruction. Steuben took the weapons from the men's hands and showed them exactly what he wanted. From initial wrinkles of his big nose when he handled a dirty or rusty weapon, he proceeded to stern admonition and then the punishment of extra drill. Soon enough every man came to the Grand Parade with his weapon shining bright, lock and stock and barrel. Woe to the man who dropped his musket into the mud!

They learned how to carry weapons on the march, so that they could move quickly and efficiently, and look formidable and soldierly. Further, a few men here and there in every campaign would be saved from having their heads blown off by a comrade marching before or behind.

Most important of all, they learned the use of one of the vital items of their equipment.

Bayonets in our army had always been useful. A man could broil a strip of beef on his bayonet, or use it to turn journey cakes without burning his fingers. In the absence of shovels, they were good for digging sinks and tent trenches on the march. In the lack of axes, they cut evergreen bedding from trees. If a man wanted to fish, he used his bayonet to turn up the sod in search of worms. If he was foraging or pillaging, the bayonet made a good tool for forcing hasps on reluctant barn doors. The bayonet had a hundred uses. The only time when the Continental Line found it worthless was in battle. Most men claimed its weight disturbed their aim, pulling the ends of their long muskets downward.

Steuben had questioned me closely on the use (or misuse) of the bayonet in the battles and skirmishes I had seen. Now he went to work. If our hundred thought they'd been driven in the drilling, they soon took a fresh view of that pleasant interlude. Steuben was satisfied with nothing less than precision in the use of the bayonet.

The Baron illustrated every action himself by taking a musket and acting as drill sergeant. To a newcomer on the scene, he might have presented a ludicrous figure, but our hundred men watched every move he made—their eyes never wandered as they watched him charge a straw butt with portly speed, feint, thrust, retrieve. Time and again he called the best of them forth from the line to demonstrate what might be done with bayonet and musket. A youngster of twenty, tall and strong, would defend himself against the charging figure of the Baron, who by army standards must be called an old man—the youngster's musket would go flying and he would find himself with the point of a knife-edged bayonet at his chest.

There came a day when the hundred men no longer lost their muskets to the Baron's thrust, or anyone else's. They had not yet learned as much about drill and their weapons and the importance of soldierly discipline in camp and on the march as their British cousins in regular regiments accepted as the basic training of a recruit, but what they knew already, they knew well.

The Baron's field show continued as the prime off-duty attraction of the encampment. Every day, even in the rain or sleet or the late snows of March, there were crowds of quiet men on the Grand Parade, watching intently. They knew their turn was coming; they wanted to be ready to learn.

There were other signs of the army's interest. It was a common sight, when one walked the regimental streets, to see men seated on benches before their huts, industriously sanding and honing their bayonets. In the dawn hours, before our assembly on the Grand Parade, you could hear in the still distance a cadence count: "ONE —TWO—THREE—FOUR! LEFT! LEFT! LEFT, GODDAMIT, LEFT!" as one of our hundred men took out a wood or water detail.

Sometimes you would see such a detail against the horizon, not lazing along in whatever grouping, but stepping out to the cadence count in *double rank and closed up*, as had never been seen in our army before.

The value that Steuben had sought in me was never needed other than to translate his military terms so our soldiers would not become hopelessly lost in a maneuver, or to translate their frontier phrases into the French that he could understand. The truculence, independence, and outright distrust toward a foreign officer never materialized. They took to Steuben as a flight of black ducks takes to a duckweed bed. Why? I believe the answer is simple: they knew a good man when they saw him and, what's more, they liked this one.

One of the handicaps we had expected actually turned into an advantage. He had only a few words of English to start with; he progressed slowly in speech, as I have said.

From the first, the hundred in the advanced drill squad were delighted when he tried to voice the commands in English, and sometimes they were convulsed when he exploded first into French and then into German. It was obvious to them that he was cursing them every way from Sunday.

"What was that there he called me, Lieutenant?" one of them might ask. "It sounded awful bad. What was it?"

"He just asked when your father and mother were going to get married," I would say, grinning.

"Now ain't that something?" the man would chortle. "That's a good one. I got to remember that one. Ain't he a bird, Lieutenant? A man that can swear in three languages, even if he ain't very good at it in English yet."

One of these incidents resulted in a valuable addition to Steuben's small staff. The Baron had shouted a command to wheel right, but had forgotten to use English. Some of the men must have guessed correctly, for they went right at the French words, but almost half of them went left, and a few thought he'd meant march to the rear. The confusion grew worse when he tried first in French and then in German to get them back into formation. I wasn't nearby, and Duponceau was at headquarters. The Baron was cursing at his best.

A young New York captain stepped from among the spectators

and asked the Baron's pardon in fluent French, then told the men to get back into formation and execute the proper maneuver. As the young captain interpreted, Steuben saw his order carried out in fine form.

This was Benjamin Walker, who became Steuben's aide and close friend and, to my relief, before long was able to take over my interpreting duties and whatever else needed doing.

These language problems recurred every day, with the Baron getting lost in foreign profanity. We all stood grinning one day while the Baron stuttered to a halt, then shouted: "*Viens*, Walker, *mon ami! Mon bon ami! Sacre!* Goddam de *gaucheries* of dese *badauds. Je ne puis plus.* I can curse dem no more."

With the exception of Wayne and a few others, our general officers resented the orders from headquarters forbidding them to drill their troops in whatever fashion had been used previously. They'd never bothered with drill before, but, being deprived of the privilege, they set their tongues to clacking.

They need not have worried, however, about another foreigner stepping into a higher command than their own. When Steuben's status was changed from "volunteer," he became, as we expected, Inspector General of the army, and although he had the rank and pay of a major general, he would not command Line troops in battle, and so threatened no brigadier general's glory.

We had another change in command that considerably bettered the fortunes of the army. The General named Greene as Quartermaster General, and that competent officer, although it was common knowledge that he had little taste for the job, worked night and day to get the men enough to eat and clothes to cover their backs.

By this time, the drill instructions written by Steuben and bound in blue covers (so universally called the *Blue Book*) were well distributed among the brigades. The brigade inspectors were familiar with the drill, by the book and by watching the hundred men.

The entire army, by the General's order, began to drill on the various brigade parades and on the Grand Parade. Morning and afternoon the hills resounded to the count, to sharp commands, to the sloshing of thousands of feet in the mud. Thanks to our efforts with the Guard Company, most of the junior officers and sergeants, and indeed most of the soldiers, had a pretty good idea of what to do because they had seen it done.

I served with Steuben through the end of March, when the drill by companies was so far progressed that it was time to drill by battalions. Then Joe Williams, who had been appointed brigade inspector for our brigade of the Pennsylvania division, was relieved of that duty to be sent to York for guns for the division. Wayne asked Steuben to release me to take his place.

To be truthful, I was more pleased than sorry to leave the Baron's staff, although that jovial gentleman and his young Frenchmen had long since endeared themselves to me. I wanted to be back with the Deerkill company, however. I had no wish to be separated from Hawk any longer by the dawn-to-midnight working hours that Steuben liked to keep.

Being close to Steuben while he worked away so industriously at his miracle during those late winter days at the Valley Forge will ever be one of the stirring memories of my life. Of late, I hear that there are small men who have sneered at him as an imposter—said indeed that he bilked the Congress of enough to support an entire brigade—admitted with a laugh that he was a good drillmaster, and by the admission damned him. I say that he was more: a warm human being, a kind friend, a good man blessed with priceless humor, and, in my belief, a great man in his assigned task. I do not think that any of those who scoff at the drillmaster in the mud could have done one tenth as much.

I divided my brigade (commanded by Colonel Hartley) into four battalions of not more than one hundred and twelve men each. The strength varied from day to day as the flux or camp fever struck the troops, but these were the basic units as ordered by Steuben.

We subdivided the battalions by companies and platoons, assigning officers to each as needed. Unemployed officers stood by to watch, then took turns in the units as the days went by.

The drill was the same as had been performed by the original hundred of the Guard Company. We progressed in the *Blue Book* as rapidly as we could. Sometimes Steuben would come riding to our parade; if we looked proficient, he would dash off to another brigade. If he didn't like what he saw, he might dismount and put us through the paces, or he might order us to report next day to the Grand Parade for a display of excellence and further lessons by the Guard Company. Wayne might come upon us at any moment, scowling, grinning, asking questions, making suggestions.

My brigade, I thought, was a good one. We were the first of the Pennsylvanians to take up the use of the bayonet. From that point, Wayne was with us almost all the day long. He'd take a musket himself and charge in sham battle with a platoon, telling me beforehand that doing something for oneself was the prime factor in learning to employ a skill.

(Who will not grant that he learned to employ that particular skill excellently? When his troops took Stony Point, they did it with fixed bayonets, without firing a shot.)

Day after day, Hawk, attended by Glennis, came with his bench to the parade. He leaned forward on his staff, never missing a maneuver. He always had good suggestions to make when I gave the men ten minutes for resting.

"Now, look you, Matt," he would say. "They're not fast enough when they deploy from column into line. That's one of the prime things you're teaching 'em. You know why?"

I shrugged. "They've got to think they're soldiers before they'll look like soldiers."

"That's not what I mean at all. You remember Brandywine?"

"How could I forget it? Another place we ran like rabbits."

"Why did we run? Why? Why? Because we couldn't get the army into the line. If we could have marched then without straggling, in formation instead of Indian file, and if every regiment had come into the line at the right time, the redcoats would still be running. You put some snap into 'em out there. Let 'em know what they're doing and why it's important that they do it. A lot of 'em still think this is some kind of play. Explain to them about Brandywine and

Germantown. Tell 'em what might have happened if the army had known then just the little bit it knows now."

I didn't share his enthusiasm, because I truly believed that centuries of military discipline, as most British regiments boasted of, could overwhelm a couple of months of tactical effort.

He kept at me on that score, until I took to arranging lecture sessions with the junior officers, the sergeants and corporals, explaining, as the Baron had explained it to me, why we did thus and so. I pointed out the obvious: that a brigade marching Indian file takes up four times as much space on the roadway as it would in columns of fours. I asked them to estimate for themselves how much longer it would take the Indian file to come into line. I stressed to them the rule that a brigade was to occupy no more space in a roadway than it would occupy upon coming into line of battle.

Hawk would listen to my talks and give them comments of his own. Indeed, they were all free to speak on any area of the drill. Hawk told them that when they commanded a detail, they should always march it in double rank and closed up, thus anticipating by a few days the General's order to that effect. He told them to talk about the reasons for every maneuver to the men in their commands, so that every soldier would know why the drills were emphasized. This was important, Hawk said, because that was the most frequent question asked by the private soldier in this army: "Why?" They had a right to know, my father said.

(Steuben had said much the same thing to me one night in his quarters. "Matt, it would be foolish to compare the soldier of America to those of Prussia or France or England. We used to say to a man, 'Do this,' and he did it. Here you have to say, 'This is the reason why you have to do this.' If he thinks the reason is good enough, then he will do it.")

Hawk's enthusiasm seemed boundless, and I caught myself wondering if perhaps he was not right in saying that Steuben was the single man the army needed, that great changes were on the horizon. Yet when I looked at the men, they were as gaunt as ever, as ill-clothed as ever, and there were so pitifully few of them in comparison to the great army that was readying for the spring campaign in the city twenty miles away.

The drums tapped a marching beat, and the four battalions were passing from column into line and from line into column. They were doing as well as the Guard Company, and I watched them proudly.

I stood at the side of the parade, having long since handed over my drillmaster's role to the junior officers and sergeants. I thought to myself: put them into red uniforms and Billy Howe would accept them.

I heard Glennis calling me from a distance, alarm in her voice. "Matt, come quick!"

She was fifty yards away, before one of the huts of the Seventh Pennsylvania. She waved to me frantically. It could only be Hawk. I ran through the slushy mud.

He was behind the hut, leaning weakly against the clay chimney, his fingers crooked into the chinking to hold him on his feet. The last light snow of the season had fallen the night before. It had not yet melted here in the shadow. At his feet, the white surface was splotched widely with bright red, frothy blood.

A hunter knows when his deer has a bullet through the lungs. I clenched my jaws and stepped to him. He smiled faintly and let me take him. He lifted his hand, tapped his chest with his forefinger, and smiled again.

I picked him up to carry him back to our hut. He was as light as a child in my arms.

When we came around within view of the parade, he turned his head that way to see the battalions wheeling. Then he looked at me and laboriously winked and smiled before he closed his eyes. I could feel his heart thumping heavily against my chest.

Doc Walden came quickly when Eben Lowry took him the word. He listened to me and Glennis, then bent over Hawk for a minute or two, listening to his breathing, checking his heart, testing his pulse. He turned away and motioned me outside.

"All right, Matt," he said softly. "You go to Wayne and fix yourself a furlough. Get one for him too. He will like that—the idea that he's coming back to the army."

"Can't you do anything, Doc?"

"No."

"You think he can stand the trip?"

276

"I do. I think he can stand almost anything to get to that Deer-kill Valley of his. It must be quite a place. Sometime when this war is over, I'm going to go take a look at it."

"I'll get everything ready," Glennis said, crying softly.

"Do that," Doc said. "We'll get some good thick mattresses with fresh straw and lots of blankets for you. You want a cart with good springs, Matt. Nothing but ruts in the roads all the way, I expect. It may be a day or so before you can move him."

"He lost a lot of blood, Doc," I said.

Walden nodded. "That's got to be expected. It will be all right, I think. He's a strong man, Matt. He had to be, to come through this winter."

CHAPTER NINETEEN

It was a warm sunny morning, the first real spring day that we'd had, and I was anxious to get on the long road northward. Yet how could I press for an early departure in view of the scene at the officers' hut?

Every man of the Deerkill company was lined outside, waiting for his turn to say good-by to Hawk. If that were all, we might have pulled away shortly after breakfast. It seemed to me that most of the Seventh Pennsylvania was there as well. There were also men from every brigade in the encampment, singly or in pairs, officers and soldiers. They stood around the huts, talking quietly until Glennis or Doc Walden told them they could go inside.

Hawk sat comfortably on his bunk, smiling easily and saying a few words to each man. His recovery from the hemorrhage seemed to me so remarkable that I could even believe he might gain strength and health under my mother's care.

I knew how weak Hawk was—Doc Walden prevented him from shaking hands with every man, as he wished to do—but his coughing seemed to have abated, and he claimed that the pain wasn't as bad as it had been.

I could have hoped for better days for him, had it not been for these farewells from his friends. Many a man came out of the hut blinking his eyes, or knuckling them to brush away tears.

Every so often while we waited, stolid Walter Luckey would come to stand beside me, saying, "It's hard to see him go, Matt. What will we do now? How can we manage without him?"

I went into the hut with Jed Palmer of the Seventh Pennsylvania, wanting to tell Doc Walden to hurry the visitors through.

I heard Palmer talking to Hawk. "When you get there, Captain, you tell your wife to fix you mush for breakfast every day, corn meal mush. That'll stick to your ribs and fatten you up so's you can get back here by the time we're ready to go after Billy Howe. You do that, Captain. Mush with lots of milk, and some honey on top if you got any."

"I thought it was turnip skins that would stick to your ribs, Jed." Hawk grinned at him.

"Ah, hell, Captain. You know as well's I do that turnip skins is all right if you ain't got one other damn thing to eat. Anything is all right if you ain't got nothing but whatever it is."

"All right, Jed. Mush it will be."

"And buttermilk, Captain. Buttermilk is good for a man that's run down a bit, like." Palmer paused. "We're going to miss you, sir. You get back as fast as you can. We'll lick them redcoats together, you and me and Wayne."

He wiped his eyes with the sleeve of his coat as he left the hut.

There were officers by the dozen who filed through the hut to say good-by, men who had known Hawk since the days at Boston. It gave me pleasure to see Steuben ride up, as always in a hurry. He dismounted; I led him inside. He exchanged a few words with Hawk in his halting English, switched to French for me to convey his regrets that so able a soldier was leaving, then left with sad eyes.

I had to go and get the cart, being overhauled and greased by a gunner in Knox's artillery. When I came back, I asked if Wayne had been there yet, because I wanted to get started. Joe Williams looked at me curiously. "Wayne ain't coming here," he said. "Didn't you know that?"

"Why isn't he, to say good-by to a man who has served him so well?"

Williams shook his head. "He's got something real important to do."

"Important!" I cried. "What in hell could be more important than properly saying good-by to one of his best officers? He'll look a long way before he finds another like Hawk."

"He knows that, Matt."

"Damned if I think he knows it! And damned if I'm not going to do something about it. When I get back, Joe, this company will go into the New York Line. Anthony Wayne can go to hell. Now we've got to leave. We can't wait for Wayne to stop doing whatever it is that's so important."

I told Doc shortly to bring Hawk out to the wagon. Glennis was already waiting, sitting very handsomely on the front seat, and dressed for once in proper female attire. The Deerkill men crowded around her, telling her they'd see her when the British were whipped, maybe come the first of August. They laughed and joked with her until Hawk came out, when they fell silent.

Hawk waved to them all, then Doc helped him into the wagon bed, where he could lie down on the comfortable thickness of three good mattresses that Doc had procured somewhere. He was tired by the leave-taking, so I wasted no time in putting the horses into their collars. I looked around for Harm Tallman and Joe Williams, to give them a few final words, but they were nowhere to be seen.

Couldn't they have stayed to see Hawk ride off? What's got into them, I wondered.

We followed the brigade road around the first group of Pennsylvania huts. This put us in full view of the Pennsylvania parade, where, as usual, both brigades were assembled for drill.

The rolling rattle of snare drums started as we came into view, accompanied by the shrill piping of two fifes, in the soldiers' favorite marching tune, *Yankee Doodle*. The two brigades marched smartly in column across the parade toward the edge of the road, then swung precisely to form line to the front.

"Can you sit up, Hawk?" Glennis asked. "It's for you."

He raised himself from the mattresses and faced the brigade lines. As we passed slowly along the road, battalion after battalion snapped muskets front in salute. The officers' commands rang crisply. Again and again, as I glanced back to see that my father was all right, I saw him raising his thin hand to his brow to return the salute.

At brigade center General Wayne waited for us, sitting his horse among a group of officers on foot. He moved his horse forward as we came up, and I saw that Harm and Joe Williams were among the officers in the group. Wayne saluted my father, his mouth splitting in his cocky grin that made him look so boyish at times.

"They look good, Captain Hill?"

"Splendid, sir, splendid."

"All right, then. Get yourself a good rest and come back to fight with 'em."

Hawk smiled weakly.

Wayne looked briefly at me. "Take good care of him," he said. "So, God speed you, Captain."

"Good-by, sir," Hawk said.

The drums rattled on, and the fifes squeaked the tune:

> *Yankee Doodle went to town,*
> *A-ridin' on a pony,*
> *Stuck a feather in his hat,*
> *And called him Macaroni.*

BOOK THREE

We had been blessed with good weather all the way, those warm days of early April that bite deep into the hidden frost and dry the roads so that traveling becomes a pleasure rather than a chore.

The grass was green in the valley as we came along the Deerkill. Above the runs and riffles, the caddis flies were fluttering in their awkward flight, swept more by the warm breeze than by their webbed wings to the safety of budding leaves and branches and rock over-hangs ashore. A hatch of caddis flies is a sure sign that the angler ought to look to his rods and lines, for the trout will be moving out to gorge themselves as the caddis worm leaves its case of stone or sticks at the bottom of the river and moves to its adult stage on the surface.

We followed the river road through the village, although I could have turned toward the ridge on any of the several woods roads that led to our house. Hawk said he wanted to go through the village.

People came out to greet us along the way, crying out to me in surprise at my coming, shouting for news of their men with the company, viewing Glennis with outright country curiosity. When they saw Hawk lying on the mattresses, however, they fell silent, staring at him with pity clear in their eyes.

He greeted them all in his harsh whisper, smiling as if he were stranger to pain and suffering. He told them one and all that he was a shade under the weather with some chest trouble—had to come home to rest up before the new campaign. They all nodded solemnly, and a few even volunteered one home remedy or another that would set him on his feet again.

285

My mother, of course, had known since late winter that we would come one day. Perhaps, as she worked in her big bright kitchen with its rows of windows facing the valley, she had formed the habit of looking down the road. At any rate, we were scarcely into the lane before I saw her on the porch, shading her eyes. Then she was running to us with that bobbing step that women must use in holding their skirts away from their flying feet.

"Go up and talk to her first, Matt," Glennis whispered. "It will be easier then, when she sees him. Go ahead, I'll hold the team."

Hawk must have heard what she said. "Let her come," he said. "She knows. Let her come."

My mother was close to us now, and I reined in the team. Hawk struggled to lift himself; Glennis helped him. My mother saw him as he managed to sit up. For an instant her face drained of blood, and I saw what might have been terror in her wide eyes. Her teeth touched her lower lip momentarily, then she smiled happily.

"You've come home, Marion," she said. She went to the side of the wagon and leaned forward to kiss him. She acted as if it were no different from the other time he had come home, simply to mend a broken leg.

He nodded, stroking her hand. "Home," he whispered.

My mother looked up at me, a question in her eyes, although her voice was banteringly sharp. "Well, you big lummox, can't you get on to the house? Your father needs rest after the journey, doesn't he?"

"He does." I nodded three or four times.

She walked beside the wagon, reaching across to hold my father's hand.

My brother Johnny was struck hardest of all. Evidently my mother had warned him and Abbie that Hawk was coming home sick, but Johnny had only to take one look to know the truth. Farmer and hunter in spite of his youth, he knew death when he saw it. He vanished into the haymow after maintaining a brave appearance in talking to Hawk. He stayed there for several hours before we saw him again. Then he came to where I was doing his chores around the barn. Helplessly, he wanted to strike back somehow.

"Why didn't you take care of him?" he cried.

"We did our best, Johnny."

"He looks starved. You let him give all his food away."

"He can't eat much, Johnny."

"Couldn't you do anything for him?"

I shook my head, then told him quietly about Doc Walden and how he'd tried all he knew to help.

"How long?" Johnny asked, crying now. "What did the doctor say?"

"Not long. Hawk wanted to see you all. Maybe getting here took all his strength. I don't know, Johnny."

"I'm scared, Matt. Don't go back and leave him. Stay with us. Will you, Matt?"

"I'll stay. Harm has the company. He'll do everything I could do."

In contrast to Johnny's understanding of how bad it was, my sister Abbie accepted the fact that Hawk was sick, clucked her tongue at his loss of weight, then set about eagerly to be his nurse. It was she who fed him the little he would eat, and she who administered his dosage of opium whenever he told her he needed it. She was with him constantly except during his worst spells of coughing, when my mother and Glennis sent her from the room.

Hawk rallied after a day's rest, got up from his bed, and insisted on spending most of the daylight hours on the porch, where the sun and warm breezes touched him, where he could see his beloved valley.

Glennis and my mother became fast friends immediately. Within twenty-four hours one would think that Glennis was as familiar to our big house as Harm Tallman or Billy Bill had ever been.

For almost the first time since I'd become so busy with the Baron, I thought of Peggy Remsen. It might have been, I told myself, that she would have been here waiting for me. I grinned. That would have been something to see—Peggy and Glennis. Peggy would have been superior, and Glennis as aggravating as only she could be.

My mother had always been somewhat distant with Peggy, and Peggy with her, as if they had taken inventory of each other and found qualities lacking. Glennis and my mother, though, talked incessantly about every subject under the sun that interest women; they worked together in the big kitchen without a trace of friction, which surprised me, because my mother's kitchen was her castle. I noticed that when Glennis took to wearing her masculine getup for helping Johnny and me with the work around the place, my mother never voiced an objection, although I am sure she would have talked at least obliquely about a lady's obligations if Peggy had worn such clothing.

As soon as it was apparent that Hawk was relaxing and resting, the general tightness among us disappeared. We could laugh again and tell stories about the lighter side of our winter at Valley Forge. (The hunger and the cold were too recent for me to want to discuss them at length with anyone.) Glennis surprised Hawk and me with an amazing imitation of the Baron, which had my mother and Johnny and Abbie rocking with laughter. Glennis puffed her slim form, looked down her nose in exact mimicry of Steuben in one of his flashes of anger, then began to mouth a flow of Germanic English so thickly and richly that you'd almost think the Baron was there. Just as quickly she switched to an imitation of Eben Lowry doing the drill, then back to the Baron swearing at him. I tried to call a halt when she announced that she would try next a re-creation of the famous conference between General Wayne and Lieutenant Hill. She had most of it right, and she showed me puffing and pouting and saying nothing but "Yes, sir," and "No, sir."

She did Wayne excellently, ranging from quiet but stern voice to raging bellow, but she said not one word about his suggestion that I get her out of camp or marry her.

"There was more to it than that," I said, laughing with the others when she finished.

She shook her head, looked steadily at me. "No, Matt. That's all."

I nodded then, smiling. "All right, that's all."

My mother looked from one to the other of us, in the way she has when she discovers that all is not exactly as she thought it was.

As I say, they got on well together. I would walk into the kitchen and find Glennis and my mother giggling and whispering like a pair of schoolgirls. While Glennis was scarcely more than that, to be sure, I suppose I was used to more dignity from my mother. The effect was pleasing, anyway, although I always had the feeling that they were

288

gossiping about me, because when I came in they'd usually shut right up, then burst out laughing.

Johnny and I went fishing one warm afternoon, because Hawk said he could go a little baked trout for supper, was anybody in the mind to catch him a few.

The water was high and brown, but the fish were feeding voraciously in the pockets behind rocks and in the long glides at the tails of the pools. We didn't bother baiting them, taking them instead on a long slim hook wrapped top and sides securely with the brown and white hairs from a deer's tail. This was a Six Nations' trick that Harm had taught us, and brought results when the fish were feeding freely. It seemed to imitate, as it was brought through the water in fits and starts, one of the dace minnows that are so plentiful in our streams.

Soon enough we had a dozen trout, running in the main the size of my two hands' spread. Before hiking up the hill to the house, we lay in the sun on a shale bank. I smoked a pipe, and Johnny shied rocks into the water.

"When you getting married?" Johnny asked.

"That's all done," I said. "I told you what happened when I went to Philadelphia. Too much was made of that. It's as easy to get in and out of Philadelphia as it was for us to catch these fish."

"Not talking about that one," Johnny said. "I mean this one you brought home." He thought Glennis an odd name, I suspected, and didn't care to use it until he became more accustomed to it.

"What put that idea in your head?" I asked easily. So many people seemed to think that this was the thing I ought to do, that I was taking the question for granted. "She's only been a widow a couple of months."

"Ma thinks you're going to marry her, sooner or later. So does Hawk. Ma says better sooner than later. I heard 'em talking. I think the girl does too."

"The girl does? What?"

I pushed myself up on both elbows.

"Thinks she's going to marry you," Johnny answered. "Easy to tell. When you ain't around, every time she says something, it's Matt this and Matt that and Matt the other thing. 'Cording to her, you trained that whole army yourself in just the last month or so, and you're friends with all kinds of generals like that Dutchman and Wayne, and with colonels and such. She says you ought to be a general yourself, because she's seen some of 'em and you'd do a better job at it. She says you built all the huts at the Valley Forge that's any good, and that they pick you for court-martials and things because you're the best officer they got."

"Good Lord, is that what she's been telling you?"

"It's true, ain't it? Hawk nods his head when she says them things. Yesterday he says that the only thing wrong with you is that you don't really want to win, and she got red in the face and said that wasn't it at all—it was just that you couldn't stand the thought of losing. And Hawk looked at her, then at Ma, then back at her, then says maybe so—he never thought of it that way. Seems to me she's all-fired interested in you for a person she ain't going to marry."

"I'll tell you what's true, Johnny. Wayne almost threw me out of the Pennsylvania division. Hamilton wanted me put before a court."

Johnny shrugged. "She and Hawk told us all about that. Hawk says sometimes you act like a damn fool, specially where women are concerned. Seems to me he's right, Matt, if you would compare that Peggy to this one."

"Seems to me you'd better all do less talking," I said easily enough. "She'd do well to remember, maybe, that poor Billy hasn't been dead long."

Johnny looked at me in surprise. "Don't you know about that, either? She and Ma cried for five minutes the first day you were here, cried over Billy, both of 'em. Then Ma tells her she's too young to make too much of it. She told Ma that she just married Billy because they were both alone and she had no place to turn, nobody to go to. Then Ma says, 'Too bad Matt didn't wake up before then.' And they both laughed a little, not much, and then Ma says, 'He's got to be nudged a little, I guess.'"

I knocked out my pipe in the shale that caught and held the warmth of the sun. "So the two of them picked you to do the nudging?"

Johnny shook his head. "My own idea. You'd ought to, Matt. Marry her myself, was I old enough."

"Well, since you've all got everything figured out for me," I said lightly, "I'll have to give it some thought."

Damned if I didn't, all the way back to the house.

In point of fact, if I compared her with Peggy, she rated very well indeed, whenever she wasn't plaguing me. She was pretty enough for any man who was taken by her boyish ways. She had worked wonders with Hawk, and for that I would ever be grateful. She had had the attention and devotion of every man of the company, and half of the rest of the encampment as well. She had my mother's love, and Hawk's, and now Johnny's and, for all I knew, my sister Abbie's as well. Why not mine?

I told myself one reason—a woman should be gentle, tender, dependent, feminine. Could she be all these things if she knew they would please me? Suppose I changed my attitude toward her? If I started to look upon her as if she were a woman like Peggy, she would respond. I would try it.

Suddenly I had a picture of myself at Peggy's cabin in those days before we went off to Valley Forge—I chopped wood, hauled water, did the barn chores, butchered meat, while most of the time Peggy stood by smiling happily. Glennis, on the other hand, would have swung ax or cleaver right beside me. I grinned. If a man was to live in our valley, he'd better have a wife that was handy with the tools he lived by.

That thought pleased me, and I whistled a gay tune while we walked the rest of the way up the hill.

Johnny gazed quizzically at me. "You don't think it's such a bad idea, do you, Matt?"

"I'm giving it due thought," I said lightly.

I might have known that my airy notions would come to naught. In the first place, in spite of my ideas of having a woman handy with tools, it seemed highly improper that when we reached the house Glennis was standing astride a length of hickory next to the woodpile, splitting it with sledge and wedges for the kitchen hearth. She had already split enough for a week's fires. She rested the sledge at our approach. Just like a man, she pulled out a kerchief and mopped her face and neck. Perspiration stained the old hunting shirt she wore.

"You shouldn't do that, Glennis," I said. "That's Johnny's work, or mine."

"Well, why don't you do it then? Seems to me one of you would have been enough to go fishing. Did you get any fish?"

"Certainly we got some fish," I said sharply. She could see the damp cloth bag hanging at my waist, bulging with trout and wet fern fronds to prevent any quick spoiling. I pulled the bag free and held its open neck forward.

She turned up her nose. "Awful small, aren't they?"

"There's plenty for all of us here. I'll clean 'em for you, and you can coat 'em in egg and corn meal and fry them in butter."

"Hawk wants his baked," she said.

"A baked fish has got to be stuffed to keep it from drying," I said shortly. "The bellies of these are too small to stuff."

"Why didn't you catch big ones?"

"We caught the ones that were feeding! Dammit, how can you catch big ones if the big ones aren't feeding? Any fisherman knows that! You go to the brook just as the sun starts behind the hills and you'll get fish bigger than these, but not now, with the sun high."

"Come in the house a minute," she said, eyeing me strangely.

I followed her into the kitchen, since I had to get one of my mother's paring knives to clean the fish. She crossed to the Dutch oven in the fireplace, flipped its door open with a poker and pointed inside. There, baking in a sauce smelling of cream and cheese and onions, was a trout that would have gone two and a half or three pounds when it flopped on the bank. Its belly was stuffed to the bursting point.

I suppose my lower jaw was hanging, for she laughed immoderately.

"Where'd it come from?" I asked.

"Oh, I just ran down to the creek and caught me a minnow with a piece of bread and a hook and a hand line. Then I put the minnow on the hook, tossed it into the deepest part of the pool, and waited." She waved her hand airily. "I was back here in twenty minutes."

"It's a nice fish," I said grudgingly.

"It's surprising that I caught it," she said, grinning. "Any fisherman would know that the big ones aren't feeding at this time of day."

I stomped glumly out without bothering to answer, leaving our fish for her to clean or give to the cats or whatever. Her hoydenish laughter followed me.

We were home four days before Hawk had a bad spell. I didn't know anything about it until the next morning when he stayed abed and I noticed that my mother and Glennis looked drawn and tired.

They had tried to give him opium against the pain, but it had made him sick, as it sometimes did. He was sleeping now, they told me.

I worked with Johnny all morning with a heavy heart, wondering how long it could last. We came in for dinner, and my mother told me that Hawk wanted to see me.

I went into the bedroom. He looked paler than ever against the white bedclothes. It was painful to look at his face while he talked, he was now so wasted. I remember thinking that maybe I ought to cut his hair; longer now than he had ever worn it, it seemed to accentuate his gauntness.

"A few things, Matt," he said in the whisper that was becoming all he could manage. "You'll be captain. Watch out for the men the best you can. They've been proud that they were always the last to run. Save that pride for them. Although it looks as if maybe the running will be over soon."

"Don't talk, Hawk," I said gently. "I know these things."

"I have to talk," he said with a show of spirit. "There's not much time and you know it. I don't have to say anything about the family. I know you too well. The girl—she'd make you a good wife, Matt. You two stop flaring at each other. Smile instead."

"Yes, sir. I have it in mind, although she gets my goat."

"Let me tell you something. Stop trying to be like Hawk Hill. Be like Matt Hill, and then you'll laugh more and take things easy, and you'll not fight with Glennis. You're a fine man by yourself—there's no need for you to be a sobersides because you're my son. I've never stopped laughing and joking in my lifetime, have I?"

"No, sir."

"Then you try it. A smile fits your face, boy, better than a frown."

He paused. "Now, I've not fretted over the way you feel about the war. Have I?"

"No, sir. You've respected my opinion."

"I'd like to know that you're changing it. I think maybe you are. Right?"

"Maybe. I know I had no hope before. But since Steuben came, and we worked so hard, I'm almost eager to try out what we did. I guess I'm changing, Hawk."

"You'll come all the way around. I know you will. And another thing I know—when the victory is in sight, I'll know it."

I nodded without speaking.

"One more thing. This is pretty bad, Matt. I want to hang on, but I can't. Get the pistol from the chest and load it for me." He lifted his hand to show me the tremor. "I couldn't load it, or I'd do it myself."

"No, sir!" I cried. "You know I couldn't do that, Hawk."

"It would be a kindness to me, Matt."

I shook my head several times. "I couldn't, Hawk."

He sighed. "All right. Albion Walden told me you would not help. And I can't load it myself. And I won't ask any of the others. All right, Matt."

Once again Hawk regained his strength, so that he was able to get out of bed and walk around on the second day. The good weather had continued except for a day or two when we had sharp winds and sudden cold rains. During the afternoon of the day that Hawk got to his feet again, I met him on the porch as I was coming in from the barn. Johnny and I had been sorting seed for planting. Hawk stood at the head of the steps, viewing them dubiously.

"Good," he said when he saw me. "You can help me down."

"Where do you want to go, Hawk?" I asked, thinking that he should have someone with him.

"Just to walk," he said. "Out by the barn, to look at the stock, to see how Johnny's coming along at being a farmer."

"Go slow," I said. "You're not strong enough yet for a lot of walking."

"I have my staff, Matt. And I'll never get any stronger."

I helped him down and watched him go off, sadly viewing the dragging steps of the man who had ever been the last to tire on the march.

My mother and Glennis were working in the kitchen.

"Where's your father?" my mother asked.

"He's walking out to the barn. He says he'll be all right."

She nodded. "The fresh air will be good for him."

I sat down to a cup of coffee. Before I'd half finished it, Johnny came into the kitchen. "What do you want me for, Matt? I've got a lot of work to do."

"I don't want you," I said. "I left you in the barn not five minutes ago."

"Hawk said you wanted me. He said you told him to tell me to come to the house."

"I said no such thing, Johnny."

"What'd he go and say it for, then?"

Hawk's asking for the pistol had been on my mind constantly. I had warned Johnny against loading it for him on any pretext, even if Hawk said he wanted to keep his eye in on a target.

I jumped up and ran into the big bedroom. I threw back the lid of the chest where Hawk kept his clothing and razors and such. The pistol, with its twin flasks of balls and powder, was kept in a cedar box. The box lay open in the chest, empty.

I ran out of the house as fast as I could go, knowing that he would manage to load the pistol. He'd always contrived somehow to do what he wanted to do. All the way to the barn I dreaded hearing the shot, but it did not come.

He had been trying to load it, all right. He'd set it into the small vise in the harness room; the powder and ball flasks were on the workbench. He'd probably figured that if he had the vise to hold the barrel steady, he'd be able to pour in powder and ball.

He had failed, because he had come to the end of his painful way. He lay on the floor where the last attack had thrown him. The bright red blood moved slowly in rivulets away from him. I knew he was dead before I touched him.

We buried him on the hillside high above the house in a natural clearing among a grove of quaking aspen that he had spared from the ax long ago, picking it for our burying ground.

"We'll like it there," he'd said. "Those trees, you know—those popple or aspen, whatever you want to call 'em—they're never silent, so it can't be lonely there."

CHAPTER TWENTY-ONE

The night came down suddenly upon the Deerkill Valley, as it seems to me it always does in springtime. One minute you will be looking at the red sun dipping toward the western mountains, and the next minute it is gone and you are standing in the soft dusk.

I walked among the dogwood trees that Hawk had brought down from the mountain and planted for my mother many years before. It would not be many weeks now before they blossomed. Hawk had always waited for their pink and white flowers to show before he would go fishing for trout. Their flowering also marked the time when the last northbound flights of ducks and geese left the Drowned Lands. The trees formed a barrier between the house and the small gravel pit on the hillside. It was a pleasant place to be always, but especially so now with the house filled by well-meaning friends who did not have the sense to go home and leave my mother alone.

They didn't need me there; they had Abbie and Glennis to serve them pie and coffee, and Johnny to shake hands as they left.

I wanted to be alone for a while. I was weary of tears and lamentations from womenfolk, and I believed I could not bear to hear another solemn recounting of what a fine man Hawk Hill had been— each of his old friends had already talked to me at length about his kindness, wisdom, honesty, strength. They meant well, but I thought it would be good for me to go off by myself to think about him. I did, for a time.

Then there were decisions that I had to put my mind to. I had always known, of course, that we were well-situated in the matters of property and money, but never had I realized how much we owned until that morning, when my mother urged me to find Hawk's will among his books and papers. She said that there were many bequests that I could take care of before returning to the army.

I found that we had title to tracts of land that I had never set foot upon; there were mortgages and notes of hand for many parcels in the Deerkill Valley; there were investments that I had not known of—in a brickyard in Highland Landing and in the gunpowder mills at Gardinerville. Perhaps most surprising of all to me was the bond of the Continental Congress of the United American States, securing a loan of five hundred pounds from "Marion Hawk Hill, as generous assistance in the prosecution of the present hostilities against England."

That one we can probably whistle for, I thought grimly, if Congress' record to date is any standard of judgment.

I was aware that someone was calling me from the house. I looked that way and saw Glennis holding a lantern, peering beyond its glow into the darkness.

"Here," I called softly, supposing that they wanted me to come in to bid farewell to the funeral guests.

When Glennis heard me answer, however, she put down the lantern and came toward me. She was a dark shadow in one of my mother's dresses, her own being too bright for a burying.

"Speak to me, Matt," she said quickly, "I can't see you."

"Here I am."

She touched my arm in the darkness, and as quickly withdrew her hand. "I believe they'll stay the night inside," she said, "if your mother doesn't send them packing."

"It's the minister," I said. "He loves to talk."

"I'm glad it's over," she said simply, "because he suffered so, but I will miss him even though I knew him only a short time. And I will miss this valley of his when I leave."

Swift and sudden alarm surged through me, and I knew for the first time in truth that I had made my decision.

"Leave?" I asked, being careful to hide the alarm. "Why should you leave? This is your home. I've never felt the need to tell you, but Billy asked me to take care of you. You'll stay here with my family, Glennis. They love you already."

"No. I have to make a new life somehow. I have the farm money waiting for me in Philadelphia. Will the British let me into the city, Matt?"

"If you went there, they'd let you in, of course. But what in the world would you do there?"

"I have cousins there. I'd stay with them until I could collect my money. Then I could start a shop of some kind. Maybe a bakery shop. I'm a good baker, Matt. You know that."

"You would sadden us all by leaving," I said. "Can't you see that this is a better place than any city?"

"No, Matt. Not this way."

Suddenly then I knew that it was time for me to speak if ever I would. I took her hand and turned her to face me. "Not this way," I repeated. "And how should we change it?"

She didn't answer, but I knew that she was waiting for me to say more, watching my face in the faint light of the lantern on the porch.

"It would take the fingers of both hands," I said, "to count up the number of times I've missed seeing what I should have. More than anything else, I suppose, I have spent my time worrying about how powerful the British are, instead of watching the men this winter who wouldn't give up no matter how sick or cold or hungry they were. I'm glad I was able to let Hawk know that I was beginning to see the forest instead of just the trees. That applies to things other than the army. I have it in mind now to follow out a suggestion from General Wayne. Will you marry me, Glennis?"

The old touch of mockery sounded faintly in her voice. "You don't have to say that just because I'm a lone widow. I'll manage, Matt, and Billy need not have told you to take care of me."

"That's not why I asked you," I told her softly. "I love you, and that's all the reason I need."

Her voice was not so sure and certain. "And how do you feel these days about your lady in Philadelphia?"

"That's long behind me, Glennis."

"Not so long," she said softly.

"Long enough. Let's not talk any more." I took her in my arms and kissed her, holding her closely and wondering why in the world

I had ever imagined that she was as straight and slim as a boy. She finally pulled her lips from mine and whispered, "Yes, Matt, yes. I thought you'd never get around to asking me."

She buried her head against my shoulder, and we stood there holding each other.

There is, it seems to me, a curious reversal in fact of that part of the burial service of the *Book of Common Prayer*, as the minister had read it over Hawk's grave: *In the midst of life we are in death*. For I believe that when death comes close to us, we deal more gently with those we love and our passions are intensified. Perhaps it is natural for man to seek love when he has just viewed death; perhaps it is a natural way of reassuring himself that though he will one day die, his kind will not.

I lifted Glennis' head from my shoulder. "Why should we wait too long?" I asked softly. "Let's speak to the minister now. There need be no banns. He can marry us as soon as you think proper, with the burying and all."

She started to speak hesitantly, then suddenly began to laugh. "Oh, Matt! Your mother thinks faster than you do. She told me earlier today to get you to ask the question while the minister was here, so we could arrange it. She said there's no need to wait for what folks would call a decent interval. Hawk wouldn't want us to wait."

"You had it all planned, then? And you didn't really care about how much I still thought of Peggy?"

"I wouldn't care about a dozen like her, Matt, as long as you kiss me that way. Now come, let's talk to Mr. Cornwall before he goes home. Then we can come back here and kiss some more."

"He'll object to speed," I said. "He's very proper."

"It's got to be soon, so we can get started back to the Valley Forge."

"We? What do you mean, we? You're staying right here."

"No, I'm not, sir. I'm going back to be with you until the campaign starts."

"We'll see about that."

"We will," she said, going toward the house, laughing. It was still the same laugh, but no longer was it hoydenish. It was now merry and bright, and I loved to hear it.

300

We were quietly married two days later, without any celebration of the event for the folks of the valley, although a goodly number of them gathered outside the church to watch us come out and to shake our hands. The only festivity was held back in the big kitchen of our house, where my mother proposed a toast to our happiness with noggins of applejack, including one for Johnny, who tossed it off with the assurance of a man and then almost choked as it hit his throat.

It would be expected that I, being a lieutenant in the Continental Army, as well as erstwhile aide to the Inspector General of that army, and presumably new commanding officer of a ranger company, would have my orders followed by my wife and family. However, when I told Glennis that she was staying home, and told my mother that she was to see that my wife stayed there, neither of them paid one whit of attention to me, but went on with their packing of things we were to take with us.

I think every family in the valley who had a man with the company paid us a visit that day to leave a large parcel to be taken to the Valley Forge. I had to draw the line at some things, limiting the gifts mostly to food and clothing, but even so, our wagon was well filled by evening.

I expect that it is given to few couples to have so pleasant a wedding trip as ours. We neither hurried nor tarried on the way, but followed the roads that brought us from the Deerkill Valley to the Delaware and then kept to those that generally were within sight of the river.

Two nights we stayed at country inns in the Jerseys, where the landlords might have been Tories from their talk, but set good tables and kept clean bedrooms. The other nights we were more than happy to camp off the road in some woodland clearing or other, which was a delight to my wife, as camping out under the stars was a strange experience for her.

We had no fear of British foraging parties so long as we were in the northern reaches of the Jerseys, but we were told that partisans were active in that country. I could judge whether a man stood for King or for Congress by his warnings about partisan raiders and thieves. Generally he blackguarded one side and whitewashed the other.

We encountered no troops, however, either regular or partisan, and we crossed the Delaware at Coryell's Ferry, heading west and then south for the Valley Forge. Here, so close to Philadelphia, there was real danger from the British, so we wasted no time once across the river. Luckily we fell in with a party of Lee's light horse, and stayed with them all the way to the encampment.

Although we had not been absent from the Valley Forge for three full weeks, we found startling changes on our arrival.

Along the roads near camp, and lounging at various huts inside it, we saw dozens, scores, of civilians, some of them with weapons and some unarmed. If they had one thing in common, it was a serious air of determination. I had not seen so many of them since I myself had been one of them on the way to Boston.

"Who are they, Matt?" Glennis asked.

"Recruits," I said. "New soldiers for the Line. Steuben will soon have 'em wishing they had stayed home."

One new set of arrivals caused universal misery. These were the millions of black gnats, as we called them in the Deerkill Valley, or midges, as I suppose they are properly named. The Hudson Valley men in the New York regiments had still a third term for them, and a most appropriate one: "shad flies." They said that the shad run brought them up the Hudson River, an explanation they staunchly maintained in spite of its being utter nonsense. You could explain all day to a man from Peekskill, New York, that since we had the black gnats but not the shad in our Deerkill Valley, therefore the flies had nothing to do with the shad. He would nod as if seeing the wisdom of what you said, then say stubbornly, "Be that as it may in your country; the shad brings 'em up the Hudson."

These pestiferous insects probably fared poorly in the sparsely settled valley of the Schuylkill in other years, but in the April days of '78 they had a rich feast. The sound of slapping, and of cursing as well, was raised from morning until night. The only thing that brought surcease was a good wind, in which they could not navigate. Windy days were scarce in April, however, and there were some among us who suffered terribly, being subject to an infection from the bites of these terrors. As for me, they seemed not much worse than mosquitoes, while Glennis seemed to notice them scarcely at all.

The men from Peekskill and other Hudson towns were correct at least in associating the flies with the fish. When Glennis and I drove through the camp on our way to the Deerkill huts, we noticed a new smell added to the hundreds with which we were already familiar. It wasn't so bad as some others, being simply the odor of fish, fresh caught.

The soldiers had enough for the first time since Germantown, enough to fill their bellies to bursting. The shad run was on in the Schuylkill, and the army was gorging on literally tons of great silver fish that came up in the nets that our men and the country people set in the river.

During spring visits to Highland Landing in other years, I had enjoyed the taste of fresh shad from the Hudson (that, indeed, being the universal item on tavern bills of fare in Highland Landing during the spring of the year). However, as soon as I talked to Jed Palmer, I discovered that I knew nothing about shad.

Having welcomed us on behalf of the Pennsylvania division, having remarked that it was about time I had showed sense enough to marry Glennis as everyone had known I would, and having managed to invite himself to dinner with us, Palmer informed us about shad. "Them buck shad, now, some folks will eat and claim to like, but not me. Come the first few days of the run, I'll eat some female shad, just like anybody else would if he was hungry. After a dozen or so of them fish in a day or two, a man gets a little particular. Right now I wouldn't eat nothing but the roe. Broiled just nice in butter, if you got any butter—and I just happened to find a firkin over to Wayne's farm the other day when he sent me on an errand—with lots of salt and pepper, there ain't a dish in the world can match it."

"And garnish it with turnip skins," said Eben Lowry, somewhat vindictively.

"Damn it, Eben, ain't you ever going to forget turnips?" Palmer growled. "The winter's over now. We ain't going to be everlastingly hearing about turnips, are we?"

"You told me they was the best thing a man could eat," Eben

said aggrievedly, "and I been trading off all kinds of good things for turnips."

"Sure I told you that, and at the time they was, too. We didn't have nothing else, did we? All right, then. But the best thing a man can eat is shad roe. I found that out. Sticks to your ribs and tastes fit for a king. You're going to have some for dinner, Matt, and you, too, Missis Hill. And maybe for breakfast tomorrow and dinner and supper and so on, until them fish stop running."

"What," asked Glennis, "is shad roe?"

"You don't know what shad roe is? I thought everybody in the Commonwealth of Pennsylvania knew that. Come to think of it, I never knew either, until this week when them fish started coming up the river. Shad roe, Missis Hill, is plain old fish eggs, that I always threw out of every trout I ever caught. That's what it is. Millions and millions of tiny little orange fish eggs."

"I'll just have the baked shad for dinner, if you don't mind, Sergeant."

And so we had baked shad, and shad roe, and then shad roe and baked shad, and shad chowder, and fried shad, until I was sick of the very word shad, and my arms were weary from slapping at shad flies. Then as suddenly as it had come, the run was over, and within a week we were thinking how nice it would be to have a juicy piece of shad to eat. Palmer even allowed that he would eat buck shad if he could get it. The shad flies were gone too.

At any rate the men weren't hungry any longer, even when the fish were no longer in full supply, because we now had a real quartermaster general, Nathanael Greene, in place of the bumbling Mifflin. There were rations for all men on hand when they were needed. The Pennsylvania division not only had received all the uniforms for which Wayne had long been screaming, but they had extra ones as well, and our Deerkill company was outfitted in blue coats with red facings just as fine as any in the army. Our men wore the uniforms with an air, although they promised themselves that on the march they'd return to their hunting shirts and buckskin breeches. They were a ranger company, they said, and they wouldn't want to be confused with plain ordinary soldiers of the Line.

Glennis and I had moved into the hut that she had shared with

Billy in a time that now seemed long ago. The first night of our return, the men had a meeting at which they elected me captain. They so notified General Wayne, and my promotion was officially noted in division orders the next day.

Doc Walden came to visit us. His own work, he said, reflected the general air of recovery in the encampment. Fewer men were dying in the camp and in the churches that had been turned into hospitals in nearby towns. Every day men who had been sick for weeks were getting to their feet and returning to duty, or going home for sick furloughs.

"What do you hear about the British?" I asked, not from any desire to be perverse or pessimistic, but simply because I knew that spirit and training, no matter how good, would avail us nothing if the King's ministers sent twenty thousand fresh regulars against us.

"Why," Doc Walden said soberly, "just what do you want to know? There's spies going back and forth all the time with the news. Billy Howe is still more interested in Mrs. Loring than in running an army. So we hear they have been having a high old time. A good soldier gets drunk every night, has a good fight for himself at least once a week. Every officer of field grade has got to keep himself two house-keepers—that's what they call 'em, housekeepers—and every general has an average of three. We had a deserter come in last week—not exactly a deserter, either, because he was Irish and only joined up with 'em because in Dublin they tied him hand and foot and dragged him off to be a British soldier—he came over to us and said things are pretty bad in Philadelphia. More courts-martial than we got, and lots of whippings and such. Them Hessians are the worst, he says. They stable their horses in houses where they're billeted, and then they cut a hole in the floor and shovel the manure into the cellar.

"This Irishman says the city stinks to high heaven. He sniffed a lot around here the day he come in—I was tending him for blistered feet he got running all the way—and smelled our various odors and says to me, 'Faith, and it's good to be gettin' fresh air in me lungs again.' So you can imagine what Philadelphia smells like. This Irish-man says he saw Sir William not long ago, fatter'n a pig and twice as lazy. He says there's a different show or play most every night in Philadelphia, with officers and pretty ladies cavorting on the stage."

"You can't trust the roads yet to carry wagons and guns, but it won't be more than a week before they'll be pretty good." Doc smiled mildly. "But the British haven't even started to get ready to come out after us. I wager we don't have to stir a leg until the middle of May. Billy Howe is a most accommodating man. I bet Mrs. Loring pouts at him and says, 'My heavens, Sir Billy, don't leave me just to go fight those silly old rebels.' And he says: 'All right, m'dear, I'll stay right here where we're comfortable.'"

I wasn't interested in the mistresses of British generals.

"Doc, did that Irishman of yours say how many troops are in Philadelphia?"

"He did. Yes, he did, Matt. That was one of the first things Colonel Laurens asked him. He said there were nineteen thousand, give or take a few hundred."

"And how many do we have here in camp?"

"Oh, say about ten thousand on all returns, counting sick and sick on leave and detailed out of here. 'Bout eight thousand fit for duty. More coming in every day, Matt."

"I know they're coming in, Doc, but the British have us outnumbered again, two to one."

Doc pulled his spectacles down on the bridge of his nose and looked at me owlishly. "Why, yes, Matt. That ain't so bad, is it? If it was four to one, I'd worry some, about most of 'em getting away during the fight, but at two to one, we can surround 'em." He and Glennis laughed gaily.

At the beginning of the winter, I would have scowled. Now I grinned at them, shaking my head at such unwarranted optimism. "Two to one is too much, Doc. And you know it, too."

"He's a captain now, my dear," Doc said to Glennis. "Man gets to be a captain, he worries even more than when he was a lieutenant. Just gets gloomier and gloomier. I better speak to Wayne, so he don't promote him to major. I don't see how we could stand it if Matt ever had the worries of a major."

I laughed with them, and joked some more, but thought ahead to the campaign and wished that for once we could stand even, man to man, with the British regulars.

CHAPTER TWENTY-TWO

How many rumors flew through that camp in the hills, and how few proved to be true! In point of fact, there were few tales, if any, believed on the first telling or even the fifth. As Joe Williams said to me, "If I hear something ten times from ten different fellers, then I might begin to believe it ain't but half a lie."

In late April, we did not credit the story that Billy Howe was going home to England and that Sir Henry Clinton was the new British commander in America. Sir Henry was in New York, or had been, as second in command. If this rumor was true, it meant that the campaign was still a long way off, since Clinton would have to relieve Howe and then spend weeks in familiarizing himself with the troops in Philadelphia. Setting an army into motion against an enemy force is a project requiring careful planning and preparation.

The rumor was true. Sir William was going home, our spies in Philadelphia reported, to tell the King's ministers why he had failed so often to crush our weak army. I wondered what excuses he could give. To my mind, there were no valid ones.

The second rumor flashed across the camp in the first bright days of May. The French had agreed to an alliance with the United American States! The envoy with the treaty was already in York to present it to Congress.

We didn't believe this one either. We were not partial to Frenchmen in general, nor to the policies of the French king in particular. (The attitude of the main part of the army toward things French is not surprising; after all, though we were fighting the British, we were in the main only a generation or two away from England itself, and many men in the army had fought in the French War.)

Lafayette had done much to remove some of the soldiery's prejudices, but against his good offices, his charming personality, and his excellence as a soldier, were set the scheming and arrogance of Conway, the bumbling inefficiency of Du Coudray—who fell off a horse and drowned—and the sourness and pettiness of De Kalb. An alliance with the might and wealth of France, however, would give such hope to our cause that even I, the thorough pessimist, could look to the future with confidence.

We heard all the details: the envoy's name was Simeon Deane (whose brother, Silas Deane, was one of the American plenipotentiaries in Paris); we knew the name of his ship, the *Sensible,* and that he had landed at Falmouth; he had sent word from Bethlehem to the General and had gone direct to York with the treaty.

We still didn't believe it. It was too good to be true. Even if it were true, I said, how long would it take the French to send troops? How long before the French fleet could clear our coasts of British men-of-war?

"It don't do any harm not to believe a story," Joe Williams cried indignantly, "but don't go poking into it to find trouble that we ain't even worried about yet. I'll find out if it's true."

"How will you find out?" asked Harm.

"I'll go ask."

"Ask who?"

Joe gave him a scornful glare. "The man who knows, of course. The General."

Harm guffawed. "Just walk up and ask him, eh? You won't get out of this, Joe. I'm going with you to make sure you do just what you said."

"Why not?" Williams said.

Off they went, after Williams had borrowed a mirror from Glennis so he might comb his hair properly.

They were back in half an hour, Williams grinning and Tallman shaking his head puzzledly.

"It's true," Williams said complacently.

"Who told you?" Walter Luckey asked dubiously.

"The General," Williams said.

"He did," Tallman said. "Damned if it ain't so. He went down to the house and in the gate and I stopped there, 'cause I got troubles enough of my own. So Colonel Laurens comes out of the house, and Joe says: 'Is the General inside?' And Laurens says, 'Yes, Major, he is.' And Joe says, 'Is he busy?' And Laurens says, 'He's always busy, but go on in.' You tell the rest of it, Joe."

"Ain't much to tell," said Williams. "I went inside, into the hall, and his wife was there, and I said, 'Afternoon, ma'am. Could I see the General a minute?' She nods and shows me the open doorway. He was sitting at a desk, working. He looks up, says, 'What is it, Major?' I says, 'There's a rumor all around camp, sir. About the French. The men don't know whether to believe it.' He nodded, smiled as if somebody had just told him King George had dropped dead, and says, 'It's true, Major.' So I says, 'Thanks,' and he says, 'You're welcome,' and out I went."

Verification came in General Orders on Tuesday, May 5:

It having pleased the Almighty Ruler of the Universe propitiously to defend the cause of the United States of America finally by raising us up a powerful friend, among the Princes of the Earth, to Establish our Liberty & Independence upon lasting foundations; It becomes us to Set apart a day, for fully acknowledging the Divine Goodness, & celebrating the important event. . . .

May 6 was the day. Those who witnessed it, I vow will never forget it.

Scarce a man in the entire army did not prepare himself as if he were about to court the most beautiful girl in his world. Barbers set up shop and clipped hair flew every which way. Men honed and stropped their razors to the finest of edges; needles flashed through rents in coats and breeches. It seemed that half the army on the evening of May 5 were knee-deep in the Schuylkill, washing shirts and stockings and underclothing. Never before had so many muskets shone so brightly, nor bayonets carried fewer rust pits.

The day started with a sermon, as ordered by headquarters, from the chaplain of each brigade. Our man, of the First Pennsylvania Brigade, was the Reverend Mr. Simpson, from the town of Easton, but formerly ministering on the frontier. He was of sober mien—a Wesleyan, or Methodist, as I believe they are most commonly called, and had reason to be soured on life at the moment. The Reverend John Wesley had announced to his American followers that "we Methodists are not republicans," thereby enjoining all of his faith in America to be Tories. Mr. Simpson, therefore, qualified as a rebel in politics and in religion.

The brigade assembled smartly just before nine on the parade, and we stood in battalion formation fronting on a square where Mr. Simpson stood patiently atop a barrel. Some of the men were muttering to each other at the prospect of standing in formation for the better part of an hour listening to a Methodist sermon, because, they said, the Methodists lived by rules, and the preacher was sure to follow the rule set by orders—divine services to end before ten o'clock. Just before ten, they said, he would finish.

Some Baptist or Lutheran in the Seventh Regiment chanted the couplet about the Methodist penchant for order:

> "By rule they eat, by rule they drink.
> Do all things else, by rule, but think."

Mr. Simpson fooled them. He smiled when Colonel Hartley gave him the word to begin. He lowered his head to start his prayer.

"Let us pray. Lord, we have all heard that Thou hast brought the French nation into this conflict upon our side. For this we thank Thee. When they come among us, give us the strength, if it be Thy will, to keep firm hands upon our republican principles," his voice dropped in volume, "and upon anything else that may not be nailed down." Heads popped up from attitudes of devotion, a startled hum went through the brigade. Colonel Hartley frowned.

"Oh Lord," continued Mr. Simpson, "it is not in the nature of Pennsylvanians to look kindly upon Frenchmen, who plagued our western borders for so many years with their red imps of Satan. Thou canst not expect us to change our natures. We know that Thou must look after the welfare of the other twelve states of this union, although this Commonwealth of Pennsylvania is capable of taking care of itself. We will welcome these French to the United American States, but we humbly submit to Thee the opinion that they should be congregated elsewhere than Pennsylvania. Amen."

310

With this startling pronouncement he jumped down from the barrel and stalked away. The brigade hummed in spite of frowning officers. Men grinned happily and nudged each other. If looks could kill, as the old saying goes, Colonel Hartley's glare would have felled the preacher before he took five steps.

"I know him," Joe Williams explained to me. "He lost his first wife to the Shawnees on the frontier. They shot her with a French musket and scalped her with a French knife."

The vast majority of our people, however, were overjoyed by the news of the French alliance. When we marched to the Grand Parade at eleven-thirty, according to orders, we found a great assemblage of visitors waiting for the military exhibition that had been promised. There were people from the countryside around the camp, there were wives and families of officers, and visitors who had come all the way from Lancaster and York for the Grand Review of the army.

By cannon signal we marched in battalion formation into line of battle, the columns moving with a precision that would have been completely impossible a few short weeks before.

Lord Stirling was in command of the right wing of the front line, Lafayette of the left wing, and Baron de Kalb commanded the second line.

Upon the heights, General Knox's artillery boomed out a salute of thirteen guns, one for each state, in honor of the King of France. Then the troops in line, starting on the right of the first line, fired a *feu de joie*, for which they had loaded with blank charges. The first soldier fired, then the next, and the next, and so on, with almost precise timing—one musket misfired—to the end of the line; the second line took up the musket salute from left to right. At the end the entire army yelled in unison, "Hurrah for the King of France!"

The thirteen guns boomed alternately a second time. This salute was for France and Spain and their allies who were friendly to us. While the cannon roared, the entire army reloaded with blank charges again, performing the ritual by the numbers, and every musket in the lines coming to the ready at the same split second. Following the cannon salute, another *feu de joie* rattled down the first line and up the second. This time the cheer was, "Hurrah for the Friendly

European Powers!" I could not help but think that those words were ill-chosen, since the cheer more or less trailed off after "Friendly. . . ."

The third running fire was for the United American States. This one the men boomed out with vigor.

The battalions were marched off the Grand Parade in a display of skillful maneuvering that had Steuben glowing with justifiable pride. I dismissed the Deerkill men to go enjoy the gill of rum that the General had decreed for every man in the army. Prisoners were freed in a general amnesty, and two soldiers under death sentence were pardoned by general order.

I returned to the Grand Parade, looking for Glennis. Every officer in the army was to be the General's guest at a banquet for fifteen hundred, to be served under tent cloth set on poles, with every lady of the vicinity invited.

I didn't find Glennis immediately, but I found someone else I knew, or thought I knew. I passed a well-dressed young man, standing alone and watching intently the march of the brigades from the Grand Parade. The fascination with which he fixed his eyes upon the precise columns of the battalions caught my attention, so that I looked back after I had passed him. He didn't notice that I was staring at him; he was far too busy watching the troops.

He looked somewhat different out of uniform, and I had seen him only once, but I was positive that this was the Captain Armstrong who had been in Peggy's house in Philadelphia, wearing the uniform of Simcoe's Rangers.

I took a step toward him, thinking to grab him and shout for the provost, but then thought better of it. Somehow or other, he might get away, and since he was assuredly a spy, I'd do better to get myself some help.

Suddenly it struck me that I was about to do for him exactly as he had done for me in Philadelphia—grab him for the gallows. I stopped where I was, thinking instantly that I would not do it. He was Peggy's fiancé; perhaps they were already married. He would surely hang if I took him.

For almost a full minute I stood there watching him, knowing that I should bring the guard, and wanting him to realize that he was being watched—wanting him to take to his legs and run away, so somebody else could grab him. Take him and he would hang; let him go, and a spy went to the city with word on our strength.

I made up my mind—no matter how distasteful it was to me, he was a spy and must be taken. I looked around. Not twenty yards away Colonel Hamilton was talking to Colonel Burr of the New York Line. I stepped up to them.

"Can I see you for a moment, sir?" I said to Hamilton. "It's a matter of importance."

"Certainly, Captain Hill." Hamilton bowed to Burr, who moved off with a smile.

"There's a spy here, sir, from Philadelphia."

Hamilton grinned. "For all of that, I'd wager there are several. Where is he?"

"That tall young man," I said. "The one with the dark blue coat and the light breeches. He's a captain in Simcoe's Rangers, sir. He's the one who caught me in Philadelphia."

"And now you catch him here," Hamilton said. "Turn about, Captain. Keep your eye on him, and I'll get a squad of the General's Life Guard."

Armstrong was still staring at the marching troops, as if he had forgotten entirely that he should keep his guard up for his own safety. I wanted to go forward suddenly and tell him to run for his life. Instead, I stood where I was and felt sick.

Hamilton was gone only a couple of minutes. He smiled at me when he came back. "The General says no, Captain. We won't touch him. We'll let him see what he came to see—everything that the Baron has done. Let him take the word back to Howe and Clinton. Let them know what they're going to face when they come out, or when we go in after them. If we took him, Hill, we'd only hang him. That wouldn't do us any good, and I doubt if he'd enjoy the process. Let him take his tale back to Philadelphia."

I waited where I was, keeping an eye on Armstrong, until Hamilton returned with two of the Life Guards, whom he told to watch the Tory officer until he was out of the encampment—to allow him to go nowhere but the Grand Parade, and to be sure that he was well on his way back to Philadelphia by sundown.

"They will have the word tonight," Hamilton said to me with satisfaction. "They will know for sure that the French have come in with us, and they will know that we have ten thousand trained men for Sir Harry Clinton. That will make them whistle, Captain."

Glennis and I went to the General's banquet, where we had fine cold salads and cold slices of beef and pork and ham, all served appropriately with good French wines. The French officers were naturally the center of attention this day, and since Steuben's three aides were fond of flirting with my wife, we were more or less surrounded by our new allies. They were confident that the war was all over except for the shouting.

Steuben joined us briefly after the banquet, glowing with wine and pride, and, I thought from his manner, something else as well. He kept nodding and saying, "Good news ve haf," again and again. I didn't think he was talking about the French alliance.

I was right—his good news concerned himself. The General addressed the assemblage as toasts were being drunk to our new allies, to the French King, to Franklin and Deane, to Beaumarchais and De Vergennes. The General announced that he himself had a toast to propose, a toast to a familiar figure at Valley Forge, but one carrying a new title from this day forward.

"I give you Major General Baron de Steuben, by order in Congress yesterday, Inspector General of the Army of the United American States."

Steuben bowed, beaming, and thirstily drank a glass of wine during the toast to him.

"Good fortune for me," he said in French. "I need the money. This is a most expensive army, most expensive."

We had major generals by the dozen in our army, but there were few of them that deserved the rank more than Steuben. As far as the pay went, he was right—with his luxury-loving habits, he really did need the money.

CHAPTER TWENTY-THREE

Being no expert on miracles or other phenomena unrelated to nature, I cannot say how the average miracle is first observed by the human eye or recorded in the human mind.

The only miracle I have had aught to do with was "Steuben's miracle," and I can aver that it had its proof and its early accounting in that spring of 1778.

The first test started in a headquarters order of May 18. There was need of course, now that our target date for British action had long since passed with no indication that the enemy intended anything but continuing to occupy Philadelphia, to know exactly what Clinton was up to, and how he would make his move. With the roads open, it was necessary to cover our encampment and to have quick and ready intelligence.

The General chose the Marquis de Lafayette for the assignment, perhaps in further honor to the new French alliance.

On a bright May morning, the French Boy led his force across the Schuylkill: Poor's New England brigade, a battery of five guns, some six hundred Pennsylvania militia under General Potter—whose name I cannot yet repeat without fury and disgust—and the flamboyant independent company of Captain Allen McLane. Also included were some fifty Oneida warriors who had come to us in defiance of their brothers of the Long House, and, added at the last minute by request of General Wayne, the Deerkill Independent Company.

We made the crossing of the Schuylkill at Swede's Ford, and headed toward the city along the Ridge Road above the river. We were approaching ground that was unhappily familiar to most of us—

the battle of Germantown had been fought not much farther along this countryside.

We reached a point called Barren Hill, a bit more than halfway between Valley Forge and the city. It was a good position, high on a hill and protected on the right by the ridge and the Schuylkill. To our left was the road by which we had advanced, and by which we could retreat if Sir William, who had not yet left for England, and Sir Henry Clinton, put their heads together and decided to come out after us.

For proper understanding of what happened to us, it is necessary to visualize the approaches and strengths of the position. On the far side of the Ridge Road was a wood lot with a few stone houses on its periphery. Behind us on the left were the possible defense positions of the Barren Hill Church and a cemetery. At our back ran a road to Matson's Ford nearer to us if we needed it than our first choice of Swede's Ford.

In front of our strong position was Levering's Ford at Manayunk. If the British came out, and we thought they would, we could pull foot in any direction and leave them facing an empty countryside.

McLane's company, our Deerkill company, and the Indians were sent forward by the Marquis to reconnoiter and picket the Ridge Road into the city. This was the likely point of sortie by the redcoats, other than the road from Germantown.

That road was far on our left flank, leading past Whitemarsh toward Matson's Ford, and farther on, Swede's Ford. Germantown Pike had to be held by a strong force. Lafayette, not yet fully schooled in the difference between Line troops and militia, sent Potter with his crew of Pennsylvania short-timers to hold the Germantown pike.

With one flank secured by the river and by the right wing of Poor's brigade, with the advance under patrol by my men and McLane's, as well as the Oneidas, and with Potter to hold the left, the Marquis supposed himself to be in fine shape to carry out his reconnaisance in force.

Poor's brigade was there, I suppose, only for a show of force. McLane and I were charged with the task of determining what Clinton and Howe were doing in the city. McLane sent spies right into Philadelphia's main streets; I had the job of patrolling roads and intercepting travelers to and from the British stronghold.

We had picked a good day for the sortie. Sir William Howe was going home, and his faithful army was giving him a celebration to end all such. They called it a *michianza*; it evidently consisted of a variety of amateur theatricals and musical shows, the whole accompanied by merrymaking, feasting, drinking, and the launching of rockets that we could see flaring above the horizon.

"They don't even know yet we're here," Harm Tallman told me upon returning from a swift patrol of the Ridge Road near Germantown. "They're having a big party for Sir William." He grinned. "Wagons loaded with beer and wine and rum are rolling into the city. We lifted a few jugs of rum."

"They'll know we're here as soon as the fellow you lifted the rum from gets into the city," I said. "So keep the men from tapping the jugs, Harm. They'll come out, and we'll have to make tracks fast."

They found out, all right, and they discovered something else that we didn't know until it was too late to do something about it.

We camped that night forward of Barren Hill, with the main force secure behind us. It was a good camp, made pleasant by the rum and the foraging of both McLane's and the Deerkill patrol parties during the day. McLane, who was a most lively and pleasant fellow, conferred with me on the posting of picket lines. We both deferred to Harm Tallman's judgment that the Oneidas would serve us well, having eyes like night-prowling cats, but that their numbers should be leavened with veteran soldiers, since Indians have a regrettable penchant for going where they please when they please.

What the British discovered, in that countryside full of their Tory sympathizers, was that Potter, supposedly at Whitemarsh and guarding the Germantown road with his militia, might just as well have been back at the Valley Forge. Wherever he was, and we never did find out certainly, he was not holding the Germantown Pike.

There have been times when I would as lief depend upon a parcel of grandmothers and children as I would upon a like number of militia. To give them whatever credit may be due them, they *did* fight on occasion, and their marksmanship was usually far better than the best the British could command, but in the main they were so unreliable as to be worse than useless to us—in this case, their general had taken them God knows where, and left us open for one of Howe's famous encirclements, such as he had used so well on Long Island and at Brandywine.

The bad news was brought to me just before dawn, when I was crouched by a watch fire sipping a cup of strong coffee and wondering what action the day would bring us.

James Dutcher had taken a patrol toward Whitemarsh during the night to ascertain that our pickets and those of Poor's brigade were hinged with the right flank of the militia position.

"British, Matt!" Dutcher said, panting for breath when he came trotting up to the fire. "Over on the left, at Whitemarsh. Thousands of 'em, moving up the road. They almost got us. We thought it was them goddam militia!"

"Whitemarsh?" I said incredulously. "They can't be. You made a mistake, Jim. Potter and the Pennsylvania militia are on that road."

"They are like hell! There's British on that road. Thousands of 'em, I tell you! They'll cut us off in another hour."

McLane came up to the fire. "What's this, Matt? What's this?"

I didn't answer him. I spoke again in disbelief to Dutcher. "Potter's there. He's got to be there. I don't hear any firing. We'd hear if there were British moving in on him."

Dutcher threw up his hands. "I tell you, Matt, he ain't there! There ain't nobody there but redcoats. We seen 'em. And nobody to stop 'em."

I turned dumbly to McLane. I still couldn't believe that Potter would let a British force move in on him without warning the rest of us. "He says there's British on the Germantown road, Mac. He says there's no sign of Potter."

"Damn the militia!" McLane cried. "You never can trust 'em to do what they've been told." He whipped out a crude map of the area and bent over the fire to study it. He kept muttering, "Damn that Potter! Damn his ignorant, cowardly soul! Damn his slow-witted mind! This is a mess, Matt, a real mess." His finger jabbed the map. "They've got us cut off from Swede's Ford and Matson's Ford both, if they control that crossroads between here and Whitemarsh. They've got us, Matt."

I came alive. "We're all right out to the right, with Poor's men and the ridge and the river. We've got do what we can to hold 'em off on the left. Just us and the Oneidas, until Poor can bring up some men."

"There's thousands of 'em, Matt," Dutcher said again.

"Well, somebody's got to hold 'em."

"You tell the French Boy," McLane said. "I'll take the companies. Use my horse, Matt. Let's go!"

In a matter of minutes, I was riding through the faint dawn light toward the main camp, cursing militia generals with every beat of the horse's hoofs.

Lafayette took the news calmly enough, seeming to think that the troops seen by Dutcher and his men were some of Harry Lee's light horse that were supposed to come up this day to aid mobility to our striking force. I insisted heatedly that Dutcher was a good man and was not mistaken. Even as we spoke, a courier rode up and jumped from his horse. There were British on the German-town road, he said. A patriot in Whitemarsh had seen dragoons.

Lafayette still thought it was light horse from the Valley Forge, but sent me and his aide, Captain Pontgibaud, to reconnoiter.

We came upon them suddenly in the growing light, between Chestnut Hill and the Barren Hill Church, far from where Dutcher had said we'd find them. It did not immediately occur to me that this was another column.

We reported swiftly back to the Marquis, whereupon he issued quick orders to one courier after another.

Since I was certain that the British were now between me and the two ranger companies, I had to stay with Lafayette. I realized that Dutcher had not been wrong in placing them where Potter should have been; there were undoubtedly two British columns, and now they had either cut us off from the fords across the Schuylkill or they were about to do so.

Then we saw the first proving of Steuben's miracle. In a matter of minutes, Poor's brigade was formed by battalions, and stepped smartly out in column to face the British who were approaching the Barren Hill Church. There was firing far on our left now, toward the Germantown road, and then we heard the dull thudding of artillery. Poor's New Englanders marched to position, then in a matter of seconds wheeled from column into line, superbly, as Steuben had taught them.

There was firing now heavily on the left and to our rear. We knew that there were at least two columns in heavy strength against us.

We had news of the third almost immediately. McLane came pounding a-horseback, saying that his farthest skirmishers had struck what must be the entire British army, *behind us.*

"It's the whole damn army, sir," McLane cried to the French Boy. "It's got to be. There's several thousand on the Germantown road, and more of 'em coming against the church, and now my men tell me they saw regiment after regiment, all behind us. We're cut off, sir!"

Lafayette nodded. He was as cool as he would have been on the Grand Parade. "So be it," he said. "If they're all around us, we'll have to get out of here as best we can."

It was apparent to all of us that our only chance of getting out of the trap that Potter and his militia had dumped us into, was to reach Matson's Ford on the river before the large British column on the Germantown road reached it. For us to do that, the British would have to be delayed somehow, because they were already closer to the ford than any of our troops excepting the independent companies and some of the Oneidas.

Lafayette acted swiftly and brilliantly in spite of his youthful inexperience. First, he decided on deception. With a couple of companies of Poor's brigade under our command, he dispatched McLane and me toward the left flank, where we had to hump it to get past the advancing British. There McLane and I gathered our own companies and proceeded to put on a show for the British column, which we could now see in full view.

Dutcher had been right—there were thousands. I estimated three thousand on the Germantown road: McLane thought it closer to four.

With four companies of men, we deployed to the woods flanking the British line of march. There we moved into line of battle, swung a company into column on the road, then swung it into line in the woods, then back to the road at a different spot, and so on. In the space of three minutes, we performed a dozen maneuvers. We did our best to look like an army of two or three thousand, instead of a couple of hundred men. We had the men firing at extreme range as fast as they could reload.

Several times I dashed out into the road, mounted on McLane's horse, with Harm and Walter hovering about me as if they were aides to a general officer. I motioned troops into line where no troops existed; I called men to act as couriers, and they dashed from nowhere to nowhere and back again. I turned my back to the advancing British and rode for perhaps two hundred yards along the woods, calling out instructions to squirrels and rabbits and chipmunks as if they were regiments of the Continental Line.

The British, who had our main body of two thousand in view all the time as Lafayette took them along the Spring Mill Road toward Matson's Ford, were completely taken in by our deception. (We learned later that they were commanded by Major General James Grant, with Sir William himself commanding the main force behind us.)

General Grant played it cautiously. Obviously he believed that Lafayette's movement on the Spring Mill Road was a feint, and that our main body of Continentals lay to his flank in the woods. Grant stopped his advance dead still several times to reconnoiter. Each time we fell back before him, but again made a great display of heavy force. Far off, from Valley Forge, there was the sound of cannon fire (the General fired guns to let Lafayette know that a relief column was being hurried) and McLane and I took the sound of the guns for exactly that. To General Grant, however, cannon fire beyond him meant that he was in direct danger of being caught between two columns. He slowed to a stop, and sent out skirmishers to test our strength.

Three factors brought us back across the Schuylkill with a loss of nine men. The first was Lafayette's boyish brilliance in parading a few companies as a heavy striking force, and the splendid acting of our men in the woods beyond Barren Hill Church.

The second was General Grant's excessive caution, when with a little speed and some initiative he could have easily cut us off from both fords and held us tightly until the main army could come up to force the surrender of our entire detachment.

The third factor was Steuben's miracle. I would not have believed it, had I not seen our two thousand men reach Matson's Ford and cross it. In the old days, every man would have been taken during a disorderly march in Indian file. This time, however, when the order came for them to make for the ford, they fell into column precisely and smoothly and swiftly, and they marched off under the very eyes of the British in such splendid formations and with such speed that they were over the ford, with the battery of artillery bearing on the crossing, before the pursuing enemy had thoroughly combed the woods at the Barren Hill Church to discover that our phantom army was only four companies now running hell-bent for the ford and the covering protection of the artillery.

Mounted rangers of Simcoe's regiment came after us; we had to turn to skirmish with them, losing three or four of the New Englanders, while the British lost a few more than that. The water at the ford was above waist-high, and we crossed it with hands linked against the pull of the current.

None of us saw the gallant General Potter again. If we had, I'm sure he would have regretted the meeting, because Harm Tallman vowed to punch him in the nose if he ever caught up with him. On the other hand, I would have called him a coward and a fool, and probably would have been dismissed from the service.

Immediately upon our return to the Valley Forge, I sought Steuben out to tell him how Poor's brigade had performed.

"Py Gott!" he exclaimed. "I tell you in de winter what I can do wit dem, and Goddam, you say 'Maybe.' Now you know I did it, eh, Matt?"

I nodded. "But I still say 'maybe,' General. They've gone back inside the city, but they'll be out again. We'll see."

"Goddam, we will!" the Baron beamed.

CHAPTER TWENTY-FOUR

The days went by and the weeks went by, and there was no sign that Sir Henry Clinton had made his decision. And when he made it, what would it be? Would he use Philadelphia as his base and come after us? Or would he shift the theater of war to the Hudson, or even south?

After the Barren Hill affair, the spirit of the camp skyrocketed. Our men, veterans of many a march against the British, sensed where the importance of Barren Hill lay. Under steady pressure and sudden danger, Continentals had made a forced march and beat the British at their own game of covering the country with military skill. They knew that if ever they were ready to meet the redcoats head-on, it was this spring of 1778. But when would Clinton move?

Our company spent more time on the march than in camp during the last days of May and the early days of June. We had plenty of company on the approaches to the city. McLane's rangers were often out with us, and the Oneidas, as well as detachments of Morgan's rollicking riflemen and Harry Lee's light horse. We ringed Philadelphia with a web of observation posts, watching for the sign that Clinton was making his move. We traveled light and fast, and had no fear of any British force excepting Simcoe's Rangers or dragoons under Tarleton or another of the capable British cavalry commanders.

Information brought back by our scouting trips must have filled a couple of ledgers in headquarters, but none of it gave any clear idea that the British were getting ready to come out.

In the first week of June, Glennis agreed that it was time for her to go home. We were seldom in the main camp, and she was alone most of the time.

Steuben, so fond of gaiety, heard that she was leaving and thereupon gave her a dinner party. He had livened the spring with his parties. She was the belle of the evening at this one, although other officers' wives were there. Steuben and his aides gave her so much attention and gallantry, that one would think she had no husband whatsoever.

The men of the company gave her a party also, on her last evening with us. It was less an affair for her, though, than it was for them, for they had procured several gallons of rum and most of them were asleep over their cups when Glennis and I walked away to enter for the last time the neat little hut that had served us as home for so many weeks.

The next day, as she was about to leave, General Wayne's orderly brought her a small package. Within it was a tiny gold medallion on a delicate chain, with a card wishing her good luck and long happiness from Anthony Wayne. She wears it daily to this day.

I could scarcely say good-by to her, and there were tears in her eyes when I held her close at the last minute.

"You be careful, Matt," she whispered.

I nodded, unable to speak because my throat was constricted.

"And take care of my boys," she said softly, looking around at the circle of Deerkill men who had gathered to bid her good-by.

"They'll be fine," I said. "Take care of yourself."

"Come as soon as ever they'll let you," she said. Then with a show of her usual gay spirit, she tilted her head at me and said, "I'll have a surprise for you."

I thought for a moment of what such a surprise might be, and naturally the first thing that came into my head was a child. I was instantly alarmed. "You're not going to have a baby, dearest? Not without me there?"

"Lord no, Matt. You just wait. You'll see when you come home. Make it soon."

Then she was on the seat of the chaise with sober Eben Lowry driving. The wheels started turning. The men of the company shouted their farewells, while I stood dumbly, watching her wave until the chaise rolled out of sight. My mind and my heart were empty.

I turned blankly to the men and told them to get ready. I was taking them down the Schuylkill on a two-day scout to see whether we could pick out concentrations of troops or baggage at any particular point on the perimeter of the city. Sir Henry had to do something soon.

By the second week of June, every sign and every message brought out of Philadelphia bolstered the belief that Clinton was about to evacuate the city and strike overland across the Jerseys for New York. The question: When?

Early morning of the 18th of June brought the news to Valley Forge. A half dozen couriers pounded into camp, all carrying the same story: during the night, all of Clinton's army had moved out, over the Delaware into South Jersey.

The sun wasn't an hour past meridian before we had struck and stored the tents we were now living in, and were on the road, heading north for Coryell's Ferry on the Delaware. The brigades were: Poor's and Varnum's and Huntington's, and Wayne's division, to which was attached Conway's brigade—that adventurer having long since left us without regrets from any of us.

The rest of the troops (Lafayette's and De Kalb's and Stirling's divisions) would follow the next morning with the artillery.

I know of no man among us who had a single regret at leaving that bleak winter home of ours on the hills above the Schuylkill. No one of us looked back.

You would assume that among these generals, Poor and Varnum and Huntington and Wayne, there could only be one to be given the command of that advanced striking force against the British march. It would be Wayne, by whatever standard applied. A fighter and a leader and a soldier through and through.

You would be wrong. There was one more general. Prisoner of the British for the year, he was returned to us on an unhappy day in May, to assume with characteristic arrogance his role as senior major general on the list—he and his dogs and his grimy slatterns whom he slipped through back doors after dark, and his love of things English and his contempt for things American, and his conniving against the General, and his ignorance of all that we had done during the past winter while he was living in luxury with his British captors. I mean Charles Lee, Major General Charles Lee, whose name I wish I could wipe from my memory, but cannot. He was the commander of the advanced striking force.

Charles Lee, he of the ugly countenance and the uglier soul, with his nondescript hounds tagging ever at his heels, with what must have been twisted dreams of grandeur swirling in his dark mind, with his sneering slyness and his faithlessness to the cause to which he'd sold his word: Charles Lee was one of those in whose sordid history I can find the reasons why we were fated to years of suffering beyond what might have been.

There is no need to name the others like him: incompetents, some of them; drunkards, others of them; pettifoggers and bumblers and nincompoops, by the baker's dozen; members of Congress who were not qualified to keep the watch in a fair-sized town; commissaries who grew rich and fat on the sufferings of our citizen-soldiers; traitors like Arnold—yet in Arnold's glory in the early years of the war I can find at least some evidence that he was a great man who stepped out on the wrong foot, as Steuben would say.

I can find no excuse for Charles Lee, because, to give the devil every bit of his due, he was brave and brilliant in his soldiering.

What was his crime? Why am I so bitter about what he did to us during those hot and muggy June days when we marched out to give Sir Harry Clinton and the vaunted British army a whipping that would never be forgotten?

Why? Because, as simply as I can put it, his crime was the same as mine. Not a great one, surely, for a captain of rangers, but one that cost us dearly because he was our commander. Major General Charles Lee believed that we could not stand to British regulars. So did I, even after Barren Hill, in spite of my father's faith and my work with Steuben.

What was the difference between me, captain of a ranger company, and Major General Charles Lee, so that his belief was a crime and mine was a mistake? It is not conceit or pride that tells me the answer: I had pledged myself to my country's cause when I came back to the army, and I would stand with my men until they beat us to the ground.

And what of Charles Lee? What would he do?

The answer is written acidly in the events of those broiling days on the sand flats of the Jerseys.

In spates of alternating heat and violent thunderstorms, we moved swiftly to the Delaware and crossed at Coryell's Ferry, west of Hopewell and Princeton in the Jerseys. There Lee detached the Deerkill company to swing to the east to join the Jersey militia, under General Philemon Dickinson, in operations against the advance guard of Clinton's army, wherever it could be found.

I admit that I have ever been less than gentle in speaking of the role of our militia in the rebellion; to me, it was always a shame upon our people that a nation that might have put ten times ten thousand men into the field against the British, had a standing army that was almost always outnumbered, and that the contribution of the great majority of our men was a few weeks' or months' service in the nondescript militia regiments that rarely turned up to fight when we needed them.

Therefore I hasten to say that the regiments from the Jerseys under command of Phil Dickinson rendered truly splendid service to their country in six days of June, 1778.

We marched south by east from Coryell's Ferry in the broiling sun and the drenching rain, ever aware that we had no idea where Dickinson and his men might be, any more than we had assurance that we would not tilt smack against British light horse around the next bend in the road. I kept scouts ahead of us at least a quarter of a mile, and I remember wishing that Billy Bill were with us to give a few added seconds of warning by his fleetness of foot.

We met our first Jersey militia on the Crosswicks Road, north of the Black Horse Tavern and east of the neck of the Delaware at Trenton. There were two companies of them, swarming like ants on a bridge that crossed a sluggish creek. One by one the timbers parted from each other and were carried off into the scrub growth that flanked the stream.

They paid us no mind after measuring us carefully in the first few seconds of our appearance. Indeed, it took a little doing to get one of their officers to talk to me. He was too busy watching every twist of a crowbar and every swing of a sledge.

I asked his pardon three times before he finally swung impatiently from adjusting the grip of a block and tackle on one of the cross members of the bridge.

"What do you want?" he said sharply. "You got men with you. Put 'em to work."

"I've got orders to report to General Dickinson, Captain. Where can I find him?"

"Ain't a captain," he said. "Just a lieutenant. Never elected a captain in this company. The men decided whoever it was might get to thinking he was more important than anybody else. I dunno where Dickinson is. Up ahead, someplace. We got to take this bridge apart. Cross her now if you're going to. She'll be down and hidden away in a couple minutes."

I nodded. "Thanks," I said. "Like to stay and help you, but my orders are to get to Dickinson as fast as we can." I paused, puzzled. "Why are you hiding the timbers? Wouldn't it have been faster to burn the bridge as it stood?"

His thin face took on a pained expression. "Burn it? Burn this bridge? Lemme tell you something, mister. My father built this bridge, fifteen year ago come August. It's the best damn bridge in Jersey. May not be big, but it's solid. Burn it, hell! Once the redcoats get across the creek and on their way to where it is they're going, we'll come back and put her up again. Every spike and every bolt, right where it ought to be. Thing like a war is temporary, mister, but my grandchildren will be crossing this bridge when you and me are long gone."

I nodded. "Makes sense."

"Makes sense! Sure it makes sense. Ain't that what the war is about? That we should have things the way we want them? Well, one of the things folks want around here is bridges built by my father, who knew how to build 'em, may he rest in peace. We aim to have 'em, too."

I nodded again, motioning Harm to take the men across the bridge.

"And another thing," the militia officer said. "I got eyes. I been looking at you and your men the last couple minutes. About to smile about the damn milita, ain't you? Know what's in your mind, for sure. You're thinking: 'They may be fine for bridges, but put 'em in a fight and see what happens.' Tell you something, mister. Here's what will happen. Them redcoats will come up here and look around. Where's the bridge? Where's the bloody bridge? We'll be in the scrub on both sides. Soon's there's enough of 'em asking where's the bloody bridge, we'll give it to 'em. Maybe get ten or a dozen of 'em before they run us. What do you think of that, eh? Ten or a dozen is pretty good for militia, ain't it?"

He paused, grinning sourly. "We'll run. Yeh, we'll run like rabbits when them big green troopers come at us. Five miles down the road, though, we'll stop and then maybe get us a few more. What do you think of that, eh?"

"I think it's pretty damn good," I said, returning his grin. "Good luck to you, Captain."

"Ain't a captain," he growled. "Men wouldn't stand for a captain." He swung around to bawl an order about the bridge.

Not so bad, I thought, as I picked up the stride of the company on the way to the Black Horse Tavern. Not so bad, at all.

Harm Tallman grunted beside me. "Looks like they might turn out to be pretty good soldiers if they wasn't already in the militia."

"Might, at that," I said.

From that point on, there wasn't a hundred yards of the Crosswicks Road that didn't show signs of the militia's work. Windrows of trees had been felled, and we had to clamber across them; culverts had been ripped up, leaving deep gaps in the roadbed that would have to be bridged with timbers before the British transport could cross them. Wherever a small stream or spring brook approached the roadway, it had been ditched to divert its path onto the road. The high water from the recent rains had done the rest. Heavy wagons and artillery would have the devil's own time on the road to Allentown and beyond.

We never reached the Black Horse Tavern. We ran into a skirmish or a battle or a ruckus, or whatever you wanted to call it. The Jersey militia was disputing the advance of what must have been Clinton's entire army.

Two regiments held a sandy ridge overlooking the road when we came up. Against them was a force of light infantry in red coats, perhaps two or three companies. In the distance, south on the Crosswicks Road, we could see dust swirling—probably dragoons or more light infantry coming up to drive the militia.

Driven they were, to be sure. We plunked ourselves into the brush and sand alongside the militiamen, fired a couple of rounds, then were up and running in the old familiar pattern.

It was different, this time. Even as I trotted down the road with our Deerkill men around me, the Jerseyites in homespun to front and rear—all of us making the dust jump—I felt like laughing. I was sure that in the skirmish (which had started about three minutes before we arrived) there had been no one killed or wounded. It seemed to be a kind of game. Wait until they come ponderously along the road, shoot at them a few times, and then run like hell!

The difference was that the Continental Line was on the way. Somewhere west and north on our flank, there were almost eleven thousand soldiers of the Line; they were coming as fast as they could. All these farmers with their ancient muskets had to do was buzz around Clinton like those pestiferous insects of their marshlands—the Jersey mosquitoes.

Take this skirmish, for example. Five minutes, no longer, had elapsed from the first flat crack of a musket until we had taken to our heels and left the British far behind. How long would it delay Clinton? A couple of hours. He'd have to be sure that the road ahead was clear, that these roadrunners who had plagued him were not the advance that he must know the General had out against him. His dragoons would comb the scrub for us; his light infantry would come cautiously along the road; his baggage train would sit where it was until word came back that the road was clear. During those two hours of delay, Line regiments were crossing the Delaware, battalions were swinging into column and striking out with the ground-eating stride that Steuben had drilled into them; the General's plans for battle were surely forming.

I reported to Dickinson when we'd put about three miles between us and the British. If he hadn't been pointed out to me, I wouldn't have known he was a general. He was a man in his middle thirties, sober of mien but with a twist of humor at the corners of his wide mouth. He was dressed as the others were, with the addition of a frock coat and a long and unwieldy sword cased in a tarnished brass scabbard. He greeted me pleasantly enough, almost with an air of sociability, as if we were meeting after church services on a pleasant June Sunday.

"Pleased to have you with us, Captain Hill," he said. "I had a courier from General Lee this morning, said you were coming. Rangers, eh? You come at the right time. We aim to do a little treading on Mr. Clinton's toes, to slow him down a bit."

"From what I saw," I said, "you'll have him crawling along."

"Have to," he said soberly. "If he gets as far as Middletown he'll have the high ground, and the General won't be able to hit him at all."

"Was that his main army we were taking pot shots at, sir?"

"Don't think so," he said. "Advance guard. The baggage train is somewheres around Black Horse Tavern and the rear guard with it. Good Lord, Captain, there's a pile of 'em. Ten thousand, what I saw and heard. Baggage train must be eight or ten miles long. Looks like half the Tories in Philadelphia with him."

I thought of Peggy Remsen, wondering if she were there.

"I'm glad to have a Line officer," he said. "Heard a lot of what went on this spring, with that Dutchman training you. These boys of mine ain't much as soldiers, but they take orders and such. Now, Captain, you watch close the next couple days. See me do anything wrong, or something that ain't military, you speak up. I can use all the advice I can get."

"I'll help all I can, sir."

"Good enough," he said with a grin. "Let's get 'em humping. There's a pine lot ahead, both sides of the road. Drop us some trees across the road, and then take us a good rest. Mr. Clinton's troopers will have to stop when they hit the trees. Maybe we can give him a hot time for a while."

Dickinson's idea of a hot time for Clinton was a joy to share, although rarely have I been so tired so often, so hot in the summer sun, so drenched by sudden showers, so hungry and so thirsty for hours upon endless hours while we tramped the Jersey road, sting-ing Clinton in every way we could.

For four days we stayed with the Jersey militia (Morgan joined us with a force of picked riflemen, and Cadwalader's Pennsylvania militia were similarly vexing the rear guard) and every day of the four saw damage done to the British progress across the sand bar-rens.

We destroyed bridges, culverts, and supplies of every kind imagi-nable. We plugged wells and springs. We hovered before and around Clinton in parties small and large, picking off his pickets, tumbling his officers from their exhausted horses, peppering his baggage train with a pair of ridiculous coehorns that were the pride of the Jerseyites. They were dwarfed three-pounders that shot screamingly wild most of the time, but served maybe once a day to knock a heavily laden wagon awry in the road, stopping the entire column.

We almost lost those coehorns to thundering dragoons a half-dozen times, but when their "artillery" was threatened, it took more than flashing sabers to put the Jersey militia on the run.

A dangerous trick that the men livened their nights with was to creep close to the British pickets, then yell at the tops of their lungs, "You're going to get Burgoyned!"

There was plenty of news in the interim. Couriers carried messages to and from Dickinson several times a day, and they were free with information for our eager ears—after all, we knew all about the British advance, because we were atop it, but the Continental Line might as well have been a thousand miles away, for all we knew of its movements.

We heard that the army was across the Delaware and was poised, waiting, at Hopewell—east of the river and northwest of Princeton. We heard that Morgan and the riflemen were now sent to harass the British right wing, strung far out to the south of us. We heard that all detachments vexing the British were evidently so slowing Clinton's march that the General had all the time he wanted to plan his blow.

We had firsthand word of the council of war held at Hopewell on the twenty-fourth of June, when the General asked his generals to give their opinions and advice.

We cursed Charles Lee then for the first time, when the courier, one of Greene's aides, described in detail how Lee had proposed what he called a "bridge of gold" for the British to use in reaching New York. No attack, warned Lee, against a British force of almost the same size. Let them move to New York, said he; it was their obvious destination, and disaster could be avoided by caution. The French alliance, said Lee, would in time reduce the British to help-lessness. Victory was assured—don't risk it in a pitched battle! Let them go on to New York unmolested.

Greene had been furious, his aide told us, but he was the Quarter-master General, and felt he should properly have no voice with division commanders in a council of war. Stirling and Knox, probably remembering that Lee had the reputation of a competent professional soldier, nodded their heads to the "bridge of gold," the safe passage of Sir Henry's ponderous column.

Steuben and Duportail were hampered by their lack of English in stressing the view that the long and tortuous British column pre-sented an opportunity for slashing attack that might never come again. Lafayette wanted to attack the baggage train and then engage the main force as events dictated.

Wayne alone stormed for battle. According to our courier, Wayne sulked in a corner during the last part of the council, thumbing the pages of a book and muttering, "Fight! Fight!" to every remark that came his way.

"Goddamit," Harm cried, "you mean to tell me they didn't listen to him? Out with it, man! What did they decide to do?"

The courier shrugged. "Study the situation some more, I guess."

"Study it! Good God!" Harm shouted. "Where are they study-ing it—at Hopewell or whatever that place is? Why don't they come up here and take a look? It's as plain as the nose on Wayne's face. The damn British are wide open. Ten miles on the road when they're moving. Hit 'em here! Hit 'em there! Hit 'em in the middle and on the ends! Generals! My God, one of these here Jerseyites could tell that we got 'em this time. We can end it right here. We can smash 'em to pieces."

"I guess they listen pretty carefully to Lee," the courier said. "They started something, though. They sent Scott out with fifteen hundred to hit the rear and left flank as well as he can. And I told you about Morgan."

"That's not much," I said unhappily. "There's high ground north, Dickinson says. If they reach it, we won't be able to touch them. They could hold us off with a couple of regiments and a few guns. They could get to New York easy as pie, and we'd have to stand off and watch 'em."

"Don't tell me about it," the courier said. "It's Lee that's done all the talking."

"Lee!" Harm exploded. "I never liked his looks first time I set eyes on him. I don't mind an ugly man, long as he don't act ugly. I wouldn't trust Lee no further than I could throw a bear, and that ain't more than fifteen or twenty feet. Bridge of gold! Matt, what in hell is a bridge of gold?"

"I dunno, but whatever it is, it looks as if Clinton's apt to cross it and get out of reach, unless somebody does something besides study the situation."

He looked quickly at me, his mouth tipping with a grin. "You want a fight, Matt? I thought this golden bridge would be right in your line of thinking. You want to take 'em on, the whole shooting match of 'em?"

"He's exposed his entire left flank and he can't turn it," I answered soberly. "Best chance we ever had."

"You want to fight grenadiers and dragoons?"

"Hit 'em now," I said. "We'll never have 'em spread out like this again."

"I'll be damned," Harm said, grinning broadly. "You come a long way since winter time, Matt."

"I had a long way to go," I said slowly.

Not twelve hours later, we got new orders. They were brought by Joe Williams, bearing a scribbled message from Wayne that the Deerkill Company was to join his advanced force at Englishtown or wherever thereabouts we might find him.

"Got to get a hump on," Williams said laconically after we had given him a mug of rum and then another immediately atop the first one. "He may be there already, trying to start a fight with these

British before anybody else gets a chance. You got a little fighting here yourselves, ain't you?"

He cocked an ear to four or five musket reports that sounded from the general direction of Monmouth Courthouse, where the British advance had slowly ground to a stop a couple of hours before.

"Jersey militia," Harm said placidly, jerking his thumb toward the sound of the shots. "Up there telling the British they're going to get Burgoyned. They ain't so bad, Joe. We had us a hell of a time the last few days. This here Dickinson, now, we could use him in the Line in place of about any general you'd want to name. He likes to hustle around the countryside. We run around a little, rip out three or four bridges, plug a few wells, chop a dozen trees across the road, then we do a little shooting at redcoats, then we run around some more. We had us a hell of a time. I'll be glad to get back to the Line, where it's apt to be quiet, with all of 'em studying the situation."

"They've stopped studying," Williams said, sipping his rum happily. "You're in for a hell of a time when you get back. Our man Wayne is tasting a fight, and the French Boy is right with him. Now, there's something I can tell you. You heard about the French Boy and Lee?"

"Lee again!" snorted Harm. "Ain't we ever going to finish hearing that name? You ain't going to tell us about that bridge of gold, are you? We already know that one."

Williams shook his head. "This is a different one. Seems the General wanted to send out this bunch to pick up the British and tickle 'em a little. Lee turned up his nose. Not enough men for him to take out. Fifteen hundred, maybe. Not good enough for the first-ranking major general. Anyways, maybe he was afraid that if he came out where Wayne was, Wayne would shoot him. So the General give the advance to the French Boy. Turns out now, there's about four or five thousand moving in on Englishtown. That's a nice respectable army. So there's old Lee, dogs and spindleshanks and all, a-belching around that he will take the command. Says it's his due, as the second-ranking general. Goddamit!"

"Why don't somebody shoot him?" Harm asked.

"Will he get it?" I asked.

"Sure, he'll get it," Williams said, scowling. "Why wouldn't he get it? Don't the General listen to him most of the time?"

"Maybe it won't be so bad," I said. "He's had lots of experience, and the Marquis has had hardly any at all."

"Experience, hell!" Harm cried. "You know he don't want to fight, and the Frenchman and Wayne both are hot for it."

"We got nothing to say about it," Williams said. "Come on, get your plunder and say good-by to these Long Faces from Jersey. We got to get to Englishtown. Maybe Lee won't get there in time to stop Wayne and the French Boy from piling into the redcoats. It's hard to stop a fight once it gets started, not till one side is licked."

We marched through hot weather and another of those drenching thunderstorms, joining the advance forces of the Continental Line at the village of Englishtown just about the same hour that Lee took over the command from Lafayette. We bivouacked with the Pennsylvanians as usual, and were greeted with the rumor that Lee had orders from the General to attack the British rear just as soon as Clinton moved out of Monmouth Courthouse. We had to attack; the superior ground at Middletown was not much more than ten miles northeast. If Clinton got there, he'd have his bridge of gold.

The British were at Monmouth Courthouse, enjoying a day of needed rest after their slow and exhausting days under the broiling sun and in the rains that had served only to soak them and their supplies, to turn the roads into sticky mud, but not to give them relief from the heat.

We faced the best of Clinton's troops—he had reversed the order of march from Allentown on; before that village, we had, with the Jersey militia, skirmished day after day with the Queen's Rangers, the two dragoon brigades, his light infantry, the grenadiers, the Royal Highlanders, and four brigades of the regular British Line. From the advance positions, Clinton had wisely brought these troops to the rear and moved his Hessians and some British regiments to the van.

In the morning, it was plain, we would move out and strike his rear—dragoons and Guards and Highlanders and rangers—the best he had.

Against him, Lee, in taking command from Lafayette, had Wayne and most of the Pennsylvania division, Scott's and Poor's and Maxwell's brigades, twelve pieces of artillery, and far to the right, Morgan's rough-and-ready riflemen, as well as various Jersey and Pennsylvania militia units scattered on all fronts.

We went to sleep in stifling heat soon after sundown, for we would be stirring long before dawn. The mosquitoes hummed and buzzed and stung. The heat seemed to roll across our bodies in waves.

"It will be a son of a bitch tomorrow," Harm murmured to me just before he began to snore.

CHAPTER TWENTY-FIVE

The next day was Sunday, the twenty-eighth of June. There was no sign of coming dawn when our camp came to life, perhaps at three in the morning. The heat was oppressive. We awoke coated with sweat, and we were not stirring five minutes before our clothing was as wet as if we had been out in rain all night long.

We had a cold breakfast of journey cakes and slabs of cold beef, washed down with plenty of water.

Then we were off, on short orders from Wayne to reconnoiter enemy activity at Monmouth Courthouse. In the darkness we approached the village and the morning fires of the British Army. The town itself was perhaps three dozen buildings. Clinton's troops were bivouacked everywhere around it.

We lay waiting for dawn. I sent no scouts forward into the darkness and the British picket lines. There were Queen's Rangers out there, and they were reputed to have cat's eyes at night.

Slowly the red sun pulled up over the Atlantic far to the east. The British camp came into dim view from our position on a pine-studded sandy eminence.

As soon as we saw details with any clarity, I knew that Clinton expected no battle today. He wanted to use the bridge of gold that Lee had so generously offered, and that Clinton's spies had probably reported to him not later than the day after Lee had made the suggestion. The Hessians under Knyphausen and two British brigades were moving out of the bivouac into the red dawn. The baggage train was forming to follow.

"Lord A'mighty," Harm said to me hoarsely. "Just supposing, Matt, we had a couple guns up here and some gunners to work 'em! Ten shots and we'd blow that baggage train into the worst mess you ever seen. Look at them wagons and carts. He brought half of Philadelphia with him."

"They'll be an hour training up," I said. "By that time, Lee will have the troops up here and guns and everything. We'll get 'em, Harm, in about an hour. And while they're trying to straighten out the mess, we'll jump 'em. My God, Harm, this is the day!"

"He don't expect a fight," Walter Luckey said, "or he wouldn't be sending them Hessians and redcoats out ahead of his wagons."

"We'll move up," I said, "and maybe we can get a good idea how many troops he's leaving in the rear guard, and who they are."

We moved through the pines to a point about four hundred yards from the troops assembling among the buildings of the village. I sent the Welch brothers and Aaron Conklin ahead as scouts.

There was a sudden rattle of ragged musketry ahead of us, and our scouts came dodging back through the pines and patches of scrub oak.

"We better pull out of here, Matt," Aaron Conklin gasped, hard put for breath. "There's a couple companies of Rangers coming for us."

"All right," I said, "I've got to report to Wayne, anyway, but we'll move back with covering fire. That baggage train isn't going anyplace for an hour or so. The fighting's going to start right here, and we might as well start it."

We went back slowly, firing at the darting green flashes of Simcoe's men as they moved forward in the scrub. We suffered no casualties, and the only harm done to us came from a ball touching the lobe of Henry van Buskirk's left ear, causing it to bleed profusely and draw deer flies on him in swarms, and from another ball that put a neat hole in Mordecai Mott's canteen.

We fell in with Wayne's advanced pickets, where I borrowed a horse from an officer and went dashing back to say that the British were on the move. I failed to find Wayne immediately—he was apparently forward with his troops—but I went back farther and found Lee. I found Lee, damn him!

I blurted out the news that Clinton was moving out, and that it was evident from the disposition of his troops that he expected no battle and wanted none. He was moving for the Middletown heights, I said, and had already spread out his army so widely that we could attack the rear immediately.

Lee nodded heartily when I told him that Clinton wasn't looking for battle; he frowned when I said the rear could be hit now.

"We can engage him, sir," I said excitedly, "and we can hold him until the General gets up with the rest of the army. We can maybe smash the rear guard by ourselves."

His sour face darkened as he glared at me.

"Who sent your company up there, Captain? Why did you engage the enemy and alert him?"

"General Wayne sent us, sir," I said, puzzled. "And we didn't engage the enemy; they engaged us."

"Why did you fire on them, sir?"

"Damn it, General, they were shooting at us! We just fired back. What should we have done?"

"Mind your tongue, sir."

He looked at me with that air that Conway used to assume with American-born officers, as much to say, "And did Congress get a look at you before they commissioned you?"

I plunged ahead. "Now's the time, sir, if it ever was!"

"Damn it, Captain, I know my business. Don't presume to tell me how to handle my command."

"Sir, I wasn't presuming anything at all. I just——"

"Back to your men, Captain. And next time fall back without engaging the enemy until you receive proper orders. You might have jeopardized this entire force. I'm not at all sure you haven't."

I left him, and I was confused and alarmed. What was he thinking of, for God's sakes? Now was the time to move in with his five thousand men. The last we'd seen of the British rear guard, after we'd lost Simcoe's pursuit, it was reduced to about twenty-five hundred men, with British regiments moving out constantly on the road to Middletown. Clinton was running, and now was the time to hit him! What in hell was Lee thinking about?

I found Wayne on a ridge overlooking the British camp. He was black-faced and furious. He had awaited, for almost two hours, the order to attack the British rear guard. He fumed and ranted, but he couldn't advance without Lee's orders.

I told him what was forward of us, finding that he now had more accurate information than I could give him. There were far fewer troops there now than had formed at dawn. Only loyalist troops and a brigade of dragoons were between us and the wagon train. There were maybe fifteen hundred of them in all. With Wayne's Pennsylvanians alone we could have overwhelmed them.

As quickly as always, he calmed himself. "Go join your company, Captain," he told me. "Be ready to move out as skirmishers when the order comes. He can't wait much longer. If he does, Clinton will get away clean."

I had no sooner reached the company than the dragoons charged with sabers flashing in the brilliant sun. Artillery boomed to left and right, but the dragoons came riding hard at the Pennsylvanians. They charged into our flank but were sorely hampered in their usual maneuvers by the nature of that scrub country. They fell back in confusion with considerable loss of horses and some troopers.

Now we had them! The knowledge surged triumphantly in my mind.

Wayne and Scott and Maxwell all knew it. To the right and left of the Deerkill company, Continental regiments wheeled precisely from column into line, as if they were still performing on the Grand Parade at the Valley Forge. Had Steuben been up with us, he would have beamed with pride.

With rhythmic clashing down the line, bayonets clicked into place. The men were ready for the charge. The artillery thundered. In the distance there was great banging of musketry from the head of the British column beyond Monmouth Courthouse, where I knew that Dickinson's militiamen were buzzing like a swarm of yellowjackets.

We kept looking back for the hard-riding courier that would signal the advance.

We kept looking back. There is the entire story. That courier never came.

Wayne couldn't wait too long. We had to advance! We had to, for the simple reason that Clinton could not be such a fool as to believe that he could continue to avoid a battle, not with the Continental Line ready to launch itself at his rear guard. He'd know that he would have to bring back the troops he'd already sent out, and down that road that went beyond the courthouse soon would come at double time the regular troops that would keep us away from the baggage train.

Wayne didn't wait. Cautiously, the line of battle moved forward. Sporadic musketry challenged our advance, but we kept on slowly. With an order from Lee, we would have charged. Instead, we inched forward. Our line bulged ahead in the center as we crossed the brushy fields that took us past the village.

Still there was no word from Lee!

Wayne sent back pleas for support, so he could attack. They were unanswered.

Finally, on our far right, late in that scorching forenoon, we could see regiments commanded by Lafayette moving forward.

Our Deerkill men grinned nervously and readied themselves for the swift advance that would drive the British helter-skelter into their baggage, into their advance columns, into chaos.

Then it happened. We could not believe our eyes. To our left and right—Scott, Maxwell, Varnum—their regiments were falling back!

"What the hell goes on?" Harm Tallman shouted. "Good God, Matt! They're pulling foot!"

Ten minutes went by, and the troops under Wayne were now alone with the village far to our right, where Lafayette's troops were in the same predicament—some of them were already forming column and marching to the rear.

What was worse, we could see before us in the shimmering waves of heat that rose from the ground and made the horizon dance, the columns of fresh British troops moving in for battle. When Clinton changed his mind, he acted quickly. There were Hessians, grenadiers, Highlanders, and heavy reinforcements of dragoons.

It must have well-nigh killed Wayne to give it, but the order came to us by courier: "Fall back to the rest of the Line regiments."

Sullenly our men went back in the suffocating heat, in good order and marching by column as they had been taught, but growling as they went. The most simple-minded of them had seen the chance we'd been given by Clinton when he thought no battle impended.

I was sick at heart, visualizing the smashing defeat that we could have given to the British two hours ago, an hour ago—indeed, within the last thirty minutes! For the first time in my service with the Continental Line, I had seen a golden victory lie there for the taking, and Major General Charles Lee—damn him!—had pulled us away from it.

Had he? It turned out that no one knew for certain. Orders and contradictory orders had flown around the field. Lafayette had apparently received a direct order from Lee to retreat, and one brigade commander reported that Lee had ordered him through a courier to "take your men any place where they will be safe."

Safe! The word goes deep. Who is ever safe in war? What officer will not move into danger or remain in danger for the sake of almost certain victory?

Was it an extra share of caution that cost us a stunning blow from which that redcoat army would never recover? Was it stupidity? Or was it a shade of treason, bred in his Philadelphia captivity and nurtured by the belief that I had myself known so well, that we could not stand against British regulars? The answer lies in the mind and heart of Charles Lee.

They were on us before we reached the main line: dragoons and light infantry, supported by the ponderously moving Hessians. We had lost the initiative; they grabbed it. We of the Deerkill company took a dragoon brigade's charge—they looked like young Tarleton's riders—at the edge of the swampy ground where we had to beat them off or be destroyed.

They fell away from our heavy and accurate firing, but not before James Dutcher and Ben Ferguson lay dead and Tim Halstead fell with a saber cut across his chest.

We got free of them, carrying Tim with us and leaving the dead men, stalwart Dutcher and smiling, quiet Ben. Jared King carried Tim in his arms beneath the broiling sun, speaking soothing words to the wounded man as he staggered along.

To this point the retreat, so pointless and so futile, had been conducted in good order and must have warmed Steuben's heart as he dashed here and there without a command of his own.

Now, however, some squads and then a few companies, a regiment or two, began to run. I believe that they did so because there was no order to stand and fight. They thought the day was lost, and they were getting out of there as fast as their legs could take them. But they were only a small percentage of our force.

We crossed a brook and neighboring swamps as swiftly as we could, well west of the village now. Beyond were other swamps and low ground, but now we were on a height of land that could be held. Here and there along the line, regiments halted and turned and faced smartly into line, ready to meet the redcoats who were now pursuing us eagerly, sensing that if they came up quickly, they could rout our entire army.

The orders came to keep retreating!

The cries of anger could be heard on every side. The men wanted to stand and fight. Lee took us back.

Disgust and despair mounted within me like a sickness.

We heard later many different details of the General's meeting with Lee. What was said exactly will probably never be known in certainty.

One report had it that the General was as cold as a midwinter's day in relieving Lee of his command and ordering him to the rear in disgrace.

Others said that the General exchanged only a few words with Lee before racing onward to try to recover the victory that Lee had thrown away.

The most popular story, the one that raced through the army in no time at all, had the General turning purple and cursing Lee for a poltroon and a fool until the leaves shook in the trees.

Whatever went on at that meeting, the General came quickly forward to us.

We were spread out like a fan, retreating in column, with some British units only a few hundred yards behind us.

The General was hailed and cheered as he rode along our swift-moving lines. The orders came quickly; his hands swept in gestures to the defensible positions we had been about to sweep through.

Entire regiments, in full proof of Steuben's miracle, wheeled out of column and into line of battle, falling behind hedgerows and other cover. All of Wayne's troops were turned in a matter of minutes and we were firing at the pursuing British legions at a rate that made the rifle barrels blister our hands.

The British slowed and stopped. The artillery on both sides resumed heavy cannonading. The noise was thunderous. The heat was deadly. The sun beat down on us intolerably. On both sides, more men were felled of heat exhaustion than by musketry or cannon fire.

Wayne was magnificent. We held the center of that first stand, and the British charged us with all the force they could muster. We knew the main army was forming behind us, and knew that the General would soon have it in position to reinforce us. We held. Not only did we hold, but, crouched behind a long hedgerow, we waited out another dragoon charge until they were almost upon us, then blasted them back into the ranks of their own grenadiers.

Wayne was everywhere, shouting orders, grinning encouragement, lifting his clenched fist in the air as a sign that we should hold fast no matter what the cost.

At my side, Teunis Ekerson kept grinning at Wayne and shouting something about Gideon into my ear. In a lull in cannonading, he yelled, "*He smote them hip and thigh. He smote them hip and thigh.*"

Now some of the main army was moving into position and taking over from the tired, heat-exhausted advance elements of Lee's morning command. Steuben was with Stirling on our left, and those troops wheeled into line of battle with a grace and precision that was a delight to see. They faced light infantry and the Royal Highlanders. Disciplined volley after volley slowed and stopped the British attack, and then, as if to raise Steuben to the heights, they moved forward with the bayonet. With a respite in the fighting on our front, we could see them charge: blades gleaming, throats shrilling wild yells, line after line of them driving the redcoats before them. For the first time, Continentals used the bayonet in battle and used it brilliantly.

"Lookit them bastards go!" Harm Tallman screamed.

Steuben's miracle!

Then it was our turn. Leaving Stirling in place on our left, Clinton sent Cornwallis against Greene's position with two regiments of the Line, a battalion of grenadiers, and both battalions of the Guards.

The artillery shook the very universe.

Now Cornwallis was fairly launched against Greene on our right, and since Wayne had taken us into an orchard near a church, where some of our division made a stronghold of an old barn, we were obliquely forward of Greene's left, in good position.

The British came at us, wave on wave, grenadiers and Guards. We fired by volleys in the fashion that Steuben had taught us. One attack after another broke against the orchard and the barn.

I am amazed that Anthony Wayne was not killed by any of a thousand balls that must have been aimed at him. He was, at that moment, the finest soldier on the field.

He raced along the line, shouting encouragement and yells of triumph alternately, as the British came forward in seemingly inexorable strength, then fell back in shattered files.

The final charge came almost to the barrels of our weapons, led by a handsome officer we later learned was Lieutenant Colonel Henry Monckton of the grenadiers. He fell but a short distance from us.

Then out of the orchard we came, running like demons as Steuben had insisted, the bayonets fixed for their deadly work. The grenadiers turned and ran. Grenadiers: they turned and ran!

That was the end of the day for us.

We lay back exhausted in that orchard under the welcome shade of the trees bursting in full leaf.

Our Deerkill men lay quietly, not able to talk above the roaring of the artillery and the incessant rattle of musketry to our left and right. They grinned happily at each other, though. They knew what we had done that day.

Harm put his mouth next to my ear and said hoarsely, "Ah, Matt, if Hawk could of been here today——"

I nodded soberly, then closed my eyes against the dying glare of the descending sun.

It had cost us. We'd lost four men killed. James Welch lay beside the stone wall at the edge of the orchard. His brother Bill sat beside the body, crying. Sergeant John Curran lay there as well. Five others —Waggoner, Andrew Secord, Mordecai Mott, Tim Halstead and Toby Garrison—had gone to the rear with wounds. Others of us had saber slashes and grazes from musket balls.

We'd have to bury Welch and Curran before nightfall. I hoped that someone could go forward before dark to find Dutcher and Ben Ferguson, although that ground was still in the hands of the British.

In spite of the sorrow in my heart for good men dead on this broiling and bloody field, I could not keep the exultation from welling within me.

We had stood to the best troops in the world! We had taken all they had to give, and then we had driven them! We had driven grenadiers and dragoons and Guards and Highlanders!

Harm was right. Hawk should have lived to see his dream come true. And, I thought bitterly, he should have had the chance to know that his faith finally was passed on to me.

Maybe he does know, I thought.

The artillery's booming slowed and gradually halted; the British moved back in exhaustion and what can only be termed defeat, because they gave up the field.

Both sides were worn out with heat and fatigue. We moved up before darkness fell, but during the night—how did they manage it when they were surely as beat out as we were?—Clinton moved his troops onto the northward road and hurried wearily for Sandy Hook and the safety of New York.

The bridge of gold that Lee had sought to give him had been turned by the General into a bridge of lead and steel.

CHAPTER TWENTY-SIX

We came over the hills from the east, Doc Walden and I, on the road that gives the Deerkill Valley its only access to the rest of Highland County.

We had come in a day and a half from North Castle in Westchester County, where the army was camped on the rolling hills around the town of White Plains. We'd crossed Hudson's River by ferry to Highland Landing. We each had furloughs of three weeks. Doc got his because he'd simply asked for it at a time when his Connecticut regiment was being reorganized and consolidated with another. When he came back, Doc said, he might very well ask Wayne if the Pennsylvanians could use a doctor from Connecticut. A general like Wayne, Doc told me, was quite apt to keep a doctor busy with wounds and such, so busy that the doctor wouldn't have time to think about all the other doctors who had stayed home to make a fortune.

My furlough came as a surprise, handed to me by Wayne himself on the last day of Charles Lee's court-martial, which was August 12, four days before. I'd spent the time since July 4 waiting to testify, but had never been called.

"Go on home to that pretty wife of yours," Wayne said to me gruffly. "You've been standing around here for better'n a month, doing nothing but curse Charles Lee for a fool and an idiot and all kinds of low-down things that you never learned the meaning of from my Pennsylvanians. Go home and kiss your wife a few times for me, and cool off a little. It's all right for Anthony Wayne to stand outside a courtroom cursing a major general, because everybody knows I'm crazy, anyway. But it won't do for one of my best captains to keep at it. Somebody like a Congressman might hear you, and then you'd be in trouble. Go home and get a good rest, Matt. Don't worry; if it looks as if there's going to be a fight, I'll send one of your boys to get you."

"They should have hanged him or shot him, sir," I said heatedly, probably still not quite aware that the paper he'd handed to me entitled me to spend three weeks with my wife.

Wayne shrugged. "Suspension from command for a year. It's a disgrace, Matt."

"We could have finished Clinton," I said. "If it hadn't been for Lee, we'd have destroyed or captured the only army in force that the British have left in America. The war would have been over, sir." I looked at the paper. "Why do I get a furlough, sir?" I asked dumbly.

"For standing in that orchard with me and driving grenadiers! That's what for. Take it and get out of here. And remember this, Captain Hill: although I hate that man inside the courtroom as much as you do for what he did to us at Monmouth, I have to say that eight months ago you would have shared with him the reasons he's given for refusing to fight at Monmouth."

I nodded unhappily. "Yes, sir."

"You had Lee's sickness, Captain. You thought we couldn't stand to 'em. But we did. Not only did we stand, but we drove 'em. They call me Wayne the Drover, because I went after those cattle in the Jerseys last winter and looked like a fool when I came back with so few of 'em. Major André wrote a poem about Wayne the Drover. I don't mind the name, if they change the reason for it. Let 'em say I drove grenadiers. Let 'em tell that about me!"

He grinned suddenly. "I watched you that day, Matt. With all the hooraw and the artillery and the rest of it, I kept it in mind to keep my eye on you. I had to. I wasn't sure about you. I thought that when Monckton led them right into our musket barrels, there was a chance that you'd think we couldn't stand. Damn it, I laughed like a loony when I saw you were the first over the wall with the bayonet. We drove grenadiers and Guards, Matt! Go home and tell your wife you're a hero."

So I was going home—was almost there. Doc came with me because his wife and children had closed the house in New Haven and gone to Falmouth in Maine to live with Doc's in-laws until the war was over. I think Doc had the idea then that he would maybe come some day to our valley as the doctor we had so sorely needed for so many years. He wanted to see the place that he'd heard so much about.

"So that's it," Doc said softly as we rested our horses on the crest of the eastern ridge. "It's all that you and Hawk and the boys ever said it was."

It was lovely. The fields of wheat and corn and oats patched the floor of the valley in ripe colors. The Deerkill twisted its blue length down the center. We heard the church bells tolling for Sunday services in the "Indian church."

I talked all the way down the winding road and across the valley and up the slope toward our big house. I pointed out this and that and the other. Doc never said more than "Um-m-m" or "Ah." He was too busy looking. I suppose any man carries on the way I did when he is showing his home country to a visitor who sees it for the first time.

"There's our house," I said, as we came around the bend in the road that brought the lane and the orchards into first view, then the house and barns.

I pushed my horse into a trot, tired as he was. Doc bounced along behind me on the bony nag he'd borrowed.

It was a sore disappointment to find the place deserted.

"They're at church," I said to Doc, somewhat apologetically, as if I had to excuse my family.

"Good place to be," Doc said. "Specially on a Sunday. Tell you what, Matt. I'll set myself on this porch here, and take in some of this view for a bit. You go get us a jug of applejack and some of that cold spring water you always brag on, and we'll just wash a little dust down while we wait for 'em."

So we did.

They were walking when they returned. I saw them come around the bend, Johnny in front with Abbie, and my mother and Glennis coming more slowly behind them.

Johnny saw our horses tied at the rail. He called back to my mother, and I saw her put her hand to her eyes to shade them against the glare of the sun. I stood up and waved.

They all ran, but it is fair to say that Glennis flew over the graveled lane. She was in my arms and whispering wild things that I could not try to understand, for Johnny was patting me on the shoulder and grinning like a fool, and my mother stood waiting her turn to kiss me, tears running freely down her cheeks. Abbie was shouting welcome and jumping up and down.

Somehow I got a word to the others between Glennis' kissing of me and my kissing of her. "That's Doc," I said.

Then I kissed my mother, and Glennis swooped on Doc and kissed him so violently that she almost knocked him down.

He nodded amiably from one to another, peering at them over his spectacles and saying mildly, "Well, now, I'm right glad I came."

We had a dinner that almost reduced Doc and myself to tears, there was so much of it and it was so good.

Johnny wanted to hear about Monmouth, and I told him the story in an account that I thought was meagre, although I must have spent ten minutes denouncing Lee every way from Sunday.

Doc spoke up when I paused for breath. "Changed some, ain't he?" He beamed at my mother. "Regular firebrand, now. Worse than that durn fool Wayne. Stick with Matt and Wayne, a body could get himself into all kinds of scrapes."

"And how is our dear friend, the Baron?" asked Glennis.

"He's about the same," said Doc. "Maybe took off a little weight, the way we been running after Clinton. Ain't no better at the King's English—excuse me, the Congress' English—than he ever was. Still don't know that he oughtn't to swear in front of ladies."

Glennis got up from the table and motioned me to follow her. She took me outside and pointed to a well-used wagon track that forked from our lane westward, continuing beyond the barn and around the shoulder of the hill where Johnny had dropped the two deer with two shots on the morning Harm and I came back from our hunting trip. The track disappeared beyond the shoulder of the hill, where a small stand of cedars gave way to hemlocks and then to oaks and maples.

I was puzzled. The far side of that hill was wooded, for the most part. The hill dropped sharply away, affording one of the best views of the entire valley that could be had from its western slope, but I couldn't understand why Johnny had put a wagon track in there. Not for hauling wood, certainly; there was too much land yet to be cleared close to the house.

"Remember the surprise I promised you?" Glennis asked happily. "Come on, Matt, and I'll show you."

She raced ahead of me, rounding the shoulder of the hill and passing from my view. Too much of my mother's fried chicken kept me to a sedate pace.

I stopped around the bend and came to an abrupt halt.

There, built into the hillside and perhaps half completed, was the house that Derrick Archer had drawn the sketches for. It was unmistakable, even with its frame unfinished.

"You like it, Matt?" she asked softly. "Did I pick the right spot? Is it what you wanted?"

I had no answer to give her but to take her in my arms and hold her tightly.

After a long time of just looking at it in delight and wonder, I took my wife's hand and went forward to examine every square foot of its spaciousness.

"You came home too soon," she whispered. "I wanted to have it finished for you."

"Too soon?" I cried. "Never too soon. I'll spend every hour I'm home working on it."

"Every hour, Matt?" she asked me, laughing.

I shook my head, reaching for her. "Not every hour."

The sun was setting when I walked along from the house toward the grove of quaking aspen. Glennis knew where I was going; she stayed with the others to listen to Doc's account of our last few months at the Valley Forge, and in the Jerseys, and in Westchester County.

The popple leaves were shivering as they always do, whispering faintly in spite of little or no breeze to move the air. They seemed to bring Hawk's voice softly back to me, and the words formed a question, the one I knew he would want to ask above all others: "How does it stand with him and his army, Matt?"

"You were right, Hawk," I whispered. "We will win it for him. And for you."

BIBLIOGRAPHY

American Archives, New York, 1885.

ANBUREY, THOMAS, *Travels through the Interior Parts of America*, Boston, 1923.

ANDERSON, TROYER S., *The Command of the Howe Brothers during the American Revolution*, New York, 1936.

AVERY, ELROY M., *History of the United States and Its People*, Cleveland, 1904.

AZOY, LT. COL. A. C. M., *Monmouth—the Battle Won at Valley Forge*, Infantry Journal.

BANGS, ISAAC, *Journal*, N.J. Hist. Soc. Proc.

BARTON, WILLIAM, *Journal*.

BAURMEISTER, CARL L., *Letters to Colonel Von Jungkenn*, Phila., 1937.

BEAN, THEODORE W., *Washington at Valley Forge*, Morristown, N.J., 1876.

BEAUCHAMP, W. M., *A History of the New York State Iroquois*, 1905. *The Iroquois Trail*.

BEERS, F. W., *History of Herkimer County*, New York, 1879.

BELL, HERBERT C., *History of Northumberland County*.

BENNETT, C. E., *Advance and Retreat to Saratoga*, 1927.

BILL, ALFRED HOYT, *Valley Forge, the Making of an Army*, New York, 1952.

BOARDMAN, REV. B., *Diary*.

BOLTON, C. K., *The Private Soldier under Washington*, New York, 1902.

BOUCHER, JONATHAN, *Reminiscenses of an American Loyalist*, Boston, 1925.

BOYD, JAMES, *Light Horse Harry Lee*, New York, 1931.

BOYD, THOMAS, *Mad Anthony Wayne*, New York, 1929.

BRODHEAD, J. R., *History of the State of New York*, 1871.

BROOKS, NOAH, *Henry Knox, a Soldier of the Revolution*, New York, 1900.

BROWN, H. E., *The Medical Department of the United States Army, 1775–1873*, Washington, 1873.

BURK, W. H., *Historical and Topographical Guide to Valley Forge.*

BURR, AARON, *Memoirs*, New York, 1858.

CAMPBELL, PATRICK, *Travels in North America*, Edinburgh, 1793.

CAMPBELL, WILLIAM W., *Annals of Tryon County, or The Border Wars of New York.*

CANFIELD, DR. JABEZ, *Diary.*

Canadian National Archives, Ottawa.

CARRINGTON, H. B., *Battles of the American Revolution*, New York, 1876.

CARTWRIGHT, RICHARD, *Life and Letters*, Toronto, 1876.

CHINARD, GILBERT, *George Washington as the French Knew Him*, Princeton, 1940.

CLARK, JANE, *Responsibility for the Failure of the Burgoyne Campaign*, Am. Hist. Rev.

CLARK, JOSEPH, *Diary*, N.J. Hist. Soc. Proc.

CLINTON, GOV. GEORGE, *Papers*, Albany, N.Y., 1899.

CLINTON, SIR HENRY, *The American Rebellion*, New Haven, 1954.

CODMAN, JOHN, *Arnold's Expedition to Quebec*, New York, 1902.

CONOVER, GEORGE S., *Seneca Villages*, Geneva, N.Y., 1889.

CONWAY, MONCURE D., *Life of Thomas Paine*, New York, 1893.

COOK, FREDERICK, ED., *Journals of the Military Expedition of Major General John Sullivan against the Six Nations*, Auburn, N.Y., 1887.

CORNER, GEORGE W., *The Autobiography of Benjamin Rush*, Princeton, 1948.

CRUIKSHANK, ERNEST, *The Story of Butler's Rangers*, Welland, Ont., 1893.

CURTIS, EDWARD E., *The British Army in the American Revolution*, New Haven, 1926.

CUSTIS, G. W. P., *Memoirs of Washington*, New York, 1859.

DAVIS, NATHAN, *Journal.*

DEARBORN, HENRY, *Journals*, Mass. Hist. Soc. Proc.

Dictionary of American Biography

DILLIN, JOHN W., *The Kentucky Rifle.*

DRAKE, FRANCIS S., *Life and Correspondence of Henry Knox*, Boston, 1872.

DUNCAN, CAPT. JAMES, *Diary*, Penna. Archives

DWIGHT, TIMOTHY, *Travels in New England and New York*, New Haven, 1821.

ELLETT, E. F., *The Women of the Revolution*, Phila., 1900.

ELMER, E., *Journal*, Penna. Magazine

EWING, G., *Journal*, Yonkers, 1928.

FARNSWORTH, AMOS, *Three Military Diaries*, Mass. Hist. Soc. Proc.

FISHER, ELIJAH, *Journal*, Augusta, Me., 1880.

FISHER, SYDNEY G., *The Struggle for American Independence*, Phila., 1908.

FITCH, JABEZ, *Diary*.

FITZPATRICK, JOHN C., *George Washington Himself*, Indianapolis, 1933. *The Spirit of the Revolution*, Boston, 1924.

FLICK, ALEXANDER C., *Loyalism in New York during the American Revolution*, New York, 1901.

FOSTER, W. B., *With Washington at Valley Forge*.

FOX, E., *Revolutionary Adventures*.

FREEMAN, DOUGLAS S., *George Washington*, New York, 6 vol.

GANO, REV. JOHN, *Biographical Memoirs*.

GARDNER, A. B., *Uniforms of the American Revolution*, Mag. of American History.

GODFREY, C. E., *The Commander in Chief's Guard*, Washington, 1904.

GOTTSCHALK, LOUIS, *Lafayette Joins the American Army*, Chicago, 1937.

GOULD, JAY, *History of Delaware County*, Roxbury, N.Y., 1856.

GRAHAM, JAMES, *Life of General Daniel Morgan*, New York, 1859.

GRANT, THOMAS, *Journal*.

GREENE, FRANCIS V., *General Greene*, New York, 1893.

————, *The Revolutionary War and the Military Policy of the United States*, New York, 1911.

GREENE, GEORGE W., *Life of Nathanael Greene*, New York, 1871.

GREENE, NELSON, *History of the Mohawk Valley*, Chicago, 1929.
The Gulph Mill, Penna. Mag. of History.
The Camp by the Old Gulph Mill, Penna. Mag. of History.

HADDEN, LIEUT. JAMES M., *Journal & Orderly Book*, Albany, 1884.

HALSEY, F. W., *The Old New York Frontier*, New York, 1901.

HAMILTON, ALEXANDER, *Works*, New York, 1904.

HAND, BRIG. GEN. EDWARD, *Orderly Book*, Penna. Mag. of History.

HARROWER, JOHN, *Diary*.

HART, A. B., *Camps and Firesides of the Revolution*.

HATCH, L. C., *The Administration of the American Revolutionary Army*, New York, 1904.

HENRY, ALEXANDER, *Travels and Adventures*.

HENSHAW, WILLIAM, *Orderly Book*.

HOW, DAVID, *Diary*, New York, 1865.

HUDDLESTON, F. J., *Gentleman Johnny Burgoyne*, New York, 1927.

————, *Warriors in Undress*, Boston, 1926.

HUGHES, RUPERT, *George Washington, Savior of the States*, New York, 1930.

JONES, JUDGE THOMAS, *History of New York During the Revolutionary War*, New York, 1879.

KAPP, FRIEDRICH, *Life of Frederick William von Steuben*, New York, 1859.

KIDDER, FREDERIC, *History of the First New Hampshire Regiment in the War of the Revolution*, Albany, 1868.

KIMM, SILAS C., *The Iroquois*, Middleburgh, N.Y., 1900.

KITE, ELIZABETH S., *Beaumarchais and the War of American Independence*, Boston, 1918.

————, *Brigadier General Louis Lebègue Duportail*, Phila., 1933.

LAFAYETTE, GILBERT MOTIER, MARQUIS DE, *Memoirs, Correspondence and Manuscripts*, London, 1837.

LAURENS, JOHN, *Army Correspondence in the Years 1777-8*, New York, 1857.

LEFFERTS, CHARLES M., *Uniforms in the War of the American Revolution*, New York, 1926.

LEMAITRE, GEORGES, *Beaumarchais*, New York, 1949.

LEWIS, A., *Orderly Book*.

LOSSING, BENSON J., *Pictorial Field Book of the Revolution*, New York, 1851.

LOWELL, EDWARD J., *The Hessians and Other German Auxiliaries of Great Britain in the Revolutionary War*, New York, 1884.

LUNDIN, LEONARD, *Cockpit of the Revolution*, Princeton, 1940.

MANUCY, ALBERT, *Artillery through the Ages*, Washington, 1949.

MARKLAND, CAPT. JOHN, *Revolutionary Services*, Penna. Mag.

MARSHALL, CHRISTOPHER, *Diary*, Albany, 1877.

McLANE, CAPT. ALLEN, *Diary*, Penna. Hist. Soc. Coll.

MELLICK, A. J., JR., *Lesser Crossroads*, New Brunswick, 1948.

Military Journals of Two Private Soldiers, Poughkeepsie, 1885.

MINER, CHARLES, *History of Wyoming*, Phila., 1845.

The Minute Book of the Committee of Safety, Tryon County, New York Public Library.

MONTRESOR, CAPT. JOHN, *Journal*, Penna. Mag. of History.

MONTROSS, LLOYD, *Rag, Tag and Bobtail*, New York, 1952.

MUHLENBERG, HENRY A., *Life of Major General Peter Muhlenberg*, Phila., 1849.

NICE, CAPT. JOHN, *Orderly Book*, Penna. Mag. of History.

NICKERSON, HOFFMAN, *The Turning Point of the Revolution*, Boston, 1926.

NORRIS, JAMES, *Journal*.

O'CALLAGHAN, E. B., ed., *Documentary History of New York*, Albany.

Orange County Muster Rolls of Militia, and other supplementary data on militia affairs in the Hudson Valley, Goshen, N.Y., library and museum.

Orderly Book of the Northern Army, New York Historical Society.

PALMER, JOHN McA., *General von Steuben*, New Haven, 1937.

PARRINGTON, V. L., *The Colonial Mind, 1620–1800*, New York, 1927.

PATRIDGE, BELLAMY, *Sir Billy Howe*, New York, 1932.

PATTERSON, SAMUEL W., *Horatio Gates, Defender of American Liberties*, New York, 1941.

PEARSON, HESKETH, *Tom Paine, Friend of Mankind*, New York, 1937.

PECK, GEORGE, *History of Wyoming*, New York, 1868.

Pennsylvania Archives

POWELL, JOHN H., *Bring Out Your Dead*, Phila., 1949.

PRIEST, JOSIAH, *Stories of the Revolution*, Albany, 1838.

RAY, FREDERICK, *Valley Forge*, 1951.

REPPLIER, AGNES, *Philadelphia, the Place and the People*, New York, 1898.

ROBERTS, KENNETH, ed., *March to Quebec, Journals of the Members of Arnold's Expedition*, New York, 1938.

ROGERS, REV. WILLIAM, *Journal*.

ROOSEVELT, THEODORE, *Winning of the West*, New York, 1894.

RUSH, BENJAMIN, *A Memorial*, Phila., 1905.

RYERSON, EGERTON, *Loyalists of America*, Toronto, 1880.

SABINE, LORENZO, *Loyalists of the American Revolution*, Boston, 1947.

SAWYER, CHARLES W., *Firearms in American History*, Boston, 1910.

358

SCHOOLCRAFT, H. R., *Notes on the Iroquois*, Albany, 1847.

SCHOULER, JAMES, *Americans of 1776*, New York, 1909.

SEYMOUR, WILLIAM, *Journal*, Penna. Mag. of History.

SHREVE, JOHN, *Personal Narrative*, Mag. of American History.

SIMCOE, JOHN, *Journal*, New York, 1844.

SIMMS, JEPTHA R., *The History of Schoharie County*, Albany, 1845.
————, *Trappers of New York*, Albany, 1851.

SMITH, FRANK, *Thomas Paine, Liberator*, New York, 1938.

SPARKS, JARED, *Correspondence of the Revolution*, Boston, 1853.

STEDMAN, CHARLES, *History of the Origin, Progress, and Termination of the American War*, London, 1794.

STEINER, B. C., *Life and Correspondence of James McHenry*, Cleveland, 1907.

STILLÉ, C. J., *Wayne and the Pennsylvania Line in the Continental Army*, Phila., 1893.

STONE, W. L., *The Campaign of Lieutenant General John Burgoyne and the Expedition of Lieutenant Colonel St. Leger*, Albany, 1877.

STOUDT, JOHN BAER, *The Feu de Joie*, Valley Forge.

STRYKER, WILLIAM S., *The Battle of Monmouth*, Princeton, 1927.

SWIGGETT, HOWARD, *War out of Niagara*, New York, 1933.

TAYLOR, FRANK H., *Valley Forge, A Chronicle of American Heroism*, Phila., 1911.

THACHER, DR. JAMES, *Military Journal during the Revolutionary War*, Boston, 1823.

TOWER, CHARLEMAGNE, *The Marquis de Lafayette in the American Revolution*, Phila., 1901.

TREVELYAN, G. O., *The American Revolution*, New York, 1903.

TRUMBULL, JOHN, *Autobiography*.

TURNER, F. J., *The Frontier in American History*, New York, 1928.

UPTON, EMORY, *The Military Policy of the United States*, Washington, 1917.

VAN CORTLANDT, P., *Autobiography*, Mag. of American History.

VAN DOREN, CARL, *Mutiny in January*, New York, 1943.
————, *Benjamin Franklin*, New York, 1937.
————, *Secret History of the American Revolution*, New York, 1941.

VAN SCHAACK, HENRY C., *Life of Peter Van Schaack*, New York, 1942.

VAN TYNE, C. H., *Loyalists in the American Revolution*, New York, 1922.

Virginia Historical Magazine, Jan., 1899.

VROOMAN, JOHN J., *Forts and Firesides of the Mohawk Country.*

WALDO, DR. ALBIGENCE, *Diary,* Penna. Mag. of History, et altera.

WANDELL, S. H., AND MINNEGERODE, M., *Aaron Burr,* New York, 1925.

WASHINGTON, GEORGE, *Revolutionary Orders,* New York, 1844.

WATSON, ELKANAH, *Men and Times of the Revolution.*

WATSON, J. F., *Annals of Philadelphia.*

WATTS, MARY, *The Adventures of a Lady in the War of Independence in America,* Workingham, U.K., 1874.

WEEDON, BRIG. GENERAL GEORGE, *Orderly Book,* New York, 1902.

WILD, EBENEZER, *Journal,* Mass. Hist. Soc. Proc.

WILDES, HENRY E., *Anthony Wayne, Trouble Shooter of the American Revolution,* New York, 1941.

WILLETT, MARINUS, *Papers,* New York Public Library.

WILLIAMS, MAJOR E., *Journal.*

WINSOR, JUSTIN, *The Westward Movement,* Boston, 1897.

WISTER, SALLY, *Journal,* Phila., 1902.

WRIGHT, AARON, *Revolutionary Journal,* Penna. Archives.

WRONG, G. M., *Canada and the American Revolution,* New York, 1935.

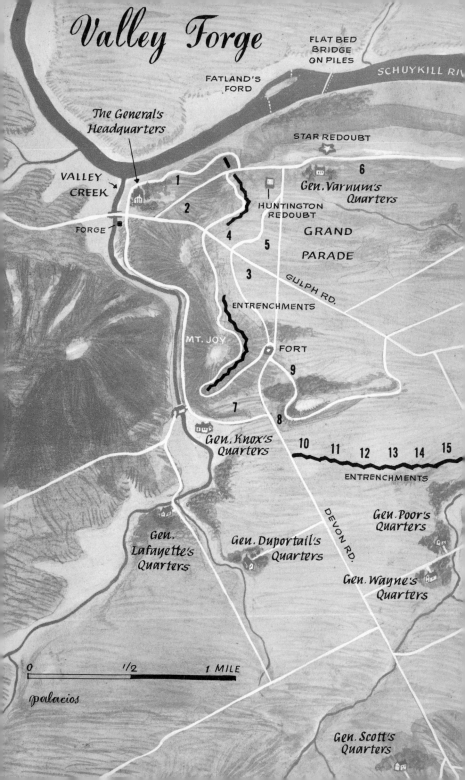

Valley Forge

FLAT BED
BRIDGE
ON PILES

SCHUYKILL RIVER

FATLAND'S
FORD

The General's
Headquarters

STAR REDOUBT

VALLEY
CREEK

1

2

6

Gen. Varnum's
Quarters

FORGE

4

HUNTINGTON
REDOUBT

5

GRAND

PARADE

3

GULPH RD.

ENTRENCHMENTS

MT. JOY

FORT

9

7

8

Gen. Knox's
Quarters

10   11   12   13   14   15

ENTRENCHMENTS

Gen. Poor's
Quarters

DEVON RD.

Gen.
Lafayette's
Quarters

Gen. Duportail's
Quarters

Gen. Wayne's
Quarters

0   1/2   1 MILE

palacios

Gen. Scott's
Quarters